AND SO THE BANSHEE CAME FOR HIM...

David shifted the changeling so that it cradled awkwardly in the crook of his left arm. Slowly he eased himself down to a wary crouch, but his gaze never left the eyes of the banshee—eyes that burned round and red like living flame. Eyes that had nothing of beauty about them, only of hatred: hatred of life. He freed his right hand and took a firmer grip on the knife.

"Greetings, Banshee of the Sullivans," he said, swallowing hard. "I can't let you have what you came for."

The wailing of the banshee faltered.

David carefully laid the changeling before him on the porch floor. "I have a child here, a *Faery* child. I don't know if he has a soul or not, but I guess I'll have to find out very shortly, unless some things change real fast. This knife—this *iron* knife—will have some effect." He raised his voice and looked up. "You hear me? I'm going to kill the changeling. The Sidhe took my brother; I claim this life for myself!"

He raised the blade...

"Delightful...it kept this reader turning pages late into the night."—Robin W. Bailey

"A FUN, FAST READ!"—A. C. Crispin

"Superlatively drawn...one of the most original heroes in modern fantasy!"—John Maddox Roberts

Worlds of Fantasy from Avon Books

THE BLACK GRAIL *by Damien Broderick*

THE CHRONICLES OF THE TWELVE KINGDOMS
by Esther M. Friesner
MUSTAPHA AND HIS WISE DOG
SPELLS OF MORTAL WEAVING

THE DRAGON WAITING *by John M. Ford*

THE FIRE SWORD *by Adrienne Martine-Barnes*

THE JADE DEMONS SERIES *by Robert E. Vardeman*
BOOK 1: THE QUAKING LANDS
BOOK 2: THE FROZEN WAVES
BOOK 3: THE CRYSTAL CLOUDS
BOOK 4: THE WHITE FIRE

100 GREAT FANTASY SHORT SHORT STORIES
*edited by Isaac Asimov, Terry Carr, and
Martin H. Greenberg*

WINDMASTER'S BANE

TOM DEITZ

AVON
PUBLISHERS OF BARD, CAMELOT, DISCUS AND FLARE BOOKS

WINDMASTER'S BANE is an original publication of Avon Books. This work has never before appeared in book form. This work is a novel. Any similarity to actual persons or events is purely coincidental.

AVON BOOKS
A division of
The Hearst Corporation
1790 Broadway
New York, New York 10019

First Avon Printing: October 1986

K–R 10 9 8 7 6 5 4 3 2 1

For Louise
    who started it

For Vickie
    who sustained it

and

For Sharon
    who said what she thought.

ACKNOWLEDGMENTS

Thanks to:
Mary Ellen Brooks and Barbara Brown
Joseph Coté and Louise DeVere
Linda Gilbert and Mark Golden
Gilbert Head and Margaret Dowdle-Head
Christie Johnson and Lin McNickle-Odend'hal
Klon Newell and James Nicholson
Charles Pou and James Pratt
William Provost and Paul Schleifer
Vickie Sharp and Mike Stevens
Sharon Webb and Leann Wilcox

PART I

Prologue I: In Tir-Nan-Og
(high summer)

A sound.

A sound of Power.

A low-pitched thrum like an immense golden harp string plucked once and left to stand echoing in an empty place.

And then, ten breaths later, another.

But it was the golden Straight Tracks between the Worlds that rang along their sparkling lengths, as they sometimes did for no reason the Sidhe could discover—and they had been trying for a very long time. Success eluded them, though, for the half-seen ribbons of shimmering golden light that webbed the ancient woods and treacherous seas of Tir-Nan-Og—and which here and there rose through the skies themselves like the trunks of immense fiery trees—were not of Sidhe crafting at all, and only partly of their World.

In some Worlds they were seen differently, and in some—like the Lands of Men—they were *not* seen. This much the Sidhe knew and scarcely more, except something of how to travel upon them—and *that* was a thing best done only at certain times.

Yet the Tracks were there, in *all* Worlds. And they had Power—in all Worlds. For Power was the thing of which they were chiefly made.

*   *   *

It was the half-heard tolling of that Power whispering through the high-arched windows and thick stone walls of the twelve-towered palace of Lugh Samildinach which awakened Ailill Windmaster a little before sunset.

At first Ailill did not know it as sound, for the song of the Track was as much felt in the body as heard with the ear: a swarm of furious tiny bees trapped in his bones and teeth, a tingling in the blood like the bubbles in artfully made wine, a dull tension in the air itself that sang to him alone.

Ailill allowed a smile to twitch at the corners of his mouth. It had been a long, long time since the Tracks had sung a song his particular Power could answer.

It was not that he lacked Power himself, that wasn't the situation at all; Power was as much a part of him as his black hair and night-blue eyes, as his tall, lean body and devious wit. But when Power came from Without as well as within, it was best to grasp it, to shape it at once to one's will—or risk the consequence. Power loose in the World was not a good thing, as all the Sidhe knew from bitter experience. For it was such random sounding of the Tracks that once of old had wrenched them from the place of their beginning and sent them wandering along the Straight Tracks to this World, where they had founded Tir-Nan-Og and Erenn and Annwyn and the other realms of Faerie that now lay scattered in the web of the Tracks like the tattered wings of dead insects.

No, unbounded Power was not a thing to be ignored, and Ailill was never one to ignore Power in whatever form it presented itself.

He sighed reflectively and folded his arms behind his head. The time for action was not yet. Sunset would be better and midnight best of all, for Ailill was night-born, and at midnight his own Power would be at its height. This particular resonance would not last that long, though; of that he was reasonably certain, and so sunset it would have to be. It was a good thing it had come today, too, for at midnight tomorrow would be the Riding of the Road, and that he would not miss in spite of certain apprehensions.

Meanwhile he studied his quarters: those apartments located high in the easternmost tower of Lugh's palace which were by tradition set aside for the Ambassador of Erenn. In particular his eyes were drawn to the high-relief sculptures worked into the four square panels of cast bronze set deep in the pale stone opposite the window: Earth and Water, Fire and Air. *Human work*, he thought with a frown. *And wondrously well done. Why can the Sidhe not do such things?*

A rampant horse first, for Earth, which was substance; to its right, a leaping salmon for Water, which was the force that bound substance together and made it move. And below them, their mirrors: the displayed eagle of Air for spirit; and for Fire, for that which bound spirit together and allowed *it* to act, the two-legged dragon called a wyvern. Framing them all was a rectangular border that bore the endlessly interlaced image of the serpent of Time which enclosed all things. Earth and Water, Fire and Air— and Time. Of these five things the world was made.

And of these, the greatest is Fire, one form of which is Power, Ailill thought. *And of Power I am very fond, indeed.*

Ailill arose then, and dressed himself in a long robe of black velvet, dark gray wool, and silver leather elaborately pieced together in narrow lozenges. A fringed cloak of black silk covered it, and a thumb-wide silver circlet bearing the fantastically attenuated images of a procession of walking eagles, worked in rubies, bound his long hair off his face.

He took himself from the palace without being seen. A close-grown grove of splendid redwoods soared about him, their summits yet less lofty than Lugh's walls, but Ailill chose a narrow gravel path that ran eastward through a tightly woven stand of stunted hazel trees, where tortured branches twisted together like the knotted brooch that fastened his cloak on his left shoulder. As sunset approached he increased his pace, Power now sparking through his body like the cracklings of summer lightning.

Eventually, his lengthening strides brought him to the low embattled wall that bordered the grove on the eastern side. Impulsively, he leapt atop that barrier, and stood transfixed as the empty immensity of darkening sky exploded before him. *Glorious*, he shouted in his mind alone, *absolutely glorious!* Ailill smiled, but no good showed in the sensual curve of those thin lips. Carelessly he stepped closer to the edge of the white marble merlon, let the rising wind send the shining silk of his cloak flapping behind him like the wings of the Morrigu. He did not fear to fall, for he could

put on eagle's shape and ride the breezes back into the High Air
—far higher than the tall palace of Lugh Samildinach that now
erupted from the wood-wrapped peak above him.

Power, he thought as he edged closer to the brink. *Raw as
rocks. Free for the taking, free for the shaping. But what to do
with it?* he wondered as his eyes narrowed and his brows lowered
thoughtfully.

All at once he knew.

He reached into the air, drew on that force he felt coiling
there, shaped it into the storm it wanted to become, and held it
poised in an indignant froth of wind-whipped clouds as he called
upon the Power and looked between the Worlds upon the homely
splatter of silver lakes, gray-green mountains, and plain white
houses that marked the Lands of Men. The sun setting behind
him—in both Worlds today, which happened but four times a
year—cast a shimmer of red light upon the landscape. But even
to Ailill's sight the shapes twisted and blurred like a torch reflected in unquiet water, obscured by the same shifting glamour
Lugh once had raised to further hide his realm from mortal eyes.

That would be an excellent place for his storm, Ailill decided,
laughing softly—even as tingling sparks shot from his fingertips
and thunder rumbled among those lesser peaks.

And so he caused it to be.

It was a delight to command such things, he thought when he
had finished. Windmaster, they called him, and not without reason: Windmaster, Stormmaker, Rainbringer—all were names that
had become attached to him, and he gloried in every one. His
mother had told him—she who had been a queen in Erenn before
his father had put her away—that a storm had raged in both
Worlds on the night he was born, and thus, just as a person's
Power was strongest at the same-hour of his birth, so did one feel
closest to the weather that had watched him into the world. He
shrugged. Whatever the reason was, he did not care; it was the
storms themselves that mattered. He was a storm child. The
storms he forged were his children—a truer reflection of himself
than the son of his body could ever be. And this was an especially
fine one.

For a long while after that he listened to the echoes of his
handiwork frolicking noisily in that other World. The Tracks no
longer called to his blood, and he relaxed into languid reverie.

Gradually, though, another sound, a gentler sound, began to creep through the grove to disturb his contemplation: the distant, muffled crunch of soft leather boots on the path that threaded the wood a short way behind him. It was a very faint sound, but clear to one of Ailill's lineage.

All at once the need came upon him to follow those footfalls, and so he did, leaping with easy recklessness from merlon to merlon as the battlement spiraled precipitously down the mountainside until at last a clearing opened among the dark shadows of the ancient oaks to his right. He paused there at the edge, masked by a gnarled gray branch that grew close against the wall—and he saw who came there, tall, golden-haired, and dressed in white: Nuada Airgetlam, who, if not yet his enemy, was certainly not his friend, and who certainly would not like his storm.

Pointless, that one would say. Irresponsible. The World shaped itself in its own good time and to its own good purpose. To impose one's will upon it without good reason was to set oneself above the Laws of Dana. It was always the same tiresome litany.

Ailill sighed and craned his neck. Nuada had knelt and was carefully inserting a hand among the ivory blossoms of an unfamiliar bush that flowered in the glade. He sprang from the wall then, silent as leaf fall, but Nuada looked up, frowning, as Ailill's long shadow fell dark upon his.

"Well, Ailill, do you like it?" Nuada asked when the other showed no sign of speaking first. "A Cherokee rose, mortals call it. I have but newly brought it from the Lands of Men."

"I like it better like this," said Ailill, languidly extending his left hand in an apparently careless gesture.

Blue flames at once enfolded the white blossoms, through which the flowers nevertheless shone unwithered.

Nuada did not reply, but the slanted brows lowered over his dark blue eyes like clouds over deep water, and he scratched his clean-angled chin with a gauntleted right hand.

". . . or maybe this way?" Ailill continued as a subtle movement of his first two fingers quenched the flames and encased the flowers in sparkling crystals of ice.

". . . or like this?" And the bush burned on one side and glittered frostily on the other.

"I like it like this," said Nuada with an absent flick of his wrist, and fire and ice were gone.

Ailill sighed and leaned back against the mossy parapet, arms folded across his chest. He shook his head dramatically. "What is it with you, Airgetlam, that you favor the things of dull mortality above that Power which is born into us, to use as we see fit?"

Slowly and deliberately Nuada stood and turned to face Ailill, eyes slitted. "Ours to *use,* not misuse . . . and as for the dullness of mortality, do you not find *immortality* dull? Were it not for mortal men I would long since have left this World from boredom."

"I find mortal men most boring of all," Ailill replied, glancing skyward in arrogant avoidance of the other's searching stare. "It is seldom indeed that they do anything worth noting."

"We shall see, we shall see," Nuada mused, his eyes shining faintly red in the reflected light of sunset, "for as the suns of our two Worlds align ever nearer to midnight and the strength of the Way to Erenn waxes, time again draws near for a Riding of the Road. Who knows what may happen when we do?"

"That Track still passes too near the Lands of Men," snapped Ailill. "This I have told Lugh more than once. I do not see why he tolerates such things."

"This is not Erenn, Ailill—or Annwyn, either," replied Nuada with a toss of his head. "What was it?—five hundred years at Arawn's court, which hardly touches the World of Men at all— and that in their past? And then straight here? Well, much can change in five hundred years, and mortal men not the least of them. It *is* true that their works intrude here, but no place is free from that now. And one thing at least may be said in their favor: They do not visit storms upon *us.* As to the Riding—*you* do not have to go. *I* ride as Lugh's vanguard this Lughnasadh."

Ailill did not reply. The sun had passed from sight. From somewhere in the darkness above them a fanfare of trumpets split the air to mark the evening.

Nuada fixed Ailill with one final searching stare, and turned his back.

Ailill frowned as he stole from the glade. He paused once at its edge, looked back, and softly snapped his fingers.

The roses took on the color of blood.

Chapter I: A Funeral Seen

(Friday, July 31)

Death was fast approaching—death in the form of old age, and it was approaching them both. Yet Patrick the priest was not concerned, not when there still remained any chance of salvation for the soul of the man sitting on the stony ground beside him. Oisin was stubborn, and his arguments were cunning, but he was a pagan, and had once been a warrior: a follower of Finn mac Cumaill, in fact, who had been the greatest champion in Ireland. Just now Oisin was defending Finn's prowess on the field of battle. The words of his boastings were a study in Gaelic eloquence.

So much eloquence, in fact, that they fairly leapt from the page of the worn blue volume David Sullivan held open in his lap.

He could see them clearly, the two old men, one thin and frail, robed and hooded like a monk, the other yet well-muscled, mail and helm and sword shining bright in the morning. It was a wonderful image.

"Daaaavy!"

The image shattered. Footsteps pounded up the rickety barn stairs behind him. *Cursed be younger brothers,* he thought. *Won't even leave you alone for thirty minutes.* David frowned at the book in grim determination.

9

Oisin sang now of the virtues of Finn, no longer simply as a warlord, but as a man accomplished in every art. It was getting good. The pagan was winning.

"Pa got the tractor stuck just like Ma said he would," Little Billy cried gleefully as he galloped past to stand perilously close to the open door of the hayloft.

David snorted irritably. He rearranged himself in the dusty old rocking chair, adjusted his wire-framed glasses, scratched his chin where a trace of stubble had *finally* begun to grow, and returned to his reading.

"That sure is a big black station wagon," said Little Billy, peering out the door and down the hill.

David ignored him.

"There sure are a lot of cars behind it, and all of 'em have their lights on, and it ain't even dark yet!"

David shook a stray lock of unruly blond hair out of his eyes and glanced up reluctantly, a little surprised to see patchy blue sky and scattered shafts of July sunlight where only a short while before clouds had held uncontested sovereignty above the familiar riverbottoms and high, rolling ridges of the north Georgia farm he called home. Wisps of clouds still hung wraithlike here and there among the dark green hollows across the valley. *Just like Ireland must be,* he thought, until he lowered his gaze toward the muddy gravel road at the foot of the hill where a line of cars crept reverently along behind a hulking black vehicle.

"It's a funeral procession," he said matter-of-factly.

Just a couple more lines . . .

"A funeral procession?"

"A funeral procession," David growled. "You ought to know that, old as you are . . . and if you ask me any more questions, you'll soon have firsthand knowledge of one—*from inside the hearse.*" His last words hung ominously in the air.

"What's a hearse?"

"That big black station wagon—except it's not exactly a station wagon: bigger for one thing; built on a stretched Cadillac frame. They're only used for funerals. Now *please* be quiet, I've only got three pages to go. Okay?"

Little Billy was quiet for almost three lines.

"They're goin' in that old graveyard across the road. Are they gonna *bury* somebody?"

David slammed the book abruptly shut, a sound like a tiny thunderclap.

Little Billy jumped, uttered a small yip of surprise and dropped the handful of straw he had been fidgeting with into the muddy backyard below. He looked up at his older brother, and their eyes met, and he knew he was in trouble.

David erupted from the rocker, setting it into riotous motion on the rough old boards. Little Billy was quicker, though, and darted down the narrow aisle between the hay bales.

"I'm gonna get you, squirt!" David cried loudly. He ran after his brother until he saw Billy's head disappear down the stairs that led to the ground floor of the barn, then stopped suddenly and tiptoed quickly back to jog noisily in place by the hayloft door. His mother's Friday wash flapped optimistically on the line below. And directly underneath . . .

Little Billy ran as if the devil himself were chasing him—down the stairs and into darkness, and then across the red clay floor, deftly leaping piles of cow manure and bales of hay as he went. Abruptly he bounded out into the broken sunlight of late afternoon and paused, his mouth slightly open in confusion. He glanced fearfully back into the gloom.

"Whoooeeeee!" cried David as he leapt from the hayloft in a sweeping arc that landed him directly behind his little brother. He made one frantic grab for the boy, but miscalculated and stumbled forward on his knees in the mud.

Little Billy shrieked, but his feet were already carrying him through the laundry and down the hill beside the house.

David recovered quickly and dodged left, skirting between his daddy's four-wheel-drive Ford pickup and his own red Mustang, hoping to ambush Little Billy as he came around the other side. But Little Billy saw him at the last instant, squealed joyously, and threw his luck into one last wild, reckless dash toward the road where the slow train of cars continued to pass obliviously.

David caught him halfway there, grasped him by the belt of his grubby jeans and jerked him quickly into the air. He locked his elbows and held the little boy above his head, kicking frantically in five-year-old indignation.

"Now that I've got you, what should I do with you, I wonder?" David glanced meaningfully at the procession and then back at his brother.

"Maybe I'll take you down the hill and give you to the undertaker and tell him to put you on ice. Would you like that, Little Billy?"

Little Billy shook his head vigorously. "No, Davy."

"Maybe I'll take you up to the house then, and hang you from the rooftop first. Would you like that better?"

"You better quit it, or I'm gonna tell Pa!"

"Pa's not here," David said fiendishly as he lowered his brother to his shoulders and began to stride purposefully up the slope.

Little Billy tried to crawl headfirst down the front of David's body, but his attempt at escape only resulted in David grabbing him by the ankles and holding him with his head bobbing up and down between David's knees. It was not an efficient mode of travel, David realized before he had gone three steps up the hill. He stopped and began to swing his brother pendulumlike between his legs, lowering him slowly until the white-blond hair brushed the long grass of the yard.

Little Billy alternately screamed and giggled, but David could feel his grip slipping. He made one final sweep and released his brother at the bottom of the arc to send the little boy scooting downhill between his wide-braced legs.

On the follow-through, David abruptly found himself peering between his knees at the bright-eyed face of a very smug Little Billy lying in the slick grass further down the hill. He suddenly felt very foolish.

Little Billy laughed. "You sure do look funny with your butt up in the air and your face down by your feet!"

"You'll look funnier when I get through with you, you little . . ."

David started to straighten up, but paused, blinking, as something attracted his attention. The air around his head suddenly seemed to vibrate as if invisible mosquitoes swarmed there, and the hair on the back of his neck began to prickle inexplicably. He froze, still bent over.

Beyond Little Billy he saw the funeral procession halt as the hearse turned into the seldom-used cemetery of the Sullivan Cove Church of God across the way. It was strange, David thought suddenly, to see a whole funeral procession at one time, from between one's legs.

The air pulsed again. David felt his eyes fill up with darkness, as sometimes happened when he stood up too quickly from a hot bath. His head swam and he felt dizzy. He blinked once more, but the darkness lingered. *Oh my God!* he thought for a panicked instant, *I've been struck blind!* But that was ridiculous. His whole body was tingling now; he could feel the hair on his arms and legs stiffening as chill after chill raced over him. And then the darkness was burned away by a hot light, as if he stared straight into the sun with his naked eyes, but with no pain.

Another blink and the world returned abruptly to normal, leaving only a faint, itchy tingle in David's eyes. He shrugged, executed a lopsided somersault, and got up to chase Little Billy.

They had nearly reached the rambling old farmhouse when their mother hollered from the back porch that David had a telephone call.

"I'll get you yet, squirt," David shouted, bounding up the porch steps.

"I just washed them pants," his mother groaned as he passed.

The screen door slammed behind him.

The phone hung on the kitchen wall next to the back door. David took a breath and picked up the receiver. Probably his father calling from Uncle Dale's, wanting him to come help with the stuck tractor. "Hello?" he said, somewhat apprehensively.

"Well, Sullivan, what're you *doing?*" came a voice young as his own, but slower and smoother, more like a lowland river than a mountain stream: his best friend, Alec McLean. An undercurrent of irritation surfaced on the last word.

"Oh, it's you, Alec," David said breathlessly, glancing nervously out the back door. "I was just trying to impose a little control on my brat of a kid brother."

"Well, why don't you impose a little of it on yourself while you're at it, and check the time every day or two. You were supposed to pick me up half an hour ago."

David shot a glance at the yellow electric clock on the wall above the stove and grimaced in dismay: It was nearly four o'clock. He rubbed his eyes absently.

Alec went on blithely. "Camping, remember? If it quit raining? Got me out of bed to ask me? Remember?"

"Son-of-a-gun!" David groaned. "Sorry. I'll be right over. I just got so engrossed in my reading that I lost track of time."

Alec sounded unconvinced. "I thought you were controlling your brother; I'd suggest a rack, thumbscrews—"

"Before that, stooge. No, really, it was one of those books I got out of that bunch the library was throwing away: *Gods and Fighting Men* by Lady Gregory. It's great stuff, Irish mythology. You know, about—"

"Not *now,* David. I'm sure I'll hear more than I want to about it anyway, before long . . . at least it's not werewolves this time," he added.

"You've got something against werewolves?" David replied archly.

"I do when my best friend tries to turn himself into one, like you did last time we went camping."

"Alec, my lad, I would prefer to forget that unfortunate episode. I'm at least a month older and *infinitely* wiser now."

"Well, I prefer to remember it—in all its excruciatingly embarrassing detail. I mean, how *could* I forget you running around up at Lookout Rock, stark naked except for the fur collar off one of your mother's old coats, smeared all over with fat from a dead possum you'd found beside the road, muttering incantations out of another one of those old library books. No, my friend, that's not an image that dies easily . . . nor, come to mention it, was it a smell that died easily—and I don't intend to let you forget it, either."

David sighed melodramatically. "I thought you were my friend."

"I am," Alec replied drily. "If I wasn't, I'd have taken my camera."

"Well, I can assure you that *this* is just a plain camping trip— a celebration of the end of this confounded rain we've been cursed with the last two weeks, if we need an excuse. And if I time it right, I may get out of having to help Pa. Uncle Dale got his truck stuck, and Pa went over with the tractor and got stuck too, and . . ."

"David?"

"Yeah?"

"Shut up and come get me."

"Oh, yeah. Guess so. Be there in twenty minutes."

"You can't get to MacTyrie in twenty minutes."

"*I* can."

"You coming in a jet or something?"

"Nah, just my Mustang."

"That's what I was afraid of. Well—try not to set the mountains on fire on your way."

"It's been raining for two weeks straight, Alec. The mountains are very, very wet." David's voice dripped sarcasm.

Alec turned serious. "Really, Mom almost didn't let me go this time, because of what she's heard about your driving—not from me, of course . . ."

"Of course."

". . . but then Dad came in and said 'Go! Get! No telling what your wild-eyed maniac friend will do if you don't!'"

David rolled his eyes toward the dingy ceiling. "Your father thinks I'm a wild-eyed maniac?"

"But he likes you anyway, otherwise he wouldn't have asked you all to put me up while they're at that conference next weekend."

David nodded. "Uh huh. No doubt he thinks you'll be a good influence on me as well, is that it?"

"Something to that effect, yes."

"Boy, is he mistaken!"

"Huh?"

"Never mind, old man," David said. "Gotta go, we're burning daylight."

David hung up the phone and flopped back against the doorjamb, grinning mischievously. *Damn, I feel good!* he chuckled to himself.

One reason, he knew, was the imminent return of good weather—just a little sunshine did wonders for his state of mind. And partly it was the promise of getting out of the house and off the farm for a while, away from the oppressive ordinariness of his family. And, too, there was the anticipation of good fellowship—he and Alec had not had a good long bull session in some time, and there were things that needed discussing.

But there was something deeper underlying it all, he realized as he started down the hall to pack. It was that rare and almost mystical elation which accompanied the discovery of some new thing that he somehow instinctively knew would be of lasting significance for the rest of his life. When it happened right, it was like the opening of a door in a high stone wall; and this particular door had opened when he had begun *Gods and Fighting Men*. From its first ringing line, the book had filled him with that same wild and unexpected joy he had felt when he'd first read *The Lord of the Rings* two years before. That book had given him "a new metaphor for existence"—that was the phrase Alec's English-teacher father had used. And now he had another.

He grinned again, in fiendish anticipation. He would tell that infidel Alec all about it—whether he wanted to know or not.

David's slim, blond mother was leaning against one of the back porch posts when he emerged from the house five minutes later. A frosted glass of ice tea tinkled in one hand; white flour patterned her faded blue Levis. She looked tired. "Somebody's dead," she observed flatly, pointing down the hill.

"Somebody's always dead."

She frowned, so that the crow's-feet in the tanned skin around her eyes deepened, as they had of late. "Don't get smart, boy!" she warned.

"Oh, I already am—got it from my mother." David flashed her his most dazzling smile as he leapt from the shadowed gloom of the low porch into the sudden glare of sun-dappled yard, his worn knapsack flapping loosely on his back as he sprinted toward the car. Little Billy was nowhere in sight.

In the harsh light the Mustang seemed somehow to shine even redder than usual, as if the steel of which it was made had been rendered red-hot by the afternoon sunshine. Its narrow chrome bumpers glittered so brilliantly they made David blink and his eyes water. Indeed the very air seemed to sparkle in some uncanny way, as if every floating dust mote were a minute, perfectly faceted diamond that materialized out of nowhere to gyrate crazily before him in a swirl of multicolored particles like iridescent dust thrown before a wind, briefly outlining every tree and leaf and blade of grass with a glittering halo of burning, scintillating color.

David stopped dead in his tracks, his mouth hanging open in curious incredulity, then wrenched off his glasses and stared at them foolishly. Though the lenses appeared clean, he wiped them on a corner of his shirttail and glanced up again, blinking rapidly.

The effect had ended.

A shrug. "Too hot, or something," he muttered to himself.

Little Billy came out from where he had been lurking behind the car. He stared at David uncertainly and extended the blue volume. "Here's your book, Davy. I'm sorry I bothered you."

David blinked again, smiled absently, and ruffled his brother's tousled hair. "No problem, kid."

Little Billy's eyes were wide, hopeful. "You're not *really* gonna give me to the undertaker, are you?"

"Couldn't get enough for you, squirt," David grinned. "No, of course not. Thanks, though, for getting this for me."

As he unslung the knapsack to stuff the book inside, David glimpsed the name neatly stenciled on the fading khaki canvas: SULLIVAN, D.

A chill passed over him, and he paused and looked up to see the crowds of people still clustered among the weathered tombstones and scruffy oak trees across the road. It was startling how clear the air had suddenly become, how much more sharply focused everything seemed. He almost felt as if he could read the names carved on the stones, count the leaves on the trees, see the tears glistening on those grief-stricken faces.

And David remembered another funeral three years before.

SULLIVAN, D—not himself, but that other David Sullivan, his father's youngest brother, after whom he had been named; David-the-elder, Uncle Dale had called him, to differentiate the two.

David-the-elder had embraced life with a burning enthusiasm not often seen in his family—and had found a sympathetic outlet for that enthusiasm in his precocious young nephew, whom he had taught to read by the age of four, and how to fish and hunt and camp and wrestle and swim and drive and a hundred other skills before David was twelve.

Then he had joined the army.

Two years later he was dead, blown to pieces where he wandered off duty on a Middle Eastern street. "An unprovoked terrorist action," the government called it. A twenty-minute funeral had marked barely twenty years of life. Not enough. But that night twenty-one shots had sounded over the family cemetery at Uncle Dale's farm, and a clench-jawed David-the-younger had fired each one into the star-filled darkness. It had been the least he could do. David felt his eyes mist over as he fished for his car keys. Once they had been David-the-elder's keys.

"You okay?" Little Billy asked hesitantly, concern shadowing his small features.

David shook his head as if to clear it, and smiled wanly, feeling too good to keep long company with such dark thoughts. "Yeah, sure."

He got in the car, cranked it, and turned on the radio. The nasal twang of some female country singer berating her long-suffering husband about "drinkin' and runnin' around" that suddenly assailed his ears sent David hastily fumbling in the glove box for a cassette instead. The song reminded him too much of home, sometimes.

Big Country, maybe—or U-2? No, that wasn't quite what he wanted. Tom Petty and the Heartbreakers? Close, but maybe something a little older. Ah—he knew just the thing.

A moment later, the Byrds's recording of "Mr. Tambourine Man" pulsed and jingled through the car. David found himself singing along as he paid token obeisance to the stop sign at the end of the gravel road and turned left onto the long straightaway that passed through his father's river bottom on its way from Atlanta to the resorts of western North Carolina. His tires chirped softly, leaving twin black streaks as he accelerated off toward MacTyrie. He frowned. There was a buzz in one of his new rear speakers.

He had already forgotten the funeral.

Seven minutes later David slid the car to a halt at the intersection that marked the effective center of downtown Enotah, where the MacTyrie road ran into Georgia 76. Twin signs pointed west toward Hiawassee and eastward to Clayton. To his right a hundred-year-old courthouse raised crumbling Gothic spires. The only traffic light in Enotah county blinked balefully overhead. Abruptly the car's engine stumbled. "Damn," he cursed as he glanced down at his gas gauge. It barely registered.

Fortunately he was in sight of Berrong's Texaco, where he had worked the previous summer pumping gas. A moment later he pulled in by the self-service pump, got out, and unscrewed the cap between the taillights. Behind the pyramid of oil cans in the station's plate glass window David saw chubby Earl Berrong nod and give him a thumbs-up sign. He grinned in turn, unhitched the nozzle, and inserted it into the car, drumming his fingers restlessly on the red paint as he watched the numbers roll by. Always something when he was in a hurry; he'd never make MacTyrie in twenty minutes now.

A Loretta Lynn song blared from a tinny speaker in the litter-strewn parking lot of the Enotah Burger across the highway, mingling discordantly with a car radio playing heavy metal—Def Leppard, maybe?—and the voices of the several youthful loiterers lounging by the service window.

One of the crowd laughed loudly, and they all looked in David's direction. A female voice called out something, but David couldn't catch it, and then the view was blocked by the bulk of a familiar black Ford pickup that pulled into the lane beside him.

His face lit up when he saw who it was.

A slender, red-haired girl stuck her head out the passenger's window. "Well, hello, David Sullivan, how're you a'doin'?" she drawled, her slightly pointed features sparkling with amused self-mockery. It was the way she always began a conversation with him.

"Well, Liz Hughes! I ain't seen you in a bear's age!" David took up the ritual greeting in his best mountain twang. He was at once delighted to see a friendly face, especially Liz's, and a little uncomfortable about the proximity of the group across the street—who might get ideas he was not quite ready for them to get yet. Liz had been a recurring theme in his thoughts lately, and David found that a touch unsettling. She'd always been a friend, but recently...

Beyond her, David could see Liz's mother talking animatedly to a red-faced Earl Berrong, who looked as though he would like to escape soon but didn't dare.

"What's up?" David asked after a moment's pause.

Liz answered promptly. "Oh, nothing much. What're *you* doing?"

"Going camping with Alec tonight, up on Lookout Rock." He hesitated. He and Liz had been good friends since elementary school, but her parents had separated the previous spring, and she had spent most of this summer with her father in Gainesville, which was fifty miles away. David was thus not quite certain how things stood or where to direct the conversation.

Liz solved the problem for him. "Gonna take me to the fair?" she asked abruptly, her eyes twinkling.

David glanced at the gas pump: eleven gallons. "I thought you might take *me* to the fair."

"Ha! Just 'cause I've got a driver's license now doesn't mean I'm gonna haul you around—though, now I think of it, I might ought to at that; we'd probably both live longer, considering your driving."

"What's *wrong* with my driving?" David glared at her as he drew himself up to his full five-foot-six, then jumped as a froth of gas shot unexpectedly out of the filler and onto his hands. He blushed furiously and looked around frantically for something to wipe them on, finally settling on his pants.

Liz raised an amused eyebrow. "Oh, there's nothing wrong with it—if you happen to live in Daytona or Talladega or somewhere. But don't change the subject. When you gonna take me to the fair?"

"When you wanna go?"

"Last time you asked me that we still went when you wanted to."

"Beggars can't be—"

"Hush, David. I want to go Sunday and try to catch the bluegrass show."

"The bluegrass show? Oh, come on, Liz. You know I can't stand that stuff."

"It's our heritage, David."

"*Your* heritage, maybe."

"Yours, too, David."

"Look, Liz, I don't feel like arguing music with you just now. I know better than to argue that subject with you any time." He sighed. "But if it'll make you happy, we can go, I guess—but I get to play my whole Byrds tape on the way."

"Ugh," said Liz, mostly to harass David, though she did not find the music at all offensive. "You limit yourself too much. But it's an even swap, I guess."

David snorted. "Limit myself indeed!"

Liz's dark-haired mother peered through the window behind her daughter. "Hi, Davy, how're you doin'? Liz'll be livin' with me for the rest of the summer, so why don't you come see her some?" She winked at him.

"Mother!" Liz hissed, her face reddening, then turned back to David. "Oh, and David, this little trip's just you and me, okay? None of your shadows."

David looked confused. "My shadows?"

"Little Billy and young Master McLean."

"My brother and my almost-brother? You got something against my brothers?"

"At some times and places, yes."

"Liz, if I didn't know you better..."

"Hush, David, not now. I'll have to check the show time and get back to you. Just be sure to bring plenty of money."

"I don't *have* plenty of money."

"Well, enchant some leaves or something. You're the one who's always calling himself the Sorcerer of Sullivan Cove," Liz called back as the pickup roared to life and rumbled away.

"Nice lookin' girl," observed Earl Berrong.

David nodded thoughtfully. "She is, I guess, now that you mention it—and getting better all the time. He handed Earl a wrinkled twenty-dollar bill, the fruit of his rather begrudged work on the farm. It wasn't much, but it kept him in gas and comic books.

"Sullivan's got a girlfriend," a male voice sang out from across the street as David got into the car.

He turned on the ignition and revved the engine, drowning the voices in the growl of dual exhausts and the Byrds singing "Eight Miles High."

"Alec, my lad," he said aloud to nobody as he shifted into second, "we gonna get at least partly that high tonight, just by walking up an old dirt road. High on life, I mean."

Six minutes later David crested the gap between two small mountains and beheld the tiny college town of MacTyrie drowsing in the valley below. A network of fields and tree-lined streams surrounded it, and above all reared the flat-topped mass of Huggins Ridge, its lesser slopes bracketing the village like protective arms. Expensive resort homes made incongruous warts along the lower ridge lines.

Closer in, a long curved bridge spanned one arm of the man-made lake that sent cold fingers probing far among the dreaming mountains. Many a once-sunny hollow lay drowned forever under that dark water, giving the otherwise pastoral landscape a quality of ominous mystery that appealed to David even when he saw it in the bright light of day. He slowed unconsciously, captivated by the image. It was as if he saw the whole valley with new clarity: The edges of things seemed somehow crisper, more sharply defined; their shapes more three-dimensional, their colors richer beneath the clear blue sky.

And how remarkably blue that sky had become! It was almost like a sheet of stained glass framed by encircling mountains. A solitary bird floated there, drifting in a lazy circle half as wide as the sky: something almost unbelievably huge. An eagle maybe— if there were eagles in Georgia. It was a little disconcerting. David blinked once, and the bird was gone, as if it had never been.

An unexpected shudder shook him as he flung the Mustang down the mountain curves and sped onto the bridge. A second tremor followed, token of another kind of fear he suppressed so deeply he did not consciously admit it even to himself: He was afraid of bridges. Unfortunately there was no way to get to Mac-Tyrie without going over one, or else going miles out of the way. The solution, then, was simply to cross them as quickly as possible. David floored the accelerator and looked out at the water, half expecting to see an arm clothed in white samite flourishing something above that silver surface. He held his breath. And then he was over the bridge. A roadside sign read MACTYRIE: 2 MILES.

Alec's house was on the first street on the left, a rather incongruous Cape Cod with dormer windows and a green shingled roof. Ivy covered most of the street side and flanked the driveway. A regiment of dogwoods that were Dr. McLean's pride screened the rest. There was precious little real yard.

Alec himself was waiting patiently beside the driveway, his backpack and tightly rolled sleeping bag stacked carefully beside him. Clad in clean jeans, hiking boots, and an immaculate black R.E.M. T-shirt, he was tall—taller than David, anyway— slender and dark-haired. And as perpetually neat as ever, David observed as he brought the Mustang to a screeching halt behind Dr. McLean's maroon Volvo. He didn't think he'd ever seen Alec look really disheveled, not even after a week of camping. As he got out of the car he cast a somewhat bemused glance down at his own scruffy clothing: a faded denim jacket from which he had ripped the sleeves, worn over his customary plain white T-shirt and faded jeans.

Alec was holding the hiking stick that David had given him for Christmas the year before. A runestaff, David had called it; he'd laboriously composed an appropriate verse, translated it into Norse runes using the dictionary as a guide, and then carved them on the ash staff:

> *Whoever holds to hinder here*
> *From Road that's right, from Quest that's clear,*
> *Think not to trick with tongue untrue,*
> *Nor veil the vision, nor the view;*
> *Look not to lose, nor lead astray*
> *Who wields this Warden of the Way.*

And as an afterthought he had carved two more lines:

> *These runes were wrought, these spells were spun,*
> *By David, son of Sullivan.*

David had capped the ends with iron in shop class, to his teacher's amusement, and had wrapped the grip with leather. Alec had not known quite what to make of it, but had been proud nonetheless, for whatever else it was, it was a thing made well and with affection. And, as Dr. McLean had observed, he was probably the only person in the country to get a runestaff for Christmas.

"Glad you could make it, old man," David began in a properly clipped British accent as he opened the trunk. He was good at accents, and at languages as well, another talent David-the-elder had encouraged.

Alec carefully laid his gear into the cramped compartment, noticing as he did David's own runestaff, a near twin to the one in his hand, almost hidden amid the clutter; then slammed the deck lid—too hard, so that David winced. "And only an hour late," he chided. "You did set the mountains on fire, didn't you? Tell me, Dr. Watson, will the headline in next week's *Mouth of the Mountains* read 'Air Force Jets Scramble as Unidentified Red Blur Terrorizes County'?"

David looked at him solemnly. "I was *delayed*, Alec. Had to get gas . . . saw Liz Hughes."

"Liz Hughes, huh?"

David nodded. "Wanted me to take her to the bluegrass show at the fair."

"The fair, huh?" Alec raised an eyebrow.

David jingled the keys. "You said something about being in a hurry?"

"Liz the one who spilt gas on you?"

David inhaled deeply, wrinkling his nose as he and Alec climbed into the car.

"Sulfurous and tormenting fumes."

Alec's brow wrinkled in puzzlement.

"Hamlet—sort of."

"Shakespeare! Yecch! That's what I go camping to forget!"

"Infidel! Heretic!"

"You don't have to live with it all the time."

David looked Alec square in the eye. "For every minute you sit there profaning the Bard, I will drive five miles an hour over the speed limit."

Alec fell instantly silent.

"Harpier cries: 'Tis time, 'tis time!" David hissed nasally in his Peter Lorre voice.

Alec bit his lower lip to keep from laughing as David turned the ignition key.

Chapter II: Trumpets Heard

Alec closed his eyes and held his breath around one final curve before the Mustang hit the long straightaway through the river-bottom below David's house. When his stomach told him it might be safe to open them again, he was greeted with the familiar sight of the Sullivan farmhouse, with its one front and two side porches, squatting halfway up a steep, treeless hill, the irregular line of outbuildings behind it seemingly the only rampart between it and the forest that grew up the mountain beyond.

David slammed on the brakes at the last possible instant and turned right.

"We *are* going to Lookout Rock, aren't we? You haven't changed your mind or anything?" Alec asked a little shakily as the car lurched to a halt in a hail of gravel a moment later.

"And where else would we go? It *is* my Place of Power, after all."

Alec relaxed visibly. "Well, that's good; I don't think I could face going anywhere else in your car."

David ignored the insult, but shot his friend a good-natured glare as he opened the door. "Nope, we'll go afoot. I just need to pick up a few things here." He tossed the keys to Alec and sprinted toward the house, leaving his friend behind to unload.

Little Billy met him in the yard, grinning like a possum. "Pa

says next time you run off like that when he's got work for you to
do, he's gonna skin you alive!"

"Ha!" David snorted as he leapt up the steps—just as his
father came out of the kitchen and onto the porch.

Stocky and shirtless, Big Billy Sullivan was covered with red
mud almost from the neck down, mud nearly the color of his
sunburned skin, and not much different from his auburn hair. *A
fire elemental*, David thought as the westering sunlight struck full
upon him. *Or a storm giant*, he added as he noticed Big Billy's
frown. He slowed reluctantly.

"I don't recall you askin' me if you could run off to Mac-
Tyrie," Big Billy rumbled.

"I was in a hurry, Pa. This is the first halfway clear day we've
had in weeks, and I told you that me and Alec were going camping as soon as there was decent weather for it."

"Or if I didn't have anything for you to do, which I did. You
knowed I needed help gettin' Uncle Dale's truck outta the mud.
But soon as you thought I might be thinkin' 'bout sendin' for you,
off you went." Big Billy folded his arms across his massive chest
and glanced into the yard where Alec continued to unload the car.

"I'm sorry, Pa, I—"

"I don't wanna hear it. But since you done got your buddy
here, you may as well run on this time. Better be back early in the
mornin', though, 'cause I'm gonna work your butt good tomorrow."

"I gather Papa Sullivan was not pleased with his oldest boy,"
said Alec when David returned a few minutes later.

David smiled and shook his head, but did not elaborate. He
had acquired a number of small bags and packages wrapped in
brown paper. "Venison," he stated simply.

"All right!" Alec exclaimed, his face suddenly breaking into a
smile. "David, my friend, there are some things you do well and
some things you don't do well, but one of the former, I am glad to
have been a part of, is your cooking of venison."

David laid an arm across Alec's shoulders and bent his head
close, whispering conspiratorially. "My pa taught me, and he
learned it from his pa. There's a secret that the men of our family
share; the women don't know and won't know. I'll pass it on to
my sons after me."

Alec raised surprised eyebrows. "Your sons? Didn't know you had any!"

"None to speak of, anyway," David said, and grinned smugly back.

"Didn't think so . . . unless you and old Leigh Smith . . . ?"

"Not likely!"

"Or Debbie Long?"

"Come on, I can do better than that!"

"Randi Huggins?"

"I *wish.*"

"So does she, so I hear."

"But she's not really my type."

Alec's eyes narrowed slyly. "Liz Hughes?"

"Alec! That would be like . . . like *incest!*"

"But they say incest is best."

"Well, it's a thing to think about, anyway."

"If I were you, I'd do more than think."

"Ha!"

"You brought it up."

"But can *you* keep it up? That is the question." David giggled and slapped his friend on the back.

Alec ignored him. "Just keeping my information current."

David began picking up his gear. "Maybe so, but I didn't expect to have to compose a dissertation on the topic. If anything changes, I'll let you know. Now, if you're through analyzing my sex life, can we get down to business?"

Alec grinned and nodded.

David shouldered his pack and pointed up the mountain with his runestaff. "That way, old man."

They began to walk—past the barn and the corn crib and the car shed, turning onto the dirt logging road that became the Sullivans's driveway further down. There were signs of "civilization" at first: beer cans and food wrappers left by parking couples who defied Big Billy's POSTED signs. David stopped at the first sharp curve in the road and gazed back down the mountain to where the family farm lay, framed by the dark and dreaming pines, a patch of light between the shady trunks. He checked his watch; it was almost six o'clock. They turned and climbed higher, soon lost the sound of the cars on the highway. The air became cooler, crisp and clean, and smelled of pine.

A little after seven they reached their destination. Halfway up the mountain, a spur trail broke off to the right, running more or less level beneath overhanging trees for a quarter mile or so before opening abruptly into an almost circular clearing atop a rock outcrop that jutted from the body of the mountain.

Once trilobites lived here, David thought as he glanced to the left where the hard stone of the mountain proper pushed through the encircling pines like the old bones of the earth wearing through the thin, tree-clad skin. A shimmering waterfall slid in what seemed like unnaturally slow motion down those black rocks to create at its bottom a small pool, maybe fifteen yards across. Mountain-born, it was always cold, even in high summer.

Without a word, the two boys picked their way among lichen-covered boulders and fallen tree trunks to the precipitous ledge that gave Lookout Rock its name. David's eyes misted slightly, as they always did when he beheld the expanses of furry-looking mountains, now beginning to purple as the sun lowered. Most of the towns were invisible, hidden behind the ridges, but here and there bits of highway showed themselves like a network of scars. The dark silver mirror of the lake lay silent and mysterious in this less populated end of the county. David's own four-times-great grandparents on his father's side had built a cabin that now lay beneath a hundred feet of that cold water. Their graves were there too. He sometimes wondered what they dreamed.

A lot of things have changed since then, he reflected as he busied himself building a small cooking fire, setting up his battered but well-loved cooking pot, and putting the almost frozen venison on to simmer with mushrooms, onions, carrots and potatoes—and a limp brown packet of the secret family seasonings. The odor soon mingled with the scent of pine trees and wet leaves, as the first breeze of evening brought the tiniest hint of chill creeping around the mountainside. It could get a little nippy on Lookout Rock, even in July.

Alec had finished setting up the tent in the traditional place at the edge of the clearing and now came over to stand beside his friend, wiping his dirty hands on his jeans. He was sweating lightly. "You don't suppose it's warm enough to go swimming, do you?" He glanced skeptically toward the pool.

David stood up and looked Alec straight in the eye. "It *is* July," he said. "It doesn't get any warmer than that. And, besides, my vainly hopeful friend, it's *never* been too cold for me to pay due respect to my Place of Power. Of *course* we're going swimming; we must placate the spirits of this place by offering our bodies naked to the waters."

Alec rolled his eyes. "Now?"

David slapped him roughly on the back. "Won't get any warmer tonight, kid. We've done it in April, so what's to worry about July?"

The wind shifted, whistling through the trees. The harsh cry of some unfamiliar bird crackled in the air. Suddenly David's eyes were itching furiously. He rubbed them and shook his head vigorously from side to side. *Smoke must be getting to them,* he thought.

"That wind feels like fall; we'll have to swim quick if we don't want to freeze our butts off," Alec sighed, rummaging in his pack for a towel before starting for the pool. He looked around for David, expecting to find him already at waterside and half undressed, but his friend had not moved; he stood staring toward the overlook, his brows lowered thoughtfully. "Davy?" he called tentatively. "Last one in's a rotten possum."

"My eyes keep tingling," David whispered, mostly to himself, as he slowly followed Alec to the edge of the pool. He felt strange, too, he realized: almost dizzy. Things seemed to slip in and out of focus. The sensation was almost exactly like the way new glasses made his eyes feel, as if something were forcing his vision, tugging at his eyes.

"Some of this cold water'll do wonders for 'em," Alec tossed over his shoulder as he skinned out of his T-shirt and started on the laces of his hiking boots.

"I hope so," David muttered absently. He cast one last backward glance toward the precipice and hastily began stripping off his clothes. A moment later both boys stood naked by the waterside. They hesitated for a moment, feeling the sly nip of wind against bare skin, knowing that the water was far, far colder. Still, there was tradition to consider—and honor.

"After you," said David.

"Your Place of Power," Alec pointed out.

David frowned, ever so slightly. Somehow that idea did not appeal to him just then, though he couldn't quite think why. He'd said the phrase himself only a moment before, had found it in some fantasy novel or other and appropriated it to designate his special place, that private place of beauty and contemplation he had claimed for his own, that he shared with no one else except by *his* choice. But now, for no apparent reason, such casual usage seemed frivolous, almost sacrilegious.

Alec cleared his throat. "Your Place of Power, I say."

David bit his lip and nodded decisively. "Right. Together then, and none of this sissy wading stuff: Jump in like men. Come on, race you to the falls."

Alec nodded in turn, and he and David simultaneously launched themselves in flat, shallow dives into the darkening water. David came up gasping as the coldness stole his breath, and ducked again, opening his eyes to let the water have a go at the annoying tingle. He felt a hand briefly brush Alec's kicking leg and struck off in the direction of the falls. A moment later, his fingers touched mossy rock, and he broke surface to see Alec's sleek, dark head emerge beside him spitting water. They both took deep breaths and started back.

David quickly found himself intensely uncomfortable, and not only from the chill of the water. The tingle in his eyes seemed to be getting worse. It was almost a burning now, and he thought he saw bright flashes in the water around him.

"Too cold for my blood," David gasped as he emerged from the water a mass of goosebumps. He gathered up his clothes and headed back to the fire to dry off and dress.

Alec stayed in a while longer, only coming out when he felt his fingers begin to numb. He wrapped his towel around his waist and made his way across the clearing, shivering all the way. David had returned to the edge of the lookout when he got there, gazing off into space again. The fading sunlight cast red highlights on David's bare shoulders.

"You look like a barbarian," Alec said as he tugged on his jeans and applied the towel to his hair. "You know, like on one of those science fiction book covers? All you need is a sword and a beautiful maiden and a fearful monster."

"And about ninety pounds of muscle and nine inches of height," David added offhandedly. Beyond him the sun touched the horizon.

"Stew smells good," Alec ventured.

David did not respond; he was gazing across space at the next high mountain over, a mountain whose nether slopes were entirely ringed by the lake—an island, but no less a mountain.

Bloody Bald, they called it, though it had a name in Cherokee. Bloody Bald, because the naked rock outcrops on its east and west flanks caught the first red rays of dawn and the last red rays of dusk.

Suddenly the half-heard, half-felt buzz was back, like some insect humming in front of David's face, and his eyes misted again, worse than ever, tingling badly. He rubbed them with his fingers, squinted, and stared into space, suddenly motionless.

For Bloody Bald shimmered as David looked at it, seeming at once to fade and to rise higher, into a symmetrical cone almost as perilously pointed as—as the steeple of a church, David thought. Misty, gray-green trees shrouded the lower slopes, merging into a sort of twisting haze of pastel colors that obscured the place where the shoreline should have been. A little higher up shadowy gardens now overlaid the naked rocks, weaving in and out of the ghostly filigree of embattled white walls which in turn gave way to the slender, fluted towers that crowned the peak like the clustered facets of some rare crystal. Pale banners flickered from the golden roofs of those tenuous pinnacles, and faint but clear came the distant sound of trumpets blowing.

It was like a watercolor painting seen through a screen of fog, like a thing seen in a dream, shaped by the mind alone. Or by the spirit.

David stood immobile, caught up.

Alec came over to stand beside him, followed with his own eyes David's rapt stare—and saw only the familiar forested peak, fuzzy with trees except at the top where red rocks blazed from purple shadows.

"David? Are you all right?"

David shook his head, wrenched off his glasses and rubbed his eyes vigorously, glanced at the ground then back into the air. He shook his head again and frowned.

"Davy?"

David turned to face his friend, and Alec could see the tension flow out of him like water, leaving a residue of incredulity—or was it fear?

"Strangest thing, Alec, I think I just had a hallucination."

"A hallucination? What *kind* of hallucination?"

"I don't know . . . I could have sworn just now that old Blood Top over there had a castle on it."

Alec folded his arms and nodded sarcastically. "Been reading those wild books again, haven't you? Finally affected your mind."

"I'm serious, Alec. It looked real. I mean *really* real—like a mixture of Mad Ludwig's castle and a Gothic cathedral transformed into glass. But now I look again I don't see a thing." He replaced his glasses and shook his head. "Must have been a trick of the light or something." David did not sound convinced.

The wind shifted then, and the smell of venison stew filled their nostrils. Suddenly hunger was uppermost in both their minds.

While David occupied himself putting the finishing touches on the stew, Alec picked up the blue volume from beside David's pack and flipped through it. "What's this book?" he asked, partly to take David's mind off his recent disturbance.

David squinted across the glare of firelight. "That's the book I was telling you about when you called. I never had a chance to finish it. Irish mythology."

"Irish, huh? You've worn out Greek and Roman and Norse and I don't know what all, so you're starting on somebody else's now?"

David seemed to have shaken off his recent confusion. "That's about it. I wish I'd run into it earlier; it's great stuff if you can pronounce the names. Got more magic than Greek and not as grim as Norse. The Irish believed in fairies—human-sized fairies. Still do, in fact, or so I gather from reading that. Well, actually, they call them the *Tuatha de Danaan,* or the "shee"— that's spelled s-i-d-h-e, by the way, but pronounced *shee,* like in banshee, I think."

"You're starting to sound like my dad."

"Sorry, 'tis just me Irish blood a'talkin' . . . now, laddie, would ye be havin' some o' me venison stew here? 'Tis made o' the flesh o' an Irish elk me brother found in a peat bog, the which he was led to by leprechauns."

Alec laughed loudly. "I'd rather have some of that deer your daddy shot last year out of season."

"I've got some of that, too, but it doesn't taste as good."

* * *

David read to Alec after supper—not that Alec really wanted him to, but David seemed to be himself again, and was off on another of his forays into strangeness, so there was really nothing Alec could do about it but just lie back and listen. He did read well, at least. Alec watched David for a long time as his friend droned on about the coming of the old gods to Ireland, about their wars with the Fir Bolg and the Milesians. The firelight cast ruddy gold onto the blond hair that brushed the collar of the sleeveless denim jacket David now wore over bare skin, laid flickering high-relief shadows on his blunt, regular features, darkened his already dark brows and lashes, so that in spite of the glasses Alec could almost imagine his friend with sword and shield in hand, checked tunic belted about his waist, marching off somewhere to fight for the freedom of Ireland.

David closed the book and looked over at Alec, who lay full length by the fire, his eyes closed, his mouth slightly open.

David walked over to him and kicked him gently on the sole of his boot. "Up, thou rump-fed runion!" he cried. "I didn't bring you up here to sleep."

"Aw, shucks! I was hoping you'd think I was really asleep and leave me alone, like any considerate person would do."

"No way."

They talked for a long time then, about Celtic mythology first, and then about the next school year, and Big Billy's tyranny, and what to make of Liz Hughes. But there was something a touch disquieting about the way David's conversation jumped erratically from subject to subject—something a little forced, as if he sought to disguise some underlying tension. It worried Alec, but he suppressed his concern, and then an unshakable drowsiness overtook him, and he crept off to the tent, leaving David awake with the stars.

A long time later Alec awoke and found David still absent. He drew aside the mesh door of the tent and saw his friend still sitting near the ledge, gazing northwest toward Bloody Bald. It was almost dark of the moon, and the night sky glittered with the constellations of summer, Cygnus foremost among them.

"Still seeing castles in the air?" Alec asked sleepily, coming to squat beside David.

"It was on the ground, not in the air, and no, I don't see it. I

must have been seeing things . . . but *damn*, Alec, it was so real!"
David pounded the rock with his fist.

"Well, you know, it could have been some kind of mirage or
something, reflecting part of Atlanta onto the mountains, or
something like that. I've never heard of mirages on a mountain,
though."

"I've never heard of castles on mountains in north Georgia,
either. All that cold water must have done something to my eyes."

Alec clapped an arm on his shoulder and shook him gently.
"No use losing sleep over, though."

"I guess not," David sighed wearily. He stood up, stretched,
and yawned. Back in the tent he flopped down atop his sleeping
bag and lay there trying to think about the magic of Ireland, trying
to picture in his mind's eye the coming of the Tuatha de Danaan.
But another image kept intruding in his thoughts, refusing to give
way: the image of a shadowy castle on a mountaintop.

Sleep claimed David finally, but he awoke again shortly before
sunrise to lie quietly with his face by the door, looking out into
the swirls of white mist awaiting banishment by the sun. A trace
of the uncharacteristic coolness remained in the air, and he snuggled gratefully into his sleeping bag, heard Alec groan and roll
over onto his back.

Yeah, just a couple more minutes and he would get up and
watch the sunrise from his Place of Power. It was the Celtic thing
to do, after all. He had learned that much from the books he'd
read: The Celts had ordered the year in certain ways, and certain
days and times of day had power—including dusk and dawn. So
what better way to make himself a part of that ancient tradition
than by watching the sun rise?

But still . . . it was warm in the sleeping bag, and he had sat up
very late waiting—or hoping—or simply *being*—he was not
certain which. He yawned. Five minutes more.

The sun had already broken the horizon when he woke again.
He sat up in the shadowed tent and cursed himself. For his eyes
were burning like fire, and far away he thought he could make out
the last fading call of trumpets. He rushed from the tent, gazed
out into mist-filled space . . . and saw nothing. The burning faded
abruptly, and he suddenly felt very foolish. David yawned and
stretched, yawned again, and crawled back into the tent. When he
awoke once more, it was to Alec kicking him none too gently in

the ribs and reminding him that Big Billy had a busy day planned for him, and if he wanted anything to eat, he'd better get up right then, or there wouldn't be anything left.

David sighed resignedly. That was always the way of it. Big Billy always had something for him to do—especially when there was something else he wanted to do more: to think over the disquieting events of the last day, for instance. Maybe tonight he'd take another look at Bloody Bald.

Small chance, he told himself bitterly; Big Billy would keep him busy right until dark—he always did. Well, David decided, he'd best get up and eat something, see if he could con Alec into a morning swim. It would be the last fun he'd have that day, that was for sure.

Chapter III: Music In The Night

(Saturday, August 1)

Uncle Dale Sullivan, whose dead youngest brother had been Big Billy's father, owned the next farm up the hollow and often "just thought he'd drop by" his nephew's house around suppertime. Full of pork chops and mashed potatoes, he and Big Billy were sitting on the side porch that overlooked the highway, discussing their day's work and watching evening creep into the valley. The soft clicking of dishes being washed in the kitchen made an almost musical counterpoint to the rhythmic squeaking of their rockers.

Bone tired from his day's begrudged labor, David slumped out of the kitchen and flopped down on the concrete steps, where he sat staring vacantly down the hill. The long, neat rows of glossy corn at the foot stirred in the soft evening breeze, their froth of tassels pale against the blue-green leaves like foam on a dirty sea. He could hear the occasional *whoosh* of a car as it came around the last curve off the high mountains to the right and accelerated on the straightaway that split the riverbottom. But he found himself straining his hearing for other sounds as well—sounds he was no longer certain he had heard. And his eyes tingled almost all the time now. He was still not sure exactly what he had seen, or if he had actually seen anything at all. It was beginning to worry him, though.

Big Billy gestured broadly with a stubby right hand. "I swear, Uncle Dale, I never could see why in the *hell* Grandpaw let them put that there highway through the middle of his riverbottom like that." He took a healthy swig from the can of Miller that sat atop a copy of *The Progressive Farmer* on the floor beside him. "No-siree," he continued, "if I had any idea why he done that, I'd sure say, but I don't. He was a strange old feller, so Daddy said."

"He was a strange 'un, all right." Uncle Dale nodded. "But he told me he let them put that road through there 'cause they wasn't nothin' would grow on it that was worth anything to anybody. He'd plant corn or cane, and it'd grow up fine and straight—except in that one place he'd get mornin' glories and sweet peas that'd strangle the life outta the corn—either that, or briars."

"Always did have trouble with briars down there," Big Billy agreed.

"So when the railroad folks come along, he let 'em follow that route, and the highway folks come after. It was the straightest way, anyhow."

"Yeah, Pa said that there was an Old Indian trail down there one time; I know I've found a good many arrowheads 'round there."

Uncle Dale leaned forward in his rocker; his voice took on a darker coloring. "Yep, Pa told me about that when I was a boy . . . but he told me something else, too, Bill—he told me that the Indians that was here before his folks settled said the trail was made by the Moon-eyed People. You know, them spooky folks the Cherokees say was here afore them—that built them ruins down on Fort Mountain, some say."

"I heard those forts were built by Prince Madoc in the year 1170," David interjected from the steps.

"That boy's a lot like his great-grandpaw was." Uncle Dale chuckled as if David were not there, but his eyes showed a gleam when they sought his grand-nephew. "Not as interested in this world as in the next—or at least in some other part of this 'un than the north Georgia mountains."

"I like the mountains just fine," David retorted. "I just don't like all the tourists we get nowadays."

"Them tourist folks brings trade, and trade brings money,

boy," Big Billy said brusquely. "Speaking of which, Dale, did I tell you I was thinking of switching to sorghum in this bottom too? The tourists love it, and old Webster Bryant over in Blairsville says he'll buy all I can work. Too late this year, but I may just take him up on it next time around."

Uncle Dale didn't answer; he was looking at David. He rocked back in his wooden rocker and crossed his ankles on the porch railing; David glanced up to see three inches of thin, white, hairless leg between the old man's socks and khaki work pants. He peered curiously down at his own bare, tanned legs, took off his glasses, and rubbed his eyes absently.

"Prince Madoc," Uncle Dale mused at length, ignoring Big Billy. "I've heard Paw talk about him once or twice, but he didn't put much stock in that story. One thing he did tell me about that old Indian trail, though, is that it's bordered by briars as far as he ever followed it—and that's a right smart ways. He's right, too; they may be little and scraggly and close in or far out, but they're there. And another thing he told me is that it goes on straight as a stick, right on over wood and water, says he got on it a huntin' one night and it like to scared him to death."

David was suddenly alert. "Did he say why?"

"Shore didn't, though I do know his dogs never come back with him that night. He made us boys and girls swear on the Bible not to go on it ourselves, 'specially not at night, and we never did. He got most of us so scared we never even mentioned it to our younguns—'course we was nearly all married and gone by then anyway . . . yore pa ever told you about it, Bill?"

"Hell no," Big Billy said sourly. He took another swig of beer and wiped his mouth on his hand. "Damn it, Uncle Dale. I ain't got time for such fairy-tale nonsense. You're as bad as the boys. Now, about that sorghum . . . I been meanin' to ask you . . ."

Little Billy came around the back corner of the house with an enormous piece of fried apple pie in his hand—which he rapidly stuffed into his mouth as soon as he saw David. "David says that fairies are as big as people and twice as beautiful," he announced loudly.

David rolled his eyes skyward.

"Damn it, and double damn it!" Big Billy exploded, slamming his fist down hard on the arm of his rocker. "I don't know what's worse: havin' boys that won't keep their mouths shut and that won't mind their own business when grown folks is talkin', or boys that won't work and just sets around all day with their noses in books. I don't give a tinker's damn about fairies and how big they are. They ain't no such things, and you both know it. If you'd read yore Bible 'stead of them funny books, you'd find that out." Big Billy picked up the copy of *The Progressive Farmer* from beside his chair, rolled it into a tube, and tossed it at David. "Here, if you want to read somethin' that'll be worth somethin' to you, read that."

The magazine unrolled itself in flight and landed in an untidy heap at David's feet.

David picked it up and shook it somewhat distastefully. Very pointedly he turned it upside-down and proceeded to peruse it with exaggerated attentiveness.

"You're readin' it upside down," observed Little Billy from the yard beside him.

David lowered the magazine, fixed his eyes on his younger brother, drew his lips back slowly, clicked his teeth precisely together one time, and looked back down at the upside-down print. His eyes tingled, ever so slightly, but—he realized for the first time—it felt good.

"Davy, could you turn the radio off? I can't sleep," Little Billy mumbled groggily into the darkness of David's bedroom.

David grunted and dragged his eyes open to see his little brother silhouetted in the doorway. A glance at his bedside clock showed it was nearly midnight.

"I don't have it on," he muttered, turning over and pulling a pillow over his head.

"You do so! I can hear it!"

"I do not! Now get back to bed."

"Da-a-a-a-vy!"

"It's *David,*" said David. "It must be the TV. Ma must be up watching the late show again. I guess she's having another one of her restless spells."

"It ain't the TV, it's comin' from your side of the house."

David levered himself up on his elbow and glared at the silhouette. "I-do-*not*-have-the-radio-on, darn it!"

"Maybe it's outside, then," Little Billy suggested hesitantly, shifting from foot to foot.

David paused, listening. "Now you mention it, I *do* hear something like music outside. Must be some couple parking down by the turn-off with the radio on loud. Pa'll have a fit if he hears it."

Little Billy's nose wrinkled thoughtfully. "Don't sound like radio no more."

David strained his own hearing. "That's true," he observed. He sat up in bed, drew the curtains aside, and looked out. A warm breeze floated over him—as warm that night as it had been cool the night before. He could see the solitary security light in the yard casting its circle of blue-white radiance onto the grass that sloped down to the cornfield. Away to the left he could make out the dirt road that came in from the hollow where Uncle David lived. He could hear the music more clearly, too, and it was strange music: not rock, nor yet country, nor what his pa called "that long-hair stuff." No, it was different: soft and sweet and low, with a hint of flutes and maybe something like guitars and a gentle jingling like bells. More than anything else, it reminded him of what little bagpipe music he had heard, only without the pipes, and a thousand times more strange. Strange, yet somehow familiar.

"Something's going on," David announced abruptly. "I'm going out to take a look."

"Not without me," Little Billy whispered loudly as his brother slipped out of bed.

"Oh no you don't! You're staying right here. I'm in enough trouble because of you already." David tugged on jeans, tennis shoes, and T-shirt, and headed for the door.

"I'll follow you anyway," Little Billy said diffidently.

David frowned, then sighed. "Okay, you can come, but *please* keep quiet. And if you say one word about this, I swear I'll cut a spancel out of your hide."

"What's a spancel?"

"A strip of skin cut from a corpse."

"But I ain't dead."

"You will be if you tell on me."

"I'll be quiet."

"You'd better."

David followed Little Billy into the hall. A floorboard squeaked like an alarm. He winced and gritted his teeth, but no sounds came from the rest of the house. He kept guard uneasily while Little Billy dashed into his own room to dress.

A moment later they stood in the yard. The mercury vapor light turned their skins an eerie green and their lips and nails blue.

"You look like Frankenstein," whispered Little Billy.

"And you look like Dracula's grandson. Now be quiet." David cocked his head. "Don't you hear it? Louder, coming from down by the highway. Come on, let's run!"

They ran down the long slope of hill, stopping at the irregular barrier of blackberry briars that fringed the bank above the corn-field. All at once the music was louder; David thought he could make out the jingle of bells and what almost sounded like voices singing. He screwed up his eyes until they hurt, staring vainly into the darkness in search of he knew not what.

And then—at the far side of that part of the field which lay beyond the highway—he saw . . . *something:* a file of pale yellow lights, winking in and out among the trees which bordered the small stream that marked the property line maybe an eighth of a mile away.

David inhaled sharply.

Little Billy stared up at him quizzically.

"Can you see anything, Little Billy?" he whispered.

Little Billy squinted into the gloom. "I can see a buncha light-nin' bugs flyin' along in a line over by the creek. Is that what you're talkin' about? Makes my eyes hurt. An' I can sorta hear some kinda singin' too." His voice trembled ever so slightly.

"Come on, then, let's take a closer look."

Little Billy hung back a moment, doubt a shadow among shadows on his face, but followed dutifully as his brother pushed through the briars, careful of the tiny thorns. They scooted down the clay slope and slipped into the welcome cover of the towering corn. As they thrust their way between the knobby stalks, the hard-edged leaves cut at their exposed skin like green knives. Finally they shouldered through the last row and crouched breath-lessly among the weeds and beer cans in the shallow ditch just below the shoulder of the highway.

David eased himself up cautiously.

Pain filled his eyes of a sudden. Pain—or light, he could not tell which—subsiding as quickly as it had come into an itching so

intense that he wrenched off his glasses and rubbed his lids furiously.

When he looked up again, the lights were closer, brighter,
following the line of the highway but a little way back from it,
angling gradually toward a point farther to the right where the
road and the fields and the mountain all converged.

"They're heading for the woods behind our house—toward
that old Indian trail Uncle Dale was talking about, I bet! Quick,
maybe we can get a better view from up there. Come on!"

David ducked back into the cornfield with Little Billy following reluctantly behind. Together they loped along between the last
row and the bank, gradually drawing ahead of the lights that were
fast approaching the highway to their left. Finally they halted at
the base of a steeper, rockier slope above which the forest began
in truth. A barricade of young maple trees and more blackberry
briars marked its edge, except at one place further on where a
dark gap showed in the leafy barrier—almost like an archway.

David hesitated, unsure, feeling somehow wary of the gap. He
glanced back, saw the lights still approaching, brighter and
brighter, and made his decision.

"Up the bank, Little Billy. Quick."

Little Billy grabbed David's pant leg. "You go, I don't wanna.
I'm scared."

David grasped his brother roughly by the shoulders. "You
want me to leave you alone in this cornfield in the middle of the
night?" The harshness of the words surprised both of them.

Little Billy stared at the ground. "No, Davy."

"Then shinny up that bank!"

Little Billy set his chin. "You first."

David frowned. "No running off?"

"Promise."

David scrambled up the bank, pausing before the thorny barrier at the top to hoist his brother the final few feet. The briars
were thicker than they had first appeared, but he kicked recklessly
through them and entered the forest, directly above the sharp
curve where the highway bent squarely east and began its tortur-
ous climb up to Franks Gap. They were only about a quarter mile
from home, so David knew he must have been in that place before, but in the bright moonlight of the summer night it seemed
different somehow, as if transfigured by that light. *Transfigured*

—*or maybe damned:* The thought was a flickering ghost in David's mind as he glanced around, saw the familiar trunks of pines and maples, the dark clumps of rhododendron and laurel. And the briars—more briars than he had ever seen, weaving in and out among the trees to the right, forming a subtle prickly barrier between himself and the house whose blue light he could dimly discern like a distant will-o'-the-wisp.

But to his left the ground was clearer and he could see that there *was* a sort of trail coming on straight up between the trees like a continuation of the line of highway. It was covered with moss and pine needles, but nothing else grew there. Indeed, it was that lack of growth that most clearly delineated it, David decided, though now he examined it closely, it appeared overlaid by a ribbonlike glaze of golden luminescence that did not quite seem to lie upon the ground. He almost thought he could make out patterns forming and reforming along that nebulous surface. But looking at it made the tingle in his eyes become almost painful, and he felt a strange reluctance to walk there. Instead, he dragged Little Billy along beside it until their way was blocked maybe a hundred yards up the mountain by the half-rotted trunk of a fallen tree.

David sat down on the log, pulling his brother down next to him. And then realization struck him like a blow: There could *be* no moonlight, for the moon had been full two weeks ago. Why, just the night before he had remarked to Alec about it being dark of the moon. Yet there was the same kind of cold, sourceless brightness in that place, like a snowfield seen in starlight—everywhere but on the trail itself. A shiver ran up his spine. The lights . . . the moon . . . the briars . . . this place . . .

Something was very wrong.

But at that moment a whisper of music reached his ears, and the first yellow lights became visible at the top of the bank.

His eyes felt as if they were on fire; his vision sharpened, blurred, sharpened again. He discovered that he was sweating, too, could feel the short hairs on the back of his neck rise one by one as more and more of the lights entered the forest, increasing in intensity and size as they came, coalescing finally into a nimbus of golden light that enfolded in its heart . . .

People.

If people they were: a great host of stern-faced men and

women riding as if in solemn procession astride great black or white horses, or horses whose smooth hides gleamed like polished steel or burnished copper or new-wrought gold. One or two of those steeds appeared to be scaled, and many sported fantastic horns or antlers, though whether these grew from the beasts themselves or were some work of artifice David could not tell.

But it was the appearance of the riders that made David's mouth fall open in wonder, for he had never witnessed such a display of color and texture and form as now passed before him like a dream from another age.

They were a tall people—both men and women—and beautiful: slim of build, narrow of chin, slanted of brow, with long, shining hair, most frequently black, and flashing eyes that seemed at once menacing and remote.

Long, jewel-toned gowns of a heavy napped fabric like velvet accentuated the proud carriage of most of the women, though here and there rode one clad in strangely cut garb patterned in elaborate plaids or checks. The majority of the men wore long hose and short, tight tunics with flowing sleeves, but an occasional one was dressed in a longer robe or in clothing of a much simpler, looser style and rougher texture. A few members of both sexes wore glittering mail or plate armor. Tassels and jewels and feathers and fringes were everywhere; and here and there was the glint of shiny metal blades and golden crowns. The host had stopped singing now, but from the bells on their clothing and their horse trappings rang out a gentle, constant melody, taking its rhythm from their tread.

At their head rode a man clad in silver armor wrought of overlapping ridged plates like fishes' scales, each one rayed with a blazing filigree of golden wire. His eyes were the color of deep still water, and the long fair hair that flowed like silk from beneath a plain silver circlet shone like the sun. He sat astride a long-limbed white stallion and bore a naked sword across the saddle before him. A white cloak swept from his shoulders, its golden fringe rippling about his ankles. The light came strongest from him.

David felt Little Billy's hand tense in his own. A quick downward glance showed the little boy staring not at the spectacle on the trail, but at David himself. A disturbing thought struck him. "See anything . . . odd?" he asked carefully.

Little Billy shook his head uneasily. "Nope. Just lights. Bright lights, like the air was shinin'."

David felt his breath catch, the copper taste of fear filled his mouth. He started to stand, to run away, but something held him back. He was seeing something strange, uncanny even—quite possibly dangerous—but no power on earth would have moved him then.

"I want to go home, Davy!"

"Hang on, kid, just a minute more. There's something I want to check out."

"Davy—"

"Hush!"

The procession drew nearer; the leader passed the two boys as if they were not there. Indeed, few of the lords and ladies paid them any heed, though some did spare them a brief, amused glance, and one or two looked slightly puzzled. But another, a man dressed more simply than most in a long robe of black and silver, reined his black horse to a slow walk and stared at them intently through eyes narrowed to baleful slits. "Hail, Children of Death," he called derisively down at them as he rode past.

The voice filled David's ears like a sound heard underwater—a sound more felt in the mind than heard in the ear. Suddenly he was frightened; chill after chill danced upon his body. He swallowed hard and rose automatically, jerking Little Billy up beside him, took a step forward. "Hello . . . Sir?" he finally managed to croak to the other's departing back.

Little Billy stared at his brother in bewilderment. "Who're you talkin' to, Davy? I don't see nobody. You're scarin' me! I wanna go *home!*"

"Be quiet!" David growled out of the corner of his mouth.

The black-clad figure jerked his horse to a dead stop and twisted around in his saddle. "You can see us!" he whispered fiercely, his voice almost a hiss. He turned to the gray-clad woman who rode nearest behind him. An enormous black crow perched arrogantly on her shoulder. "The man-child can see us!"

David suddenly felt very uneasy, but he steeled himself. "Of . . . of course I can see you," he stammered. "You're here, aren't you?"

"Who's here, Davy? You better quit scarin' me, or I'm gonna

tell Pa!" He kicked insistently at David's right foot. "C'mon, let's go!"

David grimaced at the slight discomfort, but did not move as a buzz of anticipation spread through the host like the swarming of bees. By ones and twos the mounted figures began to stop and gather round the boys, the tall shapes looming above them like the towers of some sinister citadel.

Suddenly David was afraid. Truly afraid. He began backing away, partly in response to that fear, partly in subconscious response to his brother's insistent tugs—only to discover to his horror that he could go so far and no further. Something stopped him: a vague paralysis in his legs, an unyielding surface in the very air itself. He glanced down, saw the golden glimmer that now lay beneath his feet. Somehow, in spite of his intentions to the contrary, he had stepped onto the track. *Oh my God!* he thought. *We're trapped by their magic!*

Little Billy screamed, a forlorn sound in the night, as he, too, felt that barrier press against his back. "I can't move, Davy—my legs are froze!" he cried. He released his grip on David's arm and tried to run, but only succeeded in falling flat on his face, to lie sobbing on the moss.

David squatted carefully down beside him and helped him up, all the while keeping a wary eye on the encircling host. "Hang on, kid," David whispered desperately in his ear.

The black-clad man brought his horse to stand directly in front of the boys. "And who are *you*, mortals, to gaze upon the Sidhe? —that *dares* to question the Hosts of Dana when they are about their Riding?" he barked sharply. His nostrils flared, and more than a touch of malice colored his voice.

"You are the *Sidhe?*" David cried shakily as he took Little Billy in his arms and stood up. "I thought you only lived in Ireland."

"Do you question my word?" the man snapped. "Would you have me unsoul both of you here and now?" His eyes burned like coals.

But then a shadow of thought flashed across the man's face and his chiseled features softened abruptly. He smiled a little too eagerly. "Ah, but I forgot myself, mortal lad, for time passes and we have a great distance to travel tonight. Come with us, if you would know more—and bring your brother as well. Why not?

Long has it been since we have taken two sons of men into our number. We grow bored with our own company"—he cast a dark glance toward the head of the line—"some of us, anyway." He extended a black-gloved hand which David saw was covered with tiny metal plates that tinkled slightly as he moved; minute jewels winked from its surface.

"Come back in a few years, then," David said hesitantly. He tried to sound brave, but he felt a point of fear begin in the middle of his back and slowly spread throughout his body. His pulse raced.

The man's face hardened at once. "Then you should know, *human*, that to see us is not a good thing. It is likely that we will curse you for your impertinence. It is even likely that you will die—and your brother as well."

"Not Little Billy," David cried. "He hasn't done anything to you. I don't think he can even see you."

"See who, Davy?" came a trembling whisper from where Little Billy's face was pressed against David's shoulder. "Done what? Who're you talkin' to? I want to go *home!*" The last word rose suddenly to a shriek. The little boy began pounding his brother's face and shoulders with his fists, so that David had to shift his grip to retain his hold.

"Be *still!*" he hissed through gritted teeth. "I'm not doing this for fun, believe me!"

The Sidhe-lord raised a thoughtful eyebrow, haughtily oblivious to the little boy's fear. He stared absently at David. "The little one cannot see us . . . yet *you* can," he mused. "But none of your kind can see us unless *we* will it—or unless . . ."

David caught the muttered words. "Unless?"

The dark man's eyes narrowed again, but he did not answer. "We could take him with us anyway, you know, and leave a changeling," he said after a moment. "Or we could take *you* instead, or both of you."

"Don't take Little Billy, he's my mama's favorite."

"Take me *where?*" the little boy shrieked. "You ain't takin' me nowhere." And with that he sank his teeth in David's ear, simultaneously striking out at him with renewed fury. His body twisted violently in David's arms like an enraged cat.

David could not retain his hold. Little Billy thrust himself free and half jumped, half fell from his brother's grasp. He hit the shimmering surface of the track with both feet at once—and crumpled simultaneously into a motionless pile.

David flung himself forward and knelt beside the still form, tried to feel for a pulse at his throat. He glared up at the Faery lord. "What've you done to him?" he shouted. "If you've hurt him, I'll . . . I'll . . ."

"You'll what?" the dark man asked silkily. "Nothing, I imagine—but he is only sleeping. I am tired of being interrupted at my bargaining. Now, we were discussing what you have to offer in exchange for the small one's freedom. For you should know that no one meets the Sidhe without paying the price of that meeting." He folded his arms across the high pommel of his saddle and glared intently down at David like a snake regarding an egg it intended to swallow. David could not return his stare.

"I don't think I've got anything you'd want," David said in a small voice. "Let me see . . ." He began searching his pockets and found them empty. Reluctantly he took his brother in his arms and stood up, despair a gray mask upon his face.

"Well, then, it must be yourself," the man replied, smiling maliciously.

The woman with the crow spoke then, her voice colder even than the black-clad man's. "Do not forget the Laws of Dana, Windmaster. They are mightier than any of us. You may not impose your will on the boy unless you give him some chance for escape."

An angry scowl clouded the man's features then, his mouth hardened to a thin line, but at last he spoke. "So be it, then. I will make you a bargain, boy. If you can answer three questions, I will let you go free, and your brother as well."

David was suddenly wary. "Just as we are? Not changed or enchanted or anything?"

The man looked vaguely amused. "If that is your will, exactly as you came here."

"And if I lose?"

"Then you will come with us."

David took a deep breath and nodded grimly. "I've . . . I've got a request to make, for myself, too—if I win."

The black-clad man laughed derisively. "So you would now crave favors of the Sidhe? Well, if nothing else, you are brave, mortal lad—brave or a fool."

"It *is* his right," the gray-clad woman observed pointedly.

"Ask then," the man snapped. "We can but say yes or no."

David shot the woman an uncertain smile and cleared his throat. "If I lose, you'll gain control over me, right? If I win, I'll gain nothing but a memory which I may not trust as I get older. I'd like to have something, you know, *real* from you all, so that I'll know I'm not having a dream or anything. And I'd like to ask *you all* some questions—three, I guess—in return . . . after all, I may not get another chance to see you folks."

"Do you forget so soon that you will be gaining your freedom?" the man replied sharply. "That is enough for most men to ask, and those who win it think themselves fortunate. Yet it is ever the way with you mortals that you desire more than is your right. But since you *are* a mortal and thus not likely to win, I will agree."

David swallowed hard. "Then I accept, I guess. Any time you're ready." He shifted his sleeping brother to a more comfortable position and squared his shoulders. He had to clamp his jaws together to keep his teeth from chattering.

The black-clad man thought for a moment, then spoke: "Name the stars in the sky."

David felt as if cold lightning had pierced his heart. "That's not a fair question!" he protested.

"Indeed, it is not," the crow-woman interjected. "You *do* know the rules, do you not, Windmaster? For if you do not, you insult the honor of the contest. You must ask only questions to which the answers are known among those you ask, if they have the learning for it. And since you yourself cannot answer that one, I think you had better find another question, or I will find one for you."

The dark Faery dipped his head mockingly. "As you will, Mistress of Battles. If I am to deal with fools, then I must ask foolish questions." He looked back at David.

"What animal did Queen Maeve of Connacht most love, and what animal did she most hate? Does *that* satisfy you, Morrigu?"

A low murmur rose within the host behind him, and knowing smiles crossed those beautiful, remote faces, as if the question was a familiar opening move in some ancient game.

"That's still not a fair question!" David cried. "That's two questions!"

"A coin may have two faces and yet be one coin," the dark man replied coldly. "I do not think even Morrigu will argue that point. Now answer—or come with us."

David closed his eyes, his thoughts racing frantically. The question wasn't as difficult as he had feared; the answer was in something he had read recently. He knew that Queen Maeve was a character in another book Lady Gregory had written, this one about the *Tain Bo Cuailnge*, The Cattle Raid of Cooley. He had read it last week, right before *Gods and Fighting Men*, but what was it called? *Cuchulain of Muirthme?* And he knew that Queen Maeve had gone to war over a cow, so that was probably the answer to the first part. But of the second, he was not so certain.

"The animal she most loved, I'm not sure about," he said at last, his voice quivering. "But the one she most *wanted* was the Brown Bull of Cooley. As to which one she most hated, I can't be sure about that either; I don't think the book I read said . . . but wait a minute! Cuchulain means 'the Hound of Culaign' or something like that, doesn't it? He was called that because he had to take the place of somebody's watchdog he killed. Is that it? It must be! He *was* her worst enemy, in battle at least. You were trying to trick me! You must have been! The answer must be Cuchulain!"

Behind the dark man a woman in a silver coronet bent her head toward the red-robed lady who rode beside her and whispered, "The boy has some wit about him, a rare thing indeed on this shore."

"You are correct so far," said the Faery lord. "But I have a second question, and this one will not be so easy."

"I'm ready any time," David said, trying to keep his voice steady, his bold words belying the fear that threatened to take complete control. His only comfort was the warmth of Little Billy's sleeping body against his own.

The Faery lord paused a moment. "What did the Tuatha de Danaan bring with them to Ireland?"

David's face brightened in spite of his fear. This was one he knew right off. It was in Lady Gregory, too; he'd read the section to Alec only the night before.

He took a deep breath. "Let's see," he said, looking down at the pine needles on the ground. "There was a cauldron, as I recall; and a spear, a magic spear; and a sword—magic, too; and a stone that was supposed to cry out when the true king stepped on it. I'm glad you didn't ask me their names, though, because I sure couldn't have told you."

"I will be more careful how I phrase my questions," the Faery lord replied archly, "but you are correct." A faint, ironic smile played about his lips, an eyebrow lifted slightly, but only for a moment before his forehead furrowed again, and his brows lowered over eyes that flashed like diamonds. "Let me see, this is my last chance for a changeling, so I must win with this one."

A disturbance arose among the crowded hosts, then. The white-cloaked leader had turned his horse and now rode back down the milling ranks toward the black-clad man. His searching glance barely swept across the brothers as he came to face the other. It was as if the two bright stars in Orion strove for supremacy in the night sky. The very air seemed to withdraw from between them.

"What are you doing, Ailill?" asked the white-clad man. "I did not think you interested in mortals."

"And I thought you so interested in them that you might want one or two to observe—perhaps to plant in your garden," Ailill shot back haughtily. "Besides, this one is special: This one has the Sight. So I play the Question Game with him, the stakes being nothing less than freedom for himself and his brother."

"I've seen my share of mortals," the other observed coolly, "and these do not seem particularly remarkable. But you are correct about the older one"—he pointed toward David—"he does seem to have the Sight; it shows in his eyes. He also seems to have both wit and courage to his credit, maybe even a little of the stuff of heroes. But I wonder at your reasoning, Ailill. Do you really think I want a changeling, particularly one of *your* choosing? Or are you simply trying to stir up trouble between the Sidhe and mortal men—trouble we do not need? Might you even be trying to contrive a confrontation with me? Since you know Lugh chose not to ride with us, do you test my authority as his second? What would Finvarra say, whose ambassador you are—or have you so soon forgotten?"

"I have only your best interests in mind," Ailill answered smoothly, but his tone belied the words. "That, and our brief amusement on this tiresome journey through the Lands of Men."

"Then you will not mind giving the last question to me?"

Ailill's hands strayed toward his sword hilt, and he said nothing for a moment; but his white skin took on a flush of anger, and his eyes grew as dark as his hair. David saw him open his mouth, as if to speak some bitter retort, and then take a firmer set.

"You came perilously close to breaking the Rules on the first question," the Morrigu noted. "I would be careful what I did now."

"Nor, I think, would Finvarra be pleased; *he,* at least, is a man of honor," the white-clad man added.

"I seem to have no choice, then," Ailill replied angrily, the merest trace of uncertainty coloring his voice. "If it is the will of the mortal lad, I will relinquish my last question. It is, after all, *his* decision, in the end."

David breathed a mental sigh of relief, though why he thought he was better off with this new turn of affairs, he didn't know. "If that's what you folks want to do, that's how it'll have to be, I guess. Go on and ask—and get it over with."

"Standard Rules, I presume?" the white-clad man asked the crow-woman before turning toward David and Little Billy.

"The Rules as proclaimed by Dana," the woman affirmed.

The man nodded imperceptibly, dropped the reins of his white horse, and folded his arms across his chest.

"So you think you know something about the Sidhe, mortal lad?" the Faery said. "So you think what you have read in books will suffice to save you? Well, then, let us see how good you really are. Since you were spared having to tell the names of the stars in the sky, I will ask you a simpler question: What is *my* name?"

Out of the frying pan, thought David in dismay. *How should I know his name? I might as well try to name the stars, much good it would do me. Now I know how Gollum felt when Bilbo asked what he had in his pocket. . . . Still, there must be a way; they said that if I had the right learning, I would know—but they all look alike to me!*

David studied the man carefully, taking in every detail of the silver armor, of the face and form, but could make out no special insignia, no distinctive marks that might offer some clue to his identity. The man had begun drumming his fingers on his upper arms, as if impatient. David noticed the movement, slight though it was, and looked more closely at the man's hands. The left one was encased in an articulated silver gauntlet that came up over the wrist in an elaborate flare. But the right one was different somehow; the construction was not the same—its workmanship seemed more delicate, more like a real hand. He knew that one of the Sidhe had lost an arm in battle and a new one had been made for him of silver. All at once David knew the answer to the third question.

"Your name is Nuada of the Silver Hand," he said, "or however you pronounce it. I hope that's close enough."

The man nodded and glanced back at the assembled host and then straight across at Ailill, whose diamond eyes now glinted with hints of ruby flame; but Nuada bore the brunt of that anger.

"You gave it away, Nuada. You helped him," the black-clad man snapped.

"*I* helped him? *You* gave me the question, so it's not your concern anymore, is it? He is free now." Nuada flashed a triumphant grin at his adversary and turned back to David. "You have won the contest," he said with unexpected gentleness. "You are free to go."

David sighed a long soft sigh; his knees sagged as the tension flowed so swiftly from his body that he nearly collapsed. Much of his fear had fallen away as well, and in its place came an unexpected return of some of his old cockiness.

He looked up toward Nuada, faced him eye to eye. "Don't *I* get three questions now?"

Nuada's head snapped around. "You promised him *that*, Ailill? You *are* a fool."

Ailill snorted sullenly. "I did. I did not plan on his winning."

"A fool twice over, then . . . but still, he has won fairly, and so we are bound." Nuada turned back to David. "Ask, mortal," he said, as if intoning an ancient ritual, "and if it is within our power to answer, we will. But be warned that if you seek to learn the future, only ill can come of it."

"Oh, I don't want to know the future," David replied almost casually. "I just want to satisfy my curiosity. After all, you don't just come upon the Tuatha de Danaan riding through your daddy's bottom land every day . . . and you *were* trespassing—by our laws."

"And not by ours, which are older. But ask."

"I'll put it in one question, then: Who are you, exactly; why are you here; and where're you going?" They were not the best questions he could have asked, he knew, but he hadn't really considered what would happen if he won the contest.

Nuada took a deep breath and began. "As Ailill has doubtless told you, we are the Sidhe. Among us we number some of the Tuatha de Danaan, whom men call the old gods of Ireland. Since you have not asked our separate names, I will not give them to you, though you may have mine, as you have won it, and Ailill has forfeited his, so you may have it as well. As to *what* the Sidhe are, that is beyond the scope of your question.

"But as to why we are here, by which I assume you mean in this place and not some other; that is a thing both easy to know and hard to tell. Perhaps it is best to say simply that only in a very few places does the World in which we customarily dwell touch your own, and only in those few places can we find true rest from our wanderings on the Straight Tracks between the stars. Alas! Not all such places are the same; some are more firmly rooted to your World than others, and once there were many more than now remain. But all such resting places we cherish, and this is one of them. Tir-Nan-Og, we call it: the Land of the Young."

David looked puzzled for a moment, but Nuada went on obliviously.

"And to answer your third question: Many of our kindred still dwell in Erenn, and many there have kindred here. This Track we now ride connects the two, yet that passage becomes ever more difficult as more and more the works of men breach the Walls between the Worlds. But, still, there are certain times of year— four of them, to be exact, of which this is one—when the Road is strongest and the journey less perilous. Those times we follow the Track to the Eastern Sea to greet whomever has chosen to come here. That is why we ride tonight, and where."

Nuada paused, as if considering whether or not to continue, and the strength of his gaze made David feel as if his soul were being read. "You have a sympathy for the old things, David Sullivan, that I can tell. It is now a rare child indeed, in this or any other land, who has heard of the Sidhe at all, much less Cuchulain or Nuada Airgetlam. And you have the Second Sight, as well— and that is a gift both precious and perilous. Now farewell, David Sullivan, for the Track calls us, and the Track may not be denied."

David felt his eyes tingle once more. Little Billy snored softly. All at once David felt very sleepy himself. He took a step backward, and then another. The paralysis was gone, the barrier lifted.

Nuada extended his silver hand forward and then raised it above his head in salute before gathering up his reins. He shook them once, so that the silver bells chimed, and then again, and again, and the host took up the rhythm with other bells, and with tambourines and flutes. Even the golden Track beneath them began to pulse gently. Old, that music sounded—older than man, David suspected—and filled with a heart-rending longing.

Little Billy slept quietly. David watched until the last horse had woven its way out of sight among the trees. Where the Sidhe had passed, the moss was unbroken, the pine needles unstirred. Only a faint golden glimmer remained to mark their passage, and then that too faded. He yawned again and began the walk home, his brother clutched in his arms.

As he came to the line of briars, David paused. They seemed lower, less densely tangled, less . . . vigilant. And he noticed that mortality had taken back the night: It was dark again—moonless, as it should be.

As the last light faded behind him, he did not see Ailill draw a needlelike dagger from a sheath at his waist and very discreetly prick his own right forefinger, which he then shook so that three drops of blood fell to the ground.

Nor did he see another member of the company, who had fallen unobtrusively back to ride near the end of the procession, rein his horse to a halt and turn empty silver eyes after him, and with great precision inscribe a circle in the air with the ringed fourth finger of his right hand.

Chapter IV: The Ring Of The Sidhe

(Sunday, August 2)

"I have seen the Sidhe!" David said to himself, flopping back against his pillow, arms folded reflectively behind his head.

It was not the first time those words had chimed in his thoughts that night. No, he had whispered them over and over again as he passed ghostlike through the dark forest, across the yard, into the silent house—never certain if he walked, or ran, or moved by a remnant of some supernatural power that lingered yet about him. He had seen, but still could not believe; his mind recoiled from what it had witnessed. Already his body was falling asleep around him as he strove to sort his confused thoughts. *He had seen the Sidhe!*

The Sidhe.

Impossible; or was it? That castle on Bloody Bald, the one he had almost convinced himself had all been a hallucination or the work of an overly active imagination—it was *real!* He *had* seen it, *had* heard the horns of Elfland greeting dusk and dawn.

And his eye problem—the recurring itchy tingle. Was that what had enabled him to look into that other world? They had called it Second Sight. But how did it work? More to the point, how did he get it? Certainly he had not always had it.

David yawned, stretched luxuriously, and glanced across the room to the door where Little Billy had appeared the night before. Abruptly he had a troubling thought: Exactly how much *had* Little Billy seen? What would *he* remember? The little boy *had* seen the lights and heard the music, that much was clear. Yet he had not seemed to see anything during the actual encounter, at least not if his response to David's actions was any indication. And the Sidhe had said they were visible to mortals—it was funny thinking of himself as a "mortal"—only if *they* chose, or, he supposed, if they had the Sight. For that matter, why had Little Billy not re-awakened, even when David laid him in bed? Was that more Faery magic? Or—as David was beginning to fear—something worse? He wished he'd thought to ask Nuada a few more questions, but it was too late now. He was probably lucky to get away with his skin. What had they got themselves into?

God, he was tired, he realized, as consciousness faded further —not entirely voluntarily. But there was something lingering in the back of David's mind, one more thing that he needed to recall before he could sleep—something important. But whatever it was hovered tantalizingly just beyond recall and would not focus. And as his mind dropped its guard to follow that elusive something, sleep found him instead.

Certainly it was not enough sleep, but when his mother hollered in the door that breakfast was ready and he'd better get it while it was hot because she was going to church and wasn't going to cook but once, David woke immediately, unexpectedly refreshed. Simultaneously he realized what had been bothering him the night before. It pranced into his consciousness and sat there clear as day: He had forgotten to ask the Sidhe for the promised token of their meeting.

"Crap," he said aloud as he climbed out of bed and pulled on his jeans, noting a few briars still caught in the worn denim. He paused to look in on Little Billy, who slept peacefully, a blissful smile upon his face, seeming none the worse for wear, then padded barefoot into the bathroom.

David splashed cold water on his face, ran a comb roughly through his tangled hair, and was just picking up his toothbrush when he felt a sudden burning pain against his right thigh, like when Mike Wheeler had put a hot penny down the back of his

shirt in the eighth grade. He glanced quickly down, half expecting
to see smoke, but saw nothing; stuck his hand into his pocket and
found the source of the heat—and felt it grow cooler even as he
fished it out and looked at it: a silver ring, almost a quarter of an
inch wide, entirely plain except for an indentation running completely around the circumference. Automatically he slid it onto
the forefinger of his left hand.

It fit, though perhaps a big snugly. He raised it to eye level to
examine it more carefully. Not as plain as he had thought; there
was a pattern in the indentation, an intricate knotwork of interlac-
ing lines that passed over and under each other in an endless
looping circle. He found his eyes following that pattern, fascinated. Simple it was, and yet fabulously complex. And beautiful
—the most beautiful thing he had ever seen. It never occurred to
him to wonder where it had come from. He knew. "I *have* seen
the Sidhe!" he whispered.

Little Billy trotted into the bathroom, yawning hugely, rubbing
his eyes with his fists. David whirled around, glaring, and jerked
his hand behind his back.

"Don't you ever knock?"

"Door was open. Now get, I gotta go. Ma's lookin' for you."

"So what else is new?"

Behind his back David tugged at the ring, and it came loose,
slipping capriciously from his grasp to fall to the beige tile floor
with a gentle *ping*. He snatched it on the second bounce and
stuffed it hastily back into his pocket, realizing as he did that
trying to hide it was absolutely the wrong thing to do. His brother
would be suspicious now.

"What's that?" Little Billy asked sharply.

"Oh, just a ring." David tried to change the subject. "Did you
sleep okay last night?" he asked carefully.

"Fine. Had some funny dreams, though."

Well, that's a relief, thought David.

His brother stared solemnly at him. "Where'd you get the
ring?"

"Found it. What'd you dream about?"

"Nothin' much. Where'd you find it?"

"Up in the woods."

"When?"

"When . . ." He hesitated; he was not ready for this, not when there was so much to sort out. "When me and Alec went camping a couple of nights ago."

Little Billy's eyes narrowed suspiciously. "Then how come I never seen it before? How come you never showed it to me?"

David was not at all pleased with his brother's persistence.

"I'll show you my hand on your backside if you don't hush up."

"You're hidin' somethin', ain't you, Davy? You didn't find that old ring, did you?"

David thought desperately. "I got it from the . . . from a . . . from a girl," he said finally, making up the best excuse he could on such short notice, immediately aware of how lame it probably sounded.

Little Billy raised dubious eyebrows. "You got a girlfriend?"

"Don't tell . . . please?"

"Okay," Little Billy agreed, a bit too quickly.

"Promise?"

"Yeah."

"Good. . . . Oh, and thanks."

"Had my fingers crossed," Little Billy whispered gleefully as David left him alone in the bathroom. *Teach him to keep secrets!*

So much was whirling through David's mind as he drifted down the hall to breakfast that he felt almost numb. There was the night before to consider, of course, when things he had thought unreal, or at best safely distanced, had suddenly crowded hard and near upon him, so that the entire composition of reality had shifted around him. And there was the matter of the ring, and of the lie had had just told Little Billy and already regretted. He had always preferred telling as much of the truth as he could when in a difficult situation—it made getting caught harder. *Oh well,* he thought as he slumped into the kitchen and sank down at the table that dominated the center of the room, *maybe Little Billy has already forgotten about it; at least he doesn't seem to remember last night. Thank God for that!*

That! The encounter with the Sidhe! Had it really happened? David shivered suddenly. If things had not gone as they had—if he had not won the riddle game—he would not be sitting down to breakfast now. All at once he saw his parents with a new appreciation . . . and with a trace of sadness as well, for the drabness of their lives. He knew his own would never be drab again.

David felt certain they would instantly pounce upon him. God knew they had plenty of reason, if they suspected what he'd been up to—if they could understand it at all. But, instead, his mother laid a shiny new romance novel facedown by the butter dish and got up to stick a couple more slices of bread in the toaster. Nothing out of the ordinary there. Big Billy was drinking strong black coffee with his bacon and eggs and reading the Sunday edition of the *Atlanta Journal and Constitution*. Everything normal there, too. David's guilt was still his own.

Little Billy bounced in and sat down next to him and helped himself to a pile of bacon and eggs and toast nearly as big as he was, with homemade blackberry jelly for the toast.

"You goin' to church this morning, boy?" Big Billy asked loudly without looking up.

The abruptness of the question so startled David from the apprehensive stupor into which he had settled that he nearly fell out of his chair. Fortunately nobody noticed.

"Hadn't planned to," David answered as nonchalantly as he could, pouring himself a cup of coffee, black for a change.

"Way you was talkin' yesterday, and way you been talkin' lately, you better go," Big Billy replied in turn.

David surpressed the urge to follow with the inevitable response that Big Billy didn't go either, but held his tongue. He had more important things on his mind just then than rehearsing that tired old argument.

"David's got a girlfriend," mumbled Little Billy through a mouthful of toast.

David tried to look daggers in two directions at once and found he couldn't. Too much too fast. What had possessed Little Billy to blurt out his secret like that? It was not even a true secret, either, just a hastily constructed fabrication that could not stand scrutiny. He needed time to sort things out, to get his stories straight, or he would get so far in he'd never get out. Maybe his pa had a point at that; maybe he *should* go to church. Now that David had proof of at least some supernatural creatures existing in the world, didn't it follow that there could be more?

Suddenly God was in his Heaven and all wasn't right in David's world. His ambivalent agnosticism was hanging in tatters like the scrambled eggs hanging from his fork.

"Don't talk with your mouth full, Little Billy," his mother told him. "Now don't let me have to tell you again, hear?"

Little Billy chewed noisily for a moment.

"I said *David's got a girlfriend!*" The boy looked so smug it took all David's willpower to keep from pushing his face down into his cornflakes then and there.

Big Billy slowly lowered his paper and looked up incredulously. It had taken a moment for the words to sink in.

David kicked at Little Billy under the table, missed, and got a chair leg instead. He grimaced and pretended interest in a slice of bacon.

"He's got a ring and everything," Little Billy went on, delighted by David's discomfort. David discovered to his horror that he was wearing the ring again, in plain sight. Big Billy was looking straight at it.

"Son-of-a-gun!" Big Billy exclaimed, with unexpected good humor. "It's about time!" He set his coffee cup down hard and laughed. "Sneaky old son-of-a-gun—like his daddy. Who is she, boy?" he asked conspiratorially. David was more than a little taken aback by his interest.

"Uh . . . you don't know her. She's a girl . . . a girl at school."

"You ain't been to school this summer," Little Billy pointed out.

"I didn't say it was this summer," David replied angrily, feeling as if he were rapidly digging his own grave.

"A girl!" repeated Big Billy. "Well, I'll be damned! You may make a man yet! But who is she, boy? Don't do to be ashamed of your woman." His eyes narrowed. "You ain't done nothin' you'd be sorry for, have you?"

David looked horrified. Suddenly he felt *very* uneasy.

His mother seemed surprisingly disinterested. She picked up her coffee and her romance, shuffled into the den, and turned on the TV. The raucous noise of cartoons sounded for a moment, followed quickly by the crackling hiss of fuzzing wavelengths and then somebody with an oil-on-water voice wanting to tell a nation of wretched sinners about Jee-ee-uh-sus-uh.

Big Billy changed tactics. "What's her name, Little Billy? Who's your brother's gal?"

Little Billy shrugged. "I dunno. All *I* know is he's got a ring he's been tryin' to hide, and I could hear him mumblin' last night about seein' the she."

David rolled his eyes skyward in dismay. Had he talked in his sleep as well? And so loud Little Billy could hear him from his room?

"A ring and everything! Must be serious. You give her one too, boy? Goin' steady?"

"Uh, not yet," David lied. Things were getting worse by the minute. "She just happened to have this one, so she gave it to me; it was sudden—unexpected, you know. I met her down in Atlanta at that Beta Club convention back before school was out. Nothing serious . . . really," he added lamely.

"But you just said she was a girl at school," Little Billy noted.

"Maybe I *will* go to church," David said, grasping at anything to change the subject and get himself away from the breakfast table. "I haven't been in a while."

"I 'spect that'd be a good idea," Big Billy nodded, returning to his paper. "Get yourself some practice," he added, "before that gal down in Atlanta drags you to the altar."

David got up and took a long cold shower—long because he needed to think, and cold because his wits were obviously still muddled, or he never would have got himself in such a fix. Neither helped. In the end church seemed the best option. *Any* help would do now.

Worse and worse, David thought as he eased his mother's two-year-old Ford LTD into the gravel parking lot of the First Antioch and Damascus Baptist Church, too late to sneak in unobtrusively. Normally, when he went to church at all, he accompanied Alec to the much more liberal MacTyrie Methodist; but that was usually when he'd spent Saturday night at Alec's house. David hadn't been to services in a Baptist church in maybe three years.

As soon as his mother opened her door, Little Billy squirmed between the seat back and the doorjamb and ran off to play with some of his friends.

His mother got out with considerably more grace, and David couldn't help noticing that she did cut a fine figure—when she wanted to, and spent half the morning putting it on. It was also apparent that she was completely delighted to be seen at church with her delinquent older son, since her husband—despite his talk—had not set foot in a church in eighteen years except for weddings and funerals.

David took a deep breath, straightened his tie, and opened his door. Some girls he knew from school were standing on the semi-circular steps at the door of the white frame building, watching his arrival with considerable interest and no little surprise. One of the girls pointed, and there was a chorus of giggles behind hands. David felt extremely self-conscious, and wondered what sin they imagined he had committed that was bad enough to bring him to church. An even worse thought struck him briefly, and he glanced casually down to check his fly, breathing a small sigh of relief that it was still securely fastened. He stuffed his hands into the pockets of his dark blue suit—it was getting a little tight through the armpits—and felt the coolness of the ring on his finger.

His mother was waiting a bit impatiently at the foot of the steps. She smiled at him as he shuffled up the walk. "I ain't had a chance to be escorted into church by my handsome son in a long time—not since he got to be taller'n me—and I'm gonna take it." She offered her arm and he could not refuse.

David didn't pay much attention to the sermon; he spent most of the time trying to lay out a consistent story about the nameless girl from Atlanta he had suddenly invented, and kept getting tangled up in it, especially as he had told two different versions of the story at breakfast already. *And he could not get the confounded ring off*. His finger had swollen just enough to make it stick. It sat there on his finger gleaming brightly, looking as smug as Little Billy had when he'd blurted out David's supposed secret at the breakfast table. What could possibly have possessed his little brother to tell that? He was usually reliable about secrets.

David scanned the congregation, noticing another thing he didn't like. There was Little Billy sitting over on the other side with several of his Sunday school cronies, whispering together and giggling and pointing at David.

Does everybody have to do that? David folded his arms and stared straight ahead while trying to work the ring off under his armpit. But it still would not budge. And to make matters worse, his mother expected him to hold the hymnal open for her every time there was a song or a responsive reading, which seemed to be about every other minute. He rather believed he'd prefer sitting in his pew stark naked to sitting there with that silver ring on just then. It was not that he didn't want it; he just didn't want it on *now*, in church, didn't want it too widely known. But he had an uneasy feeling that it was already too late for that.

He glared at Little Billy as his brother whispered something else into the ear of one of his cronies. Soon as they got home, he would give that little boy a talking-to he'd be a long time forgetting. It was *his* fault—for telling everything. *No, it isn't.* David knew full well it was his own, for not being straight with him, among other things, and for his lack of self-control which had led him into the woods in the first place. He was jealous, too, he realized, jealous of his real secret. But he might warm Little Billy's bottom anyway. And he wanted to take another look at that trail up in the woods, this time by daylight.

But he never got the chance.

Because Liz phoned him practically as he came in the door to tell him the music show started at two, and to ask when he could be by to pick her up, and would not hear his excuses for not wanting to go.

And then it started to rain.

And then lunch was ready.

And right after lunch the phone rang again.

"Is this Lover Boy Sullivan?" came the voice of Alec McLean.

David nearly hung up in disgust. "Sorry, there's nobody of that name here."

"That's not what *I* heard."

"What *did* you hear, then? I mean news travels fast and all, but *this* fast?"

"Then you admit there *is* news?"

Damn, thought David, *should have kept my mouth shut.*

"I have my sources," Alec continued slyly.

"So do I, but I haven't heard anything."

"Sure, sure."

"There's nothing to hear, Alec."

"That's not what your brother said at church this morning."

"I really should have given him to the undertaker," David muttered.

"What's that?"

David cleared his throat. "Little Billy has a way of . . . exaggerating."

"He also has a way of telling the truth, especially when it'll get you in trouble," Alec went on complacently.

"Look, Alec, level with me. What did you hear? From whom? And how?"

"What is this? The Spanish Inquisition? No, okay, seriously: Your brother told Buster Smith, who told his sister Carolyn, who told one of her crew, who told a mutual friend of ours who shall remain nameless as I need my spies, who told me, that you were sporting a ring at church this morning, a ring you said you got from a girl down in Atlanta—at Beta Club Convention, as a matter of fact."

So Little Billy's decided to believe that story, thought David. *Well, it's easier to substantiate—or disprove.*

"I'd hardly call it 'sporting,'" David said.

"Now, David," Alec went on, "it so happens that I was with you in Atlanta on the aforementioned occasion, and I don't recall you seeing any particular girl while we were there."

"You weren't with me every minute, either," David replied— and could have kicked himself immediately. Here he was again, starting to lay a maze of lies around the story—lies that intensified his dilemma rather than easing it. He had intended to try to be as honest with Alec as he could, given the circumstances.

"That's true. But if you're that fast a worker, well, there's a side to you I haven't seen before. No, you're not leveling with me; something's going on." He sounded hurt.

David sighed. "Look, Alec, this is too complex to go into on the phone, and besides, walls have ears, if you know what I mean—and, anyway, I've got to take Liz to the bluegrass show this afternoon."

"Oh, right, I remember you telling me about that. Well, maybe we can talk about it then; Dad's got to go anyway, to help man the gate. I can catch a ride with him."

"Ah, Alec . . . Liz—" David faltered. He could tell he'd hurt Alec by not being straight with him; no need to make things worse.

"What?"

"Never mind. . . . Look, Alec, I promise I'll give you the straight scoop at the first possible chance. You won't believe it, but I'll give it to you. Now I really do have to go—all I need is to have Liz on my case."

"Sure. Just one more thing: I was thinking about trying to get the MacTyrie gang together this evening for one more Risk game before Akin and Darrell go off to camp. Gary's finally finished the Dune board. You interested?"

"I don't think so. I doubt I'll be back from the fair until late, and . . . well, I've got some other things I need to do. Sorry."

"It's okay . . ."

"See you later, then."

David hung up the phone and squared his shoulders. He would not lie anymore, that much he had decided. To Alec, at least, he would tell the truth—as much as would be believed. If he told him that he found the ring, which was literally true, he wouldn't be lying, at least not technically, and maybe he could by slow degrees initiate Alec into the whole truth. It would take some doing, though. And there was still Liz to worry about. He tugged at the ring irritably, and was more than a little surprised when it slipped off. He started to take it back to his room, thinking that perhaps the best thing to do was simply to put it in a drawer somewhere and forget about it. But he suddenly found the idea of being separated from it incredibly disturbing, as if the ring had somehow bonded with him, to become almost a part of his own body.

An idea occurred to David then: If he put the ring on a chain around his neck, then he'd have it with him but it wouldn't show, and he wouldn't be tempted to put it on, as he would be if he carried it in his pocket. He went to look for a chain he remembered having seen in one of his dresser drawers. That would be one problem solved. But there was still the problem of what to tell Alec . . . and Liz.

Interlude: In Tir-Nan-Og

(high summer)

Three drops of blood glittering on a dry oak leaf.
Still bright, still wet after half a day in the Lands of Men.
A black ant tasted one and turned at once to ash.
Faery blood.
The blood of Ailill.

It had taken Ailill a great deal of effort to arrive at the place
where he found himself two days after the Riding of the Road on
Lughnasadh—two days by the sun of Tir-Nan-Og; though scarce
twelve hours had passed in the Lands of Men, for the cycles of
the Worlds no longer coursed in tandem, nor would again until
Samhain brought them once more into confluence: three months
by human time.

The day after the Riding he had wasted in fruitless contention
with Nuada: words first, ever more heated, and then a trial of
strength. Arm wrestling it had been, though not by Ailill's choice,
but by Morrigu's suggestion and Lugh's consent, which he could
not deny. His left arm still ached from that encounter. Silverhand
was strong, and the match had lasted from dawn until dusk with
no victor, at which time Lugh had commanded them to call off

their quarrel and to each pursue his own ends and to come back in a year and a day for final judgment.

But Ailill could not wait that long for his revenge. It had taken almost another day to find a place where he might work his summons unobserved, and that was enough time wasted. He would begin now, at midnight on the second day, when his Power was at its height.

The lakeside where he stood would have been beautiful if he had spared time to look at it. There was a beach of black sand on which tiny waves slapped with an oily sluggishness that suggested something other than water. The stuff smelled vaguely of cloves, and the handful he had dripped from his fingers sparkled amber in the moonlight. But he had had no desire to taste it.

The lake itself opened out behind him until its glittering surface merged with the starlit sky which it perfectly mirrored. Steep slopes ringed that water on the near sides, tall warrior pines marching up them to stand in file at the crest like the soldiers for which they were named, the sparse cones of branches at their summits for helms and the curling strips of hard gray bark that frayed from their trunks in ringlike semicircles for mail.

The only sound was the blurred whisper of the wind on the water and the forlorn cry of selkies among the rocks to the north.

Ailill glanced up at the sky and nodded.

Midnight. Time to begin the summoning.

It was too bad he could not work openly, too bad he could not work from the Track itself. But the Sidhe in Tir-Nan-Og seemed to have more regard for mortal men than he was accustomed to, and he had strong reason to suspect that such open action against the boy would not stand him in good stead.

He would have to play a careful game, then, and one of great subtlety. For he had heard much of Lugh Samildinach, and knew him to be of unbending nobility. Lugh would be a firm opponent of his plan, if it came to his knowledge, for even Ailill's own lord and brother, Finvarra, did not know the dark thoughts that filled the secret places of his mind. Not that he cared, really. The war would come anyway—*his* war, the war with mankind. But if he could capture the boy without Lugh's knowledge—rob the humans of what little initiative the boy's knowledge might give them—the start of that war might be delayed until a time when

Ailill himself might better orchestrate it to his own best advantage: King of the Sidhe in Tir-Nan-Og *and* Erenn.

He faced northeast, drew four deep breaths, and closed his eyes. His brow furrowed for a moment, and then he shook his head and crabwalked a dozen paces further to his right, where he repeated the procedure. *This* was it; this was the place! This time he was in perfect alignment with the blood trace he had left on the Track and the house, where another kind of Power told him the human boy was.

He knelt on the damp sand and closed his eyes again, took four more breaths, and set his Power to insinuating his consciousness through the Walls between the Worlds. A moment's work, like feeling his way through a densely leaved forest shrouded in thick fog. Once through, it was a simple matter to locate the residue of Power that still remained in those three drops of blood.

He cleared his mind, extended his Power, called into being a bridge of thought connecting himself with that tiny fragment of his own essence he had left as a focus.

Connected! Good!

Now to direct the Power, send it seeking its victim. Ailill recalled the boy's image to his mind: shorter than most mortal men, slender and supple like a tumbler or a swimmer; handsome for a human, with thick fair hair almost to his shoulders, dark brows, blue eyes, fine white teeth in a full-lipped mouth that would grin too easily. The image brightened, sharpened. Ailill felt the line of Power grow taut, exerting a firm but gentle tug against his will. He would enter the boy's mind now, fix the line of Power, and draw him from his own World exactly as a fisherman would reel in a catch.

The image was clear. The boy was standing on the porch of the hovel he called a house. Now to touch the mind, to fix the Power, just so . . .

NO! There was other Power here, Power that felt his touch and raced eagerly to meet it like flames cast upon threads of raw silk. Coming toward him. Coming nearer. Hotter and hotter. And he could not break free of that Power greater than his own that had appeared from nowhere to protect the boy.

It was almost on him. He must break the link. He must break the link. *Now! Now! Now! Now! Now!*

He failed.

The other Power had him, ripping his spirit free of his control, filling it with a twisting, crisping agony so intense it seemed as if his soul itself were aflame.

Pain. Pain. Pain. Pain. Pain.

And then oblivion.

It was morning when the tentative nibblings of a twelve-legged crab upon his outflung hand returned Ailill to himself. He was not happy. The boy was protected, this much he knew by bitter experience. By what, he had no idea, but he intended to find out. There would be no more summoning from afar—of that he was very sure indeed. But perhaps there were other means.

Somewhere on the floor of a forest path less than half a mile from David's house, three wisps of smoke rose from the blackened powder that had once been an oak leaf.

Chapter V: Fortunes

A combination regional fair, fiddlers' convention, livestock show, and arts and crafts exhibition, the Enotah Mountain Fair was held on the grounds of the county high school and lasted an entire week plus one extra weekend.

For that brief period tiny, rural Enotah County seemed to boast about the same population as Atlanta, or so it appeared to those few residents who tried to follow their usual routine amid the steady stream of motorhomes and Oldsmobile 98s. For the rest, mundane life slowed to a virtual standstill, as they indulged themselves in the only taste of outside reality—or fantasy, depending on how one considered it—many of them ever had.

It didn't take David and Liz long to take in the exhibits. They were both proud to see their culture on display, of course, but they'd seen it all before—often the same exact items year after year—and the music show developed an unexpectedly intractable sound system, so they gave up on it about six o'clock and went to get something to eat and to soak themselves in the sensory overload of the midway. David didn't really like it much; that is, he didn't like the crowds that jostled and pushed and grunted along in interminable lines, getting cotton candy on everybody and spilling popcorn all over the ground where a thick coating of mud from the earlier shower had already made walking treacherous. It reminded David of what he had read about the La Brea Tar Pits, and he almost expected to come upon a human hand sticking up out of the ooze, going down for the third and final time.

They met Alec while standing in line for the Trabant.

"I thought you guys were going to the bluegrass show," Alec said, staring intently at David, oblivious to the sour scowl that had darkened Liz's features.

David hesitated uneasily. "We were, but the P.A. system went out, so we came down here to numb our senses with sight and sound and smell. . . . You want to join us?" He cast a furtive glance at Liz, then looked quickly back at Alec and caught his friend's eyes for an instant in a subtle contact that said *bear with me and bide your time*.

Liz delivered a hard but unobtrusive kick to his shin, but it was too late.

David grunted and gestured at the ride which spun before them like a giddily drunken top. "We're gonna ride this next."

Alec forced a grin and produced a free pass. Liz didn't say anything at all, having resigned herself to a threesome.

They were finally beginning to catch the rhythm of the ride's dips and plunges and sudden changes in altitude, so that they could anticipate and indeed enhance the periodic weightless sensation they got when the Trabant would indulge in one of its precipitous dives, when the first raindrops fell.

At first David thought it was light-dazed bugs, or somebody's Coke brought illegally on the ride—it was impossible to see the drops themselves beyond the perimeter of pink and white lights that surrounded the ride, or to hear any sound above the shrill roar of four huge speakers that blared out soulless versions of tunes that had been popular five years before—but before long it was raining more seriously.

The operator tugged at the long red control lever and brought the Trabant to a halt before the passengers got entirely soaked.

"Let's go somewhere dry—fast," cried Liz, wiping a strand of sodden red hair out of her face.

David pulled up the hood of his light nylon windbreaker and pointed toward a dull green tent that was marked outside by a hand-painted sign depicting a crystal ball beneath an upraised open palm. "There's a fortuneteller; maybe we could go in there. It doesn't look too busy."

They hesitated indecisively for a moment.

"Always wanted to get my fortune told," Alec said finally.

"I always wanted to see if they were as fake as they're supposed to be," put in Liz.

"I predict, then," said David, hunching over as the rain fell harder still and people began to gravitate toward overhanging awnings, "that we will soon meet a tall, dark fortuneteller. In fact, I think we'll do it—*now!*"

He grabbed Liz's hand and they sprinted the five or so yards, deftly sidestepping people and leaping half-submerged power cables as they went, leaving Alec to follow with his customary deliberation.

They were a little surprised by the sudden cessation of sound and water under the edge of the awning, though they could still see out into a world now largely masked by the silver-lit curtain of water cascading off the scalloped edge.

David thought it a little strange that there was no one taking tickets, but even as he was about to give voice to his thought, a vertical slit opened in the curtain almost immediately beside the open-palmed sign, and a very short, very fat woman with frizzy red hair and heavily made-up eyes came out and stood imperiously before them. She folded her arms and looked them up and down.

"Come in, my children," she said in a tone that left no room for argument. The accent was thick but not entirely convincing—something between Bela Lugosi and the Bronx, New York.

The three friends looked at each other and shrugged in unison.

"How much?" Alec asked pragmatically. "It doesn't say out here."

The woman shrugged in turn, jingling a good ten pounds of silver-and-turquoise jewelry on her arms. "That depends on your fortune: no more than five dollars, no less than one."

Alec hesitated, shot a troubled look at David. "You got an extra five?"

"If I need to, yes."

Alec sighed and nodded.

"Okay," David said finally. "We'll all come, then."

"Yes, you will," the fortuneteller agreed. She turned and led the way into her tent.

"So much for a tall, dark fortuneteller," Alec muttered into David's ear.

They found themselves in a small, square waiting room whose

walls were hung with faded and stained red velvet drapes probably pirated from some defunct theater. A cheap fake-Persian car-
pet covered the canvas floor, and there were several low couches
upholstered in red plush and heavily scarred with cigarette burns.

The fortuneteller gestured for them to sit down, and studied
each of them for a long time, one hand cupping her chin, index
finger extended along her jawline. She looked longest at David,
then sighed and pointed at Alec. "You first."

Alec held back. "Can't we all go together?"

The woman's eyes narrowed a fraction. "I don't want to confuse the spirits. Now come—or not. Will you know your fate, or
hide from it?"

Alec rose reluctantly and the woman motioned him through a
slit in the back wall of the room.

David scratched his ring hand unconsciously; it was itching
even though the ring now hung upon a cheap silver-colored chain
around his neck.

"Well, she's not your typical gypsy, anyway," whispered Liz.
"I wonder if she reads palms or uses cards, or crystal balls, or the
Tarot, or what."

"Or Second Sight?" David suggested quietly.

"What's that?"

"The ability to see things not in this world. Some people in
Scotland and Ireland have it, or claim to—the people who claim
to have seen the Faeries, among others."

"Oh."

Before David could speak further, the slit parted and Alec
came back through, peering doubtfully at his palm.

"So what did she tell you?" Liz asked, looking up curiously.

"She said for you to go next—by name, as a matter of fact,
which I find interesting—and beyond that I will say no more until
we're clear of here and can all tell the tale one time and get it over
with."

Liz got up and rather self-consciously passed through the slit.

Alec sat opposite David, hands draped between his knees, his
gaze tracing the pattern of the rug.

"Very strange," he said. "Very strange."

David didn't say anything at all.

Alec continued to stare at the rug. "I don't think Liz likes
me," he said after a while.

"I think she has another problem with you, but that's discussion for another time and place. Let's not talk about it now, agreed?"

"Agreed," Alec said glumly. He looked at David. "So let's see the famous ring."

David sighed, fingering the chain. "Famous or infamous, I'm not sure which."

"Come on, let's see it."

David grimaced and reluctantly fished out the ring. Alec took it on his palm and examined it carefully, but said nothing. He looked a little puzzled.

"You sure you got this from a girl?"

"That's what I need to talk to you about," David replied as he secreted the chain.

"So talk."

"I don't quite know where to begin . . ."

"Next," Liz interrupted as she came through the curtain, a vaguely troubled expression clouding her face.

David got up and parted the barrier, aware at once of the difference in temperature between the muggy outer room and the cooler inner one, aware as well of the overpowering scent of incense faintly mixed with cigarette smoke, and of the dim light cast by four dark blue candles that stood on knobby brass pedestals in the corners of the chamber. But most of all he was aware that he could hear absolutely nothing of the outside world. He might have been transported to deep space or under water, he thought. He felt the ring warm slightly on his chest.

The fortuneteller sat behind a small round table draped with black velvet on which, true to expectation, squatted a bowling-ball-sized globe of some transparent substance. Oddly, it did not look like plastic, or really like glass. Half-seen shapes seemed to crawl about within it when David looked at it, making his eyes itch. Next to the ball was stacked a worn deck of Tarot cards with the top card turned face up to show the Magician. Lying on the velvet beside it was the Knight of Wands.

"Come in David . . . Sullivan, I believe?" The woman closed her eyes and extended a plump hand in his direction, as if hoping to find confirmation written on the air in braille.

"Right!" cried David, genuinely surprised, as he seated himself on a small stool opposite her. "How did you know?"

"I'm a fortuneteller, I'm supposed to know." The Bela Lugosi part of the accent had faded. She paused, staring more intently at David, then nodded. "For you there will be no charge."

"Why not?—out of curiosity, I mean?"

The woman threw up her hands theatrically, setting the jewelry to jingling again. "Is it not obvious, my son, that it is *I* who should seek to learn from *you?* It is many years since I have met one with the Sight."

"How could you tell?" David gasped incredulously.

The woman's manner of speech began to change imperceptibly, as if she drew from parts of herself she did not normally let awaken.

"Your eyes . . . they do not merely look, they see; and they have a gleam of silver about them, if you know how to look for it. I have not the Sight myself, but my mother did. It was she who taught me to recognize the signs."

"But I don't even know how I got it. Everything was normal until two days ago, and then . . . all hell broke loose."

"Oh? Tell me."

"I don't know if I should—you'd probably think I'm crazy."

"If I had not wanted to know, I would not have asked."

"I've seen . . . things."

"What kind of things?"

"A . . . a . . . castle on a mountaintop, for one."

"But not the main thing?"

"No."

"And you've never seen such things before?"

"No, never . . . I would have liked to, though, and that's what bothers me. I have such a strong imagination that I thought . . ."

"You were wrong. You have the Sight, and you have acquired it recently, and there are only a very few ways that could have happened without your intending it." She looked at David, read the unasked question on his face, and said, "Wait here."

The woman rose and disappeared through a rift in the curtains opposite the entrance. In a moment she returned with an ancient brown book, as weathered as an old leaf, and almost as small.

"This is *The Secret Common-Wealth,*" she said. "My mother gave it to me, and she had it from her mother, and so on back to Scotland. I have no son, nor am likely to have one, now. You are the one to take the book. It may contain answers, *some* answers, to your questions. Whether what it contains is true or not, I cannot say, but my mother believed it, and she did not lie."

David took the book hesitantly, overawed by the magnificence of such a gift from a total stranger. "I can't accept this!" he whispered.

"You must. Your fate may depend on it."

Reluctantly David secreted the volume in the pocket of his windbreaker. "I have to confess," he said, feeling rather awkward and squirming on the stool a little, "that I thought you were a fraud . . ." He cleared his throat. "Well, actually, I thought that *all* carnival fortune-tellers were frauds, but I'm not so sure about you now."

"Oh, I am a fraud," the woman said matter-of-factly, seemingly undisturbed by David's bluntness. "Certainly a fraud compared to you, if you chose to use your power—which I see you do not. But most people have so little fortune—real fortune, that is—that there is nothing for even the gifted to see. All they want to know about is love and death and money, so that's what I tell them. But one in ten thousand, maybe, has a fortune that I can read, and such are you."

"What about Liz and Alec?"

"Their fortunes are bound up with yours. They can tell you what I told them, if they so choose." She pulled a cigarette out of a silver case behind the table but did not light it.

"What about *my* fortune? Can you tell me anything?"

The woman leaned forward. "Let me see your hand."

David laid his right hand on the table.

"No, not that one, the left one—that is the hand where your fate is written."

David laid his left hand palm up on the black velvet beside the crystal ball.

"Can I see the ring as well?" the woman asked after a moment.

"What ring?" David was at once suspicious.

"This finger wants to wear a ring."

Reluctantly David slipped the chain over his head and placed the ring on the table, where—to his surprise—it glowed softly.

Abruptly the fortuneteller picked up the crystal ball and set it on the floor, as if fearful of some reaction between the two. A long time passed as she looked at David's hand, but not once did she touch it. Neither did she touch the ring. Finally she spoke.

"It's all threes and sixes," she said, "and one. You are one of the three; the three are stronger than one, yet the one is mightiest of the three. Six people you love, and those six people will cause you pain for pain you bring on them. Three weeks—the next three weeks—will see you tested—a testing such as you have never known before."

She paused then and studied his hand more carefully, following each line to its termination, examining each mound and hollow, her red-lacquered nail always a hair's breadth above his flesh. "Three years may pass, and maybe three again, before all is done and you may rest, your labors ended. But remember, David, that among these threes and sixes you are the one, prime and indivisible, and thus strong. You will have to find the pattern, but if you can pass the next three weeks and remain as you are, you will grow stronger. . . . But, David Sullivan, if you choose the wrong road at the end, there may be no more roads for you at all."

David felt his throat go suddenly dry. "You mean I might die?" he managed to croak.

The woman shrugged. "Death is always a possibility. He sits beside all of us, close or far. He is everywhere, if you look, but you are untrained in the looking, and I caution you not to. Yet you *will* see Death sitting beside someone close to you in less than two weeks' time, of that I am certain. That is all I can tell you."

The fortuneteller picked up the ring by its chain, lowered it into David's palm, and folded his hand around it. Then she took a deep breath and forced a smile. "Thank you for letting me meet you," she said. "Long has it been since I met one like you, and never in this short-sighted country. As I have told you, I ask no payment . . . but if you would touch your ring to the crystal here, I would be grateful." She stooped to retrieve the glassy sphere. "It won't hurt the ring and it might help the ball. Maybe then I'll be able to see something in it besides cheating husbands and new cars." She lit her cigarette then and, after David had complied with her request, winked at him one last time before waving him away with her free hand, her metal-linked bracelets tinkling softly.

David reached out impulsively, clasped her pudgy hand, and kissed it with unpracticed chivalry. "Thanks," he said. "If you're here next year, I'll return the book, I promise."

The woman smiled. "If I am here next year, maybe I'll accept it from you. But for now, take it, read it, study it. It may be your only strength. Now go! Compare notes with your friends."

"Well? Well?" Alec asked eagerly as David reemerged into the red-hung room. The sound of rain had faded.

"Well?" echoed Liz. "You sure were in there a long time, compared to us. What were you doing?"

"Talking shop," David replied a little too lightly. "I was getting a few pointers on lycanthropy."

"Huh?" queried Liz.

"Werewolves and such," Alec muttered.

"No, not really," continued David. "But let's not talk here."

They went outside, blinking into the glare of gaudy lights. The rain had indeed stopped, and the crowds were tentatively feeling their way back to the rides. The rich soup of mud was even worse than before.

"Ugh!" said Liz. "We gotta walk through that?"

"Let's take our shoes off; we can wash our feet somewhere later, before we leave."

"Ugh," Liz said again.

"Why Liz, don't you like the feel of mud squishing up between your toes?" teased Alec.

"I'll squish mud up against your nose if you don't shut up, McLean!" Liz flared, and then broke into laughter over her inadvertent rhyme.

David bent over, untied his sneakers, and picked them up. "I'm gonna take mine off anyway; anybody rides in my car has gotta have clean shoes." He stalked off, leaving Alec and Liz frantically pulling laces in the mud.

Fifteen minutes later they had found a place where they could talk: the unused chemistry lab of the high school building. Alec had been a lab assistant the year before and had a key no one had asked him to return, so they had crept in and were now sitting on the floor below window level, the room illuminated only by a blue mercury vapor lamp outside, exactly like the one at David's house.

"So spill it," Alec burst out.

"There's really nothing to tell," David said. "She just told me we'd be seeing a lot of each other for the next few weeks or so, and that our fates were bound up together."

David didn't want to lie to his friends, but he knew he couldn't tell them all the truth, at least not yet. This time, though, he had had time to decide on his ploy during their walk up to the lab.

Alec's eyes narrowed suspiciously. "Is that all? You talked longer than that."

"All of substance; she told me some garbage about marriage and death and cars, but nothing very specific, as you'd expect. What did she tell you guys?"

"There you go again, David," grumbled Alec, "not being straight with us, I don't think. But I guess I'll have to live with it. I think she told you a lot more than you're saying—serious stuff, too, judging by your expression when you came out." Alec tapped the metal leg of a lab stool before continuing. "All she told me was to help you during the next few weeks as much as I could—that you were under a sore trial but didn't know it yet, and would need my help."

Liz looked up in surprise. "That's almost exactly what she told me—that three were mightier than one, but one was mightiest of the three, and that one wouldn't survive without the other two. That was weird."

David looked straight into her eyes and smiled. "All the same crap."

"What did you expect from a fortuneteller?"

"I dunno. Never been to one."

"I'm not going back, either," said Liz. "Gave me the creeps, but I think she was serious. It didn't sound like what I expected to hear. It just felt . . . right."

"Yes, it did," Alec nodded.

"You'll get no argument from me there," agreed David. "Let's go wash this mud off and go home. I think we can use the restrooms up here."

It was very late when David finally got back home. Nobody was up, he was relieved to find. At last he had some time alone. He contrived a quick snack and crawled into bed with the fortuneteller's book. He needed some answers, and he needed them quick.

David looked at the cover curiously: *The Secret Common-*

Wealth, Or A Treatise Displaying The Chief Curiosities Among The People Of Scotland As They Are In Use To This Day. It was a brittle old book, very thin, and written in an archaic style that was sometimes difficult for him to make out—not surprising, when he learned that it had originally been composed in 1692. The author—a Reverend Robert Kirk—had been a Scottish minister who had become so interested in the local fairylore that he had written the first important study of the fair-folk—apparently coming to believe in them himself.

David flipped the pages rapidly; halfway through he found part of what he had been looking for:

There be odd solemnities at investing a man with the privi-ledges of the whol Misterie of this Second Sight. He must run a tedder of hair (which bound a Corps to the Beir) in a Helix about his midle from end to end, then bow his head down-ward: (as did Elijah I King 18.42.) and look back thorow his legs untill he see a funerall advance, till the people cross two Marches; or look thus back thorow a hole where was a knot of fir. But if the wind change points while the hair tedder is ty'd about him, he is in peril of his Lyfe. The usuall method for a curious person to get a transient sight of this otherwise invisi-ble crew of Subterraneans (if impotently and over-rashly sought) is to put his foot on the Seers foot, and the Seers hand is put on the Inquirers head, who is to look over the Wizards right shoulder (which hes an ill appearance, as if by this cere-monie, an implicite surrender were made of all betwixt the Wizard's foot and his hand ere the person can be admitted a privado to the art.)

Then will he see a multitude of Wights like furious hardie men flocking to him hastily from all quarters, as thick as the atomes in the air, which are no nonentities or phantasm, crea-tures, proceeding from ane affrighted apprehensione confused or crazed sense, but Realities, appearing to a stable man in his awaking sense and enduring a rational tryal of their being. . . .

There were a bunch of footnotes giving additional biblical quotations cited by Reverend Kirk, and David scanned them, but did not really notice what he read.

So! He smiled in satisfaction. *It must have been the funeral*

procession Little Billy and I saw. He recalled then, seeing it between his legs.

But that was a difficult concept for a rational man to swallow,
he realized after a moment's consideration. There was simply no
connection between the two events that he could discern, not even
the vaguest sort of cause and effect. And then there was that
business about a "tether that has bound a corpse to a bier." He had
certainly done no such thing—yet he had the Sight, which didn't
make sense, unless the bit about the tether was just a bit of nonsense to keep people from trying it willy-nilly. Probably the folk
with the Sight had enjoyed a special position in the community
and didn't want everybody getting in on the act, so they just made
up a complicated bit of apparatus to go with it.

It would take some doing, after all, to bind a corpse to a
bier with a tether of hair (and what kind of hair would be long
and strong enough for that, or to wind in a helix about one's
middle—surely not human?)—and then sneak in later and re-
move it. David giggled; it seemed he knew something that Reverend Kirk hadn't. And, he thought, it might be nice to try that
bit about giving the Sight to someone else—to Alec or Little
Billy, maybe. He reread that section to be certain he had it
right, then checked the footnotes, which he had passed over
before. The would-be seer was supposed to surrender himself
completely to the control of the Sighted one, he discovered.
The Sighted one would then assert his physical domination by
the method Kirk had described, while at the same time con-
firming his control by reciting "Everything between my hands
and my feet is mine," or some similar phrase.

Well, that's interesting, David said to himself. *Very interesting
indeed.*

He spent the next hour or so examining parts of the book he
had skipped earlier. Among them he learned about the sad fate of
Reverend Kirk: How his body had been found beside a supposed
fairy mound, and how some people had said he had been taken by
the fair-folk and a changeling left in his place; and that there had
been various attempts at setting him free, but that they had all
failed. He shuddered involuntarily, thinking how perilously close
he had come to that same fate.

His eyes had grown tired by this time, for it was very late, and
he turned out the light and snuggled down under the covers. He

then realized that his teeth felt scummy and that his mouth tasted faintly of the sour-cream-and-onion potato chips he had been eating. Wearily, he got up and went into the bathroom to brush his teeth.

As he turned on the water and got out his toothbrush, he felt a burning sensation from where the ring lay on his bare chest. At the same time he became aware of a voice sounding in his ears. It was like no voice he had ever heard before: so low as to seem almost subliminal; harsh, not unlike a growl; and strangely inflected, as if the mouth that shaped it was unaccustomed to the subtleties of human speech. Sweat sprang out on his body as he stared foolishly about the tiny room in search of the source of that voice. After a moment it spoke again, and this time he pinpointed its origin: the darkness beyond the bathroom window.

David felt a chill race down between his shoulder blades and lodge at the base of his spine; his muscles tensed, and he shuddered involuntarily. Finally he took a deep breath to steel himself and eased aside the curtain, keeping his eyes slitted, dreading what he might see.

It was as he feared.

No man's shape greeted him there. Rather, the massive head and front paws of an immense white dog stood out against the yard light's glow. Its claws rested on the windowsill, and its enormous eyes burned like red-hot coals.

They stared at each other for a moment, and then the dog began to speak again, and this time he could make out its words. "One of your own kind, David Sullivan, has said that a little knowledge is a dangerous thing. And so it is. You have a little knowledge, and you seek to make it more, and so it is a dangerous thing."

David started to say something, but found that his mouth was so dry he could not speak. He swallowed clumsily. The toothbrush slipped from his fingers and fell to the floor with a plastic clatter.

"Now it is widely known," continued the dog complacently, "that certain . . . things have become known to men—certain shards of a greater knowledge that are perhaps not entirely appropriate for them to know. Many have sought that knowledge, though few have found it, and fewer still have profited by it.

"But where *you* are different is that you have knowledge

backed by proof—the proof that lies sparkling upon your chest. And such knowledge places you in a position dangerous both to yourself—for in Ailill Windmaster you have made a powerful enemy—and to certain others who sometimes share your World."

The dog hesitated a moment, though its eyes never left David. "Thus it is that you have two choices: If you end this quest for knowledge now, when it is scarcely begun, and try to forget what you have seen and turn your thoughts to other things, there may still be time to forestall Ailill's intervention. But if you do not, never again will your life be as it has been. Do not seek to know more than you do—or be prepared to pay the consequences of that seeking."

And it was gone.

David felt the hair prickle once again on his neck and arms. He picked up the toothbrush and rinsed it off mechanically, but he found that no matter how hard he tried, he could not quite hold his hands steady. The ring continued to send forth pulses of low heat, and to glow softly. A final shudder shook him, and the coiled fear began to disperse.

Well, he thought, *maybe I'd better leave that trail alone for a while.*

Or, he added, *maybe I should memorize the fortuneteller's book.*

PART II

Prologue II: In Tir-Nan-Og
(high summer)

It is good to be an eagle, thought Ailill, who now wore that shape. Wings, longer than his man's form was tall, swept from his shoulders, caressing the air like the fingers of the most sensuous of lovers. Feathers black as his hair covered him; eyes sharp as his devious wit peered over a beak cruel as the desire for vengeance that burned within him.

It is good to fly, Ailill added to himself. *It is good to rule the air, to ride winds no mortal bird could dare, to breathe air too thin for their clumsy lungs, to fly so high that stars appear above, so high the curve of the mortal World shows when I look down.*

It is good to look down on the World of Men and think how it would be to crush them, to beat them into the iron-sodden dirt from whence they came. Or better yet, to hurl them into the cold blackness that surrounds them. Tenuous indeed is their hold on that World—if they but knew.

He blinked his yellow eyes and spiraled higher on the merest suggestion of an updraft, then drew upon his Power and looked down again, to see both worlds—the round Lands of Men clustered close and thick and fearful, bound all unknowing within the less easily described shapes of the far-flung Realms of Faerie, all laced about by the glittering golden lattice of the Straight Tracks that wrapped *all* Worlds and rose past him into space—and time as well—binding them *all* together in ways at once too complex and too subtle for even the Sidhe to fully comprehend. Though not *of* Faerie, the Faerie-born could travel upon them, if they dared—and mortal men as well, if they had the art, as none now did, except possibly that detestable boy who Nuada had virtually snatched from his hand, and who had cost him considerable trouble and no little pain in the days since.

Nuada!

Ailill felt the tendons that worked his claws tighten when that name entered his thoughts. Unconsciously he ground the edges of his beak together, then uttered a harsh shriek of rage into the cold empty air that surrounded him.

Nuada Airgetlam, whom men called Silverhand. Once King of the Tuatha de Daanan, once disarmed in the most literal sense by a blade of iron, once slain in the Lands of Men—and yet another barrier between Ailill and the war he desired between the two Worlds, between men and gods, if men chose to call them that. But there was another thing Ailill wanted now, and that thing was vengeance: vengeance against Nuada, who had thwarted his plan and made him look the fool in the bargain; and against the mortal boy, David Sullivan, who somehow bore some arcane protection about him whose nature Ailill could not discover, nor his Power break.

He was the unknown, the unloaded die, the rogue element in the orderly plan Ailill was formulating.

He is the one I must control; he is the one whose blood this body would taste this day if I gave myself to it, and if someone— or something—did not protect him. That is what I must discover, and if it is an object which protects him, then that object I must possess:

The eagle shape he wore spoke to him then, in that part of his mind where instincts had their dwelling. And what it spoke of was hunger.

Ailill gazed about himself, at the glitter of stars in the black sky, at the Worlds—both Worlds—spread below gleaming in the encompassing golden lattice.

And then he narrowed the focus of his vision, so that he gazed only into the Lands of Men.

And there he saw what his body sought.

He folded his wings and dived, felt the air thicken about him, felt his body grow warm from the force of that fall, knowing as he did so that if he put upon himself the substance of the mortal world, as he must do to remain there for more than a few hours, that the thing men called friction would burn him to nothing before he reached his goal.

But he was *not* of that substance. This body, like his man-body, was formed of the stuff of Faerie, and so was bound by the laws of that World.

Below him the land spread wide, the distant coast was a thin-edged glimmer on the horizon, the mountains faint wrinkles in the landscape.

And still he fell.

A moment later fields and rivers took clearer form, and those same mountains rose about him. Trees became distinct, and then the leaves that clothed them. Ailill saw with the eagle's eye alone now; he let the bird's own small mind take control so that instincts burned in the place of thoughts.

The eagle saw its quarry: long-eared, brown-furred, white tuft a marker of despair at its tail. Red became the color of the eagle's thoughts as the hidden part that was Ailill called upon his Power and wrapped his eagle-shape in the substance of the Lands of Men. Only thus could it feed.

The rabbit moved beneath him, running, frantic, sensing the black-winged doom that fell suddenly toward it out of a clear sky.

Now! Wings out! Tail fanned! Brake! Brake! Legs down, talons extended!

There was impact and a squeaking, and then the muffled sound of feathers brushing against dry grass.

An eagle's shape is an excellent shape—for certain purposes, Ailill thought, as he prepared to feed. *But there are even better shapes a clever man might wear to achieve his goals.*

He gave himself over to the eagle then, and red became the color of the grass as Ailill, who was the eagle, feasted.

Chapter VI: Swimming

(Saturday, August 8)

"It's hot," said Alec from his place on the edge of the Sullivans' front porch. "Too hot to spend half the day helping your dad pull the engine out of that old wreck of a truck he just bought."

"This is Georgia in August; it's supposed to be hot," David replied, taking a long draw on a Dr. Pepper and setting it down beside him in the porch swing. Down the hill and across the cornfield he could see a steady stream of traffic flashing by, as it would for the next four months. Tourist season had begun with the fair, and there was nothing he could do about it. "Wildwood Flower" would resonate in his mind for months.

"This is the Georgia *mountains* in August," Alec went on obstinately. "It's not supposed to be a hundred degrees in the shade!"

"At least there *is* shade." David gestured around the porch. "And, anyway, who are you to tell me what it's supposed to be like up here? *I* was born here; *you* moved in."

A large yellow tomcat jumped unexpectedly into the swing, upsetting the Dr. Pepper into David's lap.

Alec's face wrinkled with laughter. "Still wetting your pants, are you?"

"Damn."

"Better not let your mom hear that!"

"Damn!" David said again, louder, as he got up and disappeared into the house. In a moment he returned with a wet dishrag and mopped the swing. He had not changed his sodden white cutoffs.

He grinned at Alec. "Leastwise part of me's cool now."

"Some way to get cool!"

Silence fell on their conversation then. The air stilled. The only sounds were the muffled roar of the cars on the highway and the soft creaking of the swing. They did not look at each other. David stared into space over Alec's head; Alec methodically dismembered a daisy from one of the pots that perched precariously along the porch railing.

"You've been acting funny lately, Davy," Alec said at last. "Besides the business with the ring, I mean, which is another matter entirely. You never can seem to get around to giving me the straight scoop on *that,* and lord knows I've been trying all week." The petals continued to fall. He looked up at his friend and their gazes met: blue and gray. Alec's tone was soft and firm, but something about it hit David like a blow, as if he had just heard one of his secrets told aloud.

David frowned and blinked, breaking the contact. "What do you mean? I always act funny; it's the way I am."

"I know that," Alec replied, folding his arms across his chest and stretching his legs along the top step. "Like when you tried to turn yourself into a werewolf that time. But that's not what I mean. I can't really tell you exactly what I *do* mean, but it's like . . . like you're not all here. You seem distracted a lot, or something."

He paused, swallowed, felt for the post behind him before continuing. "I can't explain it any better, Davy, but you—well, you stare into space a lot more than you used to, and I see you looking at things funny sometimes."

David didn't say anything, but he began to rock the swing gently.

"Like you're doing now, David. You're not half listening to me. It's like we can kid around and all like we were just doing, but then suddenly you're off in space somewhere." He swallowed again and took a deep breath. "I guess that's what bothers me most—that you seem to be going somewhere I can't follow. I mean look, Sullivan, we've been friends practically forever and never kept anything from each other, and now something is bothering you, or something is happening to you, or *has* happened to you, and you won't tell me what it is. It's like a barrier where there's never been a barrier—and I don't like it at all."

He threw the completely dismembered daisy far down into the yard. The yellow tomcat ran tentatively toward it before retreating into the shadows under the house.

"I'm sorry, Alec," said David, with a sense of great effort behind the words. "I didn't realize there was any change. Would it help if I did something weird now?"

"You *are* doing something weird," Alec replied, looking up with an expression of hurt on his face that shocked David. "You're not being straight with me, and you've never done that."

"If I told you, you'd never believe me."

"I've heard that line before—and I've never believed *it!*"

David took a deep breath. "I have seen the Sidhe."

His eyes flashed for a moment as his gaze again locked with Alec's and broke as suddenly. The line of his mouth was set.

Alec shook his head and looked down. "You're right. I don't believe you."

"Then you won't believe that I got the ring from them."

"Damn it!" Alec almost shouted. He stood up angrily and began to pace the length of the porch, hands clinched into white-knuckled fists. "God*damn* it, Sullivan, will you *never* tell me the truth about that frigging ring? You got it from a girl. You got it from the fairies. Next you'll be telling me you got it from a goddamned man from Mars! For Christ's sake, Davy, don't you see I don't know what to believe? I might have believed you if that was the story you told first, but it's not, so can you blame me for not believing it now?"

The speed of his pacing increased, and then he whirled around suddenly to stand glowering at David. He was almost shaking. The swing had stopped.

"No, I don't blame you," David said softly. "I almost don't believe it myself. But I've got to do something about it—it's about to drive me crazy."

"That's *your* problem, man. *You're* the one who's been flashing it around like it was the crown jewels. I'd have kept it quiet if I didn't want people to know about it, and I sure wouldn't have told my loud-mouthed brother." Alec pounded the porch rail irritably, but the white heat of his anger was already subsiding. Somewhere in the house the telephone rang.

"Twenty-twenty hindsight."

"You could, of course, just get rid of it—and say that everything was over; that's what I'd do."

"I've thought about that, but I feel really uncomfortable without it, like something awful will happen if I don't have it with me, or if I lose it. I nearly get sick to my stomach just thinking about it. The chain's a reasonable compromise."

"Well, don't complain to me. You've made your bed, now you can lie in it."

"David? Telephone!" his mother called from inside.

"Crap," David muttered as he disappeared through the front door. Alec sat down and looked for another daisy.

"Well, David Sullivan," Liz's voice crackled on the line. "You haven't called me since the fair, so I'm taking matters into my own hands."

Her voice was firm rather than flirtatious, and David couldn't help but grin. Liz had a way about her—a plain, honest, straightforward way. That was what he liked best about her. She always said what she meant, and if it was tactful, fine; and if it wasn't, fine; and if it made her look like a fool, well, that didn't bother her too much, either. He wished he could be as straightforward, but on the other hand, Liz hadn't seen the Sidhe.

"Sorry, Liz," said David. "I've had things on my mind—and, besides, it's only been a week."

There was a flustered pause. "So what are you doing now, Davy?"

"It's *David*, Liz; David with a *D*, like in *dammit*, and I'm not doing anything except sitting on the porch complaining about the heat and fussing with Alec."

"Well, I can't help you with your fussing, except to ask you not to get a black eye if you can help it. I don't want to be seen with a boy with a black eye."

"It ain't that kind of fussing. Call it a gentleman's disagreement."

"You two, gentlemen? Ha! *You* won't even call a girl, and Alec never can seem to figure out when he's not wanted . . . but as far as your problems are concerned, I can't help you with your fussing, but maybe I can with the heat—if you'd like to go swimming down in the lake behind my mom's house. I'll even be nice and let you bring Alec."

David grinned. "That's good, 'cause he's spending the night over here tonight, and I'd hate to have to leave him to the tender mercies of my pa—or even worse, to Little Billy."

"Your folks might as well adopt him, as much as he's over there."

"His folks're out of town at some literature conference or another; I doubt the rural life would agree with him in the long run."

"Well, that's good; there *are* other people who'd like a piece of your time once and a while."

"Oh?"

"Never mind, Davy, just get your tail on over here."

"Oh, right."

"I'll see you in a little while."

"Right . . ." He hesitated, not quite knowing how to end the conversation, which, he realized, could have gone on for hours in endless exchange of taunts and inanities. But he had left an extremely unhappy Alec on the porch and wanted to resolve that. Maybe a change of locale would do the job.

"Bye," he said, feeling somewhat awkward, and hung up.

The door slammed behind him as David returned to the porch. Alec looked up, raised an inquiring eyebrow, then frowned into his third daisy.

"That was Liz Hughes wanting to know if we wanted to go swimming over at her house."

"So what'd you tell her?" There was only a trace of the former hostility, as if Alec had regained control of his emotions for a while—or suppressed them.

"I told her yes, of course. I presume you do want to go—considering how much you were complaining about the heat just now. Maybe it'll wash a little of the mad off you."

Alec frowned. "I'm not mad, I'm . . . confused—and hurt, a little, to be completely honest." He smiled wanly as he levered himself to his feet. "But I guess you really do mean well, even if you are crazy. At least I know you didn't get that ring from Liz; it ain't her style."

"Isn't, Alec, isn't," David laughed, assuming the exact into-

nation Dr. McLean used when correcting his son's grammar. "No, as a matter of fact Liz hasn't even seen it. I'd as soon she didn't, in fact; but there's nothing much I can do about it. If we're going swimming, I guess I'd better wear it on my finger, though; I'd hate to lose it in the lake."

"You got anything I can borrow to swim in?" Alec asked. "Somehow I don't think skinny-dipping is appropriate just now."

"Might be interesting, though," David mused. He laid an arm across Alec's shoulders and headed into the house. "Come on, fool of a Scotsman, I can probably find you something. We'd best get going, though, before Liz changes her mind."

David took mostly back roads to avoid the traffic, and Alec spent most of the trip with his eyes closed and his hands tightly gripping his seat belt. It took twenty minutes to get to Liz's house, an almost-new brick ranch sprawling amid a stand of pines.

Liz was waiting for them in her front yard, an incredibly large red towel draped around her body like a toga. Her auburn hair fell atop it like dark copper wire. She had always had nice hair, David thought. Her purple two-piece bathing suit—not quite a bikini, peeked out from beneath the towel.

"Well," she said in a tone of mock irritation, "it took you long enough!"

"Don't say that!" cried Alec in dismay. "I'd hate for him to take up hurrying. It's bad enough riding with him when he's just taking it easy."

David shot Alec a scathing glare and threw a friendly punch at his shoulder. The ring glittered on his finger.

"All right, boys!" Liz said firmly. "I don't allow any fighting around here."

"Yes ma'am," they replied as one, extravagantly repentant.

They had to pass through a small pine wood to reach the nearest arm of the lake, maybe a quarter mile behind Liz's house. The air there was cool and clean-smelling. As they walked through forest, they saw a half dozen squirrels and at least two chipmunks—which darted frantically about, as if they had just popped into existence and didn't quite know what to make of finding themselves suddenly alive.

"I hope there aren't any *possums* around," Alec whispered.

David elbowed him in the ribs.

Alec parried the elbow with a wrist. "Alive *or* dead."

"What's this about possums?" asked Liz from her position at the head of the line. Beyond her the gray-green shimmer of the lake had become visible.

"David tried to turn himself into a werepossum back in July."

"Alec!" David growled. "Shut up!"

"A werepossum?" Liz's tone was serious. They had reached the lake's edge, where the land descended in a series of red clay shelves to a thread of sandy beach Liz's father had had hauled in. The water was clear and smooth, reflecting the blue sky and the surrounding pine trees as well as the three tanned faces that stared into it.

"Never mind, Liz," David said. "I'll tell you later. Did we come here to talk or to swim?"

"I came to swim," said Liz, dropping her towel and running fifteen or so feet into the lake before thrusting her head smoothly under water.

"She's filled out some this summer," Alec observed.

David nodded appreciatively. "She has for a fact. Now come on, let's go find a bush and change."

"If you weren't so picky about that damn car, we wouldn't have to do this," Alec muttered as he followed David toward a clump of laurel at the top of the bank.

A few minutes later the three friends stood together on the muddy bottom, water waist-deep about their bodies, hair slicked back, beads of moisture dewlike on their limbs, sticking their lashes together.

All at once Liz snatched David's hand from under the water, bringing it up in a cloud of spray that sent Alec flinching. "So this is that ring I've heard so much about!" she cried, grasping David firmly by the wrist while she turned his hand this way and that, the water glittering on the silver circle.

David rolled his eyes at Alec. Alec shrugged noncommittally, leaving David to fend for himself.

"Who is she?" asked Liz.

"I found it."

"Oh, *another* story," muttered Alec.

"That's not what Little Billy told my brother Marvin at Sunday school," Liz remarked.

"That's practically ancient history now, Liz . . . and, besides, Little Billy's a kid. Who you gonna believe, him or me?"

"Don't ask *me*," Alec grumbled.

"Christ!" cried David, looking absently at the water lapping in and out of his navel. "Who *hasn't* he told about that?"

"You tell me," said Liz. "I've heard from three different people that you'd said you had a girlfriend but wouldn't tell her name."

"Good grief!" David sighed. "Can't I do anything without it being front page news? And, Alec, how many people have you told about me and a little trip up the mountain back in July? Will I read about that in the newspaper next week? 'Local Boy Tries to Become Werewolf—Fails—Parents Horrified.' Or maybe, 'Local Boy Sees Castle, then Psychiatrist'?"

Alec feigned dumbness, pointing to his closed mouth and gesticulating wildly. Abruptly he stiffened and fell backward into the water, only to emerge grinning a moment later, hair slicked into his eyes.

"You know," continued Liz, looking intently at the ring, "I get a kind of funny feeling about this ring—like it was something really old." She shook her head. "No . . . I don't think you got this from any girl around here; it's too weird for anybody we know."

"I told you! He got it from a girl in Atlanta."

David wrenched his hand away from Liz and thrust it under water. "Oh, come on, Alec. Let it die. Where would I have met a girl in Atlanta? I'd never been there without my folks but once before the convention, and you were with me then. And, besides, would I be *here* if I had a girl in Atlanta?" David's eyes twinkled, but he knew he was treading on dangerous ground—for several different reasons.

Both Alec and Liz looked confused.

A moment later Alec cried out and pointed toward shore. David and Liz turned, following the line of his pointing finger.

"A white squirrel!" cried Liz. "I've never seen one. Is it an albino, do you think?"

"Most white animals in this part of the country are," said David, "unless they're naturally white—which doesn't make much sense, if you think about it; I mean albinos *are* natural."

The squirrel lay precariously on the green-fringed tip of a pine branch that overhung the water—a patch of brilliance, almost snow-white amid the green needles. It reminded David of winter, in fact; it was like one snowflake on a summer day, and he felt an unexpected chill. Goosebumps rose on his back and chest and shoulders.

The squirrel did not move; it seemed to be watching them. The branch swayed gently under its weight.

"Odd," said Alec.

"Peculiar," said Liz.

"Strange," said David after a pause. "Very strange."

"But pretty," continued Liz.

"Not likely to live long, though," Alec observed. "Stands out too clearly. Easy prey for a hawk."

"Somehow I don't think so," David said, scratching his chin.

He flinched abruptly, for the ring had suddenly grown warm on his finger. Looking down, he saw that it was blazing with light.

"What was that?" cried Alec.

"What was what?"

"That glitter."

"Sun on the water, probably," said Liz, "if you saw what I saw."

"Weird."

"In the old-fashioned sense," David muttered as he ducked his head under. He entered a brown-green world marked by the pale shapes of his friends' legs, the white cutoffs he had lent Alec, and Liz's purple suit. And then his head broke water again. The squirrel was gone.

"Let me have another look at that ring," said Liz, reaching under water for David's hand.

David snatched his hand behind his back, fearful they would see its glow, but he knew from its diminished heat that it had faded. He held it up.

"Let me see if I can get some vibrations off it," Liz said suddenly, closing her eyes.

"Oh for heaven's sake," Alec snorted, turning his back and folding his arms dramatically. "Is *everybody* I know crazy as a bedbug? Vibrations! Liz, come on! Not you too!"

"Well, Alec McLean, sometimes I can pick up vibrations— impressions, whatever you want to call them. My granny taught me a little bit about how to do it before she died. . . . Well, she didn't exactly teach me, she just told me to be aware of what was there, to trust my feelings about things, and I do—and it works, most of the time. And right now I've got a feeling about David's ring."

"What are you going to do?" asked David, fascinated. He had known Liz for years and never suspected she was in any way interested in anything out of the ordinary, though she had listened to him go on about his various fixations with something besides the bemused glances he usually got, and did occasionally ask a penetrating question. Maybe she *was* a little bit psychic. It wouldn't hurt to try. He held his hand out to her.

She closed her eyes again and placed her hands on his, one over and one under, and took a deep breath. David and Alec watched incredulously.

She said nothing for quite a while, but her dark lashes fluttered, and her breath became shallow. Finally she opened her eyes; they were wide and filled with a strange light in their green depths.

"I don't know what just happened, but it was . . . strange. I just tried to picture the ring, and then to be aware of whatever images came into my mind, and I got this incredibly sharp image of an old man in gray robes looking at me, and then of two men, one in black and one in white, fighting with each other. . . . No, not exactly fighting, but *contending* somehow . . . and then they looked at me, and I got scared and quit. I've had impressions before, but this was like television!"

There was a sound then, like the howling of a thousand wolves heard from a great distance, but it was the sound of the wind, a strange wind that suddenly swept out of the high, still air and flowed among the pines on the far bank, then raced across the glassy water, stirring up a miniature tidal wave like a boat wake as it passed, and that then fled up the near bank, but not before it had whirled and eddied momentarily about the three friends so violently that they finally had to submerge themselves to avoid its touch—which was like deadly ice.

"I . . . think . . . I don't want to swim anymore today," Liz whispered.

"Nonsense," said Alec, who immediately did a back flip and swam fifty or so feet out into the again-smooth water. David followed in a moment, and so—reluctantly—did Liz. For a good while they sported about, diving the fifteen or so feet to the bottom and rising again, pulling each others' legs in an attempt to relieve the nervous tension that the eerie wind had generated.

Alec's head broke the surface next to David. He blew water out of his mouth and nose.

"Did you see that?" he sputtered.

"See what?"

"The white fish."

"White fish?" David was treading water, but faltered in his stroke. "Are you kidding?"

"He's not kidding," said Liz, coming up for air beside them, "if he's talking about the white trout I just saw."

David took a gulp of air and submerged, peering through the gloom past his friend's lazily churning legs, to where indeed a white trout swam rapidly in a tight circle. At the same time David became aware of a burning pain on his finger so sudden and intense that he almost gasped out his lungful of air. The ring was glowing white hot again; he could see it even under water, flaring like a magnesium torch.

Suddenly the trout darted straight toward him. He jerked back, but not before it grazed his ring finger and in an apparently deliberate motion swam away toward shore. The ring was hotter than ever, hotter than David had ever felt it, so hot that he almost wanted to take it off—but he knew that he would be a fool if he did.

He surfaced and looked around. Liz and Alec were where he had left them, but maybe fifty yards across the lake behind them he could see the head and part of the body of what appeared to be a great black horse swimming silently toward them. Its eyes glowed red in a way that made David shiver, and he thought he saw steam rising from its nostrils.

"Come on, you guys, let's go!" he cried, swimming frantically toward shore. "There's a horse coming straight toward us. And it doesn't look very happy!"

Alec glanced over his shoulder. "Son-of-a-bitch!" he shouted as he began to swim after David. Liz said nothing; she just swam. Behind them they could now hear the heavy breathing of the horse and the splash of the water against its head and neck as it increased its pace. David thought he could feel its hot breath on his back once or twice, and was it his imagination, or did a faint smell like burning sulfur taint the air?

They swam shoreward until they could stand and run clumsily in the shallows, mud welling up between their toes, the water sucking at their legs, hampering their efforts. They had not turned once to look back, but the snorting hiss of labored breathing sounded closer, and the dull, heavy splashing of the knees of the black horse breaking the surface as it came into shallower water became clearer and clearer.

They heaved themselves onto dry land and scrambled up the bank. Once in the perceived safety of the trees, they turned as one, half afraid of what they might see.

Below them in the shallows stood, indeed, a great black horse, staring malevolently up the bank toward them, but making no move to leave the water that lapped about its hocks. Moisture glistened on its flanks, and the devil light in its eyes had faded— at least to David's sight—to a dull, lifeless gray.

"Son-of-a-*bitch*," Alec whispered.

The horse stared at them a moment longer, then turned and swam off into the lake. The three friends watched it from the safety of the trees until it became a mere speck. Oddly, it did not walk out onto the bank on the other side of the lake, but rather continued into the open water to the right, disappearing finally around an outthrust peninsula.

"That sure was scary!" Liz said breathlessly.

"That's very true," David agreed, picking up his towel. Liz cautiously eased back to the shore to fetch hers.

"Any idea whose horse that was, Liz?" David asked when she had returned.

Liz shook her head. "Nobody around here has a black horse, and, anyway, I've never heard of a horse swimming around like that. I wonder if . . . God, I hope not . . . you don't reckon it might have had rabies or something, do you? I sure don't want to think about a rabid *horse* running around."

"Swimming around, you mean," Alec corrected. "You know, it was almost like it was in its natural habitat, though—and was chasing us off."

"Good thing you saw the fish when you did, Alec, or we might not have noticed till it was right on top of us," David put in.

Liz shuddered and hugged her towel more closely about her. "That's true . . . and you know something else? Between the horse and that strange gust of wind right before, all of a sudden I don't feel in the least like going back in the water."

"I know what you mean," said David. "It's about time for us to head out anyway. Got to get me and Master McLean home before supper, and I'd hate to have to take up hurrying . . ." He grinned at Alec.

As he and Alec returned to the clump of laurel bushes where they had left their clothes and began to change, David wondered if his eyes had deceived him, or if he had actually seen what he thought he had seen at the end of the horse's legs: not hooves—but fins. He glanced down at the ring. It was its usual cold and shiny self. Beautiful, but in no other way remarkable—except, he was now absolutely convinced, it was magic.

Interlude: In Tir-Nan-Og
(high summer)

The boy had spent the night in the company of a selkie woman. They had lain together twice: once on shore, when the boy had put upon himself the seal shape that was the woman's own; and once again in his boat, when she had shed her skin and joined with him in his man's form.

It was morning now, and he was still in the boat. The low sun glimmered through pale tendrils of pink-tinged mist that rose from an expanse of water scarcely darker. To the north was the vague blue crenulation of the forested shore. On every other side was water, motionless as ice and more silent.

A breeze stirred, twitching the fog away from the angry eyes of the gilded dragon prow, causing the limp green sail to billow apprehensively. The thick red fur of the manticore hide with which the boy had wrapped himself stirred. A strand of fair hair blew into his face and tickled him awake.

Something moved at his bare feet: A scaly silver head on an arm-long neck writhed from under the cover and hissed hoarsely, its elaborate ear flares flicking delicately. The rest followed: close-furled wings and clawed hind legs, tail whip-thin like a serpent. The boy jerked a foot back under the cover as the wyvern made a dive for it. He grunted, slipped a hand over the low side to port, and eased it into the water.

It took only a trickle of Power to call the fish: three of them. Each a hand long, they waited by the boat, tails undulating trustingly.

The first two he flung into his pet's waiting jaws. The third he cooked in his fist and ate himself, peeling the white flesh from the bones with perfect teeth, washing it down with the remnants of a flagon of the previous evening's wine.

He was considering the remaining flagon when he became aware of the summoning.

"Too good to last, wasn't it, Dylan?" he grumbled as he heaved himself up among the furs and tugged a gray silk tunic over his head. He stood up unsteadily and squinted into the shimmering red haze of the sun.

There, to the east, maybe an arrow's shot away: a glimmering strip upon the water that was quickly resolving itself into a streak of burning golden light as one of the Tracks came awake beneath the tread of one of his kindred.

Fionchadd! The name echoed in his mind alone: Ailill's call— his father.

He frowned but conjured a breeze to set the boat gliding across the lake toward that summons.

The golden haze of the Track lay on the water, stretching arrow-straight north and south until it was lost in the mist, the rift between the Worlds above it casting flickering images upon the air itself that made him recall his breakfast unpleasantly.

The Track brightened gloriously at one point, rivaling the sun, and then Ailill stepped from that glow and onto the boat amidship. The boat tipped slightly, and Ailill grasped the single mast to steady himself before sitting down.

Fionchadd automatically offered him the wineskin.

Ailill's gaze remained fixed upon the boy as he took a long draught. "You do not look happy, my son," he observed.

"I do not like waiting."

Ailill shrugged and returned the skin. "It was midnight when I left; now it is sunrise. That is not long, and you seem to have spent it well enough—or is that not the scent of selkies I smell upon you?"

The boy looked away. "So did you learn what you set out to learn? What is there in the Lands of Men to interest you?"

"You know of the boy, do you not? The human boy?"

"The one who bested you in the Question Game?"

"The one who insulted me."

Fionchadd took a sip of wine. "I know of him."

"Do you know that he is protected? I tried to summon him, to settle accounts my own way, but when I worked the summoning I met a Power greater than my own, one that almost consumed me. I have been in the Lands of Men seeking to learn the nature of that protection."

"I spent the night on a lake so you could look for a mortal boy?" Fionchadd frowned into his cup.

Ailill's brows lowered dangerously. "It is you who are answerable to me, not I to you."

"You could have told me what you were about."

"And you could then have told anyone who asked you where I was."

"I could have lied."

"You do not do that very well—nor do you hide your thoughts. They are there on your face for anyone to read."

"Perhaps so; but, then, I have less to hide than you do. Now, are you going to tell me what you learned?"

Ailill sighed and regarded his son uneasily. *Just like his mother. Just like the Annwyn-born bitch I got him on. He even looks like her. Fair as sunlight. But, then, he was born at dawn.*

"I learned some things, my son," Ailill said finally, "and I lay a geas upon you to reveal them to no one." He traced a vaguely circular symbol in the air.

Fionchadd traced a matching symbol in turn. "And what are those things?"

Ailill made a cushion out of the manticore fur and leaned back against it. "Very well: I went by the Water Road, which is less frequently traveled. In that I was fortunate, for I came upon the boy swimming with his friends. So I put upon myself the shape of a kelpie, thinking its strength and speed might be useful; also, I thought to test the boy's knowledge of such things. And I watched for a while, and then I threatened—to see if that which protects him offered protection of the body as well as of the mind."

"And does it?"

"It does. I could only approach so closely, and then it was like a wall of flame about him. But I saw what it is that effects this protection."

"And what is that?"

"A ring."

"A ring." Fionchadd raised an eyebrow. "Interesting. How do you propose to procure it?—which I assume you intend to do."

Ailill smiled grimly. "That is the problem, isn't it? I can approach only so closely, and I cannot summon him."

"Have you tried summoning one of his kinsmen? If you cannot touch him, perhaps one of them could. Or you could use one as a hostage."

Ailill's face brightened. "Now you show yourself as my son. But there may be a problem. I have tried summoning all those whose faces I saw graven in those parts of his mind reserved for the beloved. But every time I tried, there was Fire, weaker than that which protects, but still beyond my Power to quench. No, I fear the ring protects them as well."

Fionchadd regarded his father levelly. "So what is it you want from me?"

"I want you to help me. I cannot touch the boy, and I cannot touch the thing that protects him. Nor do I dare absent myself from court too often; Lugh would become suspicious, or if not he, then Silverhand. But there is a possibility that the ring protects him only from me. It might not hinder you."

"So you want me to help you capture the boy?"

Ailill nodded. "If possible. At least I want you to see how close you can come to the ring. It would be best if you began now. Go into the Lands of Men. Watch. Listen. Use whichever of your skills seem good to you. And report to me. You *do* know how to operate the Tracks, do you not?"

"Oh, aye," Fionchadd agreed absently as he began summoning another fish. "My mother taught me that art very well indeed."

Chapter VII: Oisin

"Supper!" JoAnne Sullivan called from the barbed wire fence at the top of the pasture Big Billy shared with Uncle Dale. "You men gonna stand there starin' at that sorghum patch all evenin'? Ain't gonna make it grow no faster!" She could see their varied silhouettes cut out against the lush green growth that filled the narrow, flat strip of land between the pasture and the Sullivan Cove road: Big Billy, tall and heavy-set, stomach gone to fat from too much beer and good food, but still well muscled; Uncle Dale, taller still, rail-thin, and aged like a locust fence post; and beside him in stair-step order: slender Alec; David, shorter but more solidly built; and then Little Billy, who looked like he would beat them all.

"One more call's all you're gettin', and then I'm gonna eat this stuff myself—now get up here!"

"Yes ma'am," hollered Big Billy, smiling faintly.

As they trudged up the grassy slope Alec and David fell slightly behind. Alec clapped a hand good-naturedly on David's shoulder and bent close. "Sorry about this afternoon," he said.

David shrugged. "No problem. I appreciate your concern, but I'm just . . . confused about some things, and I haven't figured them out yet."

"That's the kind of thing we used to work out together, my friend."

David nodded grimly. "I know, and I hope we can work this out too, but not yet . . . not quite yet."

They had reached the top of the hill by then, and David held up the barbed wire for Alec to climb through before following himself. Alec glanced up at his friend from the ditch beside the driveway and nodded resignedly.

"You go on up, I'll be there in a minute," said David.

Alec raised an eyebrow. "Well, don't expect me to leave anything for you; your ma's probably given up on us already, and I for one am not one to give up on your ma's cooking."

"I won't," David called to Alec's back as he took off his glasses and rubbed his eyes. Something was up again, he knew, as he surveyed the landscape. But where? Nothing met his gaze. Finally he shrugged and followed his friend toward the house. The itching wouldn't quit, though, and for a long moment David stood on the side porch looking out across the intervening fields and pastures toward the silver-red glitter of the lake far to the west, and then abruptly up the gravel road to the bulk of the mountain. His eyes were burning now, and his hand unconsciously sought the ring.

And then he saw it: right at the limits of sight, so faint as to be almost invisible against the dark forest. Just where the road marched in among the trees beyond the barn, he thought he could make out the hazy figure of a man—an old man in flowing gray robes—and that the man raised one thin arm and pointed up the mountain. It seemed, too, that the old man held a walking stick in his other hand, with which he felt his way. David blinked, and the man was gone.

David put down his glass of milk. "I think me and Alec are gonna walk up to Lookout Rock after supper," he announced as he speared a piece of roast beef and looked quizzically over at Big Billy, who was applying himself vigorously to his own generous portion.

"We're gonna *what?*" cried a shocked Alec through a mouthful of mashed potatoes. Little Billy giggled, but nobody noticed.

Alec slumped in his chair and glared at David through tired eyes. "David, my friend, I am weary to the bone." He pointed at himself with his fork. "All *I* want to do is play a couple of rounds of Risk and go to bed. I don't know how I let you talk me into putting in the whole day following you around."

"We didn't do anything but talk and go swimming."

"And help your daddy pull the engine out of that old pickup.

And, besides, hanging onto the seat while you take *every* curve between here and Liz's house on two wheels, takes it out of a body."

David snorted. "Wimp."

"If you're so set on goin' up that mountain, why don't you take Little Billy," Uncle Dale suggested. "Me 'n Alec'll play us a game or two of checkers. That be okay? You want to go hikin' up to the Rock with Davy, Little Billy?"

Little Billy looked up, wide-eyed. Milk had painted a white mustache on his upper lip. "Nope."

"Why not?" cried the old man.

"I don't like goin' in the woods."

"Why not?"

"They's boogers in there," the little boy said solemnly.

"Boogers! Why what kind of talk is that?" Uncle Dale gave David a sharp look. "Who's been teachin' you 'bout boogers?"

"Nobody; I saw one."

"Saw one!" said Uncle Dale. "Well, what did it look like?"

"Like a real shiny boy."

"A shiny boy? I never heard of a booger lookin' like a shiny boy."

"Well, it did," Little Billy said stubbornly. "A shiny boy wearin' funny gray clothes."

David felt the hair prickle on the back of his neck. Apparently his brother had seen one of the Sidhe. But if what Ailill had said was really true, that the Sidhe could make themselves visible to anyone if it were *their* choice, then why had one shown himself to Little Billy? That didn't augur well at all. "Did it say anything?" David asked cautiously.

"Nope. Just sat up there by the barn and looked at me."

"You won't go near it if you see it again, will you?" David laughed nervously, trying to mask how much his brother's remark had disturbed him.

Uncle Dale shot David another sharp glance.

"I ain't crazy," Little Billy replied, reaching for the plate of freshly baked cookies that were to be desert.

"But you will stay close to home, won't you?" David asked hopefully.

"I ain't crazy," Little Billy repeated.

* * *

The boys retired to David's room at a surprisingly early hour. Alec was asleep almost as soon as he hit the covers, but David stayed up to read for a while—hoping to find some key to the day's occurrence in *Gods and Fighting Men* or *The Secret Common-Wealth*. He'd read the latter cover to cover several times—it was not very long. But except for the business about Second Sight, which occupied almost half the book, there was very little in it that seemed relevant to his current situation. There were no magic rings in it, for instance, and no water horses. And it was difficult to reconcile Kirk's provincial Subterraneans with the sophisticated, urbane Sidhe he had met. There were certainly some things in it worth knowing, but almost none of them were either pleasant or encouraging. The stuff about changelings was particularly disturbing, for instance.

Eventually David found his eyes getting heavier and heavier. A tiredness he had not previously been aware of had fallen upon him, and as it claimed him, his consciousness followed.

But two hours later David was awake again. The clock by his bed indicated a few minutes before midnight. He glanced over at Alec, still sound asleep in the other bed, breathing heavily through his mouth, one bare arm hanging off the side.

He'll put his arm to sleep for sure that way, David thought and lay back down, only to sit up again a moment later. Jesus, he was restless! What a predicament: to be fully awake in the middle of the night. For a moment David wondered if anyone else was up, but the only sound that came to his ears was the distant wind: no TV, no radio. He looked out the window beside his bed and idly watched a single car accelerate down the highway.

"Crap," he muttered. "I was afraid it'd come to this."

Quietly David got up, slipped on a pair of corduroy jeans, tiptoed barefoot to the door, and soundlessly opened it, grateful he had had the foresight to oil the hinges. He continued down the hall into the kitchen, and thence onto the back porch which faced the mountain. For a long moment he leaned against a porch post, staring out into the yard, oblivious to the chill wind that played about his bare shoulders and feet. Absently he hugged his arms about himself and continued his vigil, not knowing what he sought, but knowing, too, with absolute conviction, that there was some reason for the sense of undirected urgency that filled him.

Slowly David became aware of a sort of sparkle in the grass, as if dew had fallen or autumn had sent a tentative vanguard of frost venturing briefly in from the north. At the same time he sensed a new brightness in the air, as if the moon had risen. He leapt lightly into the yard and raised his face skyward, seeking the source of that radiance.

It was the moon, all right, rising golden-yellow—only . . . something was wrong. Hadn't the moon been new just a few days before? And now it was full! And wasn't it in the wrong part of the sky? The familiar tingle tickled his eyes then, and he grimaced and exhaled sharply. He knew what he had to do.

When David slipped back into his room a moment later, he found Alec sitting on the side of his bed calmly tugging on his socks.

"I'm going with you, of course," Alec whispered in response to David's raised eyebrows. "I could tell by that look in your eyes at supper that you'd go up that mountain tonight with me or without me—and I'm just stupid enough to go with you. Maybe I'll get to the bottom of this foolishness yet."

David smiled but didn't say anything, just crossed soundlessly to the closet and pulled out a long-sleeved flannel shirt. "Wait and put your shoes on outside," he told Alec. "No way you can walk quiet as me through the house, and Pa's a light sleeper."

Alec nodded. A moment later both boys sat on the back steps looking out into the darkness.

"You see anything funny about the night?" David asked tentatively. He watched Alec's face closely.

Alec glanced at the sky and then back at David, noticing the scrutiny. "Am I *supposed* to see anything funny about the night? It's a night. Dark, mostly. Some stars. Land is darker than sky."

David looked hard at his friend. "Any moon?"

Alec frowned and looked back at the sky. "None that I can see. It's the wrong time of month for it, isn't it? Why?"

"Alec, how bright does it look out here to you?"

"What do you mean, how bright?"

"I mean how bright. Bright enough to read by? Bright enough to barely feel your way around in if you're not in shadow? How bright?"

Alec returned David's intense stare. "Not bright enough to read by, that's for sure."

"Alec," whispered David very slowly, "I know you're not going to believe this . . . but I see a full moon."

"Made out of green cheese or painted blue, no doubt?"

David sighed and flung his hands up in dismay; then he rose and jumped off the steps, striding decisively toward the driveway, his paces long and deliberate. Alec almost had to run to catch up.

"Damn, Sullivan, what're you *doing* fumbling around out here in the dark? Aren't you at least gonna get a flashlight?"

David turned almost savagely on his friend but did not slow down. "I don't *need* a flashlight. *I* see a full moon, and I see by its light. If you want to come along, you're welcome, but don't slow me down; there's something I gotta do tonight. I don't know what it is yet, but something magic is cooking, Alec. I know it. Maybe, just maybe, if you come with me, you'll see something too—and believe me." His voice softened. "I don't like not having you believe me, Alec. But you won't without proof, so maybe I can give you some."

Alec stared at David as he followed him toward the logging road. "I just don't want you breaking your leg in the dark or something."

"Ha!" came David's scornful voice ahead of him, at the point where the trees began to close in. "You're the one who needs to worry—especially if you don't catch up." His voice took on a lighter coloring. "There are werewolves on this mountain, I hear."

"Werepossums, anyway," came Alec's voice close behind him.

An hour or so later they reached their destination. It was impossible to tell exactly how long the trip had taken, because David discovered he had let his watch run down: It still registered twelve o'clock. The moon seemed to have moved, too, but somehow in not quite the right manner. David shrugged it off. Time was the least of his worries.

As he and Alec came into the open space of the lookout, David suppressed a chill as he recalled the last time he had been there. He glanced furtively at the sky before trotting over to stand on the overlook itself.

There was the usual gut-wrenching sensation of being suddenly very high in the air, the more so because the wind blew fallen leaves about, blurring the distinction between sky and earth, even as the darkness itself did. The waterfall roared incessantly to the left, strangely loud as it poured into the pool, its edges fringed with decaying brown leaves.

David and Alec found their customary ledge at the very tip of the lookout. Without a word they stretched out side by side, hands hooked behind their heads, gazing up at the stars. A meteor obligingly flashed out of the northwest. Alec pointed. "Did you see that? Nice one!"

"I did." David nodded.

"You know, this old rock is pretty comfortable. I could nearly go to sleep here."

"You'd freeze half to death and be stiff as rigor mortis in the morning."

"Appropriately!"

"Appropriately." David levered himself up on his elbows. "We'd best start back soon. I don't know why I wanted to come up here; I have no idea what I'd hoped to find."

"The Holy Grail?"

"This is serious, Alec."

Alec closed his eyes. "Just wake me in the morning," he sighed.

David continued to watch the sky for a while, hoping to see another meteor—or something. Somehow, though, he could not seem to muster quite enough energy to start the long trip back home. Or was it that he still felt that sense of anticipation, as in something important were about to happen? He sat up again, hunched over, wrapped his arms awkwardly about his knees, and rested his chin on them, wishing he had brought a jacket.

"Yes, it is a little cold," came a voice behind him, a voice that sang in his ears like music, though the phrase was in no way remarkable. David would never forget the first words he heard that voice speak.

He did not start when the voice sounded; rather, he very calmly and quietly stood up and looked back toward the mass of mountain —and was not at all surprised to see a robed figure sitting placidly on one of the rocks by the waterfall. His eyes tingled, too, but he scarcely noticed as he glanced one last time at Alec. His friend appeared to be sound asleep, a smile of almost abandoned pleasure curving the full lips above his pointed chin, making tiny dimples in his cheeks. David smiled in turn and slowly approached the figure. As he crossed the thirty or so feet between them, the thought came to him that he should not have been able to hear the man's speech above the roar of the waterfall beside him—yet the voice had sounded clearly, like a whisper in an empty church.

Almost without thinking David found himself sitting on a rock opposite the man. Beneath the gray-white hood the man seemed to look at David, and yet not at him; his gaze seemed fixed somewhere slightly above David's head. Slowly the man extended a hand, brushed his fingertips briefly against David's brow—and as slowly withdrew it—then raised both hands to the hood and flung it back.

David watched almost as if hypnotized, taking in every detail: the ancient and corded hands, like old tree bark; the nails perfect and almost metallic-looking, a ring on each finger. No, on all fingers but *one*—each of them silver, but all different. The rest of the body seemed indistinct, nebulous. David could not make his eyes focus on it, but he had an impression of a slender form shrouded in long gray-and-white robes of a soft fabric like velvet. If moonlight was woven into fabric it would be like that, he thought.

And the face . . . David hesitated to look full on it. It was the face of an old man, lined with a thousand wrinkles, yet still with its power and dignity about it, and still with the joy of youth playing about the lips and eyes. David realized that the appearance of age lay mostly on the surface, for the muscles and bones kept their firmness; it was more like a patina on silver or the fine network of cracks on an old painting. The hair was white, too, white as the stars in the sky, long, and infinitely fine, sweeping back from the furrowed forehead. And the eyes! David didn't know how long he looked at those eyes as the man continued to smile softly in the silence. They were silver-colored: from edge to edge, dark silver. *Blind,* David knew instinctively, but beautiful, and infinitely strange.

"You will have to look a long time to read my whole story there, David Sullivan," the stranger said at last, and a hush fell about that place, as if the world had stopped to listen.

"Who *are* you?" David managed to croak. "Why did you want me to come here?"

"Did I want you to come here?" the blind man asked calmly.

"Someone changed the moon down at my house. This isn't the real moon."

"I'm a blind man. How could I know that?"

"The same way I could hear your voice over the sound of the wind and the water," said David, rather pleased with himself.

"Well put," said the blind man, smiling again. "And since I know your name, and thereby have power over you—according to some—I will give you mine in return. When I last walked freely among mortal men I was called Oisin."

"Oisin," David said incredulously. It was a name he remembered from *Gods and Fighting Men*. The very sound of it cast shadows in his mind: of the ocean, of endless leagues of dark water sailed by a silver boat under a moon that never waned, while harp music floated softly over the waves; and then of other things: of the Sidhe, and the banshee; and the soft but threatening sheen of cold steel weapons well made.

"It is a name like any other," Oisin said quietly. "It conjures images like any other. Some day I may tell you what visions shine in *my* inner eye when I hear David Kevin Sullivan spoken aloud —or Suilleabhain, as it was in the tongue of your fathers."

David realized, then, that the language Oisin spoke was English, though strangely stressed and cadenced. There was none of that remote, heard-under-water quality he recalled from his encounter with the Sidhe. That, he suspected, was their own language rendered intelligible in his mind alone.

Oisin rapped David on the knee with his cane so that David flinched in alarm. "But I did not come here to speak of words and languages, boy. I came to speak of deeds. And particularly of your deeds, once and future."

"Deeds? I don't plan any deeds. I just want to go on living a normal life, like I was living before . . ."

"Like you *thought* you were living, you mean," Oisin interrupted sharply. "Few men of this age stay up nights reading anything at all, David, much less the sort of things you read. And you have seen things no one in this land has seen—things no one may see and remain unchanged."

"You seem to know a great deal about me," David observed suspiciously. "Buy why should I trust you? What difference does it make to you what happens to me?"

Oisin turned his face toward the cold blue sky. "That would be obvious if you knew my story. Indeed, I am surprised you do not know it, but perhaps men have forgotten. At times I forget myself. Certainly most of the Sidhe seem no longer to recall that I was once a mortal man such as you; that blood red as yours once ran in my veins."

"Your story . . . ?" David ventured uncertainly.

"I came to Tir-Nan-Og once, as a youth. Years I spent here, ageless. And then a craving came on me to return to Ireland. That grace the Sidhe granted me, but as soon as I touched the earth of that land, age fell upon me, and I withered where I stood. I can but recall with bitterness how I crept back here with my youth stricken from me by my own careless folly and by the curse of the Sidhe—how the Faery women would have nothing to do with me because I was no longer a fit lover, and how the Faery men lost interest because I was no fit opponent in their endless duels. I do not want that to happen to you, and it could—easily—in spite of the protection that is now upon you.

"Nothing changes in Faerie, David: The dead do not stay dead; the living scarcely know they are alive. What passion there is, in love and hate, in pain and pleasure, has no fire beneath it. It is only gratification of the moment, for when time does not matter, neither does anything else. The past is gone, yet the present is so like it that there is little to distinguish this year from those a thousand gone. To the Dagda, the Sons of Mil came yesterday; to him the sun will fade tomorrow. There is eternity in a moment, and a moment may span a century.

"Now look at me!" Oisin commanded fiercely. "Imagine your features cast upon mine, and ask yourself if anyone would wish this upon another of his own kind."

Almost against his will David found himself staring into the blazing gaze of the old man's blind eyes. The force of the horror and regret he found there chilled him to the core. Finally he blinked, and stared at the ground.

"Now do you see why I feel it my duty to speak to you?" Oisin asked, shifting his position slightly. "But enough of this. I have some things to tell you, and some things to ask you, but first of all I have a warning for you, and that warning is this: Beware the wrath of Ailill. He is a great threat to you and those you love."

"Tell me something I *don't* know," David snorted. "He's been after me at least once today already . . . either him or somebody—

or something—that works for him. There was this black horse that came after me and some of my friends while we were swimming. If it hadn't been for all those white animals—they weren't you, were they?"

"White animals? No, I have not lately worn any shape but my own. Now tell me of these things." Urgency filled Oisin's voice.

"Well, first there was a white dog, and then today I saw a white squirrel, and a white trout, and . . ."

"Those would all be Nuada, I think . . . or some of his minions. He is of your faction."

"My faction? *What* faction?" David shook his head. "I don't understand."

"The Sidhe are of two minds about you, David," Oisin said. "One side, of whom Ailill is chief, regards you as a threat. They say that when your people made the chariot road that passes near here, and thus it became an easy thing for great numbers of men to come into these mountains, there was then no longer a possibility of peace between the Worlds; that unless the Sidhe make a stand very soon, the day is not far off when only the Deep Waters will remain where the immortals may walk free—and there are no stars in the Deep Waters, and no moon. Ailill and his minions fear you, yet they dare not slay you, if only for fear of the wrath of Nuada and Lugh. But they would be glad to have you safely in Faerie so drunk on Faery wine that you never recall your own lands. This Ailill would have done on Lughnasadh had Nuada not tricked him—and had your answers not been so skillful. Ailill did not like that at all, for he and Nuada have become great enemies, and the rift between them grows wider by the day. Lugh is greatly vexed."

"Lugh is your king, right?"

Oisin nodded. "The Ard Rhi—for this time and this place. It was not always so, nor will it always be. Nuada was king once; he may be again, and for your sake I hope that day is soon. It is his faction which feels that you may be of service to us as you are: a youth largely untouched by the grosser things of this world." Again he rapped David on the knee. "This group feels that you may serve us best if you remain free among mortals, maybe in time to become a sort of ambassador between the Sidhe and mortal men, working in secret for their causes."

"But why would I do that? I'm mortal myself. And what would I do? Go to Atlanta and say to the Governor, 'I'm David

Sullivan, and the Irish fairies have told me to tell you not to build any more roads in the mountains 'cause they were there first'? Shoot! They wouldn't listen to the Indians; they sure won't listen to anybody they *can't* see!"

"The Indians gave us no sorrow," Oisin said wistfully. "The Nunnihe, they called us."

"But I've only seen a couple of things," David protested, "and already I'm fidgety all the time. I can't trust anything to be what it looks like. I don't mean Ailill any harm, Oisin! I don't want to hurt *any* of the Sidhe." David buried his face in his hands.

"And they wish that you—and all men of this land—would leave *them* alone." Oisin's response was momentarily sharp; then it faded into gentler tones. "Oh, it is a true thing, lad, that no one may harbor ill will toward what he does not know exists, but the taint of mortal men nevertheless intrudes more and more into Faerie. The days of the Sidhe in the land you call Ireland are nearly finished because of that intrusion. Here in these mountains the taint is less, yet now this land, too, is becoming closed—by things like the iron tracks that once lay where the chariot road now lies. Fifty years they have been gone, yet the shadow remains. The Road is still very weak there, the Walls between the Worlds very thin. For that brief distance the Sidhe must ride almost wholly in your World. And this year those Walls were thinner than ever before, only the faintest veil of glamour. Anyone with even a trace of Power could hear our music and see our lights. And such Power is in you and in your brother as well, though it still sleeps in him. What has awakened it in you, I do not know. But we have more important things to discuss now. You said you thought Ailill had been after you already?"

"If that really was him today—that water-horse thing. And there was a really weird wind, too. Could he have had something to do with that?"

Oisin shrugged. "Neither would surprise me at all; Ailill is very fond of shape-shifting, and is a master of winds and tempests as well, though it seems strange that he would attack you by daylight, for his Power is greatest at night. As I mentioned before, a protection has been laid upon you. I imagine he seeks to learn its nature, and so uses the tools he knows best. But, more importantly, he fears the threat he thinks you embody—and a frightened man is very, very dangerous."

David drummed his fingers on his leg. "But what about the ring? It's mixed up in this, I'm sure. Is it the protection you spoke of earlier?"

"Ah." Oisin smiled. "The ring. I was myself among the host that you encountered, and even as we rode away, I reminded Ailill of the promise he had made to you for a token of the meeting, and how it was an ill thing for him not to see that part of the bargain fulfilled. Oh, he was in a black mood after his double defeats, let me tell you, and he dismissed me with a shrug, saying that if tokens were wanted, someone else would bestow them.

"And then I thought of these many rings I have, each given me by a Faery lover when I was young"—and Oisin spread his fingers so that David could see the intricate metal work, the almost infinitely tiny gems—"each one of which is magic, but one alone, I knew, affords protection against the Sidhe themselves, for it was forged by a druid of the Fir Bolg and once belonged to Eochaid their king. That ring I caused to be put on your finger."

"But how. . ."

Oisin smiled simply. "One learns much magic in a thousand years, even those of mortal birth such as I was before I put away the substance of your world. Mortality is both a blessing and curse, David, for though it shortens our lives, it quickens our wits."

"You say the ring protects me?" David asked cautiously.

"It will protect you and those you love—those you *truly* love —from the Sidhe. While you possess it, the Sidhe are powerless to do you any physical harm. They may not touch you against your will, and their magic will have no power over you. But the ring has its limits. I yet retain some control over it, for instance, such as I used to bring you here, and the Straight Tracks are a greater Power and older; even the Sidhe do not understand all their workings."

"But how will I know whom it protects?"

"You have only to watch, for you are not without Power yourself. Things have Power because you give them Power, David, do not forget that. Discover that Power! Use it! There are people, for instance, to whom you have given enough of yourself, knowing or unknowing, that part of your Power is in them. Just as there are things like that, and places—Places of Power for you, like this one. There is part of you in that boy over there"—Oisin pointed to where Alec still slept—"or in that red-haired girl."

"Liz? I don't love her."

"Do you not?"

"I don't think so," David added in a small voice.

"You may be surprised then some day."

Suddenly David felt very uncomfortable; he didn't like the direction this conversation was going.

"Is there anything else I can do . . . to, you know, play it safe?"

"Iron and ash wood may be of some aid, and the Sidhe may enter no dwelling unasked. Remember that. Nor does time always run in Faerie as it does in the Lands of Men; thus the Sidhe are sometimes slow to act. This may be your strongest defense against them. Also, do not let anyone you care about be alone when you can prevent it, especially at night, for as I said, the ring has limits. And take special care of your brother; he is a prize they would covet. There are few things Ailill would not do to have him in his grasp."

"What kind of things?" David asked slowly.

Oisin straightened his back and began to rise. "Would that I had time to tell you a tenth part of them. Surely you have heard something of the Sidhe's less favorable dealing with mortals. Much that has been written is true."

He extended a hand to help David up. "Now I fear I must leave you. Already I have stayed too long, for I suspect that I am watched, and not only with eyes. Ailill knows I favor you and will do all in his power to prevent our further meetings if he learns of this one. If you find yourself truly in need of me again, it may be that I can come again at your bidding. In that event, come into the forest and break a twig from a maple tree. But do this only if you have no alternative, for it is magic of a kind, and you should have as little to do with magic as possible." He turned and started toward the waterfall.

"Wait a minute, please, before you go—I want Alec to meet you."

Oisin shook his head. "That may not be; the boy will recall nothing of this night's work. He is safer thus."

"But Oisin, I want him to see you!"

Oisin twisted half around to face David. "Do you also want to see him imperiled? More than he already is? I feel someone's thought creeping about the walls of my mind even now, so truly I must depart. I will leave you with a warning, one thing that should never be far from your thought if you would deal with the Sidhe: *This land they have claimed for their own, for the eternity of their lives,* and they *will* see that it remains so, even if they must make one last stand against mortal men. That time is not yet, David, but I fear it fast approaches, and when it comes, it may fall upon you to choose with whom you cast your lot. You could be a valuable friend then, or a bitter foe. It is up to you. Farewell, David Sullivan, most blessed of mortals."

And he turned away and walked not into the woods, but into the pool and under the waterfall. David was not surprised that the waters did not bow his head.

Most blessed of mortals. David's thought echoed the words. "Or most cursed of mortals," he added aloud as he walked slowly back to the lookout.

Alec was waking up as David came up beside him. He stretched languorously. "Darn! I didn't mean to go to sleep like that. Sorry. Why didn't you wake me?"

"Oh, I didn't notice at first; I was thinking about . . . other things." David smiled cryptically.

"Well, the only other thing I'm thinking about is a nice soft bed waiting for me a couple of miles down the road, and the sooner the better. I hope you found whatever it was you were looking for, that is, if you could find anything with the moon behind the clouds. Just look at them!"

David glanced up and noticed that the Faery moon was gone. Magic had left the mortal world for a while.

They didn't talk much on their way back down the mountain. Indeed, the cloud cover had become so heavy that they had to devote most of their attention simply to navigating the road without hurting themselves.

They managed to get into the house without waking anyone, undressed in the dark, and crawled into bed. Just as he closed his eyes, David heard the grandfather clock in the living room toll one time. He checked his watch's luminous dial: five after one. *It's running again,* he said to himself. *But how could it be only one? We left at midnight, and we've been gone hours and hours.* He started to wake Alec to tell him, and thought better of it. His friend was already snoring.

Chapter VIII: Running
(Sunday, August 9)

David could not believe how good he felt the next morning. His eyes virtually popped open at six o'clock, and he had no urge whatsoever to go back to sleep—this in spite of logic, which told him that he had, in fact, slept for less than six hours, and emotion, which told him that he had awakened with a great deal more to worry about than he had had the day before.

And, on top of everything else, it was threatening rain again, as a glance out his window told him. The sky loomed dark and ominous, promising the kind of sullen day he hated. If his father was a fire elemental, David thought, then he must be a spirit of the air, for it was bright sunlight and clear, clean air that delighted him most.

But, in spite of logic, in spite of emotion, even in spite of the weather, he was experiencing an almost embarrassing sense of well-being. It was as if some untapped spring of energy had over-flowed simultaneously into both his mind and his body. He felt—there was no other term for it—powerful. Powerful, in the most positive, most literal sense. And there was no way he could reasonably account for it. Unless, just perhaps, it was some final legacy of his meeting with Oisin.

David vaulted out of bed and stretched luxuriously, feeling

every muscle and bone and sinew slide sensuously into place. There was no trace of morning stiffness, none of the soreness he expected from the three hours he had spent yesterday tugging on a block and tackle—just pure energy.

He glanced over at the amorphous mass of rumpled bed linen that he hoped was Alec. A single foot protruded near the lower edge of the bed. Impulsively he grabbed it and tugged. There was a muffled cry, followed by a resounding thump as Alec flopped to the floor amid a tumble of sheets and coverlet.

"Rise and shine, Master McLean," David said, grinning.

"You've got to be kidding," Alec mumbled, trying unsuccessfully to extricate himself from the combination toga, sari, and cocoon into which he had wound himself during the night.

David sat back down on his own bed and watched with vast amusement as Alec finally disentangled himself from the pile and stretched himself in turn, fingers automatically trying to smooth his rumpled hair even before rubbing his eyes. "What's the matter, McLean? Not ready to face the day? *I* feel marvelous, absolutely first rate. In fact, I don't think I can avoid going for a run this morning before breakfast. You, of course, oh faithful partner, will come along."

Alec knelt on David's bed and peered out the window. "You've *got* to be kidding," he said again.

"What's the matter, kid? Rigorous rural life not agreeing with you?"

David began pilfering his chest of drawers in search of a pair of gym shorts (his customary cutoffs being too snug for running), followed almost as an afterthought by an ancient gray sweatshirt from which the sleeves and everything below the ribcage had been ripped.

Alec peered groggily into a mirror. "Got anything I can use?"

"Not much of a boy scout, are you?" David grunted as he rummaged under his bed for a delinquent running shoe. "Never seem to be prepared. Fortunately I think Sullivan's Lending Service can come through again. It'll be worth the trouble just for the novelty of seeing you do something physical for once." He snagged the shoe and reached for his gym shorts.

"One condition, though."

"I make no promises."

"Coffee."

"Afterward."

Alec flopped back onto his own bed. "Before, or I don't go."

"It'll stunt your growth."

"For which you should be grateful, seeing I'm taller than you."

David threw a pillow at him.

Alec caught it in mid-flight and, using it as a shield, advanced on David, whom he caught off guard with one foot still tangled in his shorts. Giggling like idiots, they collapsed backward onto David's bed.

"Fool of a faggot Scotsman!" cried David. "Get off me!"

"Promise me something, first."

"I promise to beat your ass for you if you don't get off me."

"Two cups of coffee."

"I can't promise if I can't breathe."

"Two cups of coffee."

"Done. Now hurry up, before Pa catches both of us and puts us to doing something obnoxious." He flung a slightly ragged pair of shorts in Alec's general direction, which his friend picked up somewhat distastefully.

"He works like that on Sunday?"

David looked startled. "It *is* Sunday, isn't it? Well, well." He slipped a hand under the abbreviated shirt and fondled the ring. "I've had this for a week now."

"What?" said a startled Alec as his head emerged through the neck of his T-shirt.

"Oh, nothing."

Alec frowned. "My butt."

"Has as its main functions keeping your legs together in a vain attempt to follow in my footsteps as I run fleet as a deer through the morning woods."

"Give me a break, Sullivan. *Nobody* feels that good this early."

"Not everybody has a magic ring, either."

"I'll make you a deal," said Alec, suddenly serious. "If I can beat you in a race, you tell me the straight story, beginning to end."

David stared at him. "I *have* told you the straight story."

"Bull." Alec extended a hand, his face serious, eyes trusting. "Deal?"

David took it reluctantly. "Deal . . . but only if you catch me."

Maybe I'll just run off in the woods and not come back! David thought as he burst out into the backyard a few minutes later with a still-groggy Alec trotting stiffly after him. He'd follow his short route: maybe a mile and a half—it'd never do to push Alec too hard. Across the upper pasture first, just skirting the woods; down the other side, into the woods proper for half a mile or so; then back to civilization on the other side of Uncle Dale's farm, where the forest intersected the Sullivan Cove road at the lake; and then another half mile back along that road to the farm. A fair mix of terrain.

It was good to get the blood pumping, David thought. He'd never considered himself especially physically oriented—the only sports he much cared for were swimming, volleyball, wrestling, and gymnastics (and auto racing, on TV), and rural Enotah County offered little along any of those lines. Lately, though, he'd grown more aware of his body, now that the eager upward rush of puberty seemed to be slowing and giving his body time to fill out instead of up. *A little more* up *would have been nice, too,* he thought wistfully, but at least his work on the farm over the summer seemed to have done him some good: His ribs were not so noticeable now, and his shirts were getting tight in the armpits. But he lacked the discipline to exercise on a regular basis. So he had started running a couple of months before, which was not like exercise at all, but like religion: a becoming of one with the natural world. A part of him wished he could study sword fighting or at least fencing, but, of course, there was no way that would be possible in this part of the country. For a moment he imagined himself in plate armor, swinging a two-handed broadsword in his gauntleted fists, a lord among men—like Nuada.

Joyfully he vaulted the low barbed-wire fence at the edge of the pasture, then jogged back to lift it for Alec to climb through. This first part of the run was gently uphill across the rounded crest of the upper pasture, maybe a hundred yards. David gloried in the feel of air rushing in his ears, the rhythm of his strides, the steady thud of his feet touching the springy ground. There was no trace of fatigue in his body this early on, just the exhilaration of moving fast on soft grass with the faint scent of pine needles coming in on every breath. Straight ahead of him the stubborn sun momentarily broke through the glowering clouds with swords of light, dolloping the stubble of cow-mown grass with greenish gold, striking fire from the tin roof of Uncle Dale's old house that huddled ancient in its hollow a quarter of a mile away.

Alec's dull staccato tread and hissing breaths sounded behind him. *Poor kid,* he thought as their route leveled briefly along an abandoned farm road before turning down the steeper slope on the far side of the pasture. It would be down this slope, in a now-broken rhythm, across (or under, or through) the fence at the bottom, and then sharply left, uphill into the woods proper, up a steep, winding path he recalled, that gradually straightened and then paralleled the top edge of the steep bank behind Uncle Dale's house where some ancestor or relative had ripped a gash in the mountain to make a level place for a barn that had never been built. A small, swift stream snaked along the bottom of that cut.

David half jumped down the lower face of the slope, being careful not to twist an ankle in some unexpected gully, then headed uphill, aiming for the gap between two lightning-blasted pine trees that marked the entrance to the wooded part of his route.

Abruptly the forest closed in about him, and the persistent sun now sent pale shafts of light shooting between the branches, shafts so bright against the gloom that they almost seemed solid. David set himself a new pace, arms pumping vigorously, breath coming steadily but a little harder as he began to exert himself. Up ahead he could see another landmark tree, to which he called an absurdly friendly greeting as he passed, surprising even himself. He could feel sweat beginning to form on his chest and back now, rolling gently down between his shoulders to pool, tickling, at the waistband of his underwear.

David's thoughts began to wander as he slowed a little where the course became steeper and more crooked. A newly-fallen limb lay athwart the trail, and he leapt over it and continued on. Behind him he could hear the steady thump-gasp, thump-gasp of a remarkably consistent Alec. He broke his stride to venture a glance over his shoulder and saw his friend pounding grimly onward, his dark hair flopping on his forehead. Alec's eyes caught David's for an instant, and he bared his teeth in friendly menace.

David reestablished his pace, but he could hear Alec's breathing becoming harder, more forceful, though it was not yet labored. *Like a little bull,* he thought. Alec was gaining, too—which was not good. Suppose David lost! Suppose Alec held him to his vow and demanded the whole incredible story from him. How could he tell his friend *that?*

A branch slapped at his face, disrupting his reverie. He checked the trail ahead; he hadn't been this way in a while, and the landmarks were not as clear as he remembered them.

"You'd *better* run, Sullivan," he heard Alec call out behind him, "'cause if I catch you, you ain't gonna like being caught!"

David quickened his pace, but the sound of Alec's running grew no fainter.

"What you gonna do, fool of a Scotsman?"

"Wring the truth out of you like a bagpipe," Alec gasped.

"Ha!" David cried. "Not bloody likely!"

They came upon a short section that was straight and level, an aisle among the pines and maples. Ahead and to the right David caught glimpses of the roof of Uncle Dale's house, much closer now. Once on that straight he increased his speed—but so did Alec.

David withdrew into himself then, concentrating, feeling only his blood racing, his legs pumping, hearing the air whistle between his glasses and his ears, noting that the lenses were steaming up a little. Where *was* the next landmark, he wondered; the trail had become extremely vague here. Oh yes, there it was, over to the left.

The trail now bent upward into the steepest part they had yet come to—that part which led most deeply into the forest before turning abruptly back upon itself. Funny, David didn't remember it being quite so steep last time, but then it had been a while since he had used this route. And it was *awfully* straight. Too straight, in fact; maybe he had made a wrong turn or something and come upon one of those old logging roads that mazed the woods. Up ahead he could see something white moving alongside the trail: the telltale flag of a whitetail deer? He supposed so; there were some in these woods.

The trail widened then; the air felt cooler. The green of the needles, the brown of the pine straw, even the gray of the patches of sky he occasionally glimpsed seemed subtly brighter, more clearly defined. David's eyes itched—but they did that almost all the time now—and he was sweating rather profusely. He could still hear Alec behind him, though; kept expecting at any moment to see his friend pull even with him, or worse, to grab him behind to wrest from him the secret he was now honorbound to reveal.

All at once David became aware of a pain in his side. No, not his side—his chest!—burning from where the ring bounced up and down atop his breastbone. He could still see the tantalizing white flash up ahead, hear the muffled rustle of its passage through the woods.

The trail leveled again, but the trees closed in ominously, and the shafts of sunlight faded abruptly like a light turned off. David slowed, suddenly frightened. Something weird was happening here. *He was on a Straight Track!* The trail *was* arrow-straight, broken only by gentle undulations, but rising steadily . . . to where? And it was glowing softly golden, its margin marked by star-shaped white flowers of an unknown species which—David shuddered when he noticed—were also glowing. Now that he was aware of it, it was obvious, and he felt an utter fool for not at least suspecting earlier; but he was not exactly used to thinking in terms of such things. His eyes were burning painfully, and he tried to veer off, to turn aside from that place of subtly disturbing otherness. But as he approached the edge of the trail, he found that he could go so far and no farther. It was as if he ran into a soft but infinitely strong barrier through which he could not pass, exactly the sort of barrier he had encountered the night he met the Sidhe.

Oh God! he thought, clutching at the ring, *I'm on one of their Straight Tracks, like Great-grandpa got on, and I can't get off! I wonder if this is a trap. . . . But I haven't done anything to them; they should know that. I haven't even told anybody about them, except Alec, and he doesn't believe me. Shit! If they've got me, they've got him too!*

Behind him David could still hear Alec gasping along. "Where you going, Sullivan?" his friend croaked. "You gone off the deep end or something? This ain't the way *I* remember."

"Veer off, Alec. Veer off!" David screamed over his shoulder as panic began to encircle his rationality.

But Alec did not veer off.

And David kept running, though he wanted to stop, to fling Alec bodily from that path, if such a thing were possible. He tried to stop—and found he could not. His legs continued working in spite of his mind's orders to the contrary. There was nothing to do but run.

In one brief instant David's whole world compressed to the sounds of feet and breath, and to alternating flashes of darkness and light that were *too* dark and *too* light as David sped past trees that grew thicker and taller than any Georgia tree had done since before man walked the earth. And there were certainly no familiar landmarks now; all that was certain was that he ran in a straight line. Up ahead the other shape that he had once thought a deer seemed to have paused beside the trail, but intervening branches made a clear view impossible. He doubted it was anything he wanted to encounter, though.

"I'll catch you sooner or later, Sullivan," he heard Alec pant. "You can't run forever."

"That may be exactly what we're doing," David shouted back.

David did run faster then, surely as fast as it was possible for him to go, until the world became a whistling blur of dark green and pale gray, centered on the pain on his chest where the ring burned white-hot. And as he passed a particularly thick and squatty live oak *(live oak? here?)* he saw with a small cry of dismay that no woodland creature crouched there, nor any monster out of his worst fears, either. Rather, the half-seen runner was a pale-skinned, blond-haired boy who looked scarcely older than himself, clad only in a golden belt and a white loincloth—a lad whose slanted green eyes and slightly pointed ears and unearthly grace of face and limb marked him, surely, as one of the Sidhe. As he passed the lad, David saw the perfect lips open and a rather too evil smile play about them, even as the boy reached toward him with one slim-fingered hand. David dodged left at the last possible instant and ran on, now pursued by two runners.

Abruptly the Track began to slant downhill. Painful shocks raced up David's legs as his feet impacted the ground with ever-increasing force. Behind him he could still hear Alec's consistent strides, and the softer but somehow more threatening tread of the Faery runner. David's heart rose for a moment as a thought occurred to him. Alec was back there; Alec would see now, and believe. But, no, his friend hadn't reacted when the boy had appeared and surely he would have. His heart sank as quickly as it had risen, for he very much feared Alec could not see that runner.

Up ahead a light showed, a break in the trees. It offered a

goal, if nothing else. Perhaps with clear sky above him he could think of a solution.

The trail leveled off again and then sloped steeply downward, and then he would be there. What he would do when he passed that goal, he didn't know. He guessed he would run onward until the Track ended or he died. That would make some obituary! No one would write a song, though, about Mad Davy Sullivan, who ran a footrace with the Sidhe. He laughed grimly, reminded of the song about the man lost forever on the Boston subway, and was suddenly jerked back to what passed for reality by the brush of hands against his shirt.

"Got you now, Sullivan!" he heard Alec cry.

Alec! He was in as much danger as David himself, perhaps worse, for his friend had no notion that this was any more than another one of David's mad indulgences. Alec was running for knowledge; David was quite literally running for his life—for both their lives.

David exerted himself one last time, imagining himself as a deer pursued by two hounds, neither of which suspected the other's presence, both with teeth snapping at his heels, each for a different reason. He could almost see mortal and Faery hands reaching toward him. But up ahead was the open place, the blue sky. *Blue sky?* He ran on down the slope toward that welcoming blue.

And then, quite suddenly, he broke free into empty space.

A pain centered on his chest shattered his senses. Golden light exploded behind his eyes. A voice screamed his name.

And then there was no ground below him at all, only thirty feet of empty air and a long, steep bank of blood-colored earth, studded here and there with bruised and broken rocks. Far below he could see the stream that flowed behind Uncle Dale's house.

In that one eternal second, when he felt he hung suspended in mid-air, before gravity woke up to his unexpected presence there, he felt something brush his neck, and twisted half around to see an inhumanly white arm pass his line of sight. There was a flash of pain again, like a knife drawn across his throat. And then he saw nothing except Alec's face frozen in an incredulous open-mouthed stare.

Then he began to fall.

He hit once; a staggering pain tore through his right thigh and hip as the earth shredded the bare flesh there; his shoulder impacted something hard, and then he was sliding, rolling, trying to slow himself with hands that ripped to tatters. And then it was his head that hit something, and the air was knocked from his lungs. Something cold and wet enfolded him; water filled his nose and ears, and then oblivion seized his consciousness and he blacked out.

He came to looking up at that same ominous and strangely remote gray sky he remembered from earlier that morning, but then Alec's face swung into view closer in, dark against the glare. He looked concerned; a drop of sweat fell from his forehead onto David's cheek to become one with that much cooler wetness that tickled capriciously about him. He was dizzy; his head spun. His head *hurt*, he realized suddenly. There was a darkness out there waiting for him; it would be so easy to fall into it, to let it hold off the pain. Stars. Stars and comets and the granddaddy of all meteor showers, his own private show going on behind his eyes.

No! David fought his way back to consciousness, opened his eyes and felt for his glasses which, remarkably, still rested crookedly on his nose. But there was too much light, too much pain. He closed his eyes again, whether to return to that place of increasingly pleasant darkness or to steel himself to rise he didn't know until he found himself trying to sit up—and cried out as agony exploded from his right shoulder, joining other bursts from his hip, his legs, his hands. His whole body ached, and an unpleasant stickiness oozed from his palms. He fell back into the water, gripping the bank with one hand, fingers digging small trenches among the pebbles.

"Davy! You okay?" It was Alec's voice that echoed metallically in his ears. Someone lifted his head, a hand worked its way into his armpit.

"Easy, boy, let me help you here," a different voice crackled.

David forced his eyes open to see another face looming above him, this one crowned with silver hair escaping the dark halo of an ancient felt hat. The smell of tobacco reached his nostrils: Uncle Dale's own personal blend of homegrown.

He felt hands in his armpits again, dragging him onto dry

land. Somebody picked up his feet, and he grunted at the pain. Then there was solid ground under him again.

"David?" he could hear Uncle Dale's voice call. "Davy, boy, you hear me?" The old man sounded strangely calm. "Don't talk, just nod if you can hear me."

David opened his mouth, but could only croak something that sounded like "hurt."

"You'll live, I think," Uncle Dale said. "Appears you've scraped yourself up some; your butt looks like a side of bacon. Maybe one of them concussions, too—leastwise you look like you're seeing stars. Now, then, you just lay there and get your breath; I don't think nothin' else is wrong."

Wrong? thought David, dimly. *Wrong? Something must be wrong.* But he couldn't remember. All he could recall was running and getting lost in the woods, and running and running and running some more, and then falling for what seemed like forever, only there was a burst of agony about every ten centuries, each in a different place. And there had been other runners . . . He tensed, felt pain again, and groaned dully as he tried to roll away from that pain, even as he felt hands forcing him again onto his back. He heard some distant shaky voice that might have been Alec's say, "Here's a blanket, Uncle Dale," then add, "I can't believe he didn't see that bank. I just can't believe it."

No, this wasn't Alec's fault, David realized vaguely, nor even his own; it was that other boy, the one who'd been after him, after the . . .

The ring!

David's fingers clutched for his throat, felt for the chain that should lie about his neck.

It was gone.

His fingers sought the ring then.

It was gone!

The Faeries had won it back, this he now knew of a certainty. It was gone. The most precious thing he owned, one of the great heirlooms of the world, maybe—according to what Oisin had said. Gone. Stolen.

And with that abandonment of hope, David abandoned consciousness as well, passing into an empty, falling blackness from which he did not return until much, much later.

* * *

The next thing David remembered clearly was waking up on the couch in the dim light of Uncle Dale's living room. His scraped thigh, the raw ruin of his hands made themselves known only by distant throbbings. Someone coughed softly, and David followed that sound through slitted eyes to see Uncle Dale sitting beside the couch, looking seriously concerned. A small transistor radio beside him whispered country music. For some reason David's vision focused on the stuffed deer head that hung above the fieldstone fireplace opposite the couch.

David rolled his eyes. *Oh God, I hurt! But I can't stay here. The Faeries have my ring. I've got to find it.* "I've got to find it!" he shouted aloud. He tried to sit up, but firm hands on his shoulders held him back.

"Now, now, boy, don't go gettin' excited. You hit yore head a good'un, and I 'spect we'd better get a doctor to take a look at it. That McLean boy's called the hospital and yore folks; he's in the kitchen makin' us some coffee right now. You hungry?" Uncle Dale stood up and started for the kitchen door.

"Hospital!" David started to shriek to the old man's departing back, but the simple effort of stretching his jaws wide made pains shoot through his head that made a perfect counterpoint to the stars that returned to cloud his vision. "Hospital," he whispered. "I can't go to the hospital. I can't! I've got to find my ring!" His voice grew louder. "I gotta go look for my ring! You didn't find my ring, did you? Oh God!" His voice sank again into a moan.

Alec came in from the kitchen with a can of Coke in his hand, which he started to hand to David. But David grabbed his friend's wrist, oblivious to the agony it cost him. "Alec, *you* didn't find my ring, did you?"

Alec gently pried David's fingers loose. "No, sorry . . . I didn't even think about it."

David sat up, though it made his eyes fill up with darkness and his head spin. Thunder pounded between his ears.

"You didn't *think* about it? What *did* you think about?"

Alec looked incredulous. "Why you, of course; you're more important than any old ring."

"You sure of that?"

"Dammit, Sullivan, you could have drowned in that creek if I hadn't been right behind you when you decided to play Mexican cliff diver with the wrong kind of cliff. You think I'm gonna be worrying about jewelry when you've got blood all over you? You could have been dying for all I knew."

"You don't understand, Alec, you really don't. It's a goddamn magic ring, and it's very, very important. You didn't even see the *chain* anywhere?"

Alec shook his head. "Sorry."

Thunder rumbled ominously outside, and the lights in the room dimmed unexpectedly. Rain tinkled on the tin roof.

"Looks like we're in for a bad'un," said Uncle Dale, motioning toward the window with his pipe. "Just what you need to make you feel better, ain't it Davy boy?... You think you oughtta be settin' up like that?"

Thunder drowned out David's grunted reply, and the lights dimmed again. Lightning flashed uncomfortably close. The tempo of the rain increased, rattling on the roof like an infinity of marbles dropped from an unimaginable height. David glanced toward a window but could see only a silver shimmer.

"A real bad'un," Uncle Dale repeated.

David stood up, swaying. "Uncle Dale, did *you* happen to see anything of my ring when you found me?"

"You mean that old ring you got from that gal? Nope, sure didn't. I ain't seen you wearin' it lately, so I figured you'd broke up with her."

David rolled his eyes, his gaze seeking Alec's. "I only had it a week!"

Uncle Dale spoke from beside the window. "A week's enough time to do nearly anything, if a man sets his mind to it—course a week of rain like this'd be more than enough for most people, but not for God, maybe. I'll tell you something, though, David. If that ring was anywhere on that bank before, it's plumb washed away by now."

"Ailill is a master of winds and tempests," David recalled Oisin saying; had he contrived this storm just for the purpose of confounding David's efforts at recovering the ring? August rain usually consisted of brief afternoon showers, the day's electricity shorting itself out in a harmless display of self-indulgent pyrotechnics. Rain this hard this early in the day was almost unheard of.

"No!" David cried suddenly. "No, I've got to find it. I've *got* to." He broke into a lurching run toward the door that lead directly from the living room onto the back porch. Alec grabbed at him as he passed, but David shoved him aside with such unexpected force that his friend sprawled backward onto the floor.

David flung open the screen as another bolt of lightning struck nearby, followed almost immediately by a blast of thunder that rang through the valley like a mile high steel gong being smashed to pieces. The world turned white for an instant, and the stars he still saw became black cutouts against that background. The scent of ozone filled the air. David's head throbbed abominably.

But he had to find the ring. It was his last chance, his *only* chance.

He didn't notice the water that pounded directly off the tin roof without benefit of gutters, for he was already soaked to the skin, and skin was mostly what he had on anyway. He began to run toward the bank, his head exploding with every footfall, his scraped leg sending it's own insistent messages of protest. But he didn't care. He must get the ring. *He must get the ring.*

The ring. The ring. The ring. The thoughts echoed the pounding of his feet. Behind him he could hear Alec and Uncle Dale calling to him.

The ring, the ring, the ring, the ring, the ring.

David found himself by the creek, but it was hardly recognizable: a swollen, frothing torrent, colored blood-red by the sticky mud that scabbed the bank above it. A thousand tributary streams flowed into it, each with its own load of silt and red Georgia clay, each one maybe carrying his ring with it to some unreachable destination.

If the Sidhe did not have it.

But he had to look; he *had* to.

David waded out into the creek, tried to run his fingers along the bottom, but it was no use. The water welled up about his forearms. Once he thought he touched it, but it was only the ring off a pop-top drink can; the water carried it away before he could toss it. He waded a couple of yards downstream, following the current that was unexpectedly strong for such a shallow stream. He felt for the bottom again, but found only coarse, rounded gravel amid larger, more jagged rocks.

Another try, another failure. It was no use, he knew: There

was too much to search, and no time, for the water was his enemy.

Another try.

Another failure.

The bank, then, he thought as he heaved his aching body out of the stream and into the cleaner, though scarcely less dense, torrents that gushed from the swollen clouds overhead.

But the bank was a treacherous wall of mud, and David could scarcely get two steps up it before he began to slip downward again. It was almost too steep to climb at the best of times—and this wasn't one of those times.

Lightning again, and thunder.

And rain.

Pain.

Noise.

His head hurt.

He had lost the ring.

He was defeated.

Wearily he slogged through the knee high creek, turning back toward the dimly discernible shape of Uncle Dale's house. Two figures stood on the back porch.

David stopped when he saw them, and then fell forward onto his knees in the mud. His hair was plastered to his head; his tattered clothes clung to his body like a wrinkled second skin. But the water that washed his face most fiercely was the salt water of his own tears.

Uncle Dale was in the yard beside him then, and Alec as well. They helped him up, helped him climb the steps onto the back porch. When they had finally got him back into the living room, he flung his arms around Uncle Dale and began sobbing uncontrollably. "I've lost it," he cried. "It's gone!"

Alec draped a blanket around his best friend's shoulders and patted him awkwardly.

David glanced sideways at his friend, and said with perfect lucidity, "It's gone, Alec, and I don't want to think about what might happen now."

PART III

Prologue III: In Tir-Nan-Og

(high summer)

Silverhand's weed seems to be everywhere, Ailill noted irritably as he strode down the high-arched length of the Hall of Manannan in the southwest wing of Lugh's palace. Ten times a man's height those arches were, and white as bone—appropriately, for each of those spans was made of the single bladelike rib of a variety of sea creature that was now extinct in Faerie. Mosaics of lapis and malachite set in a marine motif and overlaid with a veneer of crystal patterned the walls, and the floors were tiled in alternating squares of ground coral and pearls.

Between every set of arches was a waist-high vase in the shape of a giant purple murex. And in each of those vases grew one of those insipid flowers Nuada had brought from the Lands of Men.

And there is Himself, Ailill added as the fair-haired Lord of the Sidhe stepped from the shadows of one of the arches with a handful of dead leaves in his hand, at which he gazed in a somewhat bemused manner.

"At the flowers, again?" Ailill inquired to Nuada's back. "Perhaps Lugh should make you his gardener instead of his warlord."

Nuada did not look up, but Ailill saw the hard muscles of

Silverhand's back tense beneath the dirty white velvet of his tunic. The sight pleased him considerably.

"Well," the dark Faery went on, "perhaps there is something to the study of the mortal lands after all. Perhaps you have had a favorable influence on me—"

"I doubt that," Nuada observed archly, without turning around.

Ailill moved his hand a certain way and the rose closest to Nuada wilted.

Nuada whirled; a tiny dagger appeared, needlelike, in his hand exactly where the leaves had been.

Ailill was not impressed. "For you see, Silverhand," he said languidly, "I too have taken up the study of men—and a fascinating study I find it."

Nuada raised a skeptical eyebrow. "Indeed?"

"Yes," Ailill went on, "and one of the things I find most fascinating is how they can get along without Power."

"Very well, I would say," Nuada retorted.

"Perhaps." Ailill looked idly at the bush, blinked thrice in succession, and sent three more blossoms crumbling to dust. "But take an example here, Nuada. Suppose that one of us lost something. Well, then, all *we* have to do is to call upon the Power and there are half a score ways we may use to find it."

"This is not unknown to me," Nuada observed.

"Ah! But *mortals* can*not* always find things when they lose them, and one of the things I have learned in the process of my recent activities is that mortals lose things very frequently—very frequently indeed. But they do not find them nearly as often."

Nuada tapped impatient fingers on his hip. "What, in particular, are you talking about?"

"A certain ring."

"A ring?"

"A particular ring that offers some slight protection against some forms of Power."

"A *particular* ring?"

"—That is no longer in the mortal boy's keeping."

"Nor in yours, either, I would guess," Nuada replied. "Or you would have taken special care to call it to my attention by now."

"Would I?"

Nuada glared at his adversary. "There are things about that

ring you do not know, Ailill. There are things about that ring *I* do not know. Probably even things Oisin himself does not know."

It was Ailill's turn to glare. "Indeed?" he echoed sarcastically.

"And besides," Nuada replied calmly, "there is other protection to be had than the ring, protection older and stronger."

"You would not be speaking of yourself, would you, Silverhand? You are certainly older than I, if not the ring. As to stronger?" Ailill shrugged. "It is not a boast I would make, if I were you. I have not noticed that you have had any particular success in protecting the boy."

"I am as successful as I need to be. My strength has never failed me. Can you say the same?"

"My Power has never failed *me.*"

"Indeed? I was under the impression that a certain summoning of yours had not gone to your liking." He paused. "Surely you see the foolishness of what you undertake, Windmaster. Whatever you may think, mankind is no docile foe, be assured of that. You may think the Sullivan boy easy prey, but that is not necessarily true, either, even without help from our side. And be assured, Ailill, that though I do not approve of intervention in the World of Men, I will do whatever I have to in order to keep the Worlds apart. The boy will *not* be harmed."

"So you are a traitor?" Ailill sneered.

Nuada's eyes narrowed dangerously. "I would be careful how I used that word."

Ailill's eyes narrowed as well. "I listened to you once, Silverhand, and have been put to much trouble because of it. I should have known that you could not study the ways of mortals as closely as you have done and not be won to their cause."

"I have *not* been won to their cause," Nuada flared, "but I believe in making no enemies without reason, and in making allies where they may help us. I have no more desire than you to return into the High Air, or to retreat into the Hollow Hills or the Deep Waters.

"But there are ways and ways of achieving one's ends," Nuada went on, "and I also believe one should study one's foes and learn from them—and if possible seek to win their friendship. No war is yet declared between Mankind and Faerie, though I know *you* itch for battle. Yet mortal men do not know us as their enemy, they do not know us at all, except for one, and you yourself know that even his closest comrades think him both a fool and a liar. There is no honor in attacking the innocent and the ignorant, Ailill. And there is no honor in making war for your own glory. You despise mortals because they have no honor and have lost sight of truth, and yet you behave no better. And so I must stand with the lad."

"But are you prepared to die with him?"

"I seriously doubt I will have the opportunity."

"Do not be too certain of that, Silverhand."

"I have seen mortal men at war. You have not. It is a thing worth remembering."

"Perhaps I will, if it suits me."

Nuada frowned. "Then perhaps there are a few *other* things you should remember while you are so engaged: your status in this realm, for instance. You are a *guest* in this land, an ambassador of your brother, Finvarra of Erenn. Lugh Samildinach reigns in Tir-Nan-Og—yet you have defied him a hundred times over in the short time since you came here. Lugh will tolerate only so much interference."

"Interference may not be needed much longer," Ailill replied.

"Nor may Finvarra's most current ambassador," Nuada shot back as he turned his face once more toward the Cherokee roses.

Chapter IX: Hiking . . .
(Tuesday, August 11)

Fortunately David did not have a concussion, as a quick trip to the hospital had shown. But he did have a headache two days later—in the form of an early morning phone call from Liz Hughes. She had called simply to check on his recovery (which was progressing nicely), but things had quickly taken a more irritating turn.

"*No*, Liz," David said firmly and for the third time, "you *cannot* go ginseng hunting with Uncle Dale and me."

The phone receiver crackled ominously.

"But why not, Davy? I think your Uncle Dale is pretty neat, and I've never even seen any ginseng, and I think this would be a good time to combine both—kinda kill two birds with one stone."

"It's a matter of tradition, Liz. The men in my family have always been the ones who know the secret places where the ginseng grows; only now am *I* allowed to find out, and no Sullivan male has ever, *ever* taken a woman along."

"Except your Aunt Hattie." Uncle Dale sauntered into the kitchen.

David covered the phone with his hand and looked skeptically at his great-uncle.

"Who is it?" Uncle Dale asked.

"Liz Hughes," David answered hurriedly. He spoke back into the receiver, "Just a minute, Liz."

"What's she want?"

David lowered the receiver to waist level. "Oh, she wants to go hunting ginseng with us tomorrow."

"She does, does she? I think what she's huntin' don't grow in the ground, though."

"Uncle Dale, come on! I don't want her goin'!"

David could hear Liz calling his name from down by his hip.

"Better talk to her, son; don't want yore hikin' partner mad at you. Bad luck. I 'spect she'll be wantin' to go deer huntin' next, and it wouldn't do to be on her bad side—might get shot." Uncle Dale's voice was pitched a shade too loud, deliberately so, David suspected.

Reluctantly David raised the phone to his ear again.

"What was that?" Liz asked, slightly irritated.

"Uncle Dale thinks it's all right for you to go," he said glumly. "Seems Aunt Hattie used to go with him."

"Good! When do we leave?"

"*Early,* Liz. Before daylight. It's supposed to rain again tomorrow afternoon, and Uncle Dale wants to get an early start."

"So why doesn't he just wait till the weather's better?"

"That's what I asked him," David sighed in some annoyance, "and all he'd say was something about having to do it when the moon was in the right phase. You can find ginseng anytime, apparently, but only certain times are best to harvest it. And it's supposed to be most potent if you get it early in the morning while the dew's still on it, or something like that. So it's gotta start before sunup. Still want to go?" he added sarcastically.

"I'll be there when I need to be," Liz replied firmly, "and I'll be dressed right and I'll have what I need, and I bet I find some ginseng before you do."

"Maybe you will and maybe you won't," David said, hanging up the receiver before she could reply.

"That's some gal," Uncle Dale said wryly as he helped himself to a cup of the morning's coffee. "She really does remind me of yore great-aunt Hattie, rest her soul. Fine woman. Got up at four o'clock every mornin' of her married life and sent me off to the copper mines to work. Damn fine woman, though, and a sight better with a gun than I am, too, if the truth was known. You know that ten-pointer I got over my fireplace that I always said I shot?" He took David by the shoulder conspiratorially. "Well, *she* got it, really—but I never told, and she let me have my glory. But why you reckon that Hughes gal wants to go huntin' 'seng with us?"

David contemplated the floor. "I dunno. Just being pesky, I guess."

Uncle Dale looked straight at him. "I think you do know."

David leaned up against the wall and folded his arms. "Well, she's into this back-to-nature thing and all—survival skills, wilderness living, herbs and all that. She's a walking *Foxfire Book.*"

"That may be true," laughed Uncle Dale, "but there's some things to a woman's nature she's never far from. Trouble is, us menfolks are usually too late in findin' it out." He laughed again.

"I can run pretty fast," said David.

"Can you outrun one of Cupid's arrows, though? That what you was runnin' from the other day?"

David rolled his eyes. "You know that I don't want you to go, either, for that matter."

"Why, Davy boy! Why not? I been trompin' around in them woods for sixty-odd years. I ain't gonna quit now."

"That's a good reason: them sixty-odd years. You ain't as young as you used to be."

"I'm not? Well, that's a fact—but them woods is a lot older'n I am, and they can still show a man a good time."

David considered this unexpected piece of philosophy.

"But, Uncle Dale, suppose something happened to you out there?"

"What can happen? I know every rock and tree and stream for ten square miles back where we're goin'. Been there every season and every weather. They ain't nothin' there can hurt me. Bears'll run, what few there may be; ain't no cougars no more; snakes you just gotta watch for; Indians gone a hundred fifty years; what else is there?"

"Oh, things like broken legs, sprained ankles . . ."

"Heart attacks?"

"Now that you mention it, yes."

"Look, Davy, us Sullivans're long lived folks; takes a lot to kill us. You ought to know that yoreself, considerin' how busted up you was just two days ago. That even put the wind up me, if you want to know the truth. But look at you now. Just a scab or two to show for yore trouble. Few of us are ever sick more'n an aspirin'll cure, and when we die, it's usually 'cause we think it's time for us to die—none of this lingerin' in the hospital business. Shoot! Wars get more of us than anything else, and at that it takes some shootin' to catch a mortal spot."

David recalled how Uncle Dale had been wounded a couple of times in World War II, and he wasn't a young man then. He glanced out into the yard and saw the red Mustang, recalled how another war had claimed David-the-elder and nearly unleashed a bitter retort, but restrained himself.

Uncle Dale was looking intently at him. "So what else is there to be scared of?"

"Maybe there's things in the woods that you can't see."

"You been at them weird books again, ain't you, boy?"

"They're not weird; they were written by learned people."

"As learned as you'll be one day, I've no doubt. But look, David, I know they's things in the world besides what we know; I've been too close to some of 'em to disbelieve entirely, like when I seen yore grandpa's ghost that time, and I know you believe a darn sight more than I do, but *I* believe I'm gonna be all right, and that they ain't nothin' to be scared of this year that ain't been there for sixty years before."

The old man poured himself another cup of coffee and buttered a cold biscuit. "Now you tell me somethin', boy: What're *you* scared of—or is it 'who'?"

"I'm not scared of anybody," David replied sulkily.

"You're the first man alive who ain't, then. That's part of your life—that, and facing up to it. But just remember who you are and what you are, and what you believe in. That's all it takes."

"Right-makes-might is easy if you're six-foot-two and one-eighty."

"Shoot, size don't matter none. Why, when I was yore age I was littler than you. I did all right."

"Oh, it's not that, Uncle Dale," said David, drumming his nails against the wall by the phone. "I can fight okay, if I have to. It's just the hassle that bothers me, having to put up with things that I can't control, but that try to control me. I've got a whole lot bothering me right now, and I'm gonna have to start back to school real soon, and that'll only make it worse. I can't stand this being in a bunch of worlds at once, like at school, where half the town kids won't associate with me 'cause I'm too country, and half the country kids won't 'cause I'm too town, and they all think I'm weird, and the girls . . ."

"Go on."

"Oh, nothing! I just wish I could go off and not come back."

"Do it, then. Nobody's stoppin' you."

"You know I can't."

"I know you *won't*. There's a difference." The old man's voice softened. "Look, David, you are *you*: smart as a whip, good lookin', healthy as a moose, well brought up, honest. You've got a good turn, an' I don't know what else—you're everything I'd want in a son . . . and you sit there talkin' like you ain't worth nothin'. That's a bunch of crap, boy. Now tell me, what's got you so bothered?"

"I'm afraid of words, I guess, of being hassled and made fun of . . . and of something else I can't tell even you."

"There ain't never been much you couldn't tell me."

"This is one of those things, though; this is one of those things I can't even tell Alec."

"It's about that ring, ain't it?" Uncle Dale took a sip of coffee, but his gaze never left David.

David didn't say anything, but he could feel the weight of that stare.

Uncle Dale nodded knowingly. "That's it, ain't it? I thought so. Just remember one thing, boy: You ain't the only one in the family that's ever lived here, and that's ever been up in them woods of a summer night."

David looked up incredulously. "You?"

Uncle Dale shook his head almost sadly. "I told you, we didn't dare . . . but my pa did. He seen something not of this world, and, you know, that light in his eyes was just like the one I been seein' in yores lately, and it was there till the day he died."

"Uncle Dale . . ."

"Now's not the time, boy; you'd best be seein' to gettin' your gear together for tomorrow. Won't be no time for it in the mornin'."

* * *

Fog filled the lowlands the next morning, hiding the farms, the lakes, even a good part of the mountain. Ragged bits lingered higher up, too, hanging eerily among the oaks and maples. An unseasonable cold front had moved into north Georgia during the night, bringing with it record-breaking low temperatures, even scattered reports of frost. David had had to get up in the middle of the night to turn on the heat in his bedroom.

But it was still a splendid morning. Or would be when the sun rose, David thought—even allowing for Liz, who had been on time, and dressed right, and had brought everything she was supposed to bring, and had even helped his mother make coffee. And David wished he had another cup as the three ginseng hunters pushed through a patch of rhododendron and paused for a rest atop a rock outcrop twenty or so feet high from which they could look both out and down.

David sank down on his haunches with his runestaff braced across his knees and took in the view, huddling himself up in his electric orange nylon hunting jacket—the same color as the jaunty cap Uncle Dale was wearing. He could see his breath floating away in the morning air, reminding him of the fog down below. To the east the sun still hid sleepily just out of sight behind a fold of mountain.

"That sure is a pretty view," Liz commented.

"It is for a fact," agreed Uncle Dale, "and I shot my first deer from right up here, too—back before Davy's pa was born."

"Was that before or after the Flood?" Davis teased offhandedly as he continued to contemplate the view. The first ray of sunrise cast a glitter into the air, and David found himself gazing across the fog-muffled lake that filled the valley below to the nearly symmetrical cone of Bloody Bald, now completely ringed by fog. Would it happen? he wondered. Would he see what he expected to see? Funny how nearly two weeks could pass without him ever getting time to catch Bloody Bald right at sunrise or sunset.

But David had his chance now, and even as he looked, his eyes took on the expected tingle, and he saw that same mountain rise into an impossibly slender peak, saw it crowned as well with towers, battlements, windows, and arches—and dimly thought he could make out men on those battlements, and dimly, very dimly hear horns ringing in his ears to welcome the sun. And then

David blinked and it was gone, replaced by the fuzzy gray bulk of the ordinary mountain.

There was a rustle among the trees to their right just then, and the ginseng hunters turned to see three ravens take wing among the dark trunks. They watched the birds fly out into the open air, wheeling and circling above the fog.

David raised his runestaff to his shoulder like a rifle and aimed experimentally, oblivious to the slight pain that still lingered in his shoulder.

Uncle Dale laid a hand on the smooth wood and slowly but firmly pushed it down. "Don't even think such things, boy. Shootin' ravens is bad luck."

"Just playing around," David said testily.

Uncle Dale bent over to sight down the face of the rock, and as he bent the brilliant orange cap fell from his white hair and floated down to land amid the brown leaves and moss at the bottom. It rolled to a stop at the base of an ancient, gnarled oak tree.

"I'll get it," said David.

"I'll get it," said Liz, who was already on her way down the gentler slope to the left of the cliff.

"*I'll* get it," said Uncle Dale. "I was the fool who lost it."

"Why don't we *all* go," David growled irritably.

Uncle Dale cuffed him gently on the shoulder, but there was warning in the glance he shot his nephew. "And be quick about it. No sense wakin' up the whole woods arguin'."

So they all went—Liz down the western slope, David and Uncle Dale down the steeper eastern one. Uncle Dale picked up his cap and paused, peering at the ground where it had lain. Something showed in the soft earth there, the unmistakable print of a cloven hoof, pointed at the front. The old man bent to check it.

"That's deer sign, and fresh." Uncle Dale rose and looked back toward the cliff. "But we ain't huntin' deer."

Liz began to lead the way back up the steep leaf-covered slope. To their right the sheer rock face jutted out, gray and crusted with lichens, crowned with a thicket of rhododendron and laurel. Their feet rustled in the damp brown leaves. It was hard to walk quietly, and they slipped frequently. David slipped more than frequently, finally falling onto all fours in spite of his hiking stick. He straightened and looked at Uncle Dale's back a few paces ahead of him.

Something twanged in David's ears then—or was it in his mind alone? Something hissed as it flew fast through the cool damp air. Something white flashed and then buried itself in Uncle Dale's chest with a dull thud. David cried out, lunged forward desperately, aware too late of the telltale burning in his eyes.

Uncle Dale slumped forward, clutching at his throat, his head. He uttered no sound, but simply collapsed, twisting as he fell, to land half on his face in the damp leaves.

Liz, a little higher up the slope, turned and stared at him, gasping, eyes wide, her face pale beneath her red hair.

As David scrambled toward the old man, he spared a brief glance up at the cliff, to see—in plain view, making no move to hide himself—the figure of a very young man clad in white and gray and pale green clothing that was most certainly not consistent with this time or place or world. The Faery held a long white bow in his left hand, and the white fletching of the second arrow he had half-nocked in the other was identical to that of the short shaft that now protruded from the right side of Uncle Dale's chest. As Davis gaped incredulously, the youth turned and pushed soundlessly back into the bushes.

Gently David rolled the old man onto his back. "Uncle Dale!" he cried.

Liz scooted down the slope to join them. "What is it? What's happened?"

"He's had a . . . stroke, I think. Maybe a heart attack, but probably a stroke." Even as David stared at the Faery arrow, it began to fade, to vanish.

No hole was left in the old man's jacket, but David knew the damage was done. He recalled that the very word *stroke* was short for *elf-stroke*, because people had once believed that those who suffered unexpected paralysis were in fact struck by Faery arrows —usually stone-tipped arrows, if he recalled correctly from *The Secret Common-Wealth*. Evidently there was some grim truth to the legend.

David laid his hand on his uncle's chest, moved it to his neck, his wrist, searching for a heartbeat, a pulse. Both were there, faint but steady. And he was breathing shallowly.

The old man fought to rise, but somehow his body would not

obey him. His blue eyes sought David's, wide and panic-stricken, and he tried to talk, raising his good left arm and pointing to his right side; and then his eyes rolled back and he fainted.

"Quick, Liz, we've got to cover him up and get some help; there's nothing we can do here. It *was* a stroke, I think." David hesitated. "You go and get help," he said finally. "I'll stay here."

Liz stood up, flustered. "*You* go, Davy; I don't know the way too well—I might get lost."

"He's my flesh and blood," David said hotly. "I'm staying here. Just get to the top of this ridge and then follow it down. You'll come to the road that goes down by our house. It's not far, really. Get Pa, and call a doctor."

"All right, Davy, all right. If you're sure there's nothing I can do here."

"Look," David almost shouted, "one of us has got to stay, and one go. I'm gonna stay. I want to be here in case . . . in case . . ." He could feel tears welling up in his eyes as he looked down at his uncle lying flat on his back among the leaves.

David took off his jacket and spread it over the old man as best he could, thought for a moment, and removed his shirt as well, to stand shivering in a white T-shirt. He frowned up at the top of the cliff, face set.

"Here, Liz," he said at last, throwing his walking staff toward her, "use this. Maybe it'll help."

Ash, he recalled, was supposed to afford some protection against the Sidhe, and there was iron on the ends, which was also good. There was no way he could protect both Liz and his uncle, so he'd give Liz what protection he could.

Liz caught the staff easily, and to David's surprise, his eyes tingled and he thought he saw a faint white glow spread outward from where her hands touched it.

"Go on! Hurry!" he cried.

Liz turned and half ran, half crawled up the mountain side. She was gone from sight in an instant, but David could still hear her crashing through the bushes upslope.

He sat down beside Uncle Dale and stared emptily through the trees at the dissipating fog. The old man didn't seem to be getting any worse, but he didn't seem to be getting any better, either.

Damn, David thought, gazing up at the rock face again. *I shouldn't have let him come*. He clenched his hands into fists and almost looked away before he saw the Faery youth appear again upon the cliff top.

David watched fascinated as, without the slightest hesitation, the boy leapt from the cliff and floated easily down from that height. It was almost as if he had not weight enough to fall at a normal speed. The boy landed in a bent-kneed crouch, bow still in hand, and walked calmly toward David.

Frantically David grabbed a broken branch from the forest floor and held it before him. A twinge of pain ran through his shoulder, but he ignored it.

The youth laughed and continued to approach.

"That is not a very good weapon against one such as I," the Faery said. "And at no time would it be simple for you to slay me in your World. *You*, on the other hand, do not appear to be as well protected as you have been, or else my arrows would not have been able to touch the old man. Interesting. You haven't lost anything lately, have you? A ring, perhaps?" He lifted his bow and nocked an arrow.

"I'm more good to you alive," said David, trying to stall for time.

The Faery lad laughed again, but there was a hollowness to the sound, a lack of conviction that did not quite ring true to David. The youth lowered his bow and seated himself on a fallen log, motioning David to sit beside him.

It was all David could do to suppress his rage. This boy had hurt Uncle Dale—probably killed him. And he had the nerve to ask David to sit beside him?

David gritted his teeth and glared helplessly, half a mind to swing his clumsy stick in that other's face again and again, as many times as he could, and then continue with his fists. It would be good to see those too-pretty features turned to bloody pulp. Iron and ash indeed! He'd give him hot flesh-and-blood fists!

But that would be a mistake, he realized; there was more at stake here. The boy had returned for some reason and David had to find out what it was. He risked a glance at Uncle Dale's prostrate form. The old man seemed to be getting no worse. David took a deep breath and dropped the stick but continued to stare at the youth. There was something disquietingly familiar about that clean-chiseled face.

"Well, have you seen enough?" the Faery asked wryly.

"Should I stand up and turn around? Take my clothes off, maybe?"

"I've seen enough," David said grimly. "One of your arrows is in my uncle's chest. Why did you do that? What'd he ever do to you?"

"I was . . . told to do it," the boy said. "The old man is important to you; we have hurt him. He will not die unless he himself chooses to, but he will never be any better unless *we* heal him. We want only one thing in return for that healing: you."

"That's what I was afraid of . . . but why me?" David played innocent.

"I thought Oisin made that clear to you: We want you where you may do no more harm."

"You are one of Ailill's minions, then?"

The Faery's eyes narrowed haughtily. "I am my own man . . . but yes, I have some obligation to that one's service."

David sat down cautiously, finding it difficult to maintain anger toward someone so reasonable-sounding, so fair-spoken. But then his glance touched Uncle Dale, and he found his anger returning and his words coming more easily.

"So you're going to pick away at my loved ones until I give myself up?"

"That is the plan as it was revealed to me."

"What if I won't?"

"Then those you love will suffer for it." The Faery took a breath and continued, his voice earnest—David hoped sincerely so. "You cannot be everywhere, David—but you can be one place where those you love will be protected—and yourself as well." He stood up and came to sit beside David, laid a hand on David's leg so that the mortal boy shuddered.

"Come with us, lad; it's not so bad. There are women wondrous fair and quick to lust, and food like you have never tasted, and wine such as you have never drunk—though you have not drunk much wine, have you? Or tasted many women? And for sport there are hunts. You think hunting the beasts of this world a pleasure? Wait until you have hunted manticores, or taken a kraken from the depths of the sea with Manannan MacLir! You can meet your heroes, David; you can learn magic, see other worlds, even go beyond this poor round planet if you have the courage for it. Only come with us." The grip on David's leg grew tighter.

"Come for a day only; we ask for nothing more, if Faerie does not please you."

"I know what a day can be like in Faerie," David replied fiercely. "I'm not stupid; I've read about it—and I've met Oisin."

A shadow crossed the Faery's face. "Oisin, yes! A fine old man, but troublesome. He thought Ailill had forgotten he was mortal once, but Ailill remembered. Lugh has forbidden Oisin to meet with you again."

David's heart sank, but he maintained his front. "Why did he have to do that?"

The Faery shrugged. "Lugh views this matter as a contest between Ailill and Nuada alone; he does not want Oisin meddling."

"Isn't that what you're doing, though? So why don't you just kill me now and be done with it?"

"I think you know the answer to that as well as I do," the Faery boy replied. "Nuada is right about you, you know: You do have the stuff of heroes in you, even I can see it now, and something of Power as well. Killing you would be a waste. But it would be interesting to see whether that Power you hold flares to flame or passes into darkness—as your uncle's life soon will, if you do not make a decision very soon indeed."

David stopped listening; it was more than he could stand to hear. His gaze began to wander.

Abruptly something caught his attention out of the corner of his eye. He looked at it for a moment, then glanced quickly back at the Faery boy lest his expression betray him, but the lad was looking uneasily at a large raven perched on a limb above his head.

David acted.

He lunged to his left, a long body-leap, and barely managed to grasp the bow the Faery had laid aside. Quickly he regained his footing and whirled back around, gripping the bow by one delicately filigreed end. He raised it above his shoulders and made as if to strike it against the trunk of a nearby oak.

The Faery sprang up, his body tense, a feral light in his eyes. Panther-quick he leapt at David.

David swung the bow around, but Fionchadd was on him before he could complete the swing. They fell to the ground, rolling over and over in a Gordian knot of arms and legs, the bow somehow unbroken between them. All at once David found himself lying atop the Faery. And though he could touch that Faery stranger, feel the solidity of his body beneath him, it was as if the Faery could not quite touch him, though he glared up at David with bared teeth, golden sparks flashing in his green eyes, wet brown leaves sticking in his golden hair, soiling the white velvet of his tunic. David grasped the bow with both hands and brought it down across the Faery's throat. The boy intercepted it, and for a moment they struggled inconclusively.

The Faery lad was surprisingly strong, for all he was more lightly built than David, but David could feel a cold fire raging in himself, boiling up from somewhere deep inside. He thought about Uncle Dale lying unconscious behind him, of Liz wending her frightened way down a mountain, and he slowly and inexorably began to press the bow down toward the Faery's throat, resting it at last atop his windpipe, oblivious to the pain that shot through his injured shoulder.

"I told you, nothing you can do in this world can harm me for any longer than it takes to heal," Fionchadd hissed.

"What if I break this bow, then?" David said through gritted teeth. "It was when I began to threaten it that you attacked me. What's so great about this bow?"

"It is none of your concern."

"What's so great about this *bow*, dammit? You tell me, or I'll break it."

The Faery's eyes flashed fire. "It is a bow made for me by Goibniu, the smith of the Tuatha de Danaan. Rarely does he work in wood, but when he does the work is fine indeed. I prize it above all things in the Worlds I have seen, for it never misses."

"Better tell me how to heal my uncle, then, or I *will* break it."

The boy's face grew pale, almost fearful, and he grimaced. "That I may not do, mortal lad, much as I might now wish to, for I do not know the answer. I am a hunter, not a master of Power or of lore. I may shoot a man in Faerie and be drinking with him again the next night, but such is not the case in your world, and the rules which govern that difference I do not understand. I cannot help you."

David's eyes blazed. "Swear that you can't?"

"If you like."

"On your bow?"

"If you like."

"Swear, then, that all Power may be gone from this bow, and that it will never shoot true again if you lie."

"I do swear. Now are you satisfied?"

"A little."

"Let me up, then."

"Not yet. What do you know of my ring?"

"I know that you do not have it, but that its protection is evidently still upon you to some degree." The Faery hesitated, took a deep breath, chose his words carefully. "I also know that he who was sent to procure it has failed."

David's eyes narrowed. It was as if the pauses, the subtly accented words of the Faery's speech were meant to convey some second, hidden message that must remain unspoken.

"If the Sidhe do not have the ring, then where is it?"

"Somewhere in your World, I suppose."

"Swear that this is the truth."

"I swear that I do not know where the ring is; to make further oaths in ignorance would be foolish."

David grunted. "Sure?"

"It is as I have said. Now will you let me up?" The Faery sighed wearily. "There is nothing more I can do to help you."

"No, I suppose there isn't, is there?" David smiled a smile as grim as the Faery's. He withdrew the bow from the boy's throat and stood up stiffly.

Fionchadd rose as well and dusted himself off. He extended a slim right hand. David looked puzzled.

"You have bested me in a fight," said the boy. "And few have done that. I would offer you my aid, but it is sworn elsewhere and I may not break that oath. But when this song is ended, let us be friends. Maybe yet we will meet as comrades in Faerie."

David didn't know quite what to do at first or why he did what he did do, but that phrase rang in his mind as something sacred, old, and honorable—beyond good and evil. Hadn't the champion of the Tuatha de Danaan said that to the champion of the Fir Bolg when first they fought in Ireland? Hesitantly he extended his own hand, and clasped that of the Faery youth.

They looked into each other's eyes for a moment, then released each other's hands. The Faery boy took his bow from David's loose fingers. "And now I must depart," he said. "Ailill has asked of me almost more than is his right to ask." The boy disappeared into the trees before David could do or say anything further. The leaves did not rustle under his tread, but the print of his back was still visible in the soft loam of the forest floor. David sat down by Uncle Dale and waited, looking often at his hands, wondering whether or not he was a traitor.

Chapter X: ...And Later

Little Billy looked up at David, who slumped beside him in the white-walled waiting room of the Enotah County Hospital. "Will Uncle Dale die?" he asked earnestly.

A lot of people were jammed up against the walls around the waiting room, but David didn't know any of them, nor care to just then. He wished they were all somewhere else—or that he was; he was feeling very alone just then. It was mid-afternoon, and his parents had not yet returned from securing things at Uncle Dale's farm; Liz had stayed for a while after they had first brought the old man in, but then she had had to leave. Alec had phoned, but there was nothing to tell him. Nobody knew anything.

"Will Uncle Dale *die*, Davy?" Little Billy asked again, tugging insistently on David's sleeve.

"I don't *know*," David growled back, so harshly that Little Billy cowered down into his shirt collar. "I hope not," he added more softly, reaching over to ruffle his brother's hair, feeling how soft it was, realizing suddenly what a neat kid Little Billy was. And then more deeply in the pit of his stomach rose the fear that had engulfed him after the Faery boy had left, the fear that the same fate might await all the people he cared about. David found himself clenching his fists.

A brown-haired nurse came out of the room into which they had taken Uncle Dale.

"Nurse?" David called shyly, looking up.

The woman glanced down irritably, a little taken aback by the dirty hiking togs David still wore. "Yes?" she asked sharply.

"My uncle—Dale Sullivan—will he be all right?"

The nurse grimaced. "He's had a stroke, we think, but Doctor Nesheim has him stabilized. He won't get any worse at least. But he oughta know better'n to be running 'round in the woods at his age. 'Course it coulda been worse, coulda been a heart attack— but he still oughta know better." She frowned offhandedly at David, who felt himself cringe under the combination of her gaze and his own guilt. "Good thing you were with him, though," she added, before continuing down the corridor.

"Can I go see him?" David shouted after her.

"Not yet," she called back, still moving. "Maybe later."

David slumped back in his chair, folded his arms on his chest, and tried to sleep. He wished he had something interesting to read, but he had already exhausted the supply of outdated magazines in the reading room, and had hardly been in a position to snag anything at home before the trip to the hospital. Sleep was thus the only way he could think of to speed the time until he found out something about Uncle Dale's condition, or at least until his parents returned.

Two hours passed before a friendlier nurse—Talbot was the name on her plastic badge—let David in to see Uncle Dale. His parents still had not returned, and he found himself suddenly alone in the hospital room with the old man. Uncle Dale lay propped up in bed, tubes running out of his nose, a bottle of some nameless clear fluid set up leading to needles taped into his arms. He was under heavy sedation, probably had lost the use of his right side, the doctor had said. The real fear, though, was that knowing he was half paralyzed, he'd just give up and will himself to die. That didn't sound like Uncle Dale to David, but, then, he didn't know as much about his uncle as he had thought. *One thing for sure, though,* David thought, *I'll bet he never expected to die of elf-stroke.*

Uncle Dale was breathing more or less evenly, but his face had a sort of cold pallor to it, and age lay heavy upon him. Cautiously, David reached over and pulled down the covers. Curiosity had gotten the best of him; he had to know something.

David worked the hospital gown down on the side where he knew the elf-arrow had struck, right in the triangle below the outer end of the collar bone. He noticed the pale, flabby skin, the stringy muscles like old ropes, the stray coarse hairs, but look though he would, he could find no wound. Somehow, though, he knew the damage was still there, invisible to mortal eyes and machines.

David kept straining his eyes, hoping to conjure the Sight, and was finally rewarded by the faintest glimpse of a pale red X-shaped mark exactly where he was looking for it: in the outer point of the depression below the collar bone. He stared at it foolishly. There was nothing *he* could do. Help would have to come from some unorthodox direction, because no human doctor could cure an elven wound.

Abruptly a heavy arm fell across his shoulder. "We're back," came Big Billy's voice behind him. "Mama and me'll stay here tonight; you take Little Billy and go on home. We'll keep you posted."

David nodded reluctantly and shuffled out of the room, noticing in the hallway window outside that the promised rain had begun.

The glass in David's bedroom window rattled, struck by a gentle wind, and he jumped, alarmed, as the sound brought him fully awake. He had been dreaming of the Sidhe, and now found himself trying to make sense of what Oisin had said, of what that other boy had told him.

They were perilous, David knew, and some of them had it in for him—but still, they were not really evil by their own standards. He could even understand how they felt, a little; he felt the same way about the people who moved into the mountains from Atlanta and Florida, putting up their summer homes on the high places, spoiling things for the natives who didn't want an A-frame on every mountaintop but preferred inviolate wilderness where a man could walk for hours and not see another house or another person.

It was crazy, he knew, considering what he'd been through, but a part of him still wanted to watch the Sidhe ride again. They were so beautiful, so heart-breakingly beautiful . . . if he could only watch without being seen, see them just once more astride their long-limbed horses: black and silver, gold and frosty gray; see them in their silks and velvets and fine wool: wine-red and midnight-blue, forest-green and amber; hear the rustling of their mail or the bells ringing on their clothing; see their beautiful faces, cold and remote; see those fair women with hawks on their shoulders and braided hair hanging to their knees, and the clean-faced warriors with their sharp spears and silver armor; see their ghost-thin greyhounds or their great hunting dogs that were first cousin to wolves; and see those banners that floated above them unfurled by no wind of the mortal World.

One banner in particular he remembered, borne at the head of the procession: Long and narrow, maybe thirty feet long, and held aloft on a staff of ivory, it had been made of silk, or at least something as soft and shiny, red as sunrise, cut at its trailing edge into flickering flamelike dags so tenuous they might have *been* flames, and worked near the staff with the stylized image of the sun—a sun in splendor, he recalled. But this one glowed of its own light, its alternating straight and curved rays shrinking and expanding, rotating in the figures of some obscure dance in praise of fire.

The wind rattled the window again, and a patter of rain sounded on the roof. He was not at all sleepy, he realized, as he got up, turned on the light, and settled himself to rereading *Paradise Lost*.

So it was that David was still awake when he heard Little Billy talking quietly in his bedroom across the hall. He frowned, climbed wearily out of bed, and slipped into the hallway, to pause by the closed door to his brother's room. He could hear the little boy inside, talking as if in his sleep, but couldn't quite make out what he was saying. Gently David opened the door and peeked inside.

Little Billy was kneeling on his bed, peering out the window, and as he watched, David could hear him saying, "But I *can't* let you in; we can't have dogs in the house. My mama won't allow 'em."

"Come outside, then," said a voice from beyond the window.

"I can't; I'm not allowed to go outside at night, and Davy told me special not to go outside tonight."

"Your brother is a fool," said the voice.

David could contain himself no longer. He rushed into the

darkened room, lunged toward the window, stared out above Little Billy's head—and saw the shape of a huge black dog glaring back at him: a shaggy black dog with its feet on the sill, and its great black nose nearly touching—but *not* touching—the window screen. Its eyes were red as coals—a familiar red. The logical part of David's mind told him that the ledge was at least seven feet off the ground. But then he recognized the voice: Ailill, his enemy.

The dog howled and growled through bared teeth. David caught a glimpse of fabulously long fangs and a black tongue and a red throat from which a small flame seemed to issue; and then it howled again and leapt away into the yard. David watched as it ran, wolflike, toward the road up the mountain. As it disappeared into the obscuring gray drizzle, he thought he saw it joined—and in none too friendly a fashion—by another dog, a white dog. David glanced nervously down at his little brother, who still knelt beside him gazing quietly—too quietly—out the window.

"You saw that?" David asked incredulously. "Tell me what you saw, Little Billy, tell me what you remember."

Little Billy turned a white, tear-stained face toward David, a face so white and wracked with fear that David almost cried out.

David took his brother by the shoulders and held him firmly. "Look at me, Little Billy. It's me, Davy. Now tell me what you saw. I'll believe you, don't worry."

"I don't *know*, Davy," Little Billy sobbed. "I woke up and saw these red lights shinin' in the window, and I got scared and hid under the covers. But then I heard a voice sayin' not to be afraid, and I looked out again and saw they were still there, but it was the eyes of this big black dog, and I got scared again, 'cause dogs can't talk. Only this one was, and I heard it say that it wasn't just any old dog, that it was a magic dog and would make me magic, too, if I'd come with it, and that I wouldn't ever have to go to school, but could do whatever I wanted to do, and could play all the time. And I said I couldn't do that unless Ma and Pa said I could, and it told me not to ask, 'cause if I wanted to go, I had to go tonight."

"Did it ask you to let it in?"

"Yeah, and I told it we couldn't have animals in the house."

David couldn't help but smile at this simple but effective

logic. He wrapped his arms around Little Billy and held him tight.

"You did fine, kid. You did real good."

Little Billy was shaking convulsively, wracked with sobs, but David held him firm. "Tell you what," said David, "you can sleep with me tonight. I don't think I want to be alone either."

Interlude: In Tir-Nan-Og
(high summer)

Fionchadd was shooting pomegranates out of his wyvern's mouth when Ailill finally found him practicing archery in the Court of the Kraken. He stepped into the shadow of a rough-hewn pillar and for a moment watched his son unobserved. Fionchadd was almost full-grown now, but still a long way from the sort of manhood Ailill had hoped to see him achieve. *More of that Annwyn blood,* Ailill thought. *I should never have acknowledged him. . . . Still, the lad is a skillful archer,* he conceded, noting the boy's confident stance, the purposeful tension of the bare arms revealed by the simple blue-and-white-checked tunic.

Fionchadd drew to the cheek and released. The arrow flew true to its mark, striking dead center in the rough red globe which Dylan held delicately in his needle-toothed beak. But instead of piercing the pomegranate and bearing it away, the arrow was stopped in mid-flight, as, with exquisite timing, the creature snapped its jaws shut to trap both fruit and shaft. The wyvern staggered under impact but did not lose its footing. A loud crack and the drooping of the white fletching marked the final closure of its beak. Twin trails of red juice trickled across the silver scales to drip in a starfish-shaped puddle at the suckered tip of a mosaic kraken arm that curled by the wyvern's taloned feet. Balancing precariously on one elegant claw, the creature delicately extracted the arrow halves with the other. It swallowed once, the fruit a visible lump in its supple neck, then spread its wings and glided somewhat awkwardly forward to receive another from its master.

"You have become a fine archer," Ailill said, emerging from the shadows where he stood.

The boy's head snapped up, his expression clouding when he recognized his father. Dylan scurried behind him, to peer uncertainly from beneath the dark blue fringe of the boy's tunic.

"I don't like being spied upon," the boy snapped.

"Then you should use the Power."

"Why? Yours is stronger, so there's no point there; and in the case of anybody else, there's no need." Fionchadd fumbled in his quiver for another arrow. "But you spy on everyone, don't you?"

"Very nearly—but, then, everyone spies on *me*. Silverhand has been following me like a shadow."

"I understand you have been in the Lands of Men again," Fionchadd said as he nocked the arrow and drew experimental aim on a distant squirrel. "Did he follow you there?"

Ailill nodded sagely. "Oh, yes, there have been more white animals than I can count. But there is little he can do to stop me."

The boy took aim. "That you know of."

Ailill's nostrils flared. "Sometimes I doubt your loyalty to me."

His son did not reply.

"Fionchadd?"

The boy lowered the bow and glared at his father. "Sometimes I doubt your loyalty to anyone at all—except yourself."

"Those words are not good ones for you to say."

"Nevertheless, they are mine. They are all I have."

Ailill folded his arms and stared at his son. "You have failed me, boy. Twice I have sent you into Lands of Men, and twice you have failed me."

"I have provided information," Fionchadd replied quickly, "which is the main thing you sent me for. And while I was your spy I missed two hunts and almost lost my bow."

"But you have failed at the quests I set for you."

Fionchadd laid the bow carefully aside and turned to face his father. "I have *not* failed. I watched the mortal boy. I saw him meet with Oisin. I heard that one's words. When the power of the

ring awakened the Track I was there. I ran. I would have captured
the ring, if only . . ."

"Yes?"

The boy's shoulders slumped. "If only the Power of the ring
had not wrenched him from the Road."

"The chain broke, you have told me. Yet you did not see
where the ring fell?"

"I did not expect the chain to be made of iron, it burned me.
The boy was in his own World by the time I recovered from that
shock. And then it took an instant to shift my Sight."

"And what about the old man?"

"I made the arrow as you instructed. My aim was true. *You*
said not to kill him. You said the boy's fear for his family would
drive him to us. And, anyway, the fact that I could wound the old
man but could not touch the boy confirms that the ring no longer
protects anyone but the lad himself. I tried to get him to join us."

"You were not very persuasive," Ailill snorted.

"*I* am not a diplomat." Fionchadd shot back.

"I do better than you, boy! I almost have the younger brother
where I want him. There is a storm brewing in the Lands of Men,
which I can augment to good advantage."

"Lugh will not like that," Fionchadd interrupted. "He says you
spend too much time there at the expense of your other duties.
You missed his feast last night."

"I thought it more important to investigate threats to his realm
than the food on his table."

"I'm sure."

"My brother would think so."

"Uncle Finvarra would not care what you did as long as you
were not underfoot. That is, after all, why he sent you here."

"So you know my brother's mind better than I do? If you
would second-guess him, you tread on dangerous ground indeed."

Fionchadd raised an inquisitive eyebrow. "As do you, if you
would go up against Lugh Samildinach. I have seen that much
while I have been here. Shall we see who has the greater number
of friends?"

"And which are you, boy? You give your oath everywhere
else; even to the very one you are sworn to seek."

Fionchadd's face redded with indignation. "Forced to seek,
more likely. Twice the boy has bested me in combat, Father: at

running and at wrestling. It was the honorable thing to do. Even Morrigu commended me."

"They were not fair fights, though, for the ring's protection was still upon the boy. The Mistress of Battles is a fool to say otherwise."

"A very powerful fool, however," Fionchadd retorted.

Ailill raised his fist as if to strike his son, then lowered it again decisively. "Very well, boy. Since you are so concerned with her rules, I invoke the Rules: You owe me one more attempt on David Sullivan."

Fionchadd's eyes blazed. "By what right?" he demanded.

"By the Rule of Three," Ailill shot back. "Twice he has bested you. There must be a third."

"The boy is *not* my enemy!" Fionchadd shouted.

"Then you are not my son," Ailill replied, his voice chill as the space between the stars, and as hollow.

Chapter XI: What The Lightning Brings

(Friday, August 14)

"So what was it you wanted to talk to me about that was important enough to make you offer me a ride home?" asked David after Liz had carefully eased her mother's pickup truck out of the Enotah County Hospital parking lot and onto rain-slick Highway 76. Curved tails of spray rose behind her as the truck splashed through the puddles that still remained from an earlier thunderstorm. Clouds hinted at more, and soon.

"Not that I don't appreciate it," he added, "but it is a little out of the ordinary for you."

Liz frowned pensively. "Oh, I don't know where to start, David—Uncle Dale, I guess. What do you think's really wrong with him?"

"He's had a stroke, of course," David answered indignantly. "You don't recover from one of those in two days."

"I know that, dummy. But why doesn't he want to fight back?"

David slumped down in the seat and fiddled absently with the window winder. "I wish I knew, Liz, I really wish I knew. But if I did, I'd sure do something, don't you think? So why are you so curious all of a sudden? I mean, you've known him for years and years."

"Don't you ever *see* anything, David?" Liz replied, a certain amount of exasperation coloring her voice. "Does it all have to be spelled out to you? He's got a sort of something about him, that's all I can say. He fits into the world. He's part of your father's world, the real world, the farmer's world; but he's got something more—a sort of . . . a sort of magic. The same magic that you have, kind of. I think you'll grow up to be a lot like him."

David cocked an eyebrow. "I didn't know you were interested in magic."

"Don't you have anything between your ears besides air, David? Air and imagination? I'm interested in a *lot* of things you don't know about. Some of them are even your fault, and I bet you didn't know that, either. But I've been interested in the occult for a long time. I told you about my granny."

"I wonder if she knew my grandpa or Uncle Dale."

"Probably—they all knew each other up here back then. But about your uncle: I just think he's a neat guy. There aren't gonna be people like him around much longer—people who grew up here before there were cars or anything, who remember the old arts and crafts and stories."

"So you want to collect my uncle like a piece of folklore?"

"I want to *learn* from him, Davy. Surely you can understand that. You're concerned with folklore and magic and all that yourself."

David frowned absently. "Well, I don't think Uncle Dale knows any magic. And, besides, what I'm interested in is mythology, especially Celtic mythology right now, not mountain folklore—it's only a shadow of the real thing."

"Maybe so, Davy, but it's your heritage—and it may not be as removed as you think."

He looked sharply at her. "What do you mean by that?"

"Oh, you're always going on about fairies and all, like they were real—but always in Ireland during the Dark Ages, or something; but my granny said she saw 'em once when she was a girl."

"Was she Irish?" David looked at her skeptically.

Liz shrugged and reached forward to turn on the wipers. "May have been. I don't think you have to be Irish to see fairies. She said she saw a couple playing in her yard when she was a little girl up in North Carolina."

"What did she say they looked like?"

"Oh, she said they were about a foot high, had wings and all."

David snorted. "Faeries don't look like that."

"And how do *you* know? Have *you* seen them?" Liz asked indignantly.

"If I told you yes would you believe me?"

Liz hesitated. "I don't know. But I believed my granny. She never lied to me about anything else."

David turned to stare out the window of the pickup at the sodden landscape, the whole world gone dull and flat, with the merest trace here and there of tired green, aged blue, or dim purple hiding among the shadows. A few clouds hung ominously lower than the rest, like vultures waiting to devour the day. He took a deep breath. "What would you say, Liz, if I told you I thought the Faeries had caused Uncle Dale's stroke?"

Liz considered the question for a moment, her mouth a thin line. "I'd say either that you were telling the truth or were lying, and that if you were lying, either you knew you were, or you didn't. How's that?"

David smiled. "You sounded full of ancient wisdom just then."

"I got that phrase from my granny too. She *was* full of ancient wisdom. But why would the fairies want to hurt Uncle Dale?"

"To get at me," David said flatly.

Liz risked a sideways glance at him. "Why are *you* so important?"

"I saw them—not two weeks ago. I got Second Sight accidentally, and right after that I met the Sidhe and asked them for a token that the meeting was real. They gave me that ring."

"*Another* tale about that ring," Liz cried in exasperation. "David, please don't lie to me."

David sighed wearily. "I'm not! I'm like the boy who cried wolf, I guess: I've told so many wild stories nobody will believe the truth. But I swear to you, I really did get the ring from the Faeries. The fortuneteller knew it, and she knew I have Second Sight."

Liz raised an inquiring eyebrow. "What *is* Second Sight? That's twice you've mentioned it."

"The ability to see into the Otherworld, I guess you could call it. I might see a mountain, or I might see a Faery palace. But I'm the only one who knows the Faeries are here, and they think I'm a threat to them because of that."

"Are you?"

"I don't know. I don't mean to be. You're the first person I've told and I doubt you believe me either—well, actually, I told Alec, but I didn't have any better luck with him than I'm having with you. Who *would* believe it, though? You grew up in the same rational world I did, Liz. Grown people don't believe in Faeries in this country in this century."

"My granny did, and I think Uncle Dale might warm to the idea."

"If he ever warms to anything again." David paused, then continued. "Look, Liz, maybe you could use your power—or whatever it is you tried to use that day at the lake—and try to, you know, to read Uncle Dale. Maybe you'd get something that would convince you."

She turned to glare at him in spite of the rain. "You're serious!"

David nodded grimly. "Absolutely. You have no idea how serious. I would *love* to have somebody to share this with, Liz, only . . . only I think I'd be putting you in danger if I did. No, best I didn't. The Sidhe might not like it, and would be after you next."

"The Sidhe are the . . ."

". . . Irish Faeries." He paused, bit his lip thoughtfully. "Just a minute, Liz, I've got something here—" He reached into his knapsack, which rested on the floor between his legs, and pulled out something small and brown, which he laid on the seat between them. "This is the book the fortuneteller gave me—*The Secret Common-Wealth*. Got some stuff about Second Sight in there, some about the Faeries, too, though that part doesn't seem to be too accurate. Maybe it'll give you something to think about . . . but, then again, maybe I shouldn't let you look at it."

Liz laid a hand possessively on the book. "Oh for heaven's sake, David, why not?"

David's expression clouded. "Might get you in trouble. The Sidhe said they'd get at me through . . . through the people I care about."

"Me?"

"You." David took a deep breath. "Of course I care about you, Liz. You're one of my best friends. Who else could I have trusted about this, except Alec of course, and he's even more skeptical than you are."

Liz glanced at him in surprise, noticing how flushed his face had become. "Well, I was wondering when you'd admit that."

David cleared his throat awkwardly. "That's why I want you to keep my runestaff. It's made of ash, which is supposed to ward off the Faeries—of course iron is too, and crosses, but I'm not sure the last one works. They might for you, though, you being more religious and all."

"Okay, if it'll make you feel better, I'll keep the staff. Can't hurt, can it?" Liz smiled.

David smiled back. "I don't think so."

"So, how many times have you seen the . . . Sidhe?" Liz asked bluntly. "Or should I say, do you *think* you've seen them?"

David slumped down in his seat. "I haven't counted, but let's see: There was the first time, dogs at the window two different times . . . and the waterhorse at the lake. *You* saw that."

"That was pretty scary," Liz agreed. "What do you think it was?"

"A kelpie, probably, a Scottish water monster; either that or . . . something worse. The Sidhe can make themselves visible when they want to, and can shape-shift as well. Some of them are on my side, too; they're not all evil."

"They told you this, no doubt?"

David frowned. "Look, Liz, if you're gonna be sarcastic, I'll shut up. I've lived in silence this long, I can continue."

Liz shook her head unhappily. "I don't know who I'm more worried about—you, or Uncle Dale."

"Uncle Dale, I hope. I'm not likely to die of terminal Second Sight. But I may have to take the Sidhe up on their offer."

Abruptly Liz slammed on the brakes and brought the truck to a skidding halt at the side of the road. She turned and stared at David. "Their offer? *What* offer? David, what have you done?"

"They want me to go with them to Faerie. . . . You probably wouldn't know the difference if I did; they'd leave a changeling in my place."

Liz poked David in the ribs. "I'd know the difference, believe me."

David grinned, and to his surprise Liz grinned back.

"Tell you what, then," Liz said in her most practical and decisive voice as she eased the car back onto the highway, "next time I see him I'll try to read Uncle Dale. Maybe then I'll get a clearer idea of what's going on. *Something* sure is; you've been acting like a crazy man since the fair. Alec's noticed it; my mom has too—and she's only seen you twice—but she thinks you're just in love with the mystery woman."

"Well, I'm not. That much I am sure of."

Liz didn't say anything for a long moment, then let out a breath. "I'm glad to hear that," she said.

"Only woman in my life is my mama," David grinned. But he knew that was not quite true.

Fifteen minutes later the pickup slipped and slithered up the Sullivans' driveway. Liz parked as close to the house as she could get, and she and David dashed frantically across the mushy yard.

David knew something was wrong as soon as they came into the house. It was too dark for one thing, for in spite of the gloom, no lights were on in the living room. The other thing was his mother. She was sitting in her chair by the television, her eyes open, but apparently seeing absolutely nothing.

He noticed immediately that her hair was soaked, as if she'd been out in the recent rain storm, and her shirt looked damp as well. She clasped a cup of coffee in her hands, but they shook so that she had spilled part of it; dark stains marked her pant leg.

"Ma!" David cried. "What's happened?"

Behind him Liz closed the door softly and stood David's runestaff in the corner. Neither Big Billy nor Little Billy was anywhere to be seen.

His mother didn't say anything at all, simply looked up at David, horror on her face, tears running into wrinkles he had never noticed before. He could not read her thoughts, but there was something terrible going on, he knew, for her blue eyes were open wide, imploring, and her mouth as well—but no sound came forth. She simply stared into space.

"Pa!" David shouted. "Pa!"

Big Billy stomped into the room from the hall, wet about the shoulders of his khaki shirt. He was obviously shaken and his breath smelled faintly of beer.

"What's wrong with her, Pa?"

Big Billy had brought a towel and began awkwardly trying to dry his wife's wet hair and hands. "It's Little Billy, son; he's in his room. Go see."

"Oh my God!" David cried, exchanging anxious glances with Liz. "If anything's happened to him . . ."

He pushed past his father, vaguely hearing him say, "Now Mama, it's all right. It's not your fault. It's nobody's fault."

David paused at the door to Little Billy's room. He took a breath and opened it into the half-dark, steeling himself, not knowing what to expect, but suddenly grateful that Liz had followed him.

Little Billy sat on the side of his bed, soaked to the skin. He did not move, though he breathed softly, shallowly. He did not blink, either, but his eyes were fixed on some empty point in the near distance. It was like the time he had seen the black dog, only ten times worse.

David rushed over to him, and took him in his arms. "Little Billy, it's me, Davy. What's happened to you?"

Little Billy didn't say anything.

"Good Lord, he's dripping wet," Liz cried, taking a step closer. "Why isn't your father doing anything?"

"Ma's messed up too—he just doesn't know which way to go." David grasped his little brother's shoulders then shook him gently. David's eyes were tingling again, and there was something weird about the way Little Billy was staring into space. "Little Billy," he called tentatively. "Liz, turn on the lights."

Light flooded the dim room. David stared into his brother's eyes. Little Billy tried to turn away, but David held him firm, forcing their gazes to meet—and saw what he feared to see.

Beyond the frightened blue eyes that were Little Billy's, David caught a glimpse of other eyes: green, and slightly slanted. He knew, then, that he looked upon a changeling.

The Sidhe had taken Little Billy.

"What's going on?" Liz demanded. "What's wrong?"

"Getting late, Liz. You'd best be going."

"It's four-thirty, David; that's hardly late. I'm not going anywhere in the middle of this." Liz motioned toward the chaos in the living room. "I might be needed. You're obviously no good. What's happened?"

"The Faeries have taken Little Billy," David said heavily.

Liz stared at him, dumbfounded. "What're you saying? Little Billy's right in there. And he's sick—catatonic, I think."

"No."

"Yes!" Liz retorted, and without really thinking about it, she slapped David hard on the cheek. "This is no time for fantasy!"

David's eyes smouldered and he grabbed her wrists. "I'm telling the *truth*, Liz," he said between gritted teeth. "The Sidhe have taken Little Billy and left one of their own children in his place. I believe that as much as I believe that you're standing here."

Liz backed away hesitantly. "I'll go see to your mother."

"Yeah," said David, wilting, "I'd better get back to her too. At least *she's* still in this world."

A moment later they were back in the living room. David's mother had buried her face in her hands and was weeping uncontrollably. Big Billy stood beside her, hands hanging helplessly. Liz took the coffee cup and set it on the floor.

"How did it happen, Pa?" asked David.

"I don't really know," Big Billy answered slowly. "I told Little Billy to go out in the yard to get the ax I'd left out there by the woodpile—and he didn't want to go, but I made him, told him there wasn't nothin' to be scared of at his age in his own backyard. Your ma told me not to make him go, but I told her there'd been enough foolishness around, and that I was gonna speak to you 'bout scarin' him with your fool stories."

"I never. . ." began David, but his father went on:

"Anyhow, he didn't come back, and he didn't come back, and your ma come and asked me if I'd seen him. And then she looked out the window and seen him standin' out there in the rain by the woodpile lookin' up at the mountain, soaked to the skin. And she let out a holler and ran on out there and grabbed him and started shakin' him."

"Did he say anything? Has he said anything?"

Big Billy shook his head. "Nothin' you could understand, just a lot of gobbledegook, like speakin' in tongues at church—except just when your ma got there she says . . . oh shit, I can't say this, boy." He bent his head, caught his breath.

"Say it, Pa!" For the first time David noticed that Big Billy was crying too.

"She said, 'Come to your mama,' and he looked up at her and

said, 'You're not my mother.' And she busted out cryin' and come inside."

"How long ago was this?"

"Right before you come."

"Shoot," said David. "It's my fault—if I'd not . . ."

"We gotta call the hospital, boy," Big Billy interrupted. "You'd better do it, I don't think I can. . . . This is all your ma needs."

David patted his father's arm. "Sure." He cast a baleful glance out the screen door at the sky. "You'd really better go, Liz."

Liz folded her arms. "I'm staying, David."

"Liz, this is a family matter. Please?"

"Oh, all right," she said, and stomped to the door.

"I'm sorry, Liz," said David, "but I can't deal with anybody else right now. I'll get in touch with you later. But be careful."

"You *sure* I can't help?" she asked as she opened the door.

David handed her his runestaff and shook his head sadly. "No. Thanks."

She stared at the staff in puzzlement for a moment. "What's this for?"

"Protection," David said simply, as he closed the door behind her.

It was a bad thing to do, he knew, to run her off like that, and maybe dangerous as well, what with the Sidhe now taking positive action against him. But he could not be everywhere at once. Liz would be in the pickup anyway, and that was steel, which hopefully would offer some protection. And she had his runestaff, which might help her at other times, provided she remembered to carry it with her, which he very much doubted.

But what about himself and his folks? The car would help there as well, for most of the way. And, once in town, once at the hospital, there would be too many people around, he hoped—that was all he could do. And, after that, he didn't want to contemplate. Maybe he'd think of something.

Actually, he considered, he probably ought to stay at home, to look after things, and to draw off the attack, as it were—if there *was* another attack. *Somebody* had to stay, after all, and he didn't think Ailill would attack again right away; too many strange accidents would attract too much attention, which was exactly what the dark Faery's faction did not want.

He hoped.

He squared his shoulders and went over to stand before his mother. "Ma," he whispered, "it'll be all right."

She turned her tear-stained face again toward him. "You should have seen him, just standin' there in the rain, starin' at that mountain, and when he turned to me, just lookin' at me like I wasn't there, and said, 'You are not my mother,' I thought I would die. I just can't stand anything else, Davy. First you and then Dale and now this; I just can't stand it," she almost screamed.

David knelt beside her and put his arm around her. "Okay, Ma, we'll get him to a hospital and find out what's wrong. Maybe it's just shock, or something, and we'll get something to calm you down too."

"Don't worry about me," she sobbed. "All I want is my boy back. That's not Little Billy in there, David, not my Little Billy. I don't know what it is, but Little Billy's not in there. God knows I try to live a good life, but I must have sinned some way, for all this to be happening. You go look, David; that's not your brother —it's just a shell."

"He's been jumpy lately, Ma; just saw something that's scared him bad. Hospital'll be able to fix him up. May take a while, that's all." David knew he was lying extravagantly, but what else could he tell his mother? Not the truth, that was for certain.

"Shoot," said JoAnne Sullivan, "I don't know if we should even bother takin' him to the doctor—much good they did poor old Dale. They'd just say there's nothin' they can do. Oh, you should have seen him, should have heard him, David, speakin' in tongues." She began to sob again.

David leaned against the door frame. That was the second time they'd mentioned that: speaking in tongues. He thought for a minute, shutting out the panic in the room. There were three kinds of changelings, he recalled from what he had read in *The Secret Common-Wealth:* One called a stock, that was just a piece of wood enchanted to look like a real person. A stock was what the Faeries used when they took somebody and wanted everybody to think he was dead, like what had happened to Reverend Kirk.

And sometimes they left one of their own old people about to die, but this was obviously not an old Faery; David's Second Sight had proved that, and he didn't think anybody *could* grow old in this part of Faerie. No one he had seen had looked older than about thirty, except Oisin.

Sometimes, too, they left one of their own children. That was evidently what had happened here. The Sidhe had taken Little Billy and left one of their own, and it had spoken its native language in its fright. It was probably just as scared as Little Billy had been, and it didn't know any English. What his mother thought she had heard must have been the changeling's thoughts made powerful by its fear. Imagine being thrust into the world of men in the midst of a rainstorm! What kind of people would do that to one of their own children? Well, David had seen enough of the Sidhe to know something about their morality—or lack of it.

Big Billy's voice broke in upon his reverie. "Call the hospital, boy, call the hospital."

"Okay, okay," David said as he dialed the number to alert the emergency room and went back into the living room.

"Just be calm, Mama, just be calm," he heard his father saying. "You get the hospital, boy?"

"Sure did," David nodded. "But I was just thinking," he added slowly, "that I'd better stay here, do the evening chores, and keep an eye on things while you and Ma go with Little Billy, if that's all right with you."

"Yeah . . . that'd be a good idea I reckon," Big Billy answered absently.

"But you be careful, Pa. It's raining even harder than it was. Better take the four-wheel-drive, there's gonna be bad weather tonight. And you call me the minute you hear anything, all right? And don't forget to let me know how Uncle Dale's doing."

"All right. Good." Big Billy went over to his wife, took her by the shoulders. "Come on now, Mama."

"I'll take care of Little Billy," David called.

"Poor little changeling," he whispered a moment later when he came into the room where that which wore his brother's shape still sat on the edge of the bed. It grinned an honest, childlike grin, and did not resist as David began to strip off its wet clothing. David looked at it. He focused the Sight—he was beginning to learn how to turn it on and off, finally. Apparently there were times and places it worked automatically—places where magic was strong or concentrated, he suspected. But sometimes he could summon it at will, too. As David put Little Billy's pajamas on the changeling, he looked more closely at the boy, saw that other face: slimmer, more pointed at chin, the hair of unearthly fineness, the ears slightly pointed. And the long-lashed lids, he knew, covered eyes green and faintly slanted.

Yet this was different somehow, not quite like the other times he had experienced the Sight. David frowned, puzzled. Those other times he had either seen the things of the Otherworld very clearly indeed, or else he had glimpsed them as tenuously as things seen in a drifting fog. This time, though, it was not so much as if he looked on a shape—an actual form obscured by magic—as on the *memory* of a shape. There was magic afoot here, all right, but of a type different from any he had ever experienced.

David was still trying to figure things out when Big Billy came into the room, lifted the shell of his son, and carried him out to the pickup.

Two hours later Big Billy called from the hospital.

"Everything all right, Pa?"

"I reckon so." Big Billy's voice crackled over the line. "Your ma is worse off than Little Billy, I think, but they give her something to calm her down and put her in a room to sleep. Little Billy seems to be comin' round, but he's not talkin' much—or it's more like he was learnin' to talk all over again—askin' the names of things and stuff, real funnylike. I've heard of somebody bein' scared out of their growth, but I didn't think I'd ever see anybody scared out of their mind."

"Sorry you have to."

"Everything all right at home?"

"Power's flickered a time or two, but I've checked the lanterns. You staying the night?"

"Looks like we'll have to; lots of floodin' between here an' home. An' besides, they want to keep Little Billy under observation—treat him for shock. They think that he might have been hit by ball lightnin' or somethin'. Poor old Dale's a little better, though. But I tell you what, boy, I've about had it with these know-nothing doctors. Your ma and me've done decided: First thing tomorrow we're bringin' 'em home, both of 'em. We can do as good as this hospital."

"You're probably right," David muttered.

"What was that?"

"Oh, nothing."

"I was a fool," Big Billy went on reflectively, "to ask a little boy to go out in the rain like that. A damn fool."

"Maybe so," David said absently, and then hung up the phone.

The air suddenly felt empty. David frowned and went over to the refrigerator in search of something to quiet his growling stomach. Once full of coffee, cold roast beef, a peanut butter sandwich, and a handful of potato chips, he began to pace restlessly about the house, unable to stay in one place for more than a minute or two. The radio was full of static, the TV was out entirely, and reading demanded more concentration than he could muster.

He paced the house, and when that became too much, went out onto the front porch to watch the storm. Safe or unsafe, he did not really care. It was raining as if it would never cease, and he stared at that silver-laced darkness for a long time before starting back inside. He reached for the doorhandle and stopped short. His runestaff was leaning in the corner by the door. Liz had left it for him. "Oh, Christ!" he whispered. "If anything happens to *her . . .*"

But there was nothing he could do about it now, he realized glumly as he brought it inside and retreated to the final sanctuary of his room. Whatever happened would happen.

He flopped down on his bed, ran his gaze blankly over his bookcase. Idly he reached out and snagged the worn blue copy of *Gods and Fighting Men*. He wished he'd had time to scour the local libraries, and the one at Young Harris as well, for more books on Celtic folklore, but there just hadn't been time. He had prowled around in *The Secret Common-Wealth* a good bit, but all he could remember from that was something about iron and crosses, and he had doubted that those were always reliable. Still, the Faery boy had said he was under some sort of protection, and he evidently was—and fairly powerful protection at that, or else the Sidhe would have carried him off themselves by now. Maybe it *was* the ring, still protecting him from afar. But even if he *had* the ring right now, what good would it do? He couldn't fancy it undoing what was already done. No, there must be other solutions, if only he could think of them.

David flipped absently through the pages of the book. Names

and places once glorious to him flickered by. *And now I don't care*, he thought. *The glamour is gone*. He looked at the long list of names in the glossary, and thought about the changeling. "One of these people may be his father or his mother," he whispered. "I wonder where my little brother is sleeping now."

He slammed the covers.

Chapter XII: On The Mountain

David stood again on the back porch looking out at the rain, barely noticing how it stung his skin. It was falling really hard, sluicing off the tin roof in cold silver sheets, turning the yard to bog, the driveway to a blood-colored river. The sorghum patch was almost completely flooded now; only a few stray stalks of derelict cane showed above the water. The sky hung heavy, almost black. Across the drive the crosshatched shapes of trees and fences stuck up out of the mush like frozen black lightning.

He sighed and went back into the coziness of the kitchen to turn on the coffee pot.

An hour passed.

David couldn't take any more. He was going crazy with inaction and indecision. Tension throbbed in the air like thunder.

At a loss as to what to do, he slumped sullenly at the kitchen table, gazing out the window, watching the rain, the drops hard and bitter as his own despair. The riverbottoms were completely covered now, and he could only barely see the mountains across the valley. Water was creeping across the Sullivan Cove road, too, and he knew it was only a matter of time before it became impassable. David tried to imagine what the waterfall up on Lookout Rock must look like, and shuddered. It had been raining virtually all afternoon, without a letup—and that was all he needed.

He tried to remember bright, clear skies and lush foliage; green grass and soft, warm winds; and calm, cool water—not this demon-driven stuff. As if to taunt him, a gust of wind banged the screen door, forced its way inside to chill him where he sat with a quarter-cup of cold coffee in his hand. The single overhead light cast harsh shadows around the room, and David hugged himself, for the warmth had gone from the kitchen, indeed from the whole house. It felt cold and clammy as winter.

The door banged again, and David jumped. Probably the Sidhe come for him at last, he told himself grimly. *And I think if they asked I'd go . . . I'll give them credit for one thing; they sure know how to get at me: make my house an island, hide the sun, put my friends at a distance, my brother in some other world, my uncle barely in this. Shoot, what have I got to live for, anyway? There's simply no more hope.* David slammed his fist on the table so hard that the sugar bowl came uncapped.

I'll do it. I'll give myself up to the Sidhe.

It was insane, he thought, to even contemplate such a thing. And where would he go? Where did one seek the Sidhe? The Straight Track? Well, it was a thing of the Sidhe, one of their Places of Power—if it could be called a place. But he wasn't certain how to find it, nor did he know how it worked. It might lead him to Faerie, or it might lead him somewhere else, and he didn't dare risk that.

Bloody Bald? But it was an island, maybe half a mile from the nearest shore, and though David was a good swimmer, he didn't want to risk such a thing in weather like this. Idly he wondered why he had never thought of going there before, in all his sixteen years. Many a time he had been swimming in the cove, but never once had it occurred to him to swim out to the island. Nor, he realized, had anyone else he knew ever been there, or even proposed going there. It could only be the magic of the Sidhe turning men's minds away. He shook his head; he could not do that. With the weather gone wild, such a journey would be too perilous. A dead peace offering was no good.

That left Lookout Rock. Lookout Rock was his own Place of Power; he'd even called it so when such things were only a game. It was nowhere near any place of the Sidhe that he knew of, but he could see Bloody Bald from there, at least on a clear night. That was it, then: He'd go to Lookout Rock and offer himself to the Sidhe. He'd meet them, but on his own ground—not like a beggar at the back door.

He thought about the weather again. Rain. Wind. Even the road was half flooded. If he fell into the ditch, he could quite possibly drown—but then, he considered, there might be worse things than drowning. He had to die sometime, after all.

No, you fool! Don't think like that! he told himself, but was not convinced. Of course drowning would solve one problem: With him dead, maybe the Sidhe would leave his folks alone. Or would they? Had his family become so tainted by that Otherworld now, all unknowing, that the Sidhe might consider them a threat as well, even with him gone? And there was still his ring, out loose in the world, one more piece of unfinished business. He sighed. One thing was for sure, things wouldn't get any better from David's sitting here moping about them.

He went over to the stove and poured himself a cup of the last of the coffee that had been made that evening. It was mostly grounds, but he drank it, hot and black and bitter as gall. He thought for a moment, took a handful of cookies out of an open package, and crept softly into his room.

Very quietly he stripped and began to dress from the skin out in clothes more suitable to the bleak weather—warmer clothes, for the temperature had fallen with the rain so that it was sometimes perilously close to sleeting. Sleet! In Georgia! In August! Once again he recalled Oisin's saying that Ailill was a lord of winds and tempests. If he had had any doubts of *that* before, he had none now.

He finished his garb with a black rubber poncho with a hood that far overhung his face, and high hiking boots that laced close about his ankles. As he passed his dresser, he paused and opened the top drawer and took out two things: a handkerchief Liz had made for him the previous Christmas, with his initials embroidered on it in blackwork uncials; and a key fob Alec had given him with the Sullivan coat of arms engraved on one side and an Irish blessing in Gaelic on the other. He smiled wryly, stuffed them into his shirt pocket, and closed the door behind him.

His gaze flickered around the kitchen, coming to rest at last on a comfortingly familiar object: his runestaff—the one Liz had forgotten. It had some magic; it had glowed when Liz touched it. Well, maybe there was some good to magic after all. He picked it up and slung the leather strap over his wrist, thought once about taking an umbrella, but the idea seemed ludicrous. And, besides, the rain was nearly as horizontal as it was vertical.

The wind howled continuously, but the storm seemed to have let up a little—or so he thought until lightning flashed hellishly right outside, and a mighty blast of thunder rattled the windows and doors like some dark beast trying to get in. He checked them quickly, looking beyond to see if indeed something of that other world did not pace about in the yard or on the porch seeking entrance. David wondered briefly if the house would be safe while he was away, but metal screens on doors and windows, iron locks and doorknobs had worked before. He shrugged, drank the final swallow of the coffee, wincing at the flavor, and quietly opened the back door.

The wind almost wrenched the door from his hand, but he caught it before it could slam and was down the steps and into the yard almost before he knew it. One thing was for sure, he considered as he splashed across the sodden grass: He wouldn't leave any tracks. He glanced up toward the night sky, wishing for the witchlight of the Faery moon that had accompanied him the night he met Oisin, but it was not there. The rain itself imparted a sort of silver shimmer to the world, though, that was almost as alien —but still he could hardly see. *Well,* he thought resignedly, *it's uphill all the way; long as I'm going uphill and don't run into trees, I'm on the road.*

Magic, he mused. He'd had enough of magic to last him a lifetime already. He was tired of tingling eyes and burning rings, and of animals that talked, and of not being able to trust anything at face value—not even his brother. That was the heart of the problem, all right: not being able to trust anything. He could no longer be certain if a white animal was *only* a white animal, a friend *only* a friend. Even the rocks and trees were suddenly suspect.

He dismissed that stream of reasoning as frivolous in light of the day's events. *Trust,* he thought. *Ha!* Who could trust him now? He'd lied to everybody he knew, yet he couldn't expect them to believe him if he told the truth. Shoot, he wouldn't have believed them either, under the same circumstances. It was Ailill's fault—his and Nuada's, damn them both. Nuada was no better than Ailill. Yes, he was doing the right thing, all right. Better to let the Sidhe have him and be done with it.

"You hear that, Silverhand? I'm gonna talk to you! Gonna meet you man to man. You guys want me, you can have me—but at my place, and on my terms." He spoke the words low and clear into the gloom and started up the road.

The rain whipped at David, soaking him in spite of the poncho. He tried to throw back his shoulders and walk proudly and unafraid, but that notion lasted maybe ten steps before doubt settled in, weighing his shoulders down like the water that had already drenched them. Thunder rumbled like the evil laughter of giants, and the wind howled around his ears, forcing the rain into those few hidden places of his body that yet remained dry. He hunched over, pulled the hood of his poncho closer over his head and tried not to breathe too heavily. Already the cold was making him sniffle. And he had forgotten that his glasses would be utterly useless. "What the heck?" he whispered to himself. "I can see what I need to see without 'em. Almost don't need 'em anymore, anyway." He took them off, stuffed them into an inside pocket, and continued miserably onward.

He tried to blank his mind to all but the movements of his legs against the flow of water, and nearly succeeded. The wind swallowed his thoughts almost as soon as he thought them, carried them away to roll among the thunderclouds, so that he had trouble recalling much of anything beyond the endless left-right, left-right, the tiny trickles of cold sweat oozing out here and there as he exerted himself against the wind, against the ever more treacherous footing. It was probably stupid to go on the road and not under the meager shelter of the forest, he told himself. But somehow the forest did not appeal to him. He was already walking nearly blind, and at least on the road it was possible to tell where he was going.

He plodded onward for a good while, not knowing how long he had been away, nor caring, aware only of cold and the hiss of his breathing and the howling of the wind. He was half blind, half deaf, soaked to the skin, his fingers numbing as the rain grew colder, his feet freezing, so that he was less and less certain where he stepped, and his legs were getting tired too, as the water sometimes rose above his ankles even on the road. He had never tried walking uphill in a flood before—but, then, floods were pretty scarce in north Georgia. It was funny how someplace you had been a thousand times could suddenly feel different—even threatening—when you realized there was one aspect of it you hadn't seen.

David tried to sing once, "The Old Walking Song" from *The Lord of the Rings*, but he couldn't remember the words; tried a John Denver tune then, but the wind shrieked louder and he quit.

He squinted at his watch, the green numerals barely visible in the gloom, and saw that it had stopped. He shook it furiously, saw the second hand feebly creep a few degrees and stop again. Another try produced the same results, and he gave up. He felt like his watch: run down. Could hardly make his legs move, could hardly *feel* his legs. He set himself a goal: a swirl of dark water thirty feet ahead that might mark a hidden boulder. Reaching it, he set another, and then another. There shouldn't be much further to go, if he didn't miss the landmarks and pass the turnoff.

Another goal reached, and another. And then he brought his foot down on an unstable stone and staggered sideways, arms pinwheeling, his staff flying from suddenly loosened fingers to disappear beneath the torrent further to his right.

"No!" he shrieked as he leapt after it, touched it, felt it slip again from his fingers.

All at once he was near the edge of the ditch, and it was deep there, and the incline steep. He felt the earth crumble away beneath his feet, felt mud and stones carrying him downward into turbulent water, felt his feet covered, his legs engulfed. He tried to jerk himself upright, but the ooze sucked him back against the bank to lie there winded, half buried in mud, half covered by water that rose above his waist and poured down upon his head— and he could feel the current tugging relentlessly at his feet.

A long moment passed before he realized what had happened. He looked to his right and saw towering cliffs of darkness that would be blood-red clay in the daylight, but here at night they were bulwarks of sticky black muck that were already fitting themselves greedily around him. He was slipping further into the water every second. And there was a cold seeping up at him through the ground itself; he thought he could feel it covering him softly, softly. David realized that if he didn't move very soon he would drown—or be entombed by mud. And fail his quest. The Faery boy had said David had the stuff of heroes in him. *Hero?*

Ha! He closed his eyes and lay still a moment longer and thought about heroes. And he thought about dying, and a resolve grew in him. Cuchulain would never drown in a ditch by the side of the road, no sir. He'd boil the water with his own fury. Finn would laugh at it and dare it to touch him. Oisin would point a finger and it would be gone. Well, David Sullivan would not give up, either, not when he had business to attend to. The earth had already claimed one David Sullivan, and that was enough. What would David-the-elder say now, if he could see him? *Get your butt up out of there, boy, you got better things to do! I didn't teach you what I taught you to have it all end here in the mud.* Well, it *wouldn't* end here.

Ruthlessly David forced himself upright, feeling the mud pulling stubbornly at his back. His fingers brushed something smooth. *His staff!* He grasped it thankfully, poured his strength into it, used it to lever himself the rest of the way up. Water swirled about his thighs for a moment, and he almost lost his balance again, but he anchored the staff in the earth, and then he was clambering awkwardly out of the ditch.

Once back on the top he paused breathlessly, letting the rain strip the worst of the mud from his body. He glanced back down the road. It was like sighting into a long black tunnel full of ancient spiderwebs blending into a shiny floor. He turned his gaze uphill, then took a step forward. Another landmark, another goal to strive toward. All at once he became aware of a sudden warmth from somewhere to his right, and a prickling about his right hand. He stared at it curiously and noticed a faint light issuing from his runestaff: a pale ruddy radiance that glowed but did not illuminate, almost like phosphorescence. He recalled how the staff had glowed when he had given it to Liz that time in the woods. "Things have Power because you give them Power," Oisin had said. Well, this was certainly Power. Maybe it only required the presence of a little real magic to awaken more. That was interesting, but he didn't have time to waste on such speculation. His eyes were tingling. Magic was afoot.

The glow did not spread, but the warmth did, seeping slowly up his hand, through his arm, across his chest to where he felt it loosen a constriction that lay about his heart, a tightness that he had not noticed until it was lifted. The warmth continued downward, and up into his head. When it reached his eyes, his vision cleared for a moment and he saw ahead the break in the trees where the narrow track went out a short way to Lookout Rock. He had almost reached his goal.

And when he reached the place itself, David *knew* that magic was afoot, for the clouds were torn away like gossamer before a torch, and the witchmoon showed overhead. But he could see the familiar stars as well, Cygnus high in the northwest, his favorite constellation after Orion. He raised his runestaff in salute, half fearing to see the wings of the sky-swan flap in response. Stranger things had happened lately. He cleared his mind, trying not to think of arcane matters. And then he laughed. It was a good sign that such an image had come to him; it meant his brain was working again.

He walked over to the precipice, stood as close as he dared to the edge, listening to the roar of the waterfall behind him drumming on the rocks like the low song of the hosts of night on the march. Straining his ears, he could hear the faint cries of bats and night-jars and whippoorwills. Warily he glanced down, but the shapes twisted and blurred, showing at one moment clouds and at one moment moonlit mountains.

Bloody Bald reared up straight across from him, and David tried to conjure the Sight, tried to see again the castle he knew was there. But nothing changed about the mountain; whatever glamour hid it was more powerful than Second Sight. Perhaps only at dusk and dawn did it reveal itself.

David shrugged and turned his thought to other matters.

How does one summon the Sidhe? he wondered. *Stand up here and yell "Here I am, come get me"?* But he was less sure of himself now. Did he want to go through with it? Well, he'd come this far, and the Sidhe were obviously waiting for him—somebody was, or they wouldn't have been fooling with the weather. Slowly he raised his ash staff above his head, gripping it with two hands. The wind whipped his hood away, slapping damp strands of hair across his face.

"Silverhand!" David cried into air that still vibrated with the thunders of the mortal world. It almost seemed that he could see the words hanging visible in the air, as uncertain as he was.

"Silverhand!" he cried again, and put more force into the cry, but the sound again seemed muffled.

He took another breath, filled his lungs to their depths as if for a long dive, steeled his throat and vocal cords, and cried again: *"Silverhand!"* The word sprang forth, hard and clear into the night; he could almost feel it rip his mouth and throat as it burst out like the report of a rifle, could almost see the air spring aside in surprise at the presumption of its volume, could hear it echo from mountains and rocks, heard even above the falls: *"Silverhand,* Silverhand, Silverhand . . ."

He sat down then and waited, watching the lightning that played among the lowlands like lost stars.

Nothing happened.

He leaned back on his arms, his hands braced behind him . . . and abruptly jerked erect when a pain stabbed through his right hand. Something had pierced it . . . a snake?

He twisted around—and saw an ice-white raven sitting placidly preening its feathers behind him, its ivory beak the instrument of his pain.

The raven looked up at him. "Silverhand," it said.

"You?" asked David.

"Raven," said the raven.

"Raven?"

"Raven."

"I called Silverhand. Nuada of the Silver Hand," David said impatiently. He was in no mood to talk to a bird; his resolve was weakening by the minute.

"Messenger," said the raven.

David folded his arms and looked away. "I need to talk to Nuada."

"Forbidden," said the raven.

"Why?"

"Lugh's law."

David stood up and paced back and forth, precariously close to the edge. He faced the raven again. It sat implacably. David gestured around at the night. "So what is all this?"

"Power."

"Whose Power? Ailill's? Nuada's? *Lugh's?"*

"Enemy! Enemy!" squawked the raven, suddenly agitated. Even as David opened his mouth to frame another question it spread its wings and took flight.

David found himself cast abruptly into shadow. A darkness passed overhead, eclipsing the starlit sky, and then was gone.

David jerked his head up, frowning. Cygnus still blazed. He looked at another part of the sky and saw Corona Borealis, which the Welsh called Caer Arianrhod, the Castle of the Silver Wheel. It reminded him of the ring. And then his eyes took fire, and he was plunged once more into darkness.

A sound reached his ears, then: a concussion of the air, as of vast wings flapping. David looked up to see the raven fluttering frantically about, only a little above his head. And beyond it, shadowing half the sky, the outstretched pinions and dagger talons of a vast black eagle—fully forty feet from wing tip to wing tip.

There are no eagles in Georgia that big.

The eagle dipped its wings. Once. Twice. Slowly, almost deliberately. And each time those wings moved, blue lightning arced and crackled among the inky feathers at their tips, setting the creature now in such high relief that David was certain he could see every vane of every plume cut out against the heavens, now plunging it into darkness so profound that it was like a jagged rip in the sky itself.

And the size kept shifting: forty feet first, then scarcely larger than a real eagle, then spread across the sky so far and thin that the stars could be seen through its substance, then forty feet again.

A bolt of lightning struck at it from somewhere, briefly outlining it in glory.

Its size seemed to stabilize at that, but the eagle continued to float in the air, ominously aloof, still too impossibly huge to fly.

There are no eagles in the world *like that!* David thought as he blinked eyes he felt certain must themselves be blazing. A few yards below it the raven fluttered in small, confused circles, trapped, looking for escape—out, or up . . .

Or down. The smaller bird folded its wings and dove toward the sheer cliff face beyond David's feet, where it disappeared into the gloom below him. The eagle wheeled lazily and followed, abruptly dropping in pursuit like a stone. David could feel the displaced air whipping his face as the eagle fell past his vantage point. He peered cautiously over the edge.

Both eagle and raven were lost to sight in the shadow of the mountain. But a brief, high cry cut the night, and the eagle rose alone, climbing like smoke into the midnight blue sky. And then it turned its red eyes toward David.

A blast of heat seared his face, and suddenly he was running —across rocks, over fallen tree trunks, toward the sheltering forest. He barely made it, for as he dived into that protective darkness, still clutching his runestaff, he heard the whoosh of wings, felt hot breath on his neck, smelled again the odor of sulphur—only this time it was mixed with blood—and felt pain cut across his shoulders like a whip. A harsh cry exploded in his ears, like the snapping of a branch from a tree, a nonhuman cry that yet registered first surprise and then rage. Instinctively David reached down to feel inside his shirt collar, but the pain had already passed, as quickly as it had come. He felt a rent in the fabric, but there was none of the expected sticky ooze of blood on his fingers when he looked at them, only a thin smear of some black powder like soot.

It's the ring, wherever it is. It's still working. It saved me, he thought as he passed deeper into the woods, still fearing to hear at any moment the sound of wings or to feel talons or beak come at him out of the air to pierce his flesh and rend his life from him, in spite of that protection he hoped was still upon him—or take him away to Faerie, where he now realized he did not want to go. But there was no sound in the night except his own breathing; nothing unusual showed against the sky in those few glimpses he got of it.

Sometime later he came out onto the bank above the logging road that led down to his house. He was much further up than he had expected.

The eagle was waiting for him there, perched in the sturdy branches of the same ancient oak whose shelter David had just abandoned. As he stepped into the open, the bird glided soundlessly toward him, talons outstretched, seeming to grow longer, sharper, more terrifyingly pointed as they filled his vision.

Instinctively he raised his runestaff above his head, held it horizontally between his two hands—and to his surprise the eagle retreated, rising to hover impossibly slowly just out of reach above his head, wings masking the sky, claws like dire knives. He fully expected it to fall upon him, to smash him to a bloody, mangled pulp. Certainly it had mass enough to overpower him with ease—yet it did not. It simply hung in the sky, upheld by some supernatural wind.

David gritted his teeth and prayed as he continued to hold the staff aloft. *Things have Power because you give them Power.*

Oisin's words chimed in his mind, seeming to spread, to resonate throughout his body. *Iron and ash are some protection. Iron and ash. Iron and ash. Power. Power. Power.* He felt the staff grow warm.

Suddenly, beyond the eagle, David saw a vaster whiteness flash down from the night sky, to fall straight upon the back of the black eagle. He felt the eagle's shadow spread to engulf the world and stumbled backward onto the ground, covering his eyes, his staff fixed in his hands.

But the expected suffocating weight did not fall upon him. Instead there was one brief, strangled cry, and then—nothing.

When he opened his eyes again, the eagle was gone. Where it had gone, Cygnus the Swan glittered brightly in the sky overhead. A yard to his right a white feather five feet long glimmered, fading into the air even as he looked at it.

David ran then, wildly, madly, unaware when the rains returned. Relief, or fear, or both, he didn't know; he simply buried his rational mind and let instinct rule. He was in the forest, he realized at one point, for branches poked him painfully and tore brutally at his clothes and skin. The rain had lessened, but only by comparison to its former fury. He tried to stop, to think, to compose himself. But it was hard, so hard. And it was so dark he could scarcely see where he was going.

His toe struck a fallen branch, sending him sprawling forward. He retained his hold on the staff, but his other arm flailed outward, its fingers grabbing vainly at the twigs that clutched at him. One slipped through his grasp, another broke off in his fist. He fell heavily to the ground, winded, the staff beneath him. For a moment he lay motionless and gasping, trying vainly to regain control of himself.

Something warm touched his cheek and he looked up, squinting into the gloom. There was nothing there. But he knew he had felt something. Something very like a summer breeze.

As if in answer to that realization, he noticed a sparkle of light in the forest ahead of him. As he watched, it grew brighter, moment by moment, second by second. All at once he realized he was looking into a circle of light, almost like daylight, perhaps twenty feet across. He sat up, brushed his fingers across his clothes. They were dry, the mud flaked away as he brushed at it.

He fumbled his glasses out of his pocket, and put them on, realized they were filthy and tried to clean them on his shirt.

"Seeing is not really necessary when you've important things to hear," came a familiar voice scant feet ahead of him. "In fact, it is not really necessary at all."

David looked up quickly, then stared stupidly at the tri-pointed leaves of the branch he still clutched in his fist. Maple.

Oisin!

"It will not last long," said Oisin. "For it takes much Power for me to send my spirit roving in a form you can see, and more to provide an appropriate setting for any sort of discussion. But I did not come to discuss metaphysics. You have summoned me, I surmise, in a time of distress."

"Actually, it was an accident," David admitted, suddenly embarrassed. "But I'm glad you came." He stood up and took a hesitant step forward.

"You are not wearing the ring, David," Oisin said mildly, "nor do I sense it anywhere about you."

David exhaled, startled. His lips quivered, and he looked down at his feet.

"I'm sorry, Oisin, I'm sorry!" David burst out. "I strayed onto a Straight Track, and a Faery boy started chasing me, and then all at once I ran off the Track, or fell off, or something, and when I came to the ring was gone. And now the Sidhe are after my friends and family."

Suddenly he was crying, his tears falling on the warm, dry leaves. He did not fight it.

Oisin said nothing for perhaps a minute, then briefly laid both hands on David's head. "This tale is known to me already, David; and though it distresses me yet there is hope, for though you do not have the ring, I do not believe the Sidhe have it either. It does not answer my call, yet I can sense its protection still upon you, and such would not be the case if anyone else had claimed it for his own, unless he were very powerful indeed—more powerful than Ailill. That one does not have it, I am certain; you would not be standing here now if he did. For though you have Power, you cannot stand against him. No, the ring *must* remain in your world, perhaps not far from where you lost it. Seek the ring, David, first of all, for at least it will prevent further misfortune."

David shook his head despondently. "Further misfortune? How

much more misfortune can there be? I've already lost my brother and Uncle Dale." He looked up at Oisin. "Is there *anything* I can do to help them? I went up to the mountain tonight to give myself up—to Nuada. But I . . . something happened."

"Yes, I know, and I find that strange myself. But to answer your question about your brother and uncle: I fear I have no good news for you. Both of their lives are bound about with Power, Power beyond my skill to break, for only those who create such bonds may lift them. And, in any event, Lugh has forbidden my further intervention; only the fact of my previous promise to you allows me to come here this time, and at that it is only part of me you see before you. Thus, I may say little that will do you any good, except to remind you that there is always a solution to such problems if only it can be found; it is one of the Laws of Power. But knowledge of that solution must come from within yourself, David; not so much from any Power which you possess, though you have some, but from those other things that make you the person you are: your own ingenuity and determination. I can see the threads of fate patterning your destiny even as we speak." And he raised his arms into the air as if weaving some web of wind and sunlight. "Yet more than one pattern can be woven. Use your head, but follow your heart. The Sidhe are not as unlike men as they would have you think."

"You say I have Power?"

"It is as I have said, and as I suspect you are learning: Things have Power because you give them Power. How do you think you stayed Ailill long enough for Nuada to come to your aid?"

"I don't know . . . I was praying for Power, thinking about it, anyway. Hoping more than I've ever hoped before. I think I felt something . . . something strange, but I thought it was just the staff. It's made of iron and ash."

"And well made it is. Both ash and iron were factors, but most of what sustained you against the eagle was your own Power working through those things: The power of determination, of fear, and of belief. It may be a difficult thing for you to under-stand, David, but perhaps I should tell you."

"Tell me what?" David asked eagerly.

Oisin cleared his throat somewhat irritably. "I told you I did not come to discuss metaphysics, yet I see that yours is the sort of mind that will not rest until these questions are answered, so listen well: There are Worlds and Worlds, David Sullivan. This is but one. There are others that touch this one, even as Faerie does, and others that touch Faerie as well, but not this. Power is a part of all these Worlds, though mortal men seem to have forgotten that. Earth and Water, Air and Fire, of these the Worlds are made. Earth is matter; Air is spirit, more or less. The two are often linked together—more so in your world than in Faerie—for both are passive principles. By themselves they are useless, they need something to bind them together and make them act. And such are the active principles: Water, which binds the world of matter together—you would call it energy, I think—and Fire which does the same for spirit. Power is simply a force of spirit, like emotion or imagination or will to continue existing, a focusing of Fire bent to a certain purpose."

"Okay, I understand that much I think," David said slowly. "But how can a piece of wood have Power?"

"I was coming to that. The main difference between the Worlds is in the proportion and distribution of the four elements. In your world, though Air—spirit—is confined almost exclusively to living things, inanimate objects may yet contain Fire. But that Fire may only be awakened by some other fire—such as your own, for instance. You awakened the Power of the staff and added to it. These are hard things to understand, I know, and they become harder the more you study them. There are realms of almost pure matter, for instance, and realms of almost pure spirit. Faerie differs from your World mostly in the relative amounts of Fire and Earth: There is more of Fire in Faerie, more of Earth in the Lands of Man. That is why the Sidhe command Power so easily, but also why many of them fear the World of Men, for as the Sidhe may send their Power through the Walls between the Worlds and into the Lands of Men, so the substance of the Lands of Men may break through into Faerie."

"And iron and ash are two of those things, right?"

Oisin shook his head. "Not entirely. Ash is . . . the closest word is sacred, though damned might serve as well. Ash contains almost no spirit, but there is a great deal of Power in it, so much that it is both a temptation and a threat. Used properly, it can do wonders; improper use can lead to disaster.

"I will give you an example: When the Sidhe came to their World, there were no ash trees in Faerie. Then someone brought a single ash seed from the Lands of Men, just to see how it would thrive in the soil of that world. They planted it in Aelfheim, and there it grew into an ash tree as tall as the sky. Too late those folk realized that it was drawing the very substance from that World, and reaching into others as well. Finally there was only the tree and the Straight Tracks, and then, when the tree touched *them:* nothing. Aelfheim was no more. So now ash is forbidden: the thing of great Power which the Sidhe dare not touch.

"As for the power of iron: Iron is a curious thing, and almost as difficult to explain, for I have no simple words for the ideas. Iron does not exist in Faerie, and that is a fortunate thing, for in iron the fires of the World's first making never completely cool, though it may seem otherwise to mortal men. Yet the mere presence of the Power that is in the Sidhe can call forth that flame again. To the Sidhe, iron is eternally red-hot. And to make it worse, that heat may sometimes pass to that which iron touches, if left long enough. It is like the ash I told you of: Enough iron in your world in one place can sometimes burn through the barriers between your World and ours. And once it breaks through, it begins to consume the substance of Faerie. Those steel rails that once lay on your father's land broke into Tir-Nan-Og like a veil of flame, and the land there still lies hot long after they have gone. So hot, in fact, that even the Power of the Straight Track is disrupted, and that is another kind of Power entirely. Fortunately the Tracks are strong, and the burning slow, else your World might not long survive."

"So it's heat that keeps the Sidhe from touching iron?"

Oisin nodded. "Though they may touch it briefly, even as you might pass your hand through a candle flame and not be burned, if you do it quickly enough."

"Can it kill? Is its touch fatal?"

Oisin sighed restlessly. "That, too, is a hard thing to answer. For one must ask, what is fatal? Life and death are not precisely the same with your kind and with the Sidhe. In your world the body controls the spirit to a great degree. The opposite is true in Faerie: There the spirit controls the body; there one who has the skill may alter the form he wears. It is all related to that difference in proportion I told you of. And there is another thing: The spirits of mortal men are usually bound to the substance of their world alone. The Sidhe may wrap their spirits in the substance of either world *in either place*. But when wearing the substance of the world of men, the Sidhe are bound to its laws and thus may be as easily slain by iron as any ordinary mortal. That body, at least, dies; the spirit is forced to flee, but without the strength of its mortal substance to draw upon, it must find its way through the Walls between the Worlds before it can wrap itself in its original substance.

"On the other hand, if, while wearing the substance of Faerie, one should be wounded by iron, the fire of that wound would gradually consume that body. He who wore it would flee the pain of that consumption, and be forced to build another body, which can be a long and painful process, but even then the wound would never truly heal; it would be as if the spirit itself were scarred. One must then spend eternity in torment, or follow the Tracks to other . . . places, where the laws that govern such things are different. If anyone ever understands all the laws that govern all the Worlds, he will be a learned man indeed. Someday you may get a chance to walk those other Roads and find that out for yourself. The Sidhe do not own them."

David looked puzzled.

Oisin smiled sympathetically. "It is confusing, I know. But there is no time to say more now, and Lugh watches me closely. I have told you little that would be of real use to you, though much on which you may reflect. As to aiding your kinsmen, the only thing I can tell you to do is hope."

Oisin straightened and stretched. "I am sorry, David, that I could be of no more help to you. But remember that there must be a solution; every use of Power has a counter. If your kinsmen are no better for this meeting, at least they are no worse, for both may live indefinitely as they are. And you have Power of your own to see you through, and a greater power than that, even, in your two young friends. Do not underestimate them."

David released the breath he had been unconsciously holding. "How is it you know these things?"

Oisin smiled. "Magic, of course, or Power. Power calls to Power, and spirit may cast shadows the same as matter. With us such things are as obvious as the falling of leaves in autumn. Now Begone! Take the Straight Track home; it crosses the road uphill from here. Step on it and enjoy what you find. I do not think you need to fear the Sidhe tonight, for the things of this world are often echoed in that, and while I sense Ailill's hand in this storm, it is not entirely of his making. The Sidhe cannot entirely close off their World from yours, and this storm will be felt even in Faerie as a scattering of raindrops among the flowers. Now go!"

And Oisin was gone, simply not there. Once again David stood in darkness and in rain.

Funny, David thought a short while later, he had rarely been higher up the mountain than the turnoff to Lookout Rock—though the road went upward a fair way further. But the Straight Track did run lower down, so it must cross up here somewhere. He trudged on up the mountain as rain bit at him again, yet somehow its force was diminished. The road made a fairly sharp turn to the east, and ahead he could barely make out something glimmering faintly golden among the raindrops. As he drew nearer, he saw that it was indeed the Straight Track, a slash of summer day painted across the wet Georgia night with a brush of magic. Had the Sight not wakened his eyes, he would have crossed it unaware.

He stepped into that narrow belt, and it *was* day, though he could see the rain splashing on either side. The air smelled good, and the trees were dry where they overhung the Track. The way was narrow, only five or six feet wide, but David did not care; the grass was soft, the air sweet and warm, and the sun! The sun was shining. Or something was—maybe not the sun, for the light was too rich, like the light of early morning or of twilight, or of the two mixed.

David set off down the mountainside, sliding sometimes at steep places, but without concern or injury. He ripped off his muddy poncho and threw it aside as an almost irrational joy welled up inside him. He had no more answers than before, but now he thought he could face his problems. It was as though the forced stagnation of his inaction had been broken. The air elemental had won free again, only he now knew it was really Fire.

And so David rode daylight to the bottom of the mountain, to the place where the Straight Track crossed the highway. From there it was only a short walk home. The rains returned, but they had lost their force and their cold. A new gentleness permeated the drops, and overhead glimpses of sky—*real* sky—showed among the clouds.

David met his father in the backyard, dressed in his heaviest raincoat. Unexpectedly he found himself enfolded by Big Billy's thick arms in a bear hug so strong he almost had to gasp for breath.

"I was just goin' out to hunt for you, boy," Big Billy said. "I tried to call home and couldn't get nobody, and got to worryin', so I just come on home—roads wasn't as bad as they said they was. An' when I found you gone I got scared, let me tell you. Where you *been?*" There was no trace of anger in his words.

"Just out walking in the rain, Pa. I just couldn't stand staying in the house."

Big Billy laughed. "You're a bigger fool than I am, then, to do that, but right now I don't care."

"You're nobody's fool, Pa. If there's a fool in the family, it's me."

Big Billy looked curiously at his son, grinned and shrugged. "Let's not argue over that, boy. I promised I'd get back to your ma before the night's over." He glanced at the sky. "Looks like the storm might be breaking." He laid a heavy arm across David's shoulders and turned toward the house. "How're you at makin' coffee, boy? I sure could use a cup."

"I reckon I could learn pretty fast," David grinned. He had won a victory of sorts against the Sidhe, and against his own fear and doubt as well, and those were both things to be proud of. If he could only figure out how to cure Uncle Dale, and rescue Little Billy, and protect his family and friends, and . . . *No!* David told himself firmly. *Not now, not tonight.*

But as he stepped onto the porch, he thought he heard the rumble of thunder and the flapping of distant wings.

PART IV

Prologue IV: In Tir-Nan-Og

(high summer)

If there is a thing I would rather do than fly, thought Ailill, *it is to run. And if there is a thing I would rather do than run in my own shape, it is to do so in the shape of a stag. And if there is a thing I would rather do than that, it is to set myself in a contest of speed with another of a different kind.*

Thus it happened that Ailill in the form of a fine black stag had for some time been racing alongside a young white stallion he had lately acquired. They had begun their contest in a secluded, close-grown forest of lacy, tree-high ferns, where sureness of foot had been as important as speed. But now they burst out into the stark copper sunlight of a narrow meadow full of high orange grass from which spiky clusters of wine-red flowers rose on knobby stalks. Somewhere among that grass a griffin trumpeted. Lightning flashed from Ailill's antlers at that, startling the white. And then they truly began to run.

At first neither showed any clear advantage, but at last the horse began to draw slightly ahead. Ailill redoubled his efforts, masking the stag's fear of the open with his own desire for victory, and thus was almost upon the opposite edge before he knew it. The white slowed abruptly and swung away to the right to reenter the sunlight, but Ailill did not change course and suddenly found himself beneath the low, sprawling limbs and spraddle-fingered leaves at the shadowy fringe of an oak wood.

As he paused there gasping, the muffled clomping of hooves reached his ears. *Better not to be seen so,* he thought, as he called the horse to him and abandoned his antlers in favor of his own form, clothing his brief nakedness in a sleeveless hunting tunic and baggy breeches, both of tawny velvet quickly spun from a handful of grass.

And so it was that when that unknown rider urged his gold-coated stallion through one final layer of mold-webbed leaves and entered the meadow, what met that rider's eyes was a black-haired man sitting bareback on a very white horse, both of which were breathing heavily, and one of which was looking somewhat guilty as well.

"I am . . . surprised to see you here, Silverhand," said Ailill with uncharacteristic hesitation when he saw who that other rider was.

"I am surprised to see you in your own shape anywhere at all these days," Nuada replied quickly. "But I would rather see it than certain others you sometimes affect—to no good purpose, or success either, I might add."

Ailill ignored him. "Are you not afraid, Nuada, that something might happen to your pet mortal while you are wandering about here in the woods?"

"The thing most likely to happen to him is *you,*" said Nuada. "And *you* I am watching very closely right now; in fact I watch you very closely almost all the time, as doubtless you noticed when you sought to answer a summons not meant for you?"

"You cannot always protect the mortal boy," Ailill shot back. "And when I have the ring, it will not matter."

Nuada frowned. "You realize, of course, that Lugh knows about the changeling. He is not happy."

"That does not disturb me," Ailill replied complacently.

"Does it disturb you, then, that such activities are not, perhaps, entirely appropriate for an ambassador? I would remind you once again that you are a *guest* in this land—and a guest who makes himself unwelcome in Tir-Nan-Og is a fool indeed. Be warned, Ailill: If you stay in Lugh's land you are bound by Lugh's laws, for you are here by his grace, not by your right. This is not Annwyn, or even Erenn. You may not pick and choose among the inhabitants of the Lands of Men as pleases you."

"I think I have heard enough from you today," Ailill said suddenly. "In fact, I think I have heard enough from you for a very long time indeed."

"You will hear as much as it pleases me to tell you," Nuada flared, his eyes flashing dangerously.

"Then I shall have to see to it that you tell me nothing more!" Ailill cried angrily. He snapped both fists closed before him—and with his right hand drew forth a sword from his left: a sword born of Power alone. A fire sword that blazed in the forest like the burning blood of rubies.

Ailill laughed and jabbed his spurs ruthlessly into the white flanks so that blood burst forth as the stallion leapt toward where Nuada sat his own horse, unarmed.

Nuada jerked his mount aside as he saw Ailill raise the sword. The blade sizzled past his head, but left the smell of burning hair in his nostrils. The grass between them began to smoulder.

Ailill spun about in his saddle, his eyes narrowed into evil slits. He raised the sword again. Lightning flashed down to greet it, wrapped it in a nimbus of Power. Ailill smiled.

In that instant Nuada set his own fists together, and likewise called forth a blade new-forged of Faery magic: a blade of cold blue ice. And in the thick, still air of Tir-Nan-Og the two met: An arc of red flame intersected one of frosty blue.

Once. Twice.

Then, with a crackling hiss, Nuada's sword shattered into fragments.

But as Ailill continued the downward stroke, something swished past his ear and clanged loudly on the fiery hilt of his blade: a dagger cast from among the dark trees behind them. It landed clean upon the pommel so that Ailill's blade flew hissing through empty air even as Nuada swung his horse another step to the side.

Both Nuada and Ailill whirled about to see a dark woman richly clad in black and gray urging a steel-gray horse between the needlelike leaves of a thick stand of giant club moss that banked the narrow opening from which she rode. A black crow sat on the high pommel before her, an empty dagger sheath hung from her side. A moment later a second, larger figure joined her, dressed in a dark green robe, a glittering golden circlet on his black hair.

"My lord Ard Rhi," Nuada inclined his head toward the man. "Morrigu." Ailill did not follow his example.

"Airgetlam," Lugh acknowledged with an absent nod, then stared at Ailill. "And the troublemaker from Erenn. You I am glad to see, Nuada. But it would seem that some do not hold such favorable inclinations toward you, else they would not choose to violate the peace of my realm." The King of the Sidhe glanced at the Mistress of Battles beside him.

"Nor the Rules of Battle, either, Ard Rhi," the woman put in, then turned her icy gaze upon Ailill. "There may be no combat involving Power unless *I* sanction it, Windmaster. Combat is sacred, do you forget that? In combat a man risks all the gifts he has been given, and such gifts are not to be risked capriciously. You have called me a fool, but at least I still honor that trust which has been laid upon me, as you do not."

"Ailill may have called you a fool, Morrigu, but he has thought me one," Lugh added, deliberately ignoring the look of fury that burned on Ailill's face. "From Beltane to Lughnasadh have I listened to his rantings, and since then my realm has been sorely vexed by the endless contention he has caused. I have been thinking for a long while what I might have to do to put an end to his connivings. I have even been in touch with Finvarra, his king and brother."

"And?"

"Finvarra said to follow my own judgment regarding him. And now I see that judgment will not be delayed."

"And what judgment is that?" Ailill sneered.

"To order you to cease your meddling in the Lands of Men and release the mortal boy you have taken as a changeling," Lugh replied calmly. "Do this at once, or face exile from Tir-Nan-Og."

"I will not," Ailill shot back. "David Sullivan is a presumptuous mortal who has made a mockery of me and my son. I claim the right to vengeance upon him."

Lugh did not respond.

"The boy knows about us. He is a threat to your realm, do you not see?"

"I see a short-sighted fool who has spent too much time in Annwyn, where the Roads to the Lands of Men open onto older times than this," Lugh said abruptly. "And now I have heard enough of these matters. As for you, Ailill, you are no longer welcome in my realm."

"The Road to Erenn is dangerous this time of year," Ailill replied. "And, besides, I am the only one who knows where the mortal child is."

"You are no longer welcome in my lands," Lugh said again as the black-cloaked members of his guard rode from the forest and surrounded Ailill Windmaster with swords bright as sunlight.

Chapter XIII: Choices

(Saturday, August 15)

"Let's see, St. Charles Avenue with three houses, that's $1500 you owe me." Liz looked smugly up at Alec, smiling a wide, close-mouthed smile that reduced her eyes to slits and made him think of a large and self-satisfied cat—rather like the one that was crawling (illegally) among their feet as they sat around the kitchen table at David's house.

Alec groaned. "Well, I'll just have to mortgage my railroads, I guess; I don't have that kind of money."

David laughed; it was the first time he had really loosened up in what felt like ages. He leaned back from the table and folded his arms, peering at his friends over the tops of his glasses. Alec was frantically checking values on the back of his Monopoly cards while Liz held out a demanding hand.

"I really owe you two a lot," David said, suddenly serious. He felt sort of silly getting into one of his introspective moods in the middle of a Monopoly game, but when those moods came, they came, and David felt it was better to let them out.

"Yes, I know," teased Liz, "you still owe me fifty bucks from the last time you landed on Boardwalk. If I hadn't given you credit, you'd be out of the game."

"That's not what I meant, and you know it! . . . It's just that

I'm glad you guys could come up here to help me watch the invalids so my folks could go off to a movie. They *really* needed a night out by themselves, haven't had one in ages, and with all the crises lately. . ."

"We know why we're here. Now are you gonna play, or not?" asked Alec, handing Liz a stack of multicolored money, which she snatched away with exaggerated eagerness.

"Oh, yeah, suppose so." David rolled the dice.

"Shoot! Seven! That puts me where? On Alec's land there. There goes my $200 for passing GO. Can I owe you one more round, Liz?"

"With interest?"

"You won't make another round, my lad," said Alec. "The worm has turned."

"The wind has too. Listen to it," said Liz, shuddering involuntarily.

"The wind's done nothing but blow all summer—when it hasn't been raining," David observed.

"That's what it's supposed to do," Alec said drily, "by definition."

David glared at his friend. "Well, it's blown *really* hard this month."

Liz cocked her head to the right. "Remember the wind that came up while we were swimming last week—the time we saw the horse? It almost reminds me of that."

"It does, a little," David agreed, suddenly wary.

"Listen to it howl," Alec said, "loud enough to wake the dead."

"Don't say that!" cried David. "Least not around here."

"Oh, come on!"

"Okay! Okay! I will *try* to exist in the real world for just this one night. No tangents into Faerie."

Alec nodded. "Good enough. You *have* seemed to have your act together a little better the last couple of days—but I'm still worried about you."

"He's got a right to act weird," put in Liz, "with all he's been through." She got up and went to reheat the hot chocolate. "Hmm, it's nearly eleven o'clock. When'll your folks be back?"

"Heck if I know. They were going to a double feature—at the drive-in, for Christ's sakes."

"Uh-oh," said Alec, rolling his eyes. "You're liable to end up with another little brother."

"Alec!"

"Well, you could!"

"Listen, Alec, that's the least of my worries."

"I'll agree to that." He regarded the board. "You're losing, kiddo. But, then, Liz has always been lucky at games. Better not teach her how to play strip poker—or have you already?"

Liz pointedly ignored Alec's remark. "You know, this is the longest-winded wind I ever heard," she observed, looking curiously past the checked window curtains. "Must be blowing in around something, but the trees aren't bending or anything. It sounds almost like somebody crying."

David felt an unexpected shiver run down his spine. Unconsciously he rubbed his finger where the ring should be. It itched a lot. "It does sound like crying—just like some old lady carrying on at a funeral," he agreed cautiously, suddenly aware that his eyes were tingling as well.

The wind subsided abruptly, dying away to an eerie whine.

"Where does your mother keep the chocolate, David?" called Liz from the counter. "There's not enough for each of us to have a cup; I'll have to make more."

"On the cupboard."

Liz turned expressively. "Not here."

"Oh fiddle," sighed David, "let me look." He rummaged among the canned goods, finally digging out a new can of Hersheys.

The wind began to howl again.

Liz looked at David, one eyebrow raised, as he stood up and handed her the can. "It really does sound like somebody crying— you don't have any neighbors I don't know about, do you?"

David rolled his eyes and twitched the curtain aside—and began backing away slowly, arms held out rigid from his sides, fingers stretched taut.

"David!" cried Liz. "What is it?"

"Look for yourself!" he whispered.

Liz peered through the glass pane; a puzzled expression crossed her face. "I don't see anything."

"Alec, *you* look. Please!" David had backed across the room and was leaning hard against the washing machine.

Alec opened the back door and peered through the screen. Liz was still squinting out the window, trying to discern the cause of David's discomfort.

"What am I supposed to see?" Alec asked. He started to unhook the screen door.

David leapt halfway across the room to grab the handle against Alec's push. "No!" he shouted. "Don't! You'll let it in!"

Alec frowned at his friend uncertainly. "Let *what* in?"

"You don't see it? You really don't see it?" David stared incredulously.

"I see you, half crazy—and if you're acting, you're doing a damn good job."

"You don't see that woman in white standing in our backyard, not ten feet from the steps? She's the one who's howling."

"David, for the last time: No, I don't. You're putting us on."

"I *do* see a bright patch of moonlight there," Liz said hesitantly.

David slumped down at the table and buried his face in his hands.

"What is it you think you see?" Liz asked softly.

David opened one eye distrustfully and looked up at Liz from between his fingers. "It's a banshee, Liz. A real banshee. It's come for Uncle Dale's life."

"A banshee! Well, I do hear the wailing, that's real—and the more I hear the less it sounds like the wind."

"Liz, not you, too!" Alec groaned. He reached for the door again.

David sprang up faster than he could have imagined. He grabbed his friend by the shoulders, jerked him roughly back, spun him around and pushed him hard up against the doorjamb, his arms locked tight behind him. Their faces were inches apart. David's gaze burned into Alec's, his breath hissed hot on Alec's cheek.

"Believe me, Alec! For God's sake, believe me: I've got Second Sight, I can *see* it. When my uncle dies tonight, *then* will you believe me?"

"Dammit, David, I'd like to believe you," Alec replied through gritted teeth, "but banshees don't exist! If I could only see for just a minute whatever it is you think you see, I'd believe . . . I think. But I can't take this on faith."

"If you could see..." David paused as a memory played across his mind. "Alec, stand on my feet."

"Huh?"

Realization dawned on Liz's face. "Do it, Alec, do what he says."

Alec shook his head angrily. "What're you guys talking about?"

"By God, I'm gonna *make* you see, McLean. Stand on my feet." David swung Alec around so that he faced the yard and forced his friend's chin onto his shoulder.

"David, if this is some kind of game..."

"Oh, believe me, brother, it's no game. Now, put both your feet on my feet."

"Sullivan, if you don't let me go..."

"Alec, as you are my friend, my best friend, *stand on my feet!*"

"Just do what he says, Alec! Trust him."

"Okay! Okay!"

"Do it, Alec!" Liz shouted.

"*Okay!* Give me a break, will you?"

David felt Alec's whole weight fall upon his feet. "Good God, you're heavy," he muttered. He shifted his hold on his friend's tense body with his left hand and freed his right, then slapped that hand firmly on top of Alec's dark hair and shouted, "*Everything between my hands and my feet is within my power! Now see, Alec, see!*"

And Alec saw.

David knew from the shudder that ran through his friend's body that he saw. He could feel Alec's heart skip a beat, feel his muscles relax as they ceased fighting David's hold. David removed his hand. Alec staggered back, white faced, to fall heavily into a chair.

"I don't doubt you anymore, David," he gasped at last.

"I don't think I *need* to see," Liz whispered as she gently closed the inside door. "The book was right, then, wasn't it?"

David nodded. "Okay, now that you've seen, what do we do?"

"Do?" asked Liz. "What can we do against a banshee? That's one thing that wasn't in *The Secret Common-Wealth*."

"The secret what?"

"It's a book, Alec. One the fortuneteller gave me. I loaned it to Liz."

Alec's face clouded.

"She was more likely to get something out of it."

Alec nodded reluctantly. "I understand, I guess. But there's nothing in it about banshees, right? They just stay till they've done their job, is that it?"

"More or less," David sighed agreement. "But I can't just sit and wait. I've got to do *something!*" He struck the table hard with his fist. The Monopoly houses scattered.

"You can't go up against that," Alec protested. "You'd be crazy to try."

"Well, I'm not just gonna sit here and listen to it howl until Uncle Dale dies, that's for sure. Look, it's my fault he was hurt. The Faeries are after me. I know it sounds crazy, but you've seen the banshee, you'll just have to accept that now. They shot Uncle Dale with a Faery arrow—it looks like he's had a stroke, but he hasn't."

Alec was biting his knuckles. This was too much to assimilate at once. "You mean," he said, looking up, "that what you said about the water-horse, about the ring, all of that's true?"

"Yes," David answered simply, with a bit of a smile.

"You're the student of folklore, though. Don't you know what to do?"

"That's just it, Alec. I should know—I've always bragged about that—but I can't think of anything at all. Nobody ever *does* anything about banshees."

"I wish she'd just go away," Liz said edgily. "That wailing could send you off the deep end in short order." She slapped her hands over her ears and paced the length of the room.

"She will," David said almost savagely. "As soon as my uncle is dead."

"What *are* banshees?" Alec asked slowly.

David frowned and cleared his throat. "That depends. The name is from *bean sidhe,* Gaelic for *woman fairy.* According to some people, they're the ghosts of young women of particular families who have died under unpleasant or unconventional circumstances. Each family is supposed to have one. . . . I suppose I should be flattered: Ours must have come from Ireland."

The wailing continued, but at a lower pitch.

"Did you see her face?" Alec asked. "Was she human? I didn't look but a second."

David shrugged. "I couldn't tell. At least she wasn't the Scottish sort; they're ugly. But listen, I'd just sit here and let nature—if you can call it that—take its course . . . except for something Oisin said. Never mind who he is; I'll tell you later if we get out of this. Anyway, he told me that there *is* a solution, but that it lies in me, in my own Power. . . . But I can't think of a thing. None of the books I've looked at mention cures for elfshot. Yet I was led to believe there was something I could do."

Liz went back to the window, flicked the curtain aside nervously, and glanced out. "That spot of moonlight has moved closer," she observed.

"I wonder if it'll come in the house?" Alec speculated, shivering.

"I don't think so," David replied. "The screen door should help keep it out."

"I sure hope so," Liz sighed ominously. "It *is* iron, after all."

Alec sat straight up. "Does it have to have your *uncle's* life?" he asked suddenly.

"What do you mean? He's the one who's dying."

"I know, but has anyone ever tried to outwit a banshee by killing somebody else before the intended victim expired? Just theoretically, you understand."

"Alec," David cried in shock. "Nobody is going to be killed here. I'm not that crazy, and I sincerely hope you're not."

"I was thinking about the cat."

David picked up the cat from its place by the stove and rubbed its head so that it purred. He looked meaningfully into its green eyes. "I don't think banshees respond to animals. It has to be human." David's eyes took on a faraway look. "But Little Billy is *not* human . . . but he's not an animal either . . . and he's—"

"What do you mean, he's not human?" Alec interrupted. "Of course he's human!"

"No, he's not. He's not my brother," David replied quickly. "He's a changeling, a Faery child, left in place of my brother. You'll have to trust me, Alec. You've seen enough now to know I'm telling the truth . . . or would you like another look?"

Alec put up his hands, a screen before his face. "No—no, thanks! One was fine!"

"So!" David muttered. His mouth hardened in resolve.

"David!" cried Alec, grabbing his friend's arm as he passed. "You're not going to kill your brother!"

"No, I'm not going to kill him, Alec," David said wryly. "I finally have a plan—if it'll only work."

He forced his way into his bedroom, which he now shared with the changeling. It was sleeping peacefully, as it always did, except when it had to be fed or changed. It seemed to have given up trying to talk and didn't even walk much anymore, as if it had abandoned hope of adapting to an alien world. David was genuinely sorry for it. Poor thing, the shock must have really been hard on it. So much for Faery morality, to condone such things.

David paused a moment, his resolve weakening, but then squared his shoulders and picked up the small sleeping form, not bothering to bring the blanket that wrapped it. The changeling moaned and stretched. David was surprised by how light it had become; it had visibly lost weight in the few days it had been in this world, and its face looked shrunken—both its real face and the ghost face it wore when David's eyes tingled. David backed out of the room with the changeling in his arms.

"Davy!" cried Liz. "No!"

"If you don't want to watch, Liz, then don't. Maybe you should stay with Uncle Dale till this is over." He nodded toward his uncle's room. "Unless you'd like a look over my shoulder, just for proof. *This is not my brother*. Let me repeat that: *not my brother.*"

"No, thanks," she whispered fearfully as she drew away. "But I'm not going to hide in the dark. You can do whatever you think you have to. But remember that I'm gonna be there watching. And if it looks like you're gonna do anything . . . permanent, well, we'll see about that."

David did not reply, but he stared at Liz for a long moment before heading back to the kitchen.

Alec moved aside nervously when his friend strode over to one of the drawers and pulled out a long-bladed butcher knife.

"You two can watch or not," said David. "Either way, I'll be alone and responsible—"

"Actually, I think this makes us accessories," Alec interrupted.

David ignored him and went on. "If anything happens, just remember: iron and ash."

"Will I be able to see anything?" Alec ventured.

"I dunno. Try is all I can say. Maybe some ghost of Sight will linger for you."

"I'll try, Davy."

David opened the back door, shouldered the screen open without looking out, and stepped onto the porch. The banshee stood a scant two strides from the bottom steps. Her mouth was open, her lips pulled back from her gums showing uncannily white teeth. A low, low moan issued from her throat. It set David's bones to vibrating. For the first time he got a good look at her.

Although the banshee stood in the yard and he on the porch three feet higher, their eyes seemed nearly level with each other. She was tall—inhumanly tall, but then she wasn't human—and dressed in long white robes with flowing sleeves that trailed away to vapor at the edges. Her arms were raised at her sides, and she twitched them slowly to a kind of unheard rhythm, the fingers long and pale, and very, very thin. Her hair, too, was white; unbound, it flowed free in the night air, no strand quite touching any other, and it fell to below her waist. And when David finally dared look fully upon her face, it seemed close kin to a skull, though some semblance of its former beauty clung yet about it. The skin was nearly transparent, and David could see dark shadows under the cheekbones, and dark hollows where the eyes were—eyes that burned round and red like living flame. Those eyes had nothing of beauty about them. Only of hatred: hatred of life.

David straightened his shoulders, shifted the changeling so that it was cradled awkwardly in the crook of his left arm. Slowly he eased himself down to a wary crouch, but his gaze never left the face of the banshee. He freed his right hand and took a new and firmer grip on the knife.

"Greetings, banshee," he said tentatively, suddenly realizing he had no idea how to properly greet such a being, and feeling rather foolish the moment the words escaped him. His eyes burned so much with the Sight that he felt they might take fire in his head; he could feel tears forming in them.

The banshee remained where she was, but her gaze shifted down to meet his, the movements jerky, uncertain, like a lizard's. For a moment it seemed to David that the flesh fell away from her face and he truly looked upon an empty skull with burning eyes.

"Greetings, Banshee of the Sullivans, I say," he continued, swallowing hard. "Looks like you've had a long journey tonight —but it'll do you no good, I'm afraid. I can't let you have what you came for."

The wailing of the banshee faltered. She looked—there was no other word for it—puzzled.

David coughed nervously, and carefully laid the changeling before him on the porch floor. "I have a child here, a *Faery* child. I don't know if he has a soul or not, but I guess I'll have to find out very shortly, unless some things change real fast. I have no doubt that this knife—this *iron* knife—will have some effect." He raised his voice and looked up, his gaze searching the darkness beyond the banshee. "You hear me? I'm going to kill the changeling. The Sidhe took my brother; I claim this life for myself!" He raised the blade.

The banshee took a tentative step forward and extended its arms; its fingers caressed the air.

David jerked the knife toward it in a warning gesture; his eyes flashed. "Back off! I may try to kill the dead before this is over."

He glanced down at the changeling. Its eyes were open, blue on green, but the green predominated now—and by some trick they reflected a hint of the red gleam from those other eyes.

"I'm not kidding, banshee! Go back to Ireland, and leave Dale Sullivan in peace. I don't want to hurt this . . . whatever it is. Really I don't. But I will if I have to, because I know my uncle is real, half alive though he is, and I know he doesn't deserve what you people have done to him." David suddenly realized he was not addressing the banshee so much as an unseen host he imagined in the darkness.

The banshee took another step; the hem of her robe touched the bottom step.

David raised the knife higher.

"Stop!" came a voice from the shadows by the barn.

David's head jerked up sharply.

The banshee, too, turned; its wild hair flowed like water about its shoulders. The keening had quieted to a low, thin hiss, like the wind between skeletal teeth.

A woman stepped into the light before the door: A beautiful, pale-skinned woman clothed in deep blue-gray—a black-haired woman of the Sidhe.

"Who are you talking to?" David asked sharply. "Me, or the banshee of the Sullivans?"

"I speak to you both," the woman said. And he could see that rage wrapped her like a cloud, but he was unsure of its focus.

She stepped closer even as the banshee stepped back to regard her. They faced each other across the backyard, ten feet apart. David picked up the changeling and walked to the top of the steps.

"Do not harm my child!" the woman cried angrily as she turned her head slightly to face the banshee. She extended a pointed finger. "Banshee, begone! I would speak privately with this one."

The towering figure did not move.

David laughed in spite of himself. "Seems like she won't listen to you, either," he said. "But I'm still not satisfied. Is this your child, woman?"

The Faery woman looked David up and down contemptuously. "It is."

"What am *I* doing with it, then?"

"Ailill stole him from me."

"But you let him be stolen. You haven't tried to get him back. The child is sick, woman; he's probably going to die anyway. I'm just going to help him along, a little."

"Not by iron! Not wielded by mortal hand!"

David shrugged deliberately. "Talk to the banshee, then."

The woman turned her head a bare fraction. "The banshee does not concern me. All I desire is my child's safety."

"Well, why don't you just take him, then?" David said carefully. "All you have to do is help me first." He knelt and gently laid the changeling lengthwise before him—and then set the flat of the knife against its throat. It did not flinch. David was scared as hell.

The Faery woman stepped forward and stretched her hands toward the still form, brushing her fingertips across its face—then jerked them back abruptly to hold them clenched at her sides. "I may not!" she cried. "And not because of that flimsy bit of iron, either. I touched my child with Power to learn what manner of binding was laid upon him—and bitter indeed was that learning. It is as I feared: Ailill has bound him to the substance of

this World with a magic that is beyond my Power to break—
probably beyond any Power but his own."

"I don't believe you," David said, forcing his voice to remain
calm.

The woman glared at him. "Believe it, mortal. I would not lie
about such a thing as this, not with iron pricking at my little one's
throat. I have not the Power to set his proper shape again upon
him, nor to restore a mind that has already been broken once by
the switching of Worlds. Were I now to take him back to Faerie,
ensorcelled as he is, it would quickly bring upon him a madness
in which he would have to dwell through all eternity. That I dare
not risk."

David shrugged nonchalantly. "Sure you can. He may die anyway."

"I cannot take the child," the woman repeated coldly. "And
you would be a fool to harm him, for then you would have made
yet another enemy in Faerie, which I do not think you need."

"That's true," David agreed. "But what about Uncle Dale?
Surely you could cure him."

The woman shook her head. "Ailill's influence is at work
there, as well. I would be foolish to try, even if it were not forbidden."

"Forbidden?"

"Lugh has exiled Ailill and . . ."

David's breath caught in his throat. *"Exiled?"*

The Faery's face hardened. "Exiled. He leaves tonight. Lugh
no longer cares what damage the Windy One has done in your
World, he only wants him out of Tir-Nan-Og. Meanwhile, he has
forbidden the rest of us to interfere more with mortals. He feels
too much has passed between the Worlds already. I court his
wrath simply by coming here."

"But aren't you interfering now, just by talking to me?"

"I fear for the life of my child, more than I fear my king."

"So what difference would it make, then, if you were to interfere again?"

"Talk is one thing, action is another. The first Lugh might
forgive, the second he would not. I play a game as dangerous as
the one you play, and for higher stakes. Do not forget that."

David nodded grimly.

The woman said nothing at all.

He took a deep breath. "Well, then," he said thoughtfully. "If you can talk but not act, tell me two things, and I'll promise you not to harm the changeling."

"Ask. But I warn you, I may not be able to answer. Ailill's Power is involved here, and I truly do not know its limits."

"How may I drive off this"—he gestured at the banshee—"thing?"

The Faery woman cast a scornful glance at the apparition. "I can banish the spirit for a time, but she will return if your kinsman does not recover. She is bound to do that."

"Unless Uncle Dale is healed?"

The woman nodded. "It is as I have said."

"You're certain you can't heal him?"

Again a nod.

"And there's nothing *I* can do?"

"Nothing."

David considered this for a moment.

"You had another question?" the woman snapped impatiently.

"Is there *no* way I can get my brother back?"

"No way that would do you any good. . . . Fool of a mortal, do you not think that I would tell you, if it were anything you could possibly achieve? Ailill's quarrel with Nuada and Lugh is none of my doing. I hold no ill will toward you and your kin. I want only my child's safety. I . . ."

"Wait a minute!" David interrupted suddenly. "Did you just say you would tell me if it was anything I could achieve? Does that mean there *is* something that can be done?"

The woman grimaced—a strange expression on her inhumanly beautiful face. "No . . . it is impossible. The changeling now wears the substance of your world as well as the form, and even so does your brother wear the substance of Faerie. Only by bringing them face to face in the bodies they now wear might they return to their proper Worlds."

"Damn," David swore. "So all you have to do is get the real Little Billy back from Ailill—or take this one to him? Seems like you could do that. Why haven't you?"

"Do you think that if it were that simple I would not have done so?" the woman flared. "I told you. For one thing, my child would soon go mad if I returned him to Faery and did not effect the change very quickly. For another thing, I respect the law of my king. For a third, finding your true brother is no simple thing. Ailill has hidden him so that I cannot find him—perhaps in some secret place, perhaps in a form not his own. He could be wearing your brother as a ring upon his hand, for all I know."

"I'd know," said David.

"Ha!" the woman exclaimed scornfully. "If I cannot find him, do you think you could?"

"I could try. I'm supposed to be protected, after all."

"It is impossible, I say. The way to Faerie is closed to you."

David's brow creased thoughtfully. "Is there no other way? Couldn't Lugh grant me a boon or something? Couldn't I go to the Straight Track and ask him?"

"You might stand there a thousand years and get no answer. Lugh is angry, as angry as I have ever seen him, because of the contention that has been caused in his realm because of you. What you desire might possibly be within his power, but he will not listen to you. He will not listen to mortal men at all."

"Nobody?"

"Among mortals Lugh will only listen to heroes. To them only will he grant boons."

"So I need to become a hero, is that it?" David said sarcastically. "Well, *that* sounds simple enough."

Fire flashed angrily in the woman's eyes. "Say no such things in ignorance, boy. There *is* a Trial of Heroes, but it has been a very great while since a mortal man has risked it. Still, if you would undertake it, you must act tonight, before Ailill leaves Lugh's realm, and with him the knowledge you seek."

"We both seek, you mean."

"You have no time for talk, mortal lad," the woman broke in sharply. "There is a chance—a bare chance—you might succeed, and thus fulfill both our desires. But if it *is* your intention to dare the Trial of Heroes, you must act now. I myself will relay the word to those in Faerie, for the Trial is a thing ancient and sacred, and even Lugh must abide by it. Half of one hour I will give you to decide, and then I must be gone. If you truly would assay the Trial, tell me, and I will set the Rite in motion."

David took a deep breath. "But how will I know what to do? What kind of trial are we talking about? I mean, I'm not a hero, I'm not even an adult. If I thought it was something I *could* do, I'd do it, just to have an end to all this—this *Faery* stuff."

"The Trial consists of three parts," the woman said. "A Trial of Knowledge, a Trial of Courage, and a Trial of Strength. No more than this may I say. Little more than this do I know."

"But . . ."

"Time passes quickly, boy, and death hovers near—or have you forgotten? I await your decision." The Faery woman drew herself up to her full height and folded her arms.

They both faced the banshee then. She had dwindled to a mere patch of pale light, not unlike a spot of moonlight.

The Faery woman said something in a tongue David did not expect to understand, and the glimmer winked out.

"She has made a long trip in vain," the woman observed.

"I hope she doesn't have to do it again," David replied, as he withdrew the knife from the changeling's throat and slipped it carefully into his belt. He picked up the limp form and cast one last look toward where the Faery woman had stood, but she too was gone.

He turned back into the house then, leaning for a long, breathless moment against the doorjamb, realizing suddenly that he had a serious decision to make—the most serious in his life, for two lives hinged directly on it—and little time to make it in.

Alec raised an inquiring eyebrow as David reentered the kitchen.

David glanced around the room in confusion. "Where's Liz?" he panted breathlessly, as he handed the changeling to his friend and laid the knife on the kitchen table.

Alec inclined his head toward the hall. "Soon as the light vanished, she went to check on Uncle Dale." He paused. "How'd it go?"

"I have a reprieve . . . I think,"

Alec gaped incredulously. "You mean you really accomplished something with that stunt?"

"The changeling's mother came; we reached . . . an accommodation . . . didn't you see?" David added sadly.

Alec shook his head. "Not much. But what do you mean by 'an accommodation'? Do you mean you may have a solution?"

David nodded slowly. "I think so, but it's not over yet. I have a decision to make—fast—and I have to see Uncle Dale."

He met Liz coming out of Uncle Dale's room. "Uncle Dale

seems to be getting a little better," she said. "Is the . . . she . . . you know, gone?"

"Until she comes back—which, I hope, will not be for a long, long time. Now come on, I have work to do. I have to go look in on Uncle Dale one last time . . . and then I have to go out to the Straight Track."

"The Straight Track . . . ?"

David flashed them a guarded glance. "I don't have much time, folks, I'll tell you as soon as I can."

"You know, I never did get a chance to read Uncle Dale," mused Liz as they quietly opened the door into the old man's room. He was sitting propped up in bed where Liz had left him, and though his eyes were closed, a sort of vague agitation about him told David he wasn't sleeping.

"Uncle Dale," he called softly. "Uncle Dale . . . Liz, turn on that little light over there." He motioned to a night stand. "Uncle Dale, can you hear me?"

The old man opened his left eye and tried to speak, but the words were slurred, indistinguishable.

"Don't try to talk, just nod."

The old man nodded; a jerky motion, like the movements of the banshee.

"Uncle Dale, do you have any idea about what's been going on with the banshee and all?"

"David!" Liz cried.

"As close to that world as he's been tonight, I think he's aware anyway. . . . You know about the banshee, don't you, Uncle Dale?"

The old man nodded again.

"Okay, then. Good. Look . . . I may have a way to cure you, if it'll work. I just don't know—but I'm going to make the attempt. And if I fail . . . well, you won't be any worse off than you are, all right?"

Uncle Dale looked at him and nodded again. David saw the muscles in his scrawny neck and jaw grow taut. The old man's mouth contorted awkwardly, and a string of grunts and groans passed his lips, but he finally managed to wring out one single intelligible phrase. "Go . . . now . . . or I die." He closed his eyes again and fell back against the pillows.

David had no further need for decisions.

Chapter XIV: The Lord Of The Trial

Alec tapped gently on the screen door and then eased out onto the back porch, where David was sitting on the steps staring down at the yard. David had explained to him and Liz about the Trial of Heroes, and then he had asked for a moment alone to clear his head. "You ready now?" Alec asked.

"Not really." David shook his head and glanced sideways at his friend. "Know what I've been going through now, don't you?"

Alec shook his own head in turn. "No, but I don't think I ever will. It's too much, Davy—too much to put together this fast."

David sat up straight, squared his shoulders, and clapped his hands on his knees decisively. "Well, I can't put this off any longer, I've got to be going—though I haven't a clue as to how I'm going to get through this."

"I'm sure we'll think of something." Alec extended a hand toward David to help him up.

A flush of anger crossed David's face as he took Alec's hand. "We? Who is *we?*"

Alec looked surprised. "Why, you and me and Liz, of course; who'd you think?"

David froze where he stood. "Alec, don't you see what's going on, yet? Don't you remember what I've been saying to anybody who would listen for the last two weeks? It's the ring, Alec, the damned ring. It protects *me*. Even though I don't have it, it still protects *me*"—David thumped his chest—"against the Faeries. But it doesn't protect *you*, Alec—or Liz, or anybody else *unless I have it on*. You know about Little Billy and Uncle Dale now; you could find one of those magic arrows sticking out of your chest just as easy as Uncle Dale did."

"We're your friends, Davy," Alec said quietly.

David smiled grimly. "No, Alec, this is my fight."

"Dammit, Sullivan, I've already had one fight with you to-night 'cause I was wrong. Am I gonna have to have another one with you now 'cause I'm right? Let me tell you one thing, Master Sullivan: Protected or not, you confront the Sidhe on their own territory—take the battle to them, as you're threatening to do—I'm gonna be right there by your side, and so will Liz."

David had slumped against one of the porch posts, hands in his pockets, still gazing at the yard. Alec laid an arm across his shoulders and drew him toward the door. "What're you crying for, brother?" he asked.

David looked up and smiled. "'Cause I'm not alone any-more." But he knew he could not let them go.

"I really wish you folks would change your minds, both of you," David said a moment later as he riffled the kitchen drawers in search of the longest, sharpest knives he could find. Probably they would be of little use, he thought, but maybe they would provide psychological protection.

"I mean, I appreciate your concern and all," he continued. "But this is for *real*, folks. You may be risking your lives—has that really sunk into you? Even your good Baptist soul, Liz."

"We've just been over this," said Alec, reaching out to grasp his friend's arm so that David turned to look at him. Alec looked him straight in the eyes. "If *you* go, Liz and I go. Is that clear?"

David didn't say anything, but he studied Alec's face for a long, long time, and then he looked at Liz.

"You don't know what you're getting into, kids," he said softly.

"I doubt you do, either, David Sullivan," Liz shot back. "Be-sides, the fortuneteller told me and Alec to keep an eye on you—and you wouldn't want to disappoint a lady, would you?"

David snorted. "I've already disappointed a lot of ladies, Liz. Now you go get the changeling dressed. Alec, go in the living room and get Liz's runestaff—you didn't happen to bring yours, did you?"

"Matter of fact, I did. Liz asked me to, for some reason. It's in her truck."

"Better go get it, and when you get back, check in that drawer for some string. Ought to be a big roll in there."

It was not an imposing group who assembled in the Sullivans' backyard a short while later. Though they had no notion what they would be facing, they had tried to anticipate a variety of conditions and had dressed and equipped themselves accordingly. It was not so much a problem for Alec and David, for they were close enough to a size that they could wear each other's clothes; thus they both wore jeans and hiking boots (Alec in David's second best pair), and sweaters under nylon parkas. It was August, and by rights hot in Georgia, but they had no idea what sort of weather they would meet on their way to Tir-Nan-Og, and they didn't want to freeze before they'd gone two miles.

Equipping Liz had proved more of a problem, but a quick raid on David's mother's closet had produced a pair of high boots that were more or less her size, and a leather coat that looked sturdy. A slightly more purposeful image was provided by their armament: hunting knives pilfered from Big Billy's hoard, and the make-do spears Alec and Liz carried, which they had contrived by lashing butcher knives to their runestaffs. Neither of them had any notion how to use such weapons, but . . . well, it felt better. Not once had any of them considered taking any of the numerous guns with which the house was filled. Somehow, they knew, such weapons would do them no good at all.

Alec and Liz wore their backpacks, hastily stuffed with food from the Sullivans' kitchen. David carried the changeling. Though he wore a sheathed knife at his hip and another in his boot top, David was otherwise devoid of protection, for he had chosen to rely on his own Power and whatever dubious protection the ring—wherever it was—yet afforded him. He doubted seriously that weapons of any kind would be needed in the Trial.

They hesitated a moment, uncertain how or where to proceed, but an instant later the Faery woman strode out of the shadows between the barn and the car shed. Alec and Liz squinted, aware of something there yet unable to make their eyes focus clearly on anything. To David, however, the image was sharp.

"Have you decided, then?" the woman asked.

"I have decided," David said grimly.

The woman nodded. "By the look of things, I know your choice."

David cleared his throat awkwardly and felt the changeling twist slightly in his arms.

"I have set the Rites in motion," the woman said. "You are to go immediately to the Straight Track and there await what transpires."

A thought struck David, and he cursed himself for not thinking of it sooner. "Dammit, what about Uncle Dale? We can't leave him there alone; one of us will have to go back."

The Faery woman spoke then. "If you will permit it, I will look after the old man in your absence, and my child as well."

"I don't know," David said hesitantly. "Can I trust you?"

"Your success in this means as much to me as it does to you," the woman replied. "Remember that."

"But don't we need to take the changeling with us?"

"If you are victorious in the Trial of Heroes, that will not be necessary."

"But how will you know whether or not we win?"

"I will know," the woman said as she lifted the changeling from David's uncertain arms. "Of that you may be very sure indeed."

"So we've got to go to this Straight Track?" Alec asked a moment later as they trudged up the hill behind the house.

David nodded. "Yes, that's the only part I'm clear about. This is apparently a very ancient and serious ritual—come to think of it, in fact, the Sidhe seem to have a fairly ritualistic approach to life as a whole—I guess when you're immortal you *need* structure or everything goes to chaos . . . especially when you consider that some folks think they used to be gods or angels or something. They may be petty and malicious occasionally, but I think they're just remote and indifferent—most of the time anyway. Just a little too removed from us to really understand us, or care about us one way or the other. Concerned mostly with their own affairs."

Alec stared at him, amazed at the sudden gush of words.

David saw the look his friend gave him, and smiled wryly. He was scared to death, and so was Alec, and so was Liz. And Alec, at least, knew he was talking to keep his mind off what was fast approaching.

"Just consider," David went on rapidly. "Immortality might sound good to us mortals, but it has to be complicated if you're living it. Think, for instance: You could go crazy simply trying to divide your property among your offspring, or trying to get some property to divide, for that matter—there's only so much, after all, and more and more Sidhe all the time. And if you made an enemy, it could be for eternity. Think about *that!* Or what about marriage? You could get bored with the best of mates in a thousand years or so."

David let out a sigh; Alec and Liz could see him composing himself, trying to relax.

A moment later they came to the first of the thorns. David strode determinedly in among them.

Liz and Alec hung back, uncertain.

"You're not going into *that!*" came the nervous voice of Liz.

David turned and studied them. "Into what? There's some briars here, but nothing major, nothing to worry about."

"Are you crazy?" Alec nearly shouted. "There's a wall of thorns ten feet high and thick as . . . as a hedge, not two feet in front of you."

David glanced over his shoulder. The briars were there all right, but only waist high, and though there was an abundance of them between the trees, they were hardly impassable.

Illusion, he thought.

"Close your eyes," David said. "Walk straight ahead until I tell you to stop. They're not there, not like you see them. It's a Sidhe trick."

"If you say so," Alec muttered doubtfully.

"I don't see that we've got any choice but to believe him," said Liz. "We're on his ground now."

"Thanks, Liz," David replied. "Let's get going." He turned and marched forward into the thicket, glancing frequently behind him to see how Alec and Liz progressed.

They had closed their eyes as David had instructed and were fumbling their way slowly along, Alec swearing uncharacteristically as the thorns caught at his unprotected hands. Liz had worn leather gloves.

"Only about another twenty feet to the trail," David called.

And a moment later they were clear of the barrier.

David was struck anew by the otherness of the place—so different from the rest of the forest, as if the alien glamour it wore on certain nights never entirely left it, and flared again to life when the Faerie moon shone full among the trees and the Sidhe walked the earth.

"I wish I'd brought a Coke, or something," groaned Liz.

"Too late for that now," Alec replied. "I've got half a Hershey bar, if that'll help."

"You just wait," David said. "Soon as things start happening, you'll forget all about being hungry. You may never be hungry again."

Liz frowned. "What do you mean by that?"

"This is serious business, Liz; haven't I got that through to you yet? *You might not come back.* Some Faery lord might take a fancy to you and . . ."

"Oh, hush."

"They tended to like blondes, though . . ." David teased.

Alec and Liz both looked at David's fair hair.

"How will we know what to do?" asked Alec.

David shrugged. "I was told to come here and wait. So we wait. Last time I heard bells and saw light . . ." He hesitated, glancing around the surrounding woods. "But I don't know what you folks might see. It could be anything at all—or nothing at all. The Sidhe themselves control who sees them; the only people who can see the things of Faerie of their own free will are apparently people with Second Sight, like me, and it doesn't always work the same, even for me. Sometimes I can control it, sometimes I can't. I sure hope you see *something*, though, 'cause I'm gonna feel real stupid if you don't. Little Billy just whimpered and kept asking who I was talking to, so he didn't see anything, evidently, but he did hear the bells and the singing—that's what started it all, in fact—and maybe you'll do the same, assuming they don't just send a dragon or something."

"Wish they'd hurry, whatever they're gonna do," Alec whispered nervously.

David glanced over his shoulder. Far away he could make out

the familiar glow of the mercury vapor light by his house, its lonesome point of blue light somehow fighting its way among the trunks of pine and maple. It represented reality to him: his world by birth, if not by choice.

But up ahead things were different: The trees were the same, the sparse undergrowth exactly as it should be, the slope of the land itself comfortingly familiar—but close to the ground a faint golden glimmer overlaid a narrow strip of ground maybe ten feet wide, that stretched out of sight to their left and right. The Straight Track: The road to Tir-Nan-Og.

"See anything?" David asked tentatively.

Alec squinted uncertainly. "I'm not sure—maybe a little glow or something out there between those two pine trees."

"Liz?"

"Yeah, maybe a kind of goldish glitter sorta overlaying the ground—not like it was really touching it."

"Well," David sighed, "at least you can see *something.*"

David stepped into the center of the strip. His friends joined him there, their makeshift spears towering above them like pikes, giving the whole scene a vaguely martial air. Wordlessly they clasped hands with each other. Impulsively David reached over and planted a firm, wet kiss on Liz's cheek. "Take care, whatever happens. I couldn't stand to lose you."

"I think it's happening," Alec whispered as his gaze followed the Track up the mountainside.

Alec and Liz looked up.

An armored man sat on horseback a short way up the glowing trail.

He was tall—taller even than Nuada or Ailill, dressed from head to foot in close-fitting mail that faintly reflected the golden glimmer of the Track. Over his shoulders hung an open-sided tabard of deep blue and gray velvet. A boar-crested helm crowned his head, its long, intricately worked cheekpieces and nasal obscuring his face—all but the eyes and the drooping sweeps of black mustache that protruded below it. What little mouth was visible above a clean-shaven chin looked full—and very, very grim. The man was mounted on a huge, long-limbed horse whose flanks shone like blued steel. A naked sword lay crossways on the saddle before him, a burning white flame in the light of the witchmoon.

The man glared at the company as he rode forward, and David flinched under that gaze but stood his ground. Suddenly his mouth felt very dry.

"Who has come to dare the Trial of Heroes?" the man cried, his already deep voice made deeper by some acoustical trick of the Straight Track.

David swallowed, straightened, tried to look taller than he was, not so much a half-grown teenager. "I have . . . sir."

The man nodded, almost imperceptibly. "Do you dare it alone, or with companions?"

David's breath hissed, and he heard Alec and Liz inhale sharply. He had been afraid it would come to this. He had hoped —seriously hoped—that he would have to go alone, that his friends would be excluded. Not that he didn't want them along, no. But he didn't dare risk them.

"Alone," he said.

"Together," came his friends' voices behind him.

"No!" David cried.

"Three are mightier than one!" Liz whispered hoarsely.

"One is mightiest of the three," Alec added.

"Do you go alone, or with companions?" the man thundered.

David grimaced. There was no time for argument, no time for delay. "With companions," he answered reluctantly, gritting his teeth.

"Then you had best not travel blind," the Lord of the Trial said, "for not all those you meet may wish to be seen." He leveled his sword at them then, and a burst of light blazed from its point to strike full in their faces.

David cried out—not so much from fear for himself as for his friends. He heard Liz scream, Alec call out something unintelligible. And then the light was gone. He could tell by the way his friends blinked and stared that they now saw with more than human sight.

"The Trial of Heroes has begun," the man said. "The Trial is for David, but if any one of you completes the test and comes before Lugh Samildinach, King for this time in Tir-Nan-Og, it will be as if David himself had won. But know you, Alec McLean and Liz Hughes, that this is *David's* trial. *He* is the leader, *his* decisions are the ones that must stand. You may offer advice, help where it is needed, but neither of you must act without David's permission, for it is *his* knowledge, *his* courage, *his* strength that are being tested, not your own. Let the Trial of Heroes now begin. When you can no longer see me, follow the Track uphill."

Abruptly he was gone.

Chapter XV: Of Knowledge And Courage

Alec shrugged his shoulders. "After you."

David sighed, planted his runestaff on the leafy mould ahead of him, and strode forward on the Straight Track, Alec and Liz flanking him a little behind on either side.

The trail ran steadily uphill for a considerable distance, illuminated by the light of a moon that was now full. At first David was uncertain whether or not they were even on the Track, for the characteristic golden glow had faded, and the forest itself seemed no different. There was none of the unnaturally healthy plant life he remembered, none of those shifts in quality of light or air. But when he stepped to the side of the trail and made to put forth a hand between two pine trees that grew close to what he supposed to be the edge, his fingers met a resistance, and he knew then, that for good or ill, they must remain with the Track until the end.

Alec noticed it first: how their every step sent traceries of sparks scintillating among the thick blue-green moss that had slowly begun replacing the pine straw beneath their feet—sparks that haloed outward and then died away. They were pale, initially, and almost colorless; but gradually increased in brilliance as the hikers progressed. Patterns began to appear, outlined by those sparks, forming and reforming more quickly than the eye could follow: lozenges and elaborate flourishes like Arabic calligraphy, and sickening spirals of interlaced beasts that disappeared if looked at directly. The colors changed as well, became stronger, more intense, varying from red close to the hikers' feet through the whole spectrum into violet at the margin of the Track. Eventually, though, the familiar golden yellow that David remembered began to dominate and finally became pervasive, disrupted only by flashes of some other tint.

The further they walked, the more excited the sparks became, and the less confined to the area about their feet, so that for a time they walked knee-deep in a glittering cloud of floating motes that curved up more than head high on either side, obscuring any clear view except directly ahead.

After a while that part of the growth they could make out beside them began to alter as well. At first that change was marked simply by a gradual disappearance of the scruffy weeds that were a familiar but unremarkable adjunct to a normal forest; then of the taller shrubs, and finally of the pine trees themselves. In their place came taller, straighter trees, with limbs that branched forth higher from the ground. The leaves were still recognizable as oak and ash and maple, but they were unnaturally large and shiny, and there was now a greater degree of uniformity among them, as if each leaf were freshly struck from the same die.

And there were the briars that looped and whirled about those trunks like thorny snakes, forming an impenetrable screen of red stems that were sometimes thick as David's arms, with serrated six-inch thorns the color of new-cast bronze.

The floating motes within which they walked became more agitated by the moment, rising first to their waists, then to their shoulders. For a while they presented the somewhat ludicrous image of disembodied heads bobbing along on a sea of light, with their make-do spears sticking up like the naked masts of becalmed ships, and the briars looming over them like hungry sea beasts.

Finally the mist rose above Liz's head—she first, because she was shortest. A few strides further David disappeared, and then Alec. They could still see—no, *sense*—their route, rising straight and true ahead, but now a deep-pitched ringing sounded in their ears with every step. Bitter cold bit into them, then fiery heat, then cold again.

Eventually, though, the mist began to dissipate, at last revealing a lighter spot ahead illuminated by what looked like bright moonlight. As one they quickened their steps.

Immediately before them the wood opened suddenly onto a wide, grassy clearing through which the Track ran like a ribbon of golden fog. The trees fell away, but the briars remained, twisting and spiraling amid the tall, blue-shadowed grass—only now their thick stems were studded with satiny roses big as a man's head. Even in the moonlight the saw-toothed leaves on those briars shone green as emeralds, but the blossoms they bore were black.

Liz reached out impulsively to touch one of the blooms, but David hauled her roughly back, though he also felt a strong compulsion to caress the silky petals, to breathe the heady fragrance of the black roses of Faerie. Instead, he reached into the haze upon the ground, picked up something which he had just seen fall there, and held it up for Liz's inspection: an iridescent wedge of butterfly's wing, sapphire-blue, and veined with silver, smoothly cut along one side. He pressed it against the edge of one of those onyx petals—and saw it fall into two parts, as if parted by a razor. A raised eyebrow was his only comment.

They moved on then, carefully avoiding contact with the roses, and entered another wood exactly like the first.

For a long time they walked in silence.

"Neat!" Liz cried suddenly, her words shaking David from the reverie into which he had fallen.

Without really being aware of it, they had passed from the wood into a beautiful green meadow maybe a quarter of a mile across. The Track was still visible as a withered strip in the neatly cropped grass, and they could barely make out the dark line of more forest on the other side. Twenty yards away to their right grazed three low-slung beasts that looked something like armadillos and something like turtles—except that they stood man-high at their armored shoulders and had heavy, spiked clubs at the end of their tails. The sun flashed on the bright spiral patterns lacquered on their shells . . .

The sun!

But it had been night when they left—nearly midnight. What was the *sun* doing out? They *couldn't* have been walking so long; he was not even tired. In fact, David could not recall ever feeling better in his life. A sweet odor tickled his nostrils, and he inhaled deeply, appreciatively, noticing, as Liz and Alec followed him into the meadow, the waxy yellow petals and sooty black stamens of a vast profusion of huge poppies that grew alongside the trail. David regarded the animals warily and the flowers almost as carefully, wishing he could see just a tiny bit better, especially near the front feet of the most distant beast—though he had to admit his vision, with or without glasses, was nearly perfect now.

"We'll have to run," David whispered casually. "Those things don't look like they could move very fast or see very well, but I think we'd be safer if we got by them as quickly as possible. Just don't breathe any deeper than you have to, okay?"

Liz frowned uncertainly. "Is there something you're not telling us, David? Wouldn't it be better to sneak by?"

David shook his head. "I don't think so. I've got a suspicion this is more dangerous than it seems. Take a breath. Doesn't that air smell sweet? But doesn't it make you sleepy, too? Now look at that animal furthest to the right. Doesn't that look like a deer carcass to you—sort of a deer, anyway? I think these creatures are *not* vegetarians. I think they wait for the flowers to put animals to sleep and then feast on their bodies. We'd better run so the flowers'll have as little time as possible to act on us."

Alec and Liz nodded silently, and followed David's purposeful jog across the clearing. One of the beasts raised a bone-helmed head and took a tentative step forward as they passed, but the friends crossed the distance safely, and shortly found themselves again beneath the limbs of a forest.

None of them looked back to see the armored beasts abandon their grazing and move as one in a very purposeful line toward the Track.

The companions paused for a moment just inside the wood. The trees around them were low and sprawling, very like live oaks, even to the pale tufts of what in the Lands of Men would have been Spanish moss bearding them. The leaves were too small and too regular, though, and the whorled bark seemed as much carved as natural. The silence was disquieting as well, for even as the leaves brushed one another they made no sound.

They walked for a very long time in that eerie silence. David's nerves began to fray. He felt marvelous—physically—but tension was growing stronger in him by the instant. He was tired of keeping his guard up, of having to be wary every moment, suspicious of every sight and sound and even smell, and all the while knowing what would happen if he failed.

It was night again when they emerged into the next open space. A sound came to them as from a great distance, a sort of hissing roar that spoke to them of waves on some distant beach. They could see little beyond the expanse of long grass that surrounded them. The sharp-edged blades flickered alternately all white and all black as a brisk breeze teased them beneath the blue-white disk of the witchmoon.

Shapes moved out there in the dark, hunched shapes taller than a horse, with smooth pale skins and vast staring eyes that glowed orange and never blinked, and that went sometimes on two legs, sometimes on four; and which now and then leapt high above the grass, displaying three-forked tails. And there were other shapes: things too tall and spindly to be of the world David knew, or too quick, or—he shuddered—too impossibly huge.

The place was alive: Even the ground seemed sentient, for it pulsed under their feet as if the earth sought to relay to them the secrets of that unseen sea. David found himself straining his ears, half expecting to hear the cry of gulls, but the only sound was their own shallow breathing and the steady, hypnotic hiss of the Faerie Ocean.

They passed quietly. Nothing threatened them, but eyes watched their every step. And three lumbering shapes entered that place as they left it.

Another woods.

Another meadow.

Daylight.

Closer together now, and their feet no longer struck sparks as they walked—among ferns, this time. But the air had become thicker all at once, clogging their senses. The simple act of breathing made them tired. A walking pace became an agony of effort. David could feel his vitality draining away like air from a spent balloon. They moved more and more sluggishly. The air itself seemed to push against them. A step seemed to take an hour, a single breath half a day. A dragonfly flew before them, so slowly they could count the copper spots that dotted wings like vitrified night.

Sunset, and red shadows upon the bracken.

And still they walked.

Night.

And sunrise again, and the air was thinner.

But it was dark again before they could move normally.

And then light.

There were bushes to left and right, and then trees, and then bushes again.

And dark and light.

And dark and light again, alternating with mind-searing rapidity, so that for a while David lost all sense of time and space, his world narrowing to the Straight Track that continued as it had: running dead straight, and now absolutely level, though the frightened ghost of logic that lingered in the back of his mind told him that if the geography of Faerie in any way paralleled that of his own world they should have long since crested whatever mountain they had been climbing and then have descended into a valley, and now be going uphill again. But the Straight Track was obviously much further from his own world now, or the heart of Faerie much nearer. He wondered idly where he was: in Tir-Nan-Og itself, or in another realm, or in some timeless space *between* where the only certainty was the Straight Tracks.

Light. Dark. Light. Dark.

Woods. Fields. Small streams.

Flowers. Another forest.

Abruptly they found themselves standing beneath a full moon, on copper sands at the edge of a vast, still lake perhaps half a mile across; a lake whose waters gave forth a peculiar, unpleasant odor that was nevertheless vaguely familiar, almost like blood. *Exactly* like blood, in fact. David saw that the surface of that dark lake glinted red—and that the countless small wavelets which licked the copper shore moved with a strange, greasy languor that did nothing to assuage his fear. But the worst thing was the Track.

Ahead of them lay not only the familiar Track, but a crossroads from which *three* tracks diverged, one a continuation of that on which they walked, one breaking off at a sharp angle to either side.

The way to the left bent steeply back uphill toward the woods they had just left, but long before it passed into that leafy barrier it became hedged about with a threatening wall of thorns that appeared quite capable of rending the flesh from the bones of anyone so careless as to accidentally brush against them.

To the right the upward slope was gentler. Short grass pierced the copper sand there, giving way perhaps twenty yards off to a field of white lilies that glowed eerily in the half-light—lilies that became more and more plentiful as they receded, so that at the limits of sight they seemed to form a line of light at the edge of the forest.

And ahead...

The Track ahead was *not* straight. For the first time it failed to run laser-true before them. Instead it bent and twisted like the writhings of a wounded serpent as it continued on into that disturbing lake, where it manifested itself as a vague red-tinged burnishing beneath the surface.

They stopped where they stood, filled with despair.

David caught his breath, his shoulders sagging. "Jesus Christ!" he whispered.

"Well, Davy, which way?" Alec asked at last.

David shook his head. "I don't *know*. Straight ahead seems out, for obvious reasons. Of the other two, my instinct says left. That looks like the most difficult path, and thus the one most likely to test us."

Alec followed David's gaze in that direction, but then turned to look toward the right-hand trail.

"I don't know, Davy," he said. "What seems obvious might be *too* obvious. This path seems to be the *least* dangerous, and thus might be the *most* dangerous. So far we've seen nothing directly threatening. We've had no decisions to make, and had no indication that any part of the Trial had begun, much less been completed. I think this is the first test. It's the first time there's been a decision to make. But if you ask me, the right-hand path seems the best."

Liz had said nothing since stepping onto the beach, but her forehead was wrinkled in perplexity. "I don't think either of you are right," she said. "This place reminds me of something, an image from a song my granny used to sing—the one who taught me how to read vibrations. I think she called it 'Thomas the Rhymer.' It's about this fellow who runs into the Queen of the Fairies and is carried away by her—funny how I never thought of this before. But the part I'm talking about seems to fit this place perfectly—a little too perfectly, I might add." She closed her eyes and recited:

"O see you not that broad, straight road,
      that lies across the lilied way?
That is the path of wickedness,
      though the road to Heaven, they also say.

And see you not the narrow road,
      that's thickly walled with thorns and briars?
That is the path of righteousness,
      though to its end but few aspires.

And see you not that pretty road,
      that winds across the ferny way?
That is the road to fair Elfland,
      where you and I must go today."

She opened her eyes. "It's too close, Davy, too close to the song, for it not to be the way."

David shook his head doubtfully. "I don't know, I just don't know. It still doesn't quite fit. That's a lake of blood out there, not a 'ferny way.'"

Liz frowned. "That's true, but there is another verse a little further on that runs like this:

For all a day and all a night,
      he rode through red blood to the knee,
And saw he neither sun nor moon,
      but heard the roaring of the sea.

"Well, that's interesting," David said thoughtfully. "There now seems to be logical reasons for following all three routes. There's supposed to be a Test of Knowledge, a Test of Courage, and a Test of Strength. This seems to be the Test of Knowledge. But what if I'm wrong?"

"Then you'll be wrong," Alec said matter-of-factly. "Won't be the first time."

"But it might be the last—probably *will* be the last."

"It's your decision, David," said Liz. "Because whatever else we do, we have to follow one of these routes. The Lord of the Trial said to follow the Track, not follow the *Straight* Track, so we have the option at least of taking that crooked road. It may not even *be* crooked, it may only seem that way to confuse us."

David squared his shoulders. "Okay, Liz. It seems wrong to my way of thinking, but one thing I do know about the Sidhe is that though they are devious, they do not lie. Their riddles are difficult, but there's always a solution. In fact, I don't think they *dare* cheat. They use words like an artist uses a brush—only a really good artist can make you see more than one set of pictures at the same time. I . . ."

"Whatever it is, you'd better decide fast," Alec interrupted urgently, "'cause we've got company." He inclined his head upslope.

David followed his friend's gaze, just in time to see three hulking shapes shoulder their way out of the woods fifty yards behind them. Branches squealed across their shells; blunt, low-held heads swung slowly from side to side with ominous deliberation, heavy front claws scraped upon the sand as the creatures came full upon the beach. A red light shone deep within their tiny eyes, increasing in brilliance as they turned their heads toward the travelers.

"David, hurry!" Liz cried.

"They've been tracking us!" Alec whispered. "They *are* meat eaters. Make it fast, Sullivan."

David glanced about uncertainly. "I guess we'd better continue on ahead and hope the creatures won't follow us there. If nothing else, we can wait them out. Alec, lend me your staff. I want to know where I'm going."

Alec relinquished the staff somewhat hesitantly, and with that David stepped hastily onto the crooked road, hearing, rather than seeing, his friends fall into step behind him.

Though they did not seem to move rapidly at all, the creatures somehow gained five yards.

With some trepidation David eased the staff into the substance ahead of him, probing a bottom he could not see and did not truly want to visualize. To his complete amazement, the liquid—he could no longer bring himself to think of the stuff as water—drew away from it, barely a foot on either side, forming a sort of trough with the faint gleam of the Track superimposed on the copper sand at the bottom. Encouraged, he took a step, and then another, planting the staff ahead of himself again, and then once more. Alec followed him, with Liz bringing up the rear, her staff also borne low before her. Thus fortified they marched grimly forward into the tenuous rift formed by the untested Power of the makeshift spears of iron and ash that a would-be boy sorcerer had once made for pure amusement.

The Track twisted to their right, almost immediately, then to the left, and the trough grew deeper. They had to trace their way along with the staffs, ever fearful of losing the Track. It was slow going, and—with the knowledge of the creatures behind them—nerve-wracking.

The creatures had reached the edge. One lowered its nose toward the ruddy liquid but withdrew quickly. The other two shambled up behind it. One edged a tentative claw into the fluid, then jerked it back and shook it violently.

When they had gone perhaps a hundred yards into the lake David risked a look over his shoulder. "I don't think those things like the lake," he whispered. "They're still prowling around on the shore. Maybe they'll stop following us now."

"I hope so, I truly hope so," Liz replied as she followed his example. "They give me the creeps more than anything else we've seen. It's almost like they're—I don't know—aware, or something."

"Purposeful?" David suggested.

"Strange behavior for carnivores, though," Alec observed. "I'd think they'd like blood."

David raised an eyebrow. "Maybe it's not blood."

"Or maybe they can't swim."

Alec considered this for a moment. "Maybe not. They're heading back toward the woods."

David squinted across the glistening surface to where, indeed, the shell-beasts were ambling unconcernedly toward the shelter of the dark forest.

Liz whistled her relief. "Giving up, you think?"

"Maybe so," David replied decisively. "And while they're doing that, we need to put as much distance between us and them as we can."

"I'll drink to that!"

"Hush, Alec. What a thing to think of here."

"Let's move it, kids," David said firmly, and turned back toward the center of the lake, striding forward at a quicker pace than they had previously maintained.

By the time the travelers reached what seemed to be the middle of the sanguine lake, the red cliffs had risen above their heads, towering in an uneasy, jellylike tension that set all their nerves vibrating like saws struck by a hammer.

Wet copper sand squished beneath their feet, smooth as a plate, marked by no rock nor weed nor living thing, save the Track. Before them was nothing but the roiling wall of dark red, here flickering purple in the reflected blue-white light of the witchmoon, there foaming to pink where it withdrew before David's staff.

David quickened his pace as unease rose in him like the quivering walls beside him. He kept the staff before him, sweeping the viscous liquid ahead of him with a kind of grim determination, wondering how long his luck would hold, wondering when those awful walls would come crashing down around him and his friends. He dared not look back, not even to see their faces, for he feared to see the way collapse behind him as he knew it must be doing from the thick splashing sound; feared to know how closely peril stalked as they threaded a path so narrow the walls brushed their shoulders on either side, spreading alarming red stains up the sleeves of their jackets.

They walked for a long time: fearful, the rank smell of blood in their nostrils, the sickening squish of bloody sand beneath their feet. But finally—sooner than David had really expected—the walls began to lower again, and the bottom to slope upward.

A moment later the three friends stood once more upon dry sand. The Track continued on its twisted way across that beach before straightening itself at the edge of the inevitable line of trees.

David paused at the last turn and glanced fearfully back upon the lake.

And looked upon a trail that ran perfectly straight.

And on a helmed and armored figure sitting on horseback in the exact middle of it, scarcely three yards behind them. No hoofprints marred the sand behind him: the Lord of the Trial.

The Lord raised his sword and flourished it once in the air as if in salute, then paced the horse closer, so that at last David stood virtually face to nose with the animal.

The rider regarded him for a moment, and then spoke. "Hear me, David Kevin Sullivan, and know that you have passed the Test of Knowledge——not by knowing which road to take, but by knowing when to trust another's judgment above your own."

David found himself grinning in spite of himself, and turned impulsively to embrace a startled Liz. "You did it, girl. One down."

He stopped suddenly and stared at the ground, uncomfortably aware of how foolish he must look before this Lord of Power. But when he glanced up again, the man was gone. There was only the lake——and the shell-beasts still prowling slowly about the opposite shore.

The wood before them was darker than any they had seen, and more stately, beginning possibly ten yards ahead with a palisade of tall, red-trunked trees, each of almost identical thickness and height, presenting the appearance of nothing so much as a colonnade before a temple. The Track passed between two trees slightly thicker than the rest, their twined branches meeting in a pointed arch high above their heads, as if marking a gateway.

From moonlight they walked into gloom. The trail began to slope downhill, ever more steeply, as trees clustered closer to the track and more undergrowth filled the spaces between, effectively locking them into a tunnel in which the only illumination was the light cast by the Straight Track itself.

Down and down and down, ever more steeply, but continuing straight at a perilous angle so that at times they had to sit down and scoot along on their backsides or risk a foolhardy plunge into the blackness ahead.

Down and down and down.

It became darker as well, and even the trail shrank to a faint glimmer.

Darker and darker and darker.

Somewhere behind them three hulking shapes ranked themselves side by side at the juncture of three Straight Tracks and stretched their short necks skyward. One by one their mouths opened, revealing gray-white linings. Together they sent a shrill, keening cry wavering across the water.

On the opposite bank three similar shapes pricked their tiny, bone-shielded ears in response, and lumbered purposefully from the shadows of the forest, moving with absolute precision toward three sets of human footprints that showed beneath the glimmer of the Straight Track where it emerged from the lake of blood.

Darker and darker and darker.

Not until David felt fresh, cool air on his face did he realize how close the air had become in the tree-tunnel they had been pursuing. Up ahead the way lightened, the path turned level again. Eagerly David bolted toward that light.

Only Alec's flying tackle saved him from disaster. His friend's arms wrapped around his hips from behind, pitching David forward onto his knees, his arms scraping along rough rock. The breath was knocked from his lungs; he gasped, and the smell of wet stone and decaying leaves filtered into his nostrils.

"You really *like* running into thin air, don't you?" Alec grunted.

"What?" David asked, momentarily confused, then adjusted his vision to the new light in which they found themselves.

It was light in fact, but only by comparison to the darkness through which they had lately passed. For the night sky still soared above them, and the Faerie moon which never seemed to set rode again at the zenith.

And directly in front of them, inches from David's nose, a matching gulf opened in the land, seemingly as deep as the sky was high: a yawning black abyss between matching cliffs that rose unbelievably steep on either side. The jagged silhouettes of evergreens crowned those cliffs, and the narrow rocky shelf on which they had halted thrust out above the terrible darkness of the rift like fungi on an ancient tree. David looked at the rift with dread. It was not particularly wide—a hundred feet at the outside. But there was no way across.

The Straight Track simply ended, breaking cleanly off into empty air.

On the opposite cliff, etched brightly by the moonlight, the topmost branches of pale-barked trees rose above a stone archway composed of three immense rough-hewn boulders. The glow of the Track took up again there and continued through the opening. But in the empty distance between: nothing.

"Damn!" Alec cried. "It *was* the wrong turn, it must have been. We can't go on from here."

"No, it wasn't," Liz replied. "It *couldn't* have been. The Lord of the Trial said we had passed the first test."

David squinted into the darkness. "There has to be a way across."

He struggled to his feet and as he did so, he dropped the staff he was still carrying. The end with the iron butcher knife lashed to it fell forward into the darkness above the gulf.

"No!" David cried, grabbing frantically after it. But it did not topple into the giddy darkness below them; rather, the staff rested in apparent defiance of gravity with two-thirds its length lying unsupported in the air above the abyss. The air rang with a gentle *ping* like the tinkling of a glass windchime.

And from the point of the knife sparks began to appear, a panoply of glittering motes borne into the night that began to spread in all directions until at last they limned, faint but clear, the shape of the most insubstantial-looking of bridges, arching across the chasm and butting neatly against the opposite cliff. It was steep—almost a true half-circle, like an oriental bridge—and narrow, no more than a foot and a half wide. Nor was there any rail. A bridge it was, but a perilous one, scarcely more than a glimmer in the air.

"We can't cross *that*," Liz groaned incredulously.

"We've no choice, the way I see it," was David's choked reply. "And, besides, we can't go back. Those shell-things may still be back there, or others like them."

Fear had begun to coil in the pit of David's stomach as the dark places of his mind began to creep open. He couldn't do it. He *knew* he couldn't; the bridge was too steep, too narrow, *too high!* His hidden fear, the one thing he had never revealed even to Alec, was upon him: the terror of bridges. High places were fine, for he could wander around the ledges on Lookout Rock completely fearless. But being high up and *unsupported*, with nothing but empty space below him—that set his gut to writhing and his balls to seeking sanctuary inside his body. Unfortunately, he knew he had no choice.

And the bridge itself, so insubstantial it was barely there— surely it would not support his weight. David reached cautiously down and snagged the staff, fearing that the whole span would collapse at the slightest touch, or that the faint traceries that defined it would wink out.

Neither thing happened. What disconcerted him, though, was the way he could feel the whole structure tremble at that most delicate of touches. *Would* it support his weight? Would it support *any* of their weights?

For a moment neither of them spoke. None of them dared admit what they knew they must.

Finally Alec broke the silence. "All right, so who's first?"

David drew a ragged breath, his face pale as death. "Me, of course."

"Not necessarily, David," said Liz behind him.

David whirled around. "What do you mean?"

"I was thinking," she said. "Something you don't seem to be doing."

David opened his mouth to say something scathing—he was so tense, so scared—but Liz cut him off.

"No, David, let me finish. Be rational. This is a *really* shaky bridge. It might not bear our weight."

"Which is why I should go first," David shot back. "I'm heaviest; if it'll hold me, it'll hold you."

"Which is why the *lightest* should go first," Liz continued. "Meaning me. *One* of us has to get through. If the heaviest goes first, and it breaks, none of us will make it. If the lightest goes first, there's a greater chance somebody'll get through. Remember the conditions: As long as one of us succeeds, the Trial will be a success."

"But it has to be David's decision," Alec pointed out.

"Right. So David can decide. But I've told him what I think."

David had scarcely heard the argument. Either way, first or last, it meant walking—crawling, really—across that frightful gulf. That was what he most feared.

"David." Alec's voice was sharp.

"Oh, right." David's forehead furrowed, and he paced the narrow ledge. Fearless now; but only a few feet beyond he knew he would be quaking jelly.

"I don't like either option, but you're right, Liz: Lightest should go first. That's my decision....Liz, you *are* lightest, right?"

"That's what I just said, David."

"Well, it doesn't hurt to be sure."

"*I* weigh a hundred and seven pounds, David."

"I was just being sure, Liz."

She shook her head suspiciously.

"And you, Master McLean?"

"One-twenty-eight."

"Davy?"

"One-thirty-five."

Liz raised an eyebrow. "But Alec's taller."

"Only by three inches, and I'm more muscular."

Alec glared at him.

"Okay, okay, this is not the time to play macho-man."

"Right," David said decisively. "Okay, Liz, take off. I'd suggest hands and knees."

"Next time remind me to bring a rope," Alec muttered.

"Next time I will," David replied archly.

Liz approached the juncture of bridge and ledge cautiously, set one foot tentatively upon the sparkling surface—and felt it tremble in response to that contact. Her breath caught. "I don't know if any of us can make it, David."

"One of us has to. Otherwise the Trial will end. And there has to be a possibility of victory."

"Okay, but none of you start until I get across. *All the way across.*"

Liz knelt on all fours and braced her staff crossways between her two hands. She slid one hand onto the narrow span before her, then the other.

One knee. Two.

The bridge shook. Both David and Alec could see the glimmer scintillate.

One foot. Five feet. Ten. Twenty.

Liz was halfway across.

"Oh no," she called just as she reached the apex. "It's downhill now, and that's going to be even harder." She flattened herself onto her stomach and scooted, her elbows and knees hooked around the angled edges. The staff she kept crossways in front of her, forcing it downward against the substance of the bridge in hope that whatever small bit of extra friction was thus generated would help slow her descent. It worked for several feet, but halfway down the far slope she began to slide. One foot slipped sideways into air. She screamed and ground the staff into the bridge even more forcefully, which slowed her enough for her to right herself. The last third was more falling than sliding, and then she found herself lying facedown on the ledge on the other side.

"You *okay?*" shrieked a terrified David.

Liz stood up and dusted herself off. "Scrapes and bruises. Watch out for the downslope, it's slick as glass."

David rolled his eyes in despair.

Grimly Alec lowered himself onto all fours and eased onto the span. He'd had foresight to take his shoes and socks off, figuring the extra grip that would provide might come in useful, especially as he'd left the staff with David and wouldn't have it to use for balance.

Disgusting, thought David, when he saw the ease with which Alec accomplished the crossing. This time there was no slipping.

"What're you waiting on?" cried Alec when he had reached the other side. "It's easy. Easy as falling off a . . ." He clapped a hand on his mouth.

"A log?" David called back, trying to mask his fear with levity. But it was no use; he was petrified. Never in his life had anything so completely unnerved him as the prospect of crossing that hundred-foot arch. A glance over the edge of the cliff showed him nothing but blackness: no bottom, *nothing.* Suppose there *was* no bottom, suppose it just went on forever. He could imagine that, imagine fear knotting his whole body more and more tightly into itself until he simply winked out of existence in this universe and popped out again somewhere else, and kept on falling . . .

"Come on, David!"

Finally he said it. "I'm scared!"

"Scared? *You?*" Alec called back. "I've seen you scale ledges higher than this up on Lookout with scarcely a thought."

"But I knew where the bottom was, and I had solid ground under my feet."

"David!"

"I've never told anybody this, Alec. Bridges scare me. Haven't you ever noticed how I always speed up on bridges?"

He could see Alec's mouth drop open as realization dawned upon him.

"You've *got* to cross, David!"

"Okay, okay! Just give me a minute."

"Come *now,* David! *Now,* or you'll never do it."

"I think the bridge is fading!" Liz cried in such genuine alarm that David could detect it even across the gulf between them. A part of his mind wondered at the uncanny ease with which he had been able to hear across the distance.

"It is!" Alec cried.

"Now, David! *Now!"*

David stared at the bridge. It *was* becoming more transparent. Darkness showed through the near end.

"David, behind you!" Alec's voice carried shrill across the distance.

David spun around.

An armored head three feet wide thrust through the undergrowth a scant ten yards behind him.

"Now, David. Now!"

The creature advanced. Slowly. Methodically. Its eyes never left David. Moonlight glittered on the pearlescent whorls painted on its shell.

"David!"

David glanced back at the bridge, then at the creature.

It took a step.

For no logical reason he could think of he faced it, crouching warily before it, the make-do spear ready in one hand.

Another step. Eyes never leaving its quarry.

"No! This ends now!" David cried suddenly, and then hurled the spear at the beast.

It struck in the flaccid, grainy hide at the juncture of neck and carapace, and remained there, bobbing up and down. The merest puncture it looked, yet thick, evil-smelling blood welled out below the shaft. The acrid scent of burning flesh filled the air as the wrinkled skin around the wound began to blacken and curl away. The creature reared onto its stubby hind legs and screamed, a cry that tortured the silence like a dull sword thrust slowly into rusty metal.

David stood in frozen awe.

The creature collapsed back onto front feet which could no longer support it. No trace of light showed in its eyes. Its fellows began lumbering toward it.

David rushed forward and seized the spear, wrenching it from the surprisingly yielding flesh. The stench was nearly overpowering.

And then he ran.

All at once he was on the bridge.

It gave beneath his weight. He thought he felt one knee slip through. But he was moving, that was the important thing; crab-crawling his way across like the others, staff pushed before him. He could feel the substance slick beneath the heels of his palms, against his chest. Close before his eyes was a complexity of slowly moving lights defining the surface, glowing lines connecting the major nexi. But even as he looked, even as he scooted forward and up, the lights began to pale. Whole lines winked out. More and more space showed between.

Somehow he was in the middle. Downhill was a slide; he had seen that, but his nerve was frozen. He could not go forward, and he could not go back, for there *was* no back. Ahead, fifty feet, David could see the eager, expectant faces of his friends. But he dared not relinquish control. And to make matters worse, his grip was slipping, and not straight ahead, either, the sharp angles that marked the shoulders of the span were rounding. The cross-section was becoming circular! And David could feel himself slipping sideways.

"*David!*"

"Loosen up! Let go! Slide!"

He closed his eyes, loosened his grip imperceptibly, gave himself the gentlest of forward nudges with his feet . . .

An instant later he felt Alec's arms around him, pulling him to safety. Nothing had ever felt so warm, so welcoming, so solid before.

"You made it, old man." Alec grinned.

David sank to the ground, shuddering uincontrollably. "I did, didn't I?" His breath was coming fast, and he flung himself backward, chest heaving, staring up at the distant, star-studded sky.

A face swung into view above him, neither Alec nor Liz; a face half masked by an intricate helm.

"You have passed the Trial of Courage," said the Lord of the Trial, "not by defeating the Watcher or crossing the bridge, but by allowing your friends to precede you, knowing they might have to complete your quest alone—and trusting them enough to believe they would. It takes courage to put one's fate in another's hands."

David sat up and glanced back at the bridge, and was not surprised to see that it had vanished completely. Where it had abutted on the other side two shell-creatures were now feasting on the flesh of their fellow. A chill shook him, then another.

"What were those things?" he gasped.

"Watchers? Guardians? Keepers, perhaps?" the Lord replied cryptically. "By iron alone may they be slain. You are at the fringe of Tir-Nan-Og itself now; there is no further need for them to shadow you. Your last Trial will be of another sort entirely. It awaits you through the arch."

Alec laid an arm across David's shoulders and pointed to the ground beneath them, at the golden glitter of the Straight Track. It was brighter, brighter than it had ever been.

Behind them the Lord of the Trial was no longer to be seen.

"Two down," Alec panted.

"And one to go: the Trial of Strength, I would guess."

"Quicker begun, quicker ended," Liz sighed.

"Right," David sighed in turn, as he heaved himself up. "So, onward, children—onward and into the breach."

The trilithon gate rose before them, and then they were under it. Ahead stretched an arching passage in the wood. It was dark, but from where they stood they could already see light at the far end.

By some unspoken agreement they began to run.

An instant later they burst out into the blazing sunlight of a grassy glade possibly five acres in extent. Ahead, looming above even the highest of the trees on the far side, David could for the first time make out the shape that had haunted his dream: the impossibly slender cone of the surrogate Bloody Bald. He could not reckon the distance, for though the mountain appeared tiny, he seemed able to make out the smallest detail of the faceted, sharp-buttressed towers and pearly walls, the gold-laced pinnacles and high-arched windows, and the riotously tumbling gardens and ominous forests that enwrapped it.

"Neat!" said Alec.

"And restful," Liz added.

"Not for long, I'm sure," David put in distrustfully. But even he had to admit it was a beautiful glade. The brilliant green grass was short, almost like a lawn beside the Track. Small bushes bearing thick, spiky leaves, and gray boulders crudely carved with scowling human faces were scattered about in artful clumps, each accenting some slight hill or hollow. At no place were all of them visible at once.

The Track continued onward, and they followed it somewhat reluctantly, wanting to stop and rest but knowing they dared not.

Through the middle of the glade flowed a small stream maybe twenty feet across. A narrow strip of coarse silver sand bordered it on either side. They paused there uncertainly, wondering what hidden perils might lurk beneath its innocuous surface. Though shallow, it flowed rapidly, and was remarkably clear; yellow and red rocks flashed on its bottom, and once David thought he saw the flickering silver forms of a school of tiny, blue-finned fish dart past. He *did* see a hand-sized octopus almost as green and transparent as fine jade. Of that there was no doubt.

The air was still. Empty. No sound disturbed the peace of that place except the gentle gurgle of the stream.

And one other sound.

For issuing from the woods ahead came an almost subliminal jingling, and a distant buzz that finally coalesced into the sound of warpipes at full cry.

Chapter XVI: The Stuff Of Heroes

Abruptly the sky darkened as if masked by clouds, though none showed against its pristine vault. Black shadows crowded in among the distant trees. The sun still shone, but its light lacked strength or conviction. It was like predawn twilight and early evening and the eerie half-light of a solar eclipse all at once, and yet like none of these things.

Alec jerked David's sleeve, gesturing toward the line of trees straight ahead, his mouth agape in uncertain wonder. David nodded, for he too had seen what approached: light, a body of ghostly yellow-white radiance almost like phosphorescence, pale at the center, scintillating into colors at the edge. But the light did not illuminate. Rather, there was the dark forest on the one hand, and the light on the other, and an almost tangible interface between them.

As the light drew nearer, the jingle of bells became louder. The ground shook as if many horses trod upon it, and the sound of pipes, too, grew in volume. And then voices joined in with that skirling, the voices of men singing of battle and of war—at least that was how it sounded, though the language was strange—and warpipes howled in that music like thunder in the mountains on a hot summer day. David could not make out the words of the song, but they filled him with wonder and with dread.

Alec pointed to the Track ahead of them. Its edges had begun to glow even more brightly, flaring into a brilliance like white flame—white as the star-shaped flowers that sprang up alongside it in the vanguard of the Sidhe. Shapes appeared, centered in the nimbus of light, winking in and out among the trees at the edge of the meadow: the Sidhe themselves.

The whole host of Faerie seemed to be part of that riding, a panoply of glittering jewels and metals, brightly patterned fabrics and richly woven textures, furs and feathers, banners and pennants and musical instruments, swords and spears and helms, and thin golden staffs bearing strange carved and gilded insignia that glowed with their own light and cast their glow about the host.

The singing grew louder, more drivingly intense. A darker motif wove its way into the melody, and the rhythmic jingle of the horses' bells altered subtly to follow. There was a hint of tambourine and drum in the music, now, and of someone playing a harp, but the strings were plucked high and strange, almost discordant.

One by one the Host of the Sidhe forded the stream and continued up the Straight Track toward the mortals. Closer and closer they came, and still they sang.

When the last of the host cleared the trees and came full into David's sight, he forgot Alec, forgot Liz, almost forgot Little Billy and Uncle Dale. For the company parted and he saw who rode hindmost among the host of Faerie: Ailill, his enemy.

Ailill sat a white stallion whose golden mane hung halfway to the ground, and it seemed to David that tiny flames issued from the horse's nostrils and that its hooves struck sparks from the mossy turf. Ailill himself was dressed in black and silver, save for a band of red jewels about his head and the thick border of red-and-silver-embroidered eagles that edged his cloak. Arrogance showed cold across his handsome features, but the ornate silver scabbard that hung by his side was empty.

A company of twenty grim-faced warriors rode close about the Lord of Winds. The horses they bestrode were black. Each man bore a black lance pointing skyward, and each wore a black cloak wrapped tightly around him. Black mail gleamed on throat and legs and arms. Plain black helms capped heads of black hair. Their mouths were open and they sang with the others, their voices now high and clear, now dark and ominous.

Hope flickered within David for a moment, as he saw the form that rode point to the armored company. It was a silver-armed figure in white and gold, and the golden fringe of its snowy cloak swept the ground: Nuada of the Silver Hand.

The Morrigu was there too: the Mistress of Battles. Her crow sat on the saddle before her, black as her hair. Her tight, low-cut gown was red as blood, and its trailing sleeves were lined with cloth the color of flame. She was beautiful the way a slim-tipped dagger is beautiful.

But then David looked at Ailill, and saw that the dark Faery was glaring back at him, hatred in his eyes.

The song ended abruptly, cut off on a single note—as a life may end on a single sword thrust. Somewhere, someone began to pluck a harp one string at a time, soft and sad.

David's heart sank, but he squared his shoulders and strode forward to meet that company. Alec handed David his runestaff, and he held it braced before him in his two hands. He knew he must look ridiculous to stand thus before such a company, bruised and dirty—but he knew he had no choice now but to brazen it out.

Nuada reined in his horse. The armed company that accompanied him slowed to an uneasy halt.

David looked up into the glittering gaze of the Faery lord, glanced back at Ailill, then took a deep breath and addressed Nuada.

"Hail, Lord of Faerie," he said, and choked for a moment as fear welled up anew inside him.

"Hail, mortal lad," Nuada said wryly. "You seem to have a facility for meeting the Sidhe at their Riding."

"His business is with *me*, Silverhand," Ailill interrupted.

"And what business is that?" Nuada retorted sharply. "You are an exile now, or soon will be. You have had business enough with mortal men."

Ailill ignored him, but fire blazed in the dark eyes beneath his dark hair, as he folded his arms across the bronze eagle's head atop the high pommel of his saddle and leveled his gaze upon David. "You *are* a fool, then, are you not? More so than I had ever guessed, to challenge the Sidhe to the Trial of Heroes. Two Trials you have passed, so I have heard, but the Trial of Strength yet awaits you. And that Trial I have claimed for myself, as is my right. Your challenge *was* directed at me, was it not? Even if you did not so speak it?"

David gulped. "I suppose so," he answered weakly.

"Good, then it is mine to choose the nature of that Trial. You have come too far to go back now, and your fate is upon you, though not in the manner I had planned. No matter. The end will be the same. I am the champion of Erenn, you see; I am . . ."

"You are my prisoner until I rid my lands of you," a now-familiar voice interrupted from behind the mortals. "*I* determine what you are and what you are not, what you will do and what you will not do."

David whirled around to see the Lord of the Trial riding slowly up the Track toward the company.

When he had almost reached the host, the Lord lifted his helmet and handed it to a young man in blue and gray livery who rode forward to take it. A circlet of interlaced gold gleamed forth upon his black hair.

A rustling murmur caused David to turn again toward the host, to see them kneel as one body in obvious obeisance to the tall shape that loomed before them.

"The Ard Rhi," someone whispered.

The Ard Rhi! David thought. The High King: Lugh Samildinach himself, High King of the Sidhe in Tir-Nan-Og. Lugh was the Lord of the Trial.

For a moment Ailill stared at the mounted figure who faced him. "Nevertheless, the Rules do not forbid me to contest with the boy," he said, "for the Rule of the Trial is beyond even the Law of Lugh Samildinach. But I was about to add that the Trial of Strength would not be with me, but with my son." He raised his head and shouted, "Fionchadd, come here."

There was a buzz from within the assembled multitude, which quickly parted as a green-clad figure rode from where it had remained unobtrusively among the ranks. It was a youth, David saw, seemingly little older than himself, golden-haired and slender—almost his own size, in fact.

The boy took off the long-peaked cap that had shadowed his face, and David gasped as he recognized the clean-chiseled features beneath it: It was the same boy who had shot Uncle Dale. And now he realized that it was also the same half-glimpsed face that had belonged to the Faery runner who had chased him what seemed like a very long time ago. That race had started all this, in fact—all the bad part of it anyway.

The boy's face flushed angrily. "What is it you would have of me, Father?"

"Twice I sent you on missions for me, missions a mere child could have achieved—yet you failed," Ailill said. "But third time pays for all, and by the Rule of Three you owe me a third. I demand that you avenge your honor."

"You are right, for once," Lugh agreed, in a voice that allowed no argument, "though not in the manner of honor. The Trial must be a fair contest, a striving among equals. Your son and David are of a size and almost of an age, allowing for the difference between the Worlds. And Oisin's ring is lost in the Lands of Men and has no power here. Yes, Ailill, I think you have the right of it: Third time pays for all. Do you agree?"

Ailill glared arrogantly at Lugh, his mouth hardened to a thin line. "Even I must bow to the Trial of Heroes; for that which rules it is mightier than anyone here."

Lugh ignored the glare and looked to Morrigu. "Lady of Battles?"

Morrigu inclined her head slightly. "Long is it since we have observed the Rite. Yet it must be done in accord with strictest honor, or not at all. Fionchadd is the more fit opponent. If it is David's will to try with him, let it be so."

Lugh turned again toward David. "Is it so?"

David stared at Fionchadd, then at Alec and Liz, both of whose faces mirrored bewildered concern. He felt dead. Numb. He stood as if paralyzed, ten steps from . . . from what? Doom? Or immortality? He could stay in Faerie—that had always been an option. Surely with eternity for the searching he could find Little Billy. But then what about Uncle Dale? And Liz and Alec —did he have the right to make that kind of decision for them? If he aborted the quest now they could be friends forever, maybe in Liz's case more than friends. Not until that moment had he realized how much he loved them.

"I choose the Trial of Strength with Fionchadd," he said at last, his mouth dry as dust.

Lugh glared imperiously down at David. "You do not look very strong," he said. "What can you do?"

David hesitated only a moment; as for once the right words came to him. "I can run and wrestle and swim," he said.

"He can indeed," Fionchadd put in. "And he has bested me at the first two. For my part I would try with him at swimming."

Lugh nodded slightly, then spoke in a voice clear as a trumpet: "As Lord of the Trial, it is my duty to decide the form of the Trial of Strength, and this is my decision: Let it be as Fionchadd wills. Having competed already at running and wrestling, let the final Trial be swimming."

Lugh looked Ailill straight in the eye then. "But I have a stake in this as well," he said. "The Trial will be a test of strength and will. If David wins, he may perhaps gain that which he seeks, and the desire for such gain is a powerful incentive. But what if Fionchadd wins? Then I owe the mortal no boons. He and his friends will be doomed to eternity as my guests in Tir-Nan-Og—and Ailill will have paid no price for the suffering he has caused, yet he is not without guilt. Therefore let it be a contest to the death as well. It is *Fionchadd's* death I claim if he loses. On him I lay the death of iron: a time of torment in the Dark Realm from which only his strength of will may free him."

A hush filled the ranks; even the harp stopped for an instant.

"As you will have it, Ard Rhi," Fionchadd said quietly.

Ailill's face turned white. "Fool of a boy!" he screamed. "Twice fool, and thrice."

Morrigu silenced him with a glance. "It is not your decision. The Rite is in motion."

David looked around uncertainly. "But . . . there's nowhere here to swim."

"A small matter in Tir-Nan-Og." Lugh smiled grimly. "Do you see that stream? That is your river. That you will swim, this bank to the far bank."

"I still don't see how this is supposed to work," David found himself saying nervously, trying not to think of what he had just heard. "The stream is only twenty feet or so across. Why, I could wade it!"

"Not if you are no higher than my finger is long," said Lugh.

"You mean you'll shrink us?"

"Or expand the land around you; it comes to the same thing. Sometimes I myself am not certain which occurs. Now let the contestants come stand by the stream, and we can end this matter."

Lugh's gaze swept the crowd. "Morrigu, shape-shifting is an

art you practice almost as frequently as Ailill, and with somewhat more pleasing results; can you shift a man's size as easily as his shape?"

The dark-haired woman stepped forward then, a disquieting smile upon her fair face. "That I can do, Lord, and that I will do most gladly."

"David Sullivan, Fionchadd MacAilill, come forward," commanded Lugh.

David looked at Alec and Liz. Alec smiled sadly and stuck out his hand. David took it, squeezed it, but went on to enfold his friend with both arms in a hearty hug.

Liz he hugged likewise, regretfully aware of how nice her body felt against his. As he broke away, he was surprised when she pulled him back and kissed him firmly on the mouth.

A moment later David was standing on the sand at the side of the stream, water lapping about the toes of his boots. Fionchadd came to stand by his side. The boy's face was grimly emotionless. David could not imagine what thoughts hid behind those eyes. Was the Faery boy favorably disposed toward him, as David had some slight reason to suspect, or was he truly an enemy? And what was the relationship between the boy and Ailill? Father and son, certainly, but was that love between them, or hatred, or some curious combination of the two?

"Prepare yourselves," the Morrigu snapped.

Prepare yourselves? he thought. He glanced at Fionchadd in confusion, and then realization dawned on him: The boy had sat down and was tugging off the green, thigh-high boots he wore beneath his short green tunic. David felt his face coloring. *Well, of course,* he thought, *you can't swim very well fully clothed.* But he had brought nothing to swim in, and there were people around —ladies around—*Liz,* for God's sake! A corner of David's mind knew that bathing suits were a modern invention, that in olden times people had customarily swum naked. But it seemed like an insignificant thing to be concerned about now, when lives were at stake. Reluctantly he unzipped his jacket.

A moment later he stood beside Fionchadd, blushing furiously in his Fruit-of-the-Looms. The Faery boy wore only a narrow white loincloth, but seemed totally unconcerned about his state of undress. David sized up his opponent. The Faery boy was an inch or two taller than he, and more finely boned. But long smooth muscles wrapped the boy's arms and legs, and the firm, graceful curves of his chest and shoulders hinted at the sort of strength that was good for endurance.

David wondered suddenly if he *could* win. So far the trappings of the contest had distracted him from the thought that should be centermost in his mind: Victory. It was for Little Billy, he did this, and Uncle Dale, and now for Liz and Alec.

"Face me!" came the unexpectedly harsh voice of the Morrigu. "Look me in the eyes! Both of you! Now!"

David found he had no choice but to obey. The Power in the woman's voice seemed almost the equal of Lugh's, perhaps even stronger in its own way.

The eyes he gazed into were gray. Gray as evening. Gray as the steel of swords. Gray as cannons and arrows and unpolished armor. Gray as the netherworld of death.

The Morrigu blinked—or he did. And David stood again beside Fionchadd looking down at the ridiculously small stream; his face registered the confusion he felt.

Lugh's voice rang loud in their ears. "When I give the word, you will dive forward. The Power will come upon you then."

David shrugged, glanced at his friends. Alec gave him a thumbs-up signal. Liz blew him a kiss, and he grinned in spite of himself.

"Ready."

He tensed himself, crouching bent-kneed, poised for a long, shallow dive. The notion of throwing himself with full force into what appeared to be three inches of water was daunting indeed. But that was logic, and logic was not the pillar of stability it once had been.

"Now!"

David's body took over for him, for which he was grateful. And he flung himself forward, fully expecting to feel the sharp stones of the stream bed impact his chest, drive the air from his lungs. Instead, there was a brief strange sensation of falling, like a dive from a great height, and suddenly he was in deep water, twenty yards or more from shore.

There was a commotion beside him—in front of him—as Fionchadd wasted no time in forging considerably ahead. One part of David's mind wanted to stop, to gaze skyward, to see if the towering forms of the Sidhe looked down upon him. But there was no time for that now. Fionchadd was already two body-lengths ahead of him, and pulling away. David gave himself over to the task at hand.

He was not a trained swimmer, he knew. But he'd been doing it since he was a child, and had been told (by David-the-elder) that he had a natural gift for it. Water thus held no fear for him, and he often swam far out into the lake. He had raced Alec some, too, but always in fun, never for real.

And then he quit thinking, just let his body take over. Stroke. Stroke. Kick. Kick. *Breathe*. Stroke. Stroke. Kick. Kick. *Breathe*.

He was gaining. But not fast enough.

Ahead he could see Fionchadd's supple form gliding smoothly through the water, disturbing the surface almost not at all as he plunged his narrow hands into it.

Stroke. Stroke. Kick. Kick. *Breathe*.

They were into the current now, and it was all either of them could do to keep from being completely overwhelmed by it. Vast waves appeared from somewhere, towering high above their heads before crashing down upon them.

Another wave fell atop him, plunging him far under water. Something brushed against him, but he tried not to think what it might be. And then he was on the surface again, and Fionchadd not so far ahead as he had been.

More waves, and then the waters smoothed, and then waves again.

The water rose abruptly under him, bearing him upward, higher and higher, then plunging him down. Up and down. Up and down. It was like swimming in a stormy area.

All at once a wave crashed upon him, harder than any before, and he felt himself knocked half senseless, felt himself drifting nervelessly toward the bottom as bubbles trickled from his mouth to tickle his nose. His lungs hurt. His head hurt. He was drowning, he realized.

Drowning in two feet of water.

And then David remembered what Fionchadd had said about the Stuff of Heroes, how David was himself of that substance. From somewhere images came unbidden in his mind: Beowulf in his contest with Brecca, amid the monsters of a cold northern sea; Leander who had dared the Hellespont each night for love of a lady whose very name was Hero; Bran the Blessed who had *waded* the Irish Sea.

Ruthlessly he kept his arms and legs in motion. Ruthlessly he kicked toward the surface, ignoring the pain in his lungs, the buzz in his ears, the red blurr that filled his eyes.

Abruptly he surfaced and rolled over onto his back, coughing, finally dragging in long, blessedly cool breaths of sweet air. He looked for Fionchadd but the boy was nowhere to be seen.

Despair filled David until he saw the Faery's head break the surface near his own, victim of the same killer wave. For an uncertain moment their gazes met, and then both set forth again, but Fionchadd had lost most of his advantage; David was nearly neck and neck with him now, and the boy seemed to be tiring.

David rationed his own energy but maintained his pace. The shore was in sight, a thin dark line through the wet blur of water and hair that continually obscured his vision. But he was tiring, falling further and further behind. He needed an incentive, he realized, and so he once again set his imagination free to conjure images, dark images, this time. The things he most feared, the things he knew would happen if he did not succeed:

Uncle Dale lying in bed, head rocked loosely back, eyes staring at nothing, a line of thin spittle trickling from his open mouth, while the banshee stood beside him, her rictal smile greedy upon her face.

Little Billy, a bodiless wraith of hopeless fear, torn from his own world, maybe even his own shape, a disembodied child-voice crying in the wind: "Davy! Davy! Davy!"

Alec and Liz, dressed in the strange clothes of Faerie, besotted on Faery wine, eyes dulled by an endless succession of days wherein nothing changed.

His parents wondering how two sturdy sons could have vanished without a trace.

Fionchadd—Fionchadd would die if he won. Well, he had wanted to kill him once, when he saw the elf-arrow stuck in Uncle Dale's chest. But they had made a sort of peace, somehow. "Let us be friends when this song is ended," the boy had said. Well, there was still one more verse. And he still owed the boy one.

They were even now, neck and neck, and the shoreline was close, maybe fifty yards away. David took a breath, and withdrew into himself, summoning energy from every nerve, every muscle, every cell. And one thing more: his rage. He had never entirely set it free, but he did now, sent it spreading fire throughout his body.

And his body obeyed, knifing fiercely through the water, each movement born of the deadly flame of anger that drove him now, each flame consumed driving him closer to his goal.

Pulling him ahead of Fionchadd, finally.

David glanced sideways, saw a look of real, incredulous fear cross the Faery boy's face.

That was what finally did it: the fact that the boy considered his own defeat a real possibility. A final show of strength would do it now. *Now!* David told his body, and every part of him suddenly unified into one whole as he poured his last precious reserves of energy into the effort.

Sand brushed his fingertips.

Another stroke.

Again.

And then he was scrambling to his feet, to fling himself breathlessly against the coarse sand of the shore. He rolled over onto his back, chest heaving, eyes glazed. Somehow he was his own size again.

But had he won? Or not? An eerie silence hung in the air.

"Way to go, Davy! You did it!" familiar voices cried. A feeling strangely like elation filled his mind, replacing those darker images that had pushed him to . . . *victory,* he supposed. But he was tired, and too numb to think.

Someone was helping him sit up, warm, tanned hands gripping his arms. Somebody forced a drink into his mouth, a spicy richness that sent new fire racing through his body as soon as he touched it to his lips, so that he was now able to rise shakily to his feet. Someone draped a tabard across his shivering shoulders, and he fingered the fabric absently. Velvet. Midnight-blue and gray.

"Hold!" a voice thundered.

"The Trial is not ended!"

Chapter XVII: The Justice Of Lugh

Not ended! David's thoughts were awhirl. *Not ended! What?*

"It was a trial to the *death*," came Lugh's grim voice. "No life has yet been taken. You, Alec McLean, give your friend your knife. Fionchadd's life is his."

Someone—Alec?—thrust a knife into David's hand, and he raised his head groggily, staring stupidly at the weapon.

Two of the black-clad guards pulled Fionchadd upright. The Faery boy's body sagged between them, dripping wet, his eyes as unfocused as David's. Water sheened his white skin; he breathed in great gasping pants. With obvious effort Fionchadd stretched a trembling arm toward David. "You have won fairly. My life is yours. And know that . . . that I bear you no ill will, for my fate is of my own doing. The song is over."

Still half dazed, David felt someone leading him forward. One of the guards pulled Fionchadd's head back, exposing his throat. David could see the pulse beating there.

He set the knife to that smooth flesh, felt Fionchadd's breath brush hot against the back of his hand, saw the boy close his eyes in resignation. He set his own mouth grimly. Was he really doing this? He was human, mortal, *civilized*. Could he really kill a man like this? And not just a man but a man he knew, sort of, had talked to, who had had a life before their meeting—but who would have no life afterward.

"No!" he cried, and flung the knife to the sand.

"It is a strong man, David Sullivan, who can set an enemy free, perhaps to best him again," said Lugh. "By this you have passed your final Trial."

"By this you have cost me the last of my honor!" cried Ailill behind him.

David whirled to see the dark Faery seize the makeshift spear from a startled Liz. Pain darkened Ailill's face as gray smoke poured from between his fingers; the smell of burning flesh filled the air—all in the second before Ailill spurred his horse to a brutal charge straight at David.

The company fell back, calling out in alarm.

David stood frozen, staring at black death bearing down upon him. He screamed. Other voices screamed in his head. "No!" he heard Liz and Alec cry as one.

Time slowed.

David saw Ailill on the white horse, the smoking hand that grasped the spear, the glittering eyes of the Faery lord. The blade pointed straight at his heart showed red hot as Ailill's fury awakened it.

And he could not move.

There was no sound save the snorting of the horse and the pounding of hooves on the sand.

And still the spear came on.

Although David could not move, the horse could—and did, but in an unexpected manner. Something, a small stone maybe, upset its balance, and it broke its gait.

Fire flashed across David's side, and he looked down in amazement to see the velvet tabard slashed crosswise and a thin line of red oozing from a long, clean cut in the skin that overlaid his ribs.

Two screams rang in his ears.

Abruptly the pain was gone.

He turned, stared, and saw Fionchadd lying on the sand beside him. The boy's eyes were open, but Liz's knife-pointed runestaff protruded from his pale, still chest. The tiniest hint of white smoke spiraled upward from the wound to mark the sky; a single rivulet of blood trickled across the white flesh to color the sand.

David wanted to cry out, but his jaw locked. He felt his gorge begin to rise and clamped a hand across his mouth as he jerked his eyes away.

Silence hung in the air like a threat of thunder.

Wordlessly Nuada dismounted and with his silver hand yanked the spear from the wound, then spread his white cloak across the boy's body. He turned to face Ailill.

"Madman!" he whispered.

"Idiot!" a woman's voice shrieked.

"Fool!"

"Murderer!" The cries were a rising tide of anger.

"Kinslayer!"

"Kinslayer!" another voice took up the call, and then others joined in a chant that rang across the plain: "Kinslayer! Kinslayer! Kinslayer!"

Despair filled Ailill then. Despair and horror—and fear. His pride broke, and he spurred the horse to a gallop and made to follow the Straight Track across the empty field.

But even as he flashed past, David caught a blur of movement to his left, and saw Alec thrust his runestaff directly into Ailill's face.

The Faery lord cried out, his eyes stretched wide in horror, for the fear of iron came upon him. He jerked back, sending the startled horse rearing beneath him. He held the reins firmly, but was unprepared when the horse bucked sideways; *that* move unbalanced him and he slipped from the saddle. But he was on his feet again, almost as he struck the earth, and running toward the Track.

Another stood there before him, though: a black-haired woman of the Sidhe, dressed in blue, and beside her an empty-eyed child in green pajamas. Straight in front of Ailill she stood, proud and queenly, barring his way.

The Faery woman! Yet it was no defensive Faery woman this time, but a great lady of the Sidhe. Vengeance was in her gaze and triumph in her carriage as her fingers worked before her.

All at once Ailill found his way blocked by a terrible wall of swirling flame that leapt man-high from the tall grass about him and spread rapidly to either side in a threatening arc. An intricate, cagelike mesh of icicles took form within that barrier, through which the colored fires leapt and wove, constantly melting and refreezing even as the flames were extinguished and rekindled.

And so Ailill stood confounded, facing arcane fire on the one hand and the fires of iron that could bind him in torment on the other. Reluctantly he stumbled forward to stand before the king, head bowed.

Without a word, Nuada stepped forward to stand beside Ailill.

"So it is to be my justice at last," Lugh said calmly. His stern gaze swept the crowd, "Then hear you all the justice of Lugh Samildinach, High King for this Time in Tir-Nan-Og!"

Lugh's eyes bored into the dark Faery. "You, Ailill, are a fool. Even as you pass from my realm, you still contrive plots and deceptions. It was a plot of yours that started this trouble, for you should never have made that bargain with the mortal boy. But having made it, you should have stayed by it—this any honorable man would do. And now a plot of yours has finished it again, as is fitting, but that gamble has cost you a son—a high price to pay for victory. Nor is that the worst of your offenses, Ailill, for you have been guilty of another crime as well—a crime against my own house."

"My lord, I have not . . ." Ailill protested.

Lugh motioned the Faery woman forward, who came, bringing the surrogate Little Billy with her.

"Now I know—we all know—that you took a changeling; the proof of that we see before us. Is this not so?"

Ailill made no move to acknowledge Lugh's question.

"No matter," said Lugh. "We all know the truth of it. The Sidhe could use some of the thick blood of mortals to strengthen our own; that I also acknowledge. But you did it without my consent; indeed, you flaunted it in my face, even refused to return the boy when I ordered it, and thus set your will above my own, for which you earned this exile. And what is even worse than that is that you left one of our own in the child's place when a log would have served as well. What could have possessed you to do that?"

Ailill's nostrils narrowed haughtily. "Were you indeed as well studied in the ways of men as you claim, Ard Rhi, you would know that mortal men have more ways of looking at illness now than when we were mighty in the land. Had I left a stock they might have grasped the heart of our deception, and that would have made trouble for us far beyond what this boy would cause. I had to use a child of our own people."

Lugh drew himself up to his full height. His fingers grasped his jeweled reins so tightly that they snapped, sending a rain of sapphires and topazes glittering to the ground. "Is it *this* you are telling me, Ailill?" he thundered: "that you deemed a child of the Sidhe to be of less import than a child of mortal men? *I know the last number of the people I rule,* do not forget that. Did you truly think that I would overlook the theft of a true-born son of Faerie? No, Dark One, you have been too much in your own counsel, for though you took the child, and the mother not willing, you failed to inquire closely enough as to who that woman might be—and in that you erred most grievously."

"A woman is a woman," flared Ailill. "A child is a child."

"A woman may also be a daughter of a king," said Lugh, quietly. "Not all of my house choose to remain at court."

Ailill's face went white beneath his ruby circlet.

Lugh smiled. "You had best not give an heir to the King of the Sidhe as a changeling without the king's consent. I have my own plans for his fosterage."

There was a sound of laughter among the assembled company, then, and Ailill's face flushed red.

"Yes, Ailill, your true nature comes forth at last. I do not know what we will do with you, but we will see whether we can lessen the harm you have already done. I do not see the human child anywhere."

Oblivious to the pain it cost, Lugh jerked the ash spear from Nuada's hand and leveled its still-glowing tip at Ailill's heart as two guards grabbed the dark Faery on either side. "Now, *where is the boy?*"

Ailill glared at him and muttered something in a low voice. It was a spell, David knew instinctively, and probably a very Powerful one, for it hushed the crowd, and the air itself seemed at once to thicken and go flat, as if Ailill's words had a material existence and were too heavy for the air alone to contain.

The white horse that Ailill had ridden so proudly only a short while before stamped its feet as if disturbed by the presence of so much Power. It danced sideways, nervously, its eyes rolling in fright and its tongue lolling from its mouth. All at once it snorted and reared up, fell heavily to earth, and reared again—and remained standing on its hind legs as it suddenly became a naked five-year-old boy with blond hair and blue eyes. Confused recognition broke forth on that small face, as Little Billy stood there staring wide-eyed, not quite believing he had won free from the horse-shape that had enwrapped him.

David could contain himself no longer. He ran forward, knelt before his brother and gathered him into his arms. "Little Billy, it's me, Davy!"

"Davy! Davy!" cried Little Billy in turn as tears wet both their faces.

Lugh also smiled as he saw the blue-clad woman kneel and embrace her own child, whose eyes, too, blazed with new life—and they were his own green eyes now, shining joyfully in his own face.

David hugged his brother tightly. Somebody handed him a cloak, and he threw it around his brother's shoulders. Alec surreptitiously returned David's clothes, and while the attention of the crowd seemed diverted, David began slipping them on under his tabard.

"We still have things to consider," continued Lugh, "including whether or not banishment is sufficient punishment for our rebellious friend here. He has slain his son, a grievous thing, but I wonder whether that is now enough?"

The blue-clad woman stepped forward then, resting a hand on the pommel of Lugh's saddle. "Lugh, my father," she said, "may I offer my counsel in this?"

"I am always glad to hear your advice, daughter," said Lugh.

"Well, then, since Ailill is so fond of shape-shifting, let me take him into my care, and lay on him the shape of a black horse, and make of him a mount for my son to ride until he be of an age to bear weapons." She smiled triumphantly at Ailill, but there was warning in her smile as well.

"There is great justice in this," said Lugh. "So shall it be."

The woman's eyes caught David's then, and lingered there a moment before flickering over Alec and Liz and Little Billy. She smiled cryptically. "I think perhaps these fine folk will be dealing with the Sidhe again."

"I hope not," sighed Lugh, "but I fear you are correct. We have seldom met with mortals so lively in these last centuries. Now," the High King continued, "are there any *other* boons to be craved, while I seem to be holding court?" His gaze rested on David.

David opened his mouth. "I . . ."

"*I* crave a boon, Ard Rhi," Ailill interrupted.

Lugh raised an eyebrow. "*You?*"

"I would ask one thing, and as it has a bearing on the death of my son, it is a thing I have a right to know."

"And what is that?"

"Never in five hundred years have I missed a blow, not with sword nor spear nor lance. How is it, then, since the ring of Oisin lies lost and useless in the Lands of Men, that my blow nevertheless missed?"

"Perhaps it was your choice of mounts," said Lugh. "Or perhaps you are simply not as skilled as once you were."

"Or perhaps it is because the ring is *not* lost and useless," came the voice of Nuada. The silver-armed Faery reached into the breast of his tunic and drew out something round that glittered in the morning sun of Tir-Nan-Og. "I too have more shapes than one, Ailill, but the shape of a white trout may sometimes be more useful than that of a soaring black eagle when we travel the Lands of Men."

Nuada turned toward Lugh. "Long have I been watching Ailill, seeking to learn exactly how serious a threat he posed to our relations with men. And so I watched David, too. Thus I became a trout in the stream into which David fell when the ring's Power broke him free of the Straight Track. The chain parted in that fall and the ring rolled into the water where I was. It was then a simple thing for me to swallow while the boy lay unknowing. The ring is not a thing entirely of our understanding, Lugh, for we did not make it. I feared my feasting might cost me, but it did not, for I bore David no ill will, and I did not actually claim the ring for my own. Until this Riding I have kept it in an iron box, which this silver arm allows me to touch."

Nuada stepped forward and returned the silver band to David. "I *am* sorry, David Sullivan, for much ill has befallen you because of this ring. And in truth I thought for a time to return it to you. But until you actually give it to another of your own volition, it is yours, regardless of who holds it. And until that time, you, at least, are under its protection."

"But why didn't you give it back?" cried David. "You put me through bloody hell for no good reason!"

"So I did," replied Nuada. "For I see a time not far off—

much closer in fact, than I had even guessed—when we will need someone to serve our cause among mortals—not as a traitor, I would not ask that, but as an ambassador. You, David Sullivan, I thought might be that person. I sensed Power alive in you from our first meeting, which I thought strange, since Power normally slumbers in your kind unless awakened by some outside agency. My curiosity was aroused, then. And when I learned you had somehow acquired the Sight as well—"

"I thought that was because I looked between my legs at a funeral procession," David interrupted.

Nuada smiled faintly and shook his head. "What would we do without Reverend Kirk? But no, that is doubtful. It may have been the spark, for the Laws of Power are capricious, but I think something else was at work there—though I still have not been able to set a name to it."

"I can set a name to it," a female voice cried harshly. "For that name is mine."

"Morrigu?" Nuada stared incredulously at the red-clad Mistress of Battles.

"And why not? I, too, see war a-making between Faerie and the Lands of Men, and I do not like the odds. I, too, think an advocate among humans might be useful to ward off such a conflict. Indeed, I have often been in that World of late seeking such a one—even more frequently than you, Airgetlam, though my preferred shape is that of crow. And on one of those occasions I happened to see a burial in progress, and our young friend here regarding those proceedings from between his legs. The foolishness of his position called to my mind the foolish phrases the Scotsman had set down in that book of his, and I could not help but be curious. And when I saw the boy's face, and knew who he was—the twice-great-grandson of a mortal man with whom I once had lain—I knew that I had found my goal. There was Power in him already, for it is the heritage of his house. It was thus a simple thing for me to call it forth again. And I added the Sight for good measure—as a further testing, if the truth be known, to see of what metal the boy was made."

"And which metal was it?" asked Lugh.

"I have not decided," Morrigu replied. "Iron, perhaps, for the fires of the world's first making certainly flame in him. Or maybe gold, for the glory of learning which never fades from him. Or possibly silver for the power a ring of that metal once had over him."

"Or maybe mercury for the way he slipped through Ailill's fingers," suggested Lugh. "Or lead like a fisherman's sinker for the network of plots that seem to be tangled about him."

"Perhaps," said the Mistress of Battles. "Or perhaps he is not the one we need at all."

David found himself blushing in spite of himself, but then he realized he had forgotten something: the most important thing, the reason he had come here!

"Milord Ard Rhi? I . . . I mean Your . . . Majesty?"

"Speak, mortal boy."

"I . . . well . . . this is all very interesting, but you do recall why I went through all this in the first place: so that I could crave a boon of you?"

Lugh raised an eyebrow. "That is the way I recollect it."

David squared his shoulders. "I have a boon, then . . . I mean, I *crave* a boon."

Lugh's eyes twinkled above the sweeps of his mustache. "Ask, and if it be within my Power to grant, I will."

"I ask that you—or someone skilled in Faery magic—please heal my Uncle Dale. He was wounded by a . . ."

"By a Faery arrow," finished the High King. "This I know. But you yourself have already helped cure your uncle. For one of the Laws of Power states that if a man be wounded by a thing of Power forged in a World not his own—unless he die from that wound—it has power over him only so long as he whose Power is in that weapon lives."

David looked confused.

Nuada came to his aid then, and pointed to the white-draped body of Fionchadd. "With the death of the slayer, the spell itself dies. The death of Ailill's son, who was the instrument of your uncle's wound, has broken the Power of the arrow within him. The old man sleeps the sweet sleep of mortals. When he wakes tomorrow, he will be healed."

Lugh regarded David. "I would speak to you now, mortal lad. And I think I would like to speak to you again in a few years' time, when you have gained more wisdom. For I think I begin to see something of what Nuada saw in you: more a helper than a foe, and truly something of a hero as well. But the time for that is not yet. Until then, you do pose a problem. It is customary to blind those who look upon the Sidhe unbidden, and I could do that now . . ." He raised his hand, then hesitated. "But I have always thought that rather—shall we say—shortsighted, so I will simply lay a ban on all of you that you may speak of nothing you have seen or heard today to any dweller of your world save yourselves."

Lugh surveyed the host one final time and grasped the ragged ends of the broken reins in one closed fist. A nod of his head, a narrowing of his eyes, and the break was mended. He shook the leather strips experimentally, setting the bells upon them to jingling. "Well, unless someone *else* has a boon they want to crave, let us now proceed," he cried. "It seems we no longer have need to ride to the Eastern Sea, for Ailill will not be leaving after all. But there is still time to make that journey today, if we depart at once. If anyone objects to such an outing, let his voice be heard." He fixed Ailill with a burning stare. "I believe my daughter and I will lead the procession a while, in the absence of my honor guard," he said, and added almost as an afterthought, "Nuada, since you are so fond of mortals, you may escort our guests back to their home."

Nuada nodded and remounted. From somewhere three white horses appeared, saddled and bridled with red leather. Nuada motioned David and his friends to mount, which they did with ease by virtue of the Power of that place. "These horses never tire, never lose their way, and never throw a rider," Nuada said, "not even if that rider has never sat a horse before."

Nuada shook his reins, the bells chiming softly as the smaller procession formed. Somewhere the harp music began again; somewhere was the dull buzz of warpipes coming up to cry, and a tentative run on a chanter.

David had held his peace as long as he could. He urged his horse close beside that of the High King. "Can I come back next year and watch, at least?" he blurted out.

The Ard Rhi raised an eyebrow. "With your lips bound, who can worry about your eyes? If you are at the right place and time mayhap you will see us."

Lugh turned once more to face the milling host. "Now let us ride, Lords and Ladies of the Tuatha de Danaan and the Sidhe!"

Nuada's small company watched as the greater host passed

down the Straight Track which had been David's road to Faerie. David looked down at the head of his brother who sat in the saddle before him—now wearing a yellow tunic belted at his waist. He ruffled his brother's hair. "I wonder how we'll explain your wardrobe," he teased. Then he added, "How've you been, kid?"

"Sleepy," said Little Billy. "Real sleepy." He paused. "And I've got to get Pa's ax."

"You can get it in the morning," said David.

Alec whistled. "That was something else!"

"That's an understatement," nodded Liz.

"Three are mightier than one," David grinned.

"But one is mightiest of the three," cried Alec and Liz in unison.

David scratched his finger where the ring once again was set, and watched the Sidhe ride away, a line of glittering lights against the edge of the forest. It was twilight again. And he saw a smaller party ride closer by, entering the woods that marked the shorter route to Tir-Nan-Og. Amid that company rode Ailill, under heavy guard.

The Dark One said nothing as he passed, but his eyes betrayed his thoughts, and Nuada sighed before he set his horse onto the Straight Track. Ailill would take some watching.

Epilogue: In The Lands Of Men

(Monday, August 17)

David stood staring at Uncle Dale's wound. Little remained of it now, only a tiny white circle which was rapidly darkening to the color of his flesh. The old man's face was relaxed, his breathing peaceful.

Quietly David turned and reached for the doorknob.

Someone coughed in the room. "Thank you, boy," rasped a wonderfully familiar voice.

David whirled around and dashed quickly to the bedside. The old man's words were thick, but clear; he raised his arm—his right arm—high enough to pat David on the hand. His grip was weak but firm, and there was warmth in the hand. "You'd better not tell yore folks 'bout me," Uncle Dale said. "You don't know nothin' 'bout this, but I'll be better in the mornin'."

"Whatever you say," David smiled. "Whatever you say—and thanks for holding out."

"I knew you could do it, boy. I never doubted."

A moment later he was snoring.

David smiled again and quietly stole from the room. A glance in his own room across the hall showed Little Billy also asleep. The little boy would remember nothing of his time in Faerie,

Nuada had told him. That and the journey home would seem like a dream. His last clear memory would be of lightning.

He glanced at the clock on the wall as he rejoined his friends in the kitchen. It was a little after one. Time had passed, but not enough. How much time *had* they spent in Faerie? he wondered. Days and days it had seemed, and yet no time at all. He found himself looking at the ring. *The circle of Time that encloses all things:* another thing Nuada had told him.

Car doors slammed in the yard. Laughter floated clearly in from outside. David and Alec and Liz exchanged knowing looks —and began a mad scramble back to the table.

"Let's see, you had landed on Boardwalk again, hadn't you David?" Liz said as they returned to their places.

"Oh no! Not that old ploy," David replied. "Why look, Liz, your hotels are all over the floor, and I bet you don't remember where they were, do you?"

"Want to bet, David Sullivan?"

"Why, Liz, you know I'm not a gambling man," David said —and rolled the dice.

Historical Note

As is probably evident to the reader, *Windmaster's Bane* owes a considerable debt to the folklore and mythology of Ireland and Scotland. What is perhaps less obvious is the debt the novel owes to the folklore of an entirely different culture: the Cherokee Indians of the southeastern United States. It was Cherokee folklore that provided the collaborative evidence which solidified the notion that one could, indeed, write a Celtic fantasy set in the Appalachian Mountains.

There is the matter of the piled stone fortifications on Fort Mountain, for instance. These structures are usually attributed to Prince Madoc of Wales, who supposedly founded a colony in Mobile, Alabama in the year of 1170, and later worked his way inland. The Cherokees, however, attribute them to the "moon-eyed people." It was my efforts to learn more about these mysterious folk that first led me to James Mooney's *Myths of the Cherokee*. Alas, Mooney's book provided little illumination on the matter of the "moon-eyed people," but it had something better: the Nunnehi.

According to Mooney, the Cherokees believed in a race of spirit people called the Nunnehi, a word meaning something like "the immortals," or "the people who live everywhere." The Nunnehi lived in "townhouses" high in the mountains, or under water. They were fond of music and dancing, and usually helpful to humans—at least to the Indians, on whose side they fought as recently as the mid-nineteenth century. With the Nunnehi, I had both a link to the Sidhe of Irish mythology and to Tir-Nan-Og, the paradise to the west. The rest, as they say, is history.

TFD
Athens, Georgia
12 April 1986